Corner Booth

ISBN-13: 978-1508979791
ISBN-10: 1508979790

Fonts: Garamond, Berton, Liam
Cover photos: mediaphotos/istockphoto.com and AndyL/istockphoto.com
Cover Art: Chautona Havig
Edited by Haug Editing

The events and people in this book, aside from any caveats on the next page, are purely fictional, and any resemblance to actual people is purely coincidental. I'd love to meet them!

Connect with Me Online:

Twitter: https://twitter.com/ChautonaHavig
Facebook: https://www.facebook.com/chautonahavig
My blog: http://chautona.com/blog/
Instagram: http://instagram.com/ChautonaHavig
Goodreads: https://www.goodreads.com/chautonahavig
BookBub: https://www.bookbub.com/authors/chautona-havig
Pinterest: https://pinterest.com/chautonahavig
Amazon Author Page: https://amazon.com/author/chautonahavig
YouTube: https://www.youtube.com/user/chautona/videos
My newsletter (sign up for news of FREE eBook offers): https://chautona.com/news

All Scripture references are from the NASB. NASB passages are taken from the NEW AMERICAN STANDARD BIBLE (registered), Copyright 1960, 1962, 1963, 1968, 1971, 1972, 1973, 1975, 1977, 1995 by The Lockman Foundation

Fiction / Christian /Romance

~Dedication~

To every woman who ever felt inadequate and every girl who didn't know how to shut out the lies of society or a man who wormed his way into her heart only to crush it. There is One who loves you—finds you beautiful and precious. Hold fast to Him and allow Him to wash away all the ugliness and leave only the beauty of truth—that you are His workmanship, created in His image. He loves you with an everlasting love.

I am always left a little breathless at that thought, aren't you?

Wind whipped at her back as Carlie Denham rushed for the door at The Fiddleleaf Café. She stepped inside and crowded behind a group of would-be diners waiting for a table. "Busy," she muttered, as she shook out her hair and tried to kick a stray leaf from the heel of her boot.

"Yeah, twenty-minute wait for a table," a woman near her groused. "If I didn't love their turkey wrap so much, I'd leave."

After making a mental note to try the turkey wrap, Carlie inched her way to the hostess desk to add her name to the wait list. The right corner booth caught her eye and distracted her. A server laid a check tray on the table where a man sat with papers laid out and a laptop open. "Oh, just a minute. Be right back—maybe."

Three steps from the corner booth, she hesitated—until her stomach rumbled. An over-sized train station style clock in the middle of the room buoyed her courage. Her lunch hour would become effectively her lunch quarter-hour if she didn't hurry.

"Excuse me?" As the man put his finger on a spot on the paper he had been examining, she continued before she lost her nerve. "There's a crowd out there waiting for tables. I saw your server bring your check. Would you mind terribly if I joined you while you finish? It would speed things up for them and—"

The man didn't say a word, but he began gathering the stacks of papers spread across the table and scooted to the edge of the booth as if to leave. Dismay filled Carlie's heart. "No, I wasn't—I'm sorry. I'll—"

He gestured for her to take the other side of the booth and set the papers in neat stacks on the bench beside him. Without even a glance her way, he passed her the menu tucked behind the condiment tray, took a bite of The Fiddleleaf's famous cheese toast, and went back to reading pages of something—what she didn't know. The papers looked like exactly that—college papers. Carlie stared for a moment, shrugged out of her coat, and took her seat. "Thanks."

Uncertain what to do with a stranger for a lunch companion— much less one who had hardly acknowledged her, Carlie flipped open the menu and found the turkey wrap the woman had mentioned. It came with choice of soup or salad. She slid her eyes to the soup that came with it. *Red lentil soup—perfect. Hot, hearty, comforting. Exactly what I need on a cold*—a burst of rain splattered the window behind her—*rainy afternoon.*

The moment Carlie set down the menu, the man's hand rose, as if he'd been waiting for it—all while he continued to read and make notes on the papers before him. A minute passed—two. Still, he sat with the hand in the air until the server approached the table.

"How can I help you?"

Carlie smiled. "I'd like to order, please."

The woman whipped out her order pad and blinked twice before asking, "And what can I get for you today? Will this be on the other check, or—"

"No, a separate one, thank you." Carlie gave her order, requested a cup of plain tea, and sank back into the corner of the booth as the woman left. She gave her companion a friendly smile as she murmured, "Thanks again. I'm Carlie, by the way."

The man nodded, and he took another bite of toast. Though his eyes never met hers, she could see he was handsome—sort of. *There's something appealing about his face, anyway.* As she waited for her tea, she glanced around the café, taking in his features whenever he fell into her line of vision.

With his head bent half the time, Carlie had a fine view of his hair. Cut, style—everything seemed very conservative with just a dash of flair. In fact, there was something almost European about it—that and the sports jacket that hung from the hook on the side of the booth. *Is it really tweed?* Carlie didn't know exactly what tweed looked like, but she'd know the minute she could get to a computer. Her fingers slid over her phone as she made a note to Google tweed, and she cursed herself for being too cheap to invest in a data plan.

"Next year." She flushed as she inadvertently spoke her thoughts, but the man hardly shifted. "I didn't mean to say that—just thinking aloud." *Then again, who am I kidding? I'll have it ordered by next week now.*

Why she bothered commenting, Carlie didn't know. It seemed

ridiculous when her lunch "partner" didn't acknowledge anything at all. He wasn't deaf—that seemed certain.

Her tea arrived and the wild and irrational idea of taking a quick sip, so she'd burn herself presented itself. Would he ask if she was all right if she did? Then again, was it worth the pain just for that? Couldn't she ask him a yes or no question? No, he'd just shake his head or nod. Maybe his name…

Before she could decide if it was worth the awkwardness, her soup arrived. A large plate held the handled soup bowl and a tiny bowl of cumin and cilantro spiced rice. As if the arrival of her food was a signal, the man stacked his papers, slid them in his messenger bag, folded the laptop, and stowed it as well. Grabbing his sport coat, he stood and slipped it on over a turtleneck sweater.

What kind of man wears turtlenecks—much less cabled turtleneck sweaters? He's too young for such an old style, but somehow it works on him—that European thing again, she supposed. There it was once more, that wave of hair at the front, sliding down over his forehead as he grabbed his coat and flipping back effortlessly again. *Why don't more men embrace their wavy hair like that?*

He nodded at Carlie, hazel eyes barely meeting hers before he grabbed his check and bag and turned to leave. He'd made it three steps from the booth before Carlie called out, "Thanks again!"

She saw him wave as he turned the corner and smiled to herself. *He's a strange man, but there* is *something distinguished about him.*

Her wrap arrived and distracted her. *Whoa, that woman was right. This is seriously delicious stuff.* With each bite, she worked to identify the spices in the sauce, but aside from Dijon mustard and possibly ginger, she failed. Bite after bite disappeared. She cleaned the plate. Ate the last bite of soup. Sipped the last drops of tea. No check.

Twice, she tried to signal the server. Twice, she failed. Twice, she stared at her phone—*twice a minute is more like it,* Carlie mused to herself. Frustrated, she jumped from the bench, grabbed her purse and coat, and strode to the hostess desk. Her server rushed up to her as the hostess neared the desk. "Is something wrong?"

"I just need my check. Everything was delicious."

The woman offered a smile as she said, "Your check? It's paid."

"Paid?" Carlie frowned. "Do you mean the man?"

"Don't you know him?" The server—the name on her tag said Janice—looked confused.

"No. Do you? Do you know his name?"

"Sure, he comes here every Wednesday."

Carlie stepped closer. "Can you please tell me?"

"Sorry, I'm not allowed to do that." She glanced around her to see that no one overheard and added, "It would be an invasion of Dean's privacy if I told you his name." With a wink, she turned. "Thanks for coming and have a nice day."

Dean burst through the door of the men's Bible Study. "Good evening, everyone. I apologize for my tardiness."

"Look who decided to grace us with his presence." Greg Teigen looked up from his reading of James chapter three. "You're late on purpose, aren't you?"

"The infernal staff meeting ran late—again. It took more effort than it should have, but at last they agreed to table the discussion of this year's Reformation Gala. Why we discuss it, no one knows. The entire staff is fully aware that no changes will be made. The board will not approve anything that isn't 'traditional.' In the end, I suggested that we pray about it and vote next week. The Lord was merciful, and it worked."

Greg swept the room with his eyes. "Notice that he ignored the question? Conviction speaking, perchance? Or is he just avoiding the possibility of it?"

"I apologize, what was the question?"

"I asked," Greg said again, "if you were late on purpose. I mean, this *is* James chapter three… You know, 'teachers will incur a stricter judgment' and all that? If the professor among us doesn't, who will?"

"Quite amusing. I'm sure you're aware that the Greek word there—"

From the head of the table, the study leader coughed. "Let's get back to our reading now. Glad you could make it, Dean."

The longer Greg read James, the more uncomfortable Dean became. *James certainly had issues with speech. Much of his instruction to "the twelve tribes" relates to controlling the tongue—not sinning with the tongue. That is well and good, but how does this affect those of us whose professions require constant speech?*

"I've always said you chose the perfect profession—your two loves. Talking and the Bible."

Dean jerked his head toward Greg. "Pardon me?"

The table erupted in laughter. The leader smiled. "See, Dean. You talk when you don't even know you're doing it. It's like breathing or something."

His heart sank. *Wonderful. Now I've made myself an object of amusement with my lack of self-control.* The memory of his lunch changed the course of his thoughts. *However, this afternoon, I didn't. Today I kept quiet.* "Yes, yes. I need to learn to listen. I dominate conversations. I don't know when to 'be silent' or 'to speak'. And yes, it most definitely is an occupational hazard." Such confessions stung, and Dean couldn't help but add, "However, it is a part of my job, and I do enjoy my work."

"But you'd learn what your students know if you'd just be quiet and listen to them now and then," one of the other men said. "But I don't know if you know how to do that."

"I did it today…" Though he knew he sounded a bit belligerent, Dean smiled at the memory.

"Dean Sager listened instead of talked. This I gotta hear." Greg leaned forward. "C'mon. I want to hear the story."

"Isn't that counter to tonight's lesson? Aren't I supposed to be listening?"

"Well, since we all know you can't for long, how about you share when you did."

Despite the leader's blunt words, Dean heard love beneath them. "All right. This afternoon I was seated at The Fiddleleaf—as I am every Wednesday—correcting papers. All seemed quite normal, but then a woman asked if I would mind a lunch partner. If I recall correctly, she wanted to avoid a long wait for a table."

"Easy way to cut in line," someone murmured. Dean ignored him.

"Because my mind was concentrated on a particular point in the paper, I didn't speak at all. I suspected I'd lose my train of thought, you understand. So, I moved my papers out of her way and returned to my work. Didn't say a word. I planned to apologize when I'd finished with the task at hand. But then she ordered Jonathan's favorite meal."

All eyes turned to Jonathan Lyman. The man smiled. "Turkey wrap—comes with the best red lentil soup you've ever had. Delicious."

"Yes," Dean agreed. "Her choice brought Jonathan to mind—the way he often knows and understands people because he listens so well. I decided that since I would likely never see her again, it might be an excellent opportunity to attempt it—listening, I mean." He ducked his head. "In fact, I fear I only managed *not* to talk. I doubt I listened as much as I held my tongue. Somehow, I managed not to say a word the entire time." Disbelieving eyes stared back at him as Dean finished. "I do not exaggerate. I didn't even say goodbye. It was a strange experience—fascinating, but strange."

The leader perked up at those last words. "What about it did you find so interesting?"

"Unfortunately, she didn't say much. She introduced herself and thanked me for sharing the booth. I think that might have been when she mentioned talking to herself. I didn't quite understand that one. However, she did watch me." One of Jonathan's eyebrows rose. "By that, I mean to say that I was aware that as she sat and ate, she assessed everything I did. Fascinating experience."

"Assessed, huh. Is that professor speak for 'checking you out'?"

"Amusing, Greg. I can't say what she observed, but I do think she found my clothing style confusing. She kept staring at my sweater and jacket."

"You always do take your fascination with C.S. Lewis to an exaggerated degree."

The leader interrupted their repartee with a question. "I would like to know what you learned from this—if anything. You wanted to see what choosing to be a 'Jonathan' for a meal was like. So, what *was* it like?"

"As I stated, I found it interesting to observe her reactions to me. I don't think I've ever seen that." Dean felt his neck flush as he admitted, "Most likely because I rarely pay attention. She was curious, but she didn't pry. I had dozens of questions I wished to ask. Not asking *any* of them may be one of the most difficult things I've ever done."

This time, Greg asked a serious question. "If you had it to do over again, would you?"

"I've been pondering that question all afternoon," he admitted. "Unfortunately, I doubt I will never know. My initial instinct is to say 'yes,' but I know that it would be terribly difficult. Additionally, saying yes is simple when considering the unlikelihood of ever seeing her again. One cannot type 'Carlie' into Google and click the single entry that appears in order to send a lunch request. Can you imagine? 'Miss Carlie, I would greatly appreciate your presence at The Fiddleleaf next Wednesday. It is my wish that you spend your lunch break talking to me. I, on the other hand, will not speak. I will just observe you and listen.'" Dean shook his head. "We all know that even if the impossible were possible, a message such as that would likely earn me a restraining order and seventy-two hours in a psychiatric ward."

"Miss, huh…" The teasing returned to Greg's tone. "So, just how old is this Carlie?"

Dean shrugged. "I would surmise approximately mid-twenties. It is difficult to ascertain. She possesses the rare gift of one of those timeless faces. She has probably looked very much the same since she was sixteen—old for her age then—and will likely appear twenty years younger by the time she reaches middle age."

"I think that's Dean-speak for, 'And she's gorgeous, too.'"

As much as he would have preferred to deny it, truth overrode his embarrassment. "That would be a correct assessment."

Greg sat back and swept his arms out to the others. "Am I right, or did Dean choose the *wrong* time to decide to let someone else get a word in edgewise?"

"That is a little unjust," Dean protested. "I allow others to speak. This discussion is a case in point."

"When you need to come up for air—"

Dean shook his head and appealed to the other men in the room. "I leave it to you."

"Well, let's see. We made it through half of James *before* you got here and through the second half of chapter three *after*. What do you think?" The study leader grinned at his chagrin. "Don't feel too badly about it, Dean. Your love of discussing the Word blesses us all. Even when it morphs into interesting stories about how you tried to apply Scripture to your life."

"I didn't," he admitted, against his own prideful inclinations. "I tried to apply a curiosity to my life—Jonathan's personality."

Jonathan snickered.

"I apologize, Jonathan. I hope you understand—that isn't what I meant."

The study leader shook his head. "I know you. You've read James at least once a day since last week, haven't you?"

"Well, yes. I hardly see—"

The man held up his hand to silence Dean. "I think it's safe to say that James' words influenced your decision at least a little."

All the way home, Dean's study leader's words echoed through his thoughts. *"I think it's safe to say that James' words influenced your decision at least a little."*

"Unfortunately, I will likely never know. The odds of seeing her again are slim, and I wouldn't want to be *rude.*" He pondered that thought. "Yes, I would, of course, need to introduce myself at the very least. And I would be foolish if I thought I could do that without continuing with a conversation." The desire welled up in him, but Dean stuffed it back down as he pulled into his personal parking space. "Oh, well. It was an illuminating experience. I can say that for it."

The salon door mocked her as Carlie reached for the handle. *Why did I promise to come?* As she stepped inside, her heart sank at the sight of her friend's future sister-in-law. A pedicure and Rhonda's self-centered chatter, when all she wanted was a long bath and quiet—it seemed to be one of life's proverbial cruel jokes.

A receptionist beamed—much too brightly and energetically for a place that billed itself as "serenity in the city"— and asked, "Do you have an appointment?"

"I'm with Teresa Weldon's party."

"Oh, right this way."

Teresa waved, wiggling pink toes as a technician scrubbed the old skin from her heels. "I was afraid you'd back out!"

"No, sorry. Phone died, got back to work late from lunch, so had to stay—just everything that could go wrong did." She frowned at the already dying phone. "I need a new battery. Mine won't stay charged."

"I would go crazy without my phone." Rhonda, paused with a dramatic flair before adding, "But I suppose some people are fortunate enough not to have people texting or calling every few minutes." As if on cue, Rhonda's phone rang, and she waddled, toes in the air, away from the others.

Carlie took the opportunity to apologize again for being late. "I thought I'd call from the subway, but then the battery..."

"No worries. Rhonda and I were planning the bachelorette party. We're thinking two weeks from Thursday."

"What has Rhonda finally decided?"

Teresa glanced toward the door before whispering, "I don't know, and I need you to find out. Eric heard her say something about a stripper. He told her not to do it, and I just made a big deal about how horrible it was that Andrea had one—said I'd walk right out if anyone ever insulted *me* that way, but she wasn't very forthcoming about her own ideas."

"Got it. I'm on it."

Rhonda returned a minute later and stuck her feet in the air, waiting for the technician to finish whatever needed to be done to them next. "So, that was the venue for the bachelorette party. We're in. Now to find the decorations. I spent all afternoon looking for just the right things, but there is a serious lack of adequate and quality shopping opportunities. It's almost criminal."

Teresa, visibly desperate to change the subject, turned to Carlie. "So, besides working late because of a late lunch, how was your day?"

"Actually, that lunch was the best part of my day. I had an interesting lunch date with a stranger." The moment she spoke, Carlie regretted it. *Rhonda is going to pounce in five... four...*

"So, Carlie finally dumped her loser boyfriend and had a blind date?"

Less than three! Impressive. She shook her head. "No—"

"Internet date then," Rhonda insisted.

"Rhonda, let *her* tell it!"

Carlie zipped a look of gratitude toward Teresa before continuing. "I actually just did what Teresa is always trying to get me to do. I asked a guy if I could share his table."

"Well, we all have such unique ways of meeting new people, don't we? I'm impressed, Carlie. I don't think I'd have the guts to ask a strange guy to buy me lunch."

"I didn't—" Carlie sighed and continued. "Anyway, he agreed—sort of—so I ended up eating with him."

"Well, that's an interesting way to meet someone. Did you enjoy your lunch?"

Okay, I'm done. This is getting weird. She says all the right things, but there's such an edge to them. I can just tell Teresa about it later—when my phone has a charge, for instance. And she clearly doesn't listen. I already said I did. "Yeah. It was nice, and I didn't mean for him to, but the guy even paid for mine when he left. He had to have asked for the check because I never got it."

"So, what is this wonderful and generous stranger's name?"

Again, with the attitude. Oy. "Dean." *There. I know his name at least. That's a plus.*

"Dean what?"

Of course, you'd ask. "I didn't catch it. I mean, it was such a casual meeting at a table." She sent imploring eyes in Teresa's direction. *Help me out here, Teresa. I don't want to talk about it!*

"So, how did you ask him if you could sit there? Was there any kind of spark or...?"

"Um, I'm in a relationship... if you remember? You know, Blaine, the guy everyone but me hates?"

"That's because you're too good for him. He's such a jerk."

Carlie looked to Teresa for help, but her friend shrugged. "He doesn't treat you well, Carlie. You have to admit it."

"You guys just don't get him. And that's fine."

Rhonda broke in with yet another awkward question. "So, what does he do? This mysterious lunch date, I mean."

I don't know! I didn't talk to him! He was just a guy who had a bench I could park my butt on while I waited for some food. Fully aware that she'd never hear the end of a statement like that, Carlie opted for what truth she did know. "Well, he's some kind of teacher. I didn't catch what he taught, but he was grading some seriously long papers—five or more pages."

"Well," Teresa asked, "do you know if he eats there often?"

"Yeah... Every Wednesday."

Rhonda picked up the questionnaire baton with, "Are you going back? I mean, if he's there every Wednesday..."

"I thought about it, but I don't know," Carlie admitted. "I mean, it might be nice to try to pay for his lunch. It's kind of weird to have a stranger buy your lunch for you."

"My parents had an elderly couple buy our whole family ice cream once." Teresa sighed. "That was back when we were on food stamps and Dad hadn't worked in months. It was so cool."

"Is he nice?" Rhonda seemed to have forgotten the part about passing the baton to the next relayer.

"Well, he let me sit at his table, and he paid for my lunch, so yeah... he's nice."

Questions bombarded her, one after another. "Where does he work?" "What are his hobbies?" "Is he good looking?"

Frustrated, Carlie threw up her hands and the truth spilled from her before she could stop it. "Look, I don't know. He didn't say a word to me the entire time I was there. It's the strangest lunch I've ever had. All I can tell you is that he was nice. I don't know how to explain that, but it is what it is."

Understanding lit Teresa's eyes, and she shot Carlie an apologetic look. Turning to Rhonda, she said, "Hey, didn't you ask a guy to switch seats with you on a plane so you could have the window seat and all because he was cute?"

Translation: "Sorry for pestering you about it, Carlie." Carlie smiled at Teresa the next time her friend looked her way. *That's why Eric loves you— why everyone loves you.*

The girls agreed to meet on Saturday for final dress fittings and went their separate ways. All the way home, Carlie debated with herself over whether she'd go back the next week. The idea of Blaine finding out made her hesitant. *It's not like it's a real date. It would just be reciprocation. Then again, who wants the drama with Blaine?*

She rode the subway in stony silence all the way to the end of her line. *Of course, Blaine can go out with as many girls as he wants—whenever he wants. He just wants me sitting there when he's ready for me. Still, I did imply I'd be monogamous, regardless of whether he is. And he's speaking to me this week. It would be crazy to get him all worked up if he found out. He'd totally misunderstand.*

Decision made, she got off at her stop and walked the four blocks to her shabby apartment building. But the moment she stepped in the door, Carlie stared around the lonely little apartment and sighed. *With Teresa getting married, another friend might be nice. He seems like such a nice guy. And he's interesting.* A new thought hit her. *I can go just once more. I don't have to make a decision about any further than that. We can talk, and I can see what I think then. It's just lunch, after all. I'll tell Blaine myself. He can just deal with it.*

Once more, she made a decision and felt satisfied with it—right up to the moment when she saw a bright red circle around the second Wednesday in October on her fridge calendar. "And, I have a dentist appointment. What are the odds? That answers that question. By the following week, it'll be too awkward." She pulled a frozen burrito from her freezer and tore open the package before popping it in the microwave. "Now, for dinner."

While the turntable in the microwave spun, one last moment of indecision reared its head, but she shot it down. "No!" She jumped, startled at the sound of her own voice. "One lunch with *anyone* is not enough to decide to cancel an appointment over—especially since he might not even *want* someone interrupting his work like that. I mean, I haven't actually talked *with* him—just *to* him—barely."

Thirty-six papers on the meaning of Psalm 22 throughout the Bible lay spread out before Dean as he ate his potato soup and worked. "If I read one more *Eli, Eli, lama sabbath-ani,* I'll refer them all for tutoring in Hebrew," he muttered, as yet another student butchered Jesus' quote.

Janice appeared for his bowl. "You're muttering today. Kids not doing their work?"

He jabbed his pen at the paper. "Another student didn't take two seconds to check his spelling of a foreign word. This is *seminary!* They shouldn't require reminders to check their spelling at this level."

"Tell me how you really feel," she joked. Janice pointed to his bread and fruit plate. "Need a refill there?"

He hesitated, stared at the half-stack remaining, and nodded. "I'll be here for a while."

Two seconds after she'd turned to leave, Janice leaned back over his shoulder. "She's here!"

"Who?"

"That girl from last week. She jus—ooh, she's coming your way." With that, the server disappeared.

Carlie appeared before Dean could react. "Hey… can I—"

Dean cleared the table even as she asked. *Should I talk—introduce myself? Listen again? This is—*

"—sit with you again?"

As he raised his eyes to look at her, Dean realized he'd never be able to keep silent if he made eye contact. So, he continued rearranging his papers to make room for her and passed the menu. *Now, what will keep her talking? Perhaps I shouldn't leave so quickly this time.*

He tried to catch her reflection in the glass partition that separated their booth from the waiting area, but to no avail. The server arrived and asked if she'd like to order, but the woman insisted she'd need a little time. Janice's tone sounded amused—even a bit delighted.

You assume that because I don't bring dates here at lunchtime that I never have any. And the truth of my lack of dating prowess has nothing to do with your assumptions. I am not a desperate, pathetic dweeb. He frowned at that thought. *Did I just prove that I* am *a dweeb by using the word, dweeb?*

Her voice cut into his thoughts. "—thought I'd come back and see if you were here again. It seemed like some kind of routine, so I thought it was worth a shot. And," she added, as she tossed her coat onto the seat and slid into the other side of the booth, "I thought I could buy *you* lunch this time."

Not if I leave first, Dean mused. Two seconds—four—eight—half a minute passed. Dean felt his resolve weakening with his desire for another attempt at listening. *Perhaps if I ask a few leading questions. That would not qualify as* conversing, *would it?* The moment he thought it, Dean dismissed the idea. *As if I have that kind of self-control. Once I begin, I can't stop, and I know it.* The empty plate of fruit before him reminded Dean of Janice's promise for more. *Perhaps when she returns, I can offer some. A nice segue…*

A glance at her nearly destroyed his resolve. Carlie spoke just in time. "I almost didn't come—had a dentist's appointment. So, I figured I'd never get to repay you for lunch last week. Then they called to re-schedule. My dentist—get this—had an emergency dental appointment *for himself!* What are the odds? So, I came here instead."

Janice appeared again, passed him bread and fruit, and took Carlie's order. However, in an attempt to decipher a paragraph on the reasons Mark and Matthew may have used for their slightly different spellings of "Eli," he missed the exchange. Only the vague hint of something beneath the words registered. *And I missed it, of course.*

"So, you teach something, right? What do you teach?"

Kill me now. How could anyone expect me not to discuss my work? I teach the Bible! But a new resolve—strength even—welled up in him. Dean pulled a copy of the class syllabus from his bag and passed it to her with one of the better graded papers.

"Oh! *Introduction to the Books of Poetry.* So… you teach at…" She flipped open the folder. "Logos Theological Seminary. I have a friend that works there—in admissions. She's great. Maybe you know her? Desiree Ross?"

He did know Desi, but Dean managed not to say as much. He just smiled and tried to continue reading—and marking—paragraph after paragraph.

"I thought about trying some of their online classes. Our church in Morganfield wasn't all that... um... deep. I just realized a couple of years ago that I don't even know all the books of the Bible, much less in order. I keep trying to memorize them, but..." She sighed. "And memorizing Scripture too. I remember John 3:16 and Psalm 23—never read Psalm 22, I don't think."

Dean reached for a notepad and began scribbling down the books of the Bible in segments. Books of Moses, History, Poetry—every one. Then he added, on the back, a list of recommended passages to memorize and passed it across the table. *Let's see how sincere you are about it.*

"Oh, I have all the books listed at the beginning of my Bible, but—oh." He glanced up in time to see understanding brighten her face. "You broke it up into sections. That would be easier. Thanks. So, these five books here..." She flipped the paper and pointed. "These are what you teach?" He felt her attention shift. "Wait. Job? Isn't that about the guy God let the devil torture? Why is that poetic?"

You could be one of my students. I recall more asking that question than not. However, not answering became a form of pedantic torture. He ached to explain, to show, to instruct. *To flaunt your knowledge, you mean.* That thought sent his mind spinning in dizzying directions.

"I guess I could just try to take *your* class online..." Her food appeared before she could say anymore.

As he flew through his papers, Dean realized that at the speed he now worked, he'd have to leave sooner than he liked. So, he slowed, rereading paragraphs that he knew he'd skimmed too quickly. And as she neared the end of her meal, he zipped through pages belonging to his better students.

Talk. Say something!

"I have to admit," she replied as if she'd heard his thoughts. "I don't look forward to telling my boyfriend that I ate with another man—again—today. He's not going to take it well."

Another reason for you to sit, listen, learn, and keep silent. Perhaps she'll return. This could prove to be an excellent experiment, and her having a boyfriend removes the awkwardness that might come with misunderstanding. His inner self protested. *On the other hand, her boyfriend isn't likely to appreciate her spending her Wednesdays with another man—even one who doesn't speak. Once she tells him, it'll be the end of this.*

He felt it—a shift in her. That feeling that comes when someone is ready to leave. Dean shoved his papers in his bag and held out his hand for the syllabus and the paper she'd been reading. Carlie held them out of reach.

"I could hold it hostage until you tell me your name…"

He waited, hands extended, and stared first at her and then at the papers in her hands. She hesitated. Another glance at the paper brought a smile. Carlie peered in the syllabus once again and glanced back up at him. "Nice to meet you, Dean Sager. *Professor* Sager. She frowned. "Th.D.—is that *Dr.* Sager then?" Without waiting for an answer, she added, "I think I told you last week, but in case I didn't, my name is Carlie. Carlie Denham." With that, she passed the pages to him and watched as he stood, pulled on his coat, and grabbed his messenger bag. "You're an interesting man, Professor. I'm dying to know where you acquired your sense of style and what made you want to become a seminary professor." She leaned forward. "And how are you even *old* enough for that?"

With a smile and a nod, Dean turned and caught the eye of Janice across the room as he did. She met him at the register. "Nice lunch? Was everything okay?"

"Everything was perfect as usual." Just then, a cry of protest came from the booth. "I believe our guest just discovered that I thwarted her attempt to cover my lunch. Have a lovely day, Janice."

Before he could get through the door, Janice called back after him, "Thanks! See you next week."

A wave back showed Carlie standing at the register, frowning at him. *And if that wasn't a fine way to inform Carlie that I am here* every *week, I don't know what is.*

"—gotta cancel for next Friday." Blaine pulled her close as he shifted on her couch. "Tina got us tickets to that big five concert thing."

A dozen changes of mind over the previous three days had culminated in a couple of decisions. First, she would *not* tell Blaine about the lunches. Second, she would not return. But something about the nonchalant way he dismissed their date in favor of someone and something else rankled more than usual. *I can never tell if it's worse that he's honest enough not to hide it, or that he doesn't care enough about my feelings at least to pretend it's something else.*

"Whatever. So, what did you do this week?"

A rare compliment took her off guard. "You're so great, Carlie. So many girls get all bent out of shape when a guy—"

"Did I tell you I had lunch at The Fiddleleaf last week?"

Blaine stared at her for a second before shaking his head. "Um… no…"

"Yep! They were totally packed—twenty-minute wait on my break—so I just did what Teresa's always trying to get me to do and asked someone if I could join him."

"That's smart," Blaine agreed. Then it came. He stiffened, scooted back, and crossed his arms over his chest. "Wait, you ate lunch with a strange dude?"

"Well, in that I didn't know him, so he was a stranger, I guess. He was just a guy who got his check as I arrived, so I joined him. He even paid for my lunch. Nice of him, wasn't it?" *You wouldn't have. We both know that. You might have stiffed me with your check if you thought you could get away with it.*

"I don't think I like a strange guy buying you lunch."

Carlie stood and went to make popcorn. "Well, I guess that's too bad, because it happened. Twice."

That did it. Blaine jumped up and stormed after her. "What!"

"Well, I went back this week. The server said he comes every Wednesday, so I—"

"So, you asked the server about him? Just who is this guy?" Blaine's voice rose with every word until the tenant above them stomped on the floor as a reminder that their arguments were audible to most of the complex.

"His name is Dean. He's a theology professor at Logos, and—"

"Oh, an old guy." Blaine snuggled up to her, wrapping his arms around her waist from behind. "You had me worried for a minute."

Despite repeatedly ordering herself *not* to react, Carlie's mouth refused to cooperate. "Actually, he's not much older than me, I don't think. Nice guy."

"And you went out with him twice?" Blaine shoved her away from him. "Just who do you think you are? You're with *me*, remember?"

I think I'm the stupidest girlfriend on the planet to put up with this. Just who do you think you are lecturing me about letting a guy buy me lunch when your side girlfriend is buying you concert tickets? A few other choice thoughts formed, but Carlie did manage to control those. *Every time you slip, just once, your mouth becomes a cesspool of linguistic garbage.*

The thought made her smile. The smile made Blaine mad. The combination—not pleasant. He stormed to the door and demanded that she promise never to see Dean again. The hypocrisy of it all brought out a stubborn part of her that Carlie hadn't felt in a long time. "Um, sure. I can do that."

Blaine relaxed and shut the door quietly behind him. "I knew you'd see reason."

"Just as soon as you decide that you won't be spending all your free time with your little harem of dates. Otherwise, I'm going back. Deal with it."

She'd often wondered if Blaine would ever lose control and hit her. That had been her dividing line for the eight months they'd been together. And at that moment, seeing him shake with rage, she expected the worst. Instead, he stormed out the door and slammed it behind him. From the apartment upstairs, she heard what sounded like, "Good riddance!"

At halftime, Dean jumped up to grab snacks from the fridge. "Want anything, Larry?"

His stepfather hesitated before saying, "Yeah… I'll take another IBC. This one's about gone. Thanks."

With a bowl of Chex mix between them, and each holding a root beer bottle, the men chatted while waiting for the game to begin. "Do you remember last week—the girl who ate with me at the café?"

"Dark hair, porcelain skin, chocolate eyes? Yeah, you described her in exquisite—and as well as any Harlequin author ever could—detail."

"Amusing. Regardless, I thought it would interest you to know that she returned this week."

Larry shifted and stared at him. "The dark-haired girl came back? How did she know you'd be there?"

"I can't say for certain, but I suspect the server shared that bit of information." Dean repressed a smile. "She sat with me again and informed me that she intended to pay for *my* lunch this time. And—"

"Wait. You paid for her lunch? You didn't tell me that." Larry folded his arms over his chest and nearly knocked the root beer from his hand. "Since when do you do something like that?"

"A whim? And I did so again."

"Paid for her lunch? Why? I—"

Dean groaned in exasperation. "Aaargh. May I tell the story? No, I didn't speak—again." His forehead furrowed. "I suppose, then, I should say I *didn't* do it again." He shook his head. "I'm confusing myself—and you. Although, I suspect you are accustomed to that."

"Very funny. So how did it go this time?"

"Better, I think. It was certainly more *difficult*, but she opened up a little. I interacted just enough to encourage it, I think."

Larry didn't respond—not at first. He mulled over Dean's words for just a few seconds. Those seconds felt like hours. "So, what did you think of it this time? Is she interesting or did you learn… something…?"

"Carlie—that's her name—is interesting, actually. She gave the impression that she was reared in a religious home, but I didn't learn much more than that. She suggested that she didn't learn much in church as a child. I can't express it well, the way she phrased things implied that she came from a 'We attend church on Sunday, and they will teach you how to behave as a Christian' family. As if they didn't speak of Jesus the rest of the week. Anyway, she's from Morganfield."

"Kentucky, huh. Does she have an accent or…?"

"It's gentle—just a hint of one. I would very much like to hear her sing, however. She has one of those rich, deep, almost masculine voices."

"I see." Larry reached for a handful of the Chex mix. "So… when are you going to ask her out?"

"Why would I?"

"C'mon, Dean. I can see your interest even without the way you talk about it. You're fascinated by this girl."

Dean started to protest and stopped himself. *Am I? I wouldn't have thought so, but perhaps. No, this experiment has simply shown me an alternate side of conversation, and I enjoy it. That is—yes, it's just that.* "No, I don't think so—not like you assume. What truly intrigues me is the novelty of not directing a conversation. I learned tiny little things I might not have had I not been forced—self-enforced, I grant you—to simply sit and listen. That was much more difficult than I'd ever imagined, but it was rewarding."

"But maybe there's more to—"

"She has a boyfriend, Larry."

Again, there was just that brief hesitation before his stepfather responded. "You guys sure managed to talk about a lot in such a short time—just over lunch."

"You can share a lot when you are the only one speaking," Dean mused. He remembered a thought he'd had and added, "Larry, when I was dying to explain a few things to her, I felt quite—well, like a know-it-all. Is that how I'm perceived?"

"I'd say you love to share your knowledge, *both* for the love of the Bible *and* because you enjoy knowing things that others don't."

"In other words, I'm a *benevolent* show-off. So encouraging."

Larry's laughter nearly drowned out the sportscaster as he announced the kickoff.

All morning, Carlie deliberated over whether to go to the café again or just to let the experience die. She primarily leaned toward the latter—mostly due to the drama it would create with Blaine. *It's what I get for telling him. I just had to be all "in your face" about it. Now he's gonna ask, and he'll flip if I do.*

But, despite the reasons piling up on the "con" side of her list, a small part of her knew she'd yield and go. "Blaine'll have to deal."

"What?"

Carlie looked up from the stack of sweaters she'd been folding for the past twenty minutes and stared at her co-worker. "Did you say something, Chandra?"

"I asked what Blaine will have to deal with now?"

That's what you get for talking to yourself. The temptation to shrug off the question presented itself, but Teresa had been busy for the past two weeks with last minute wedding details, her mother became belligerent every time she mentioned Blaine's name, and she *needed* to talk out the situation with someone. "Well, I kind of don't blame him—somewhat." Carlie carried the stack of sweaters to the display and arranged them before returning to work on the blues. "A couple of weeks ago I went to The Fiddleleaf—remember?"

"Yeah. Lunch with the mute guy."

"Well, I went back last week. And I told Blaine. He was ticked."

Five, four, three, two, one...

"What!"

Right on time. "Yeah, well, wouldn't you be upset if your boyfriend

25

had lunch with another girl?"

"*I* would, but *your* boyfriend does it all the time, so why does he complain if you do? Talk about a stupid, sexist pig!"

"Yeah, well, he's *my* sexist pig," Carlie retorted with a hint of humor. *C'mon, don't make me get defensive. I'm not in the mood.*

"Look, Carlie. Obviously, there's something about this guy that makes him worth putting up with, but from an outside perspective, he's not worth it. I gotta admit that there are times I worry about you."

"Well, that's not necessary. With all his faults, he's not abusive."

Chandra crossed her arms over her ample chest—or tried—and dropped them to her hips when that failed. "Look, girl. There is more than one kind of abuse, and cheating on you, in front of your face, definitely fits. Carlie, he says the meanest things to you!"

"Yeah, well, that's probably my fault—"

"Classic abused line."

Frustrated, Carlie carried the sweaters to the shelf and shoved them in place. "Fine. Whatever."

A minute later, Chandra moved to her side. "Look, I'm sorry. I just care about you, okay? Is everything okay with you guys now?"

She nodded. "For now. But I'm trying to decide if I want to go back or not."

"Go back? Oh, to the restaurant? Why? You said he didn't even talk."

"That is what was so weird and cool about it. He didn't, but he's such a fascinating guy. I want to see if I can get him to talk to me." She blushed. "Weird, right?"

"So... I thought you said this guy dressed all weird. And that he wasn't that good looking. So, what makes him so fascinating?"

That, Carlie couldn't answer. "I don't know. I just want to go back. Like I said. Weird."

At that point, she knew exactly what Chandra would do. The woman grabbed the pile of tangerine sweaters that Carlie had folded and carried them to the shelf. Once more, Carlie counted down mentally. At two, Chandra called back, "Well, you've only got twenty minutes to decide."

"That's just it," she muttered. "I know I *have* decided. I just keep thinking that eventually I'll change my mind."

The clock on Dean's wall refused to budge. Surely, he'd been discussing Ryan Flichman's paper for three hours—explaining yet again why David felt forsaken by God even when God had not actually left him. "You cannot state that God did actually forsake him if it isn't true.

While *feelings* are real, they do not always reflect truth. David seems to have struggled with depression, so his psalms reflect that."

"But it *says*—"

"And Solomon says a lot of things in Ecclesiastes that demonstrate a lack of clear thinking, because they contradict what he says elsewhere. That is the purpose of that book. And the purpose of Psalm 22 is to demonstrate that though we may feel despair, God has not truly left us. Look here…"

Again, over and over, he drove home the finer details of the passage until Ryan leaned back. "So, what you're saying is God *inspired* David to write how *David* felt to show us that He doesn't do what *David* thinks He has done. Right?"

Finally! Dean screamed to himself. "Y—"

"Then why does Jesus—?"

Dean managed to stop himself from letting his head fall and bang on the desk in frustration. "I—" The alarm blipped on his phone. "I'll add this to this afternoon's discussion, but I have to leave now." The disappointment in Ryan's eyes made him add, "Ryan, these are important questions. I'm pleased you are searching for truth, but you still cannot say that God actually forsook the man after His own heart if He didn't. You must say that *David* said God did."

"Oh! Well, why didn't you say that in the first place?"

This time, Dean's head did drop to the desk. He covered by screeching, "Ouch!" and holding up his pen after fumbling around on the ground. "I have a terrible habit of not rolling my chair back before I lean down."

To his relief, Ryan expressed concern and left the office completely oblivious to the frustration Dean covered at great sacrifice to his appearance. "I'll probably have a mark on my forehead. That should make for stimulating one-sided conversation."

"What?" His top student stood in the doorway, a paper in her hand.

Dean flushed. *That'll hide my new injury but not the injury to my pride.* "I was chastising myself for a foolish action that resulted in this." He pointed to his forehead as he asked, "What may I do for you?"

"Well, here's Tiff's paper. She's doing better. I got her through the worst of it, but it's hard without telling her *what* to write."

"I appreciate that. I'll let the office know. How many hours was this one?"

"Only three." She dropped it on his desk and Dean swept it up into his messenger bag. She eyed it. "Going to take yourself out to lunch again?"

"Yes."

"Well, have fun…"

He winced at a hint of something in her tone. *Please don't form a crush on me, Amy. I don't need the hassle this year.* Dean grabbed the bag and hurried around his desk. "It's infinitely stimulating trying to eat and avoid splattering my students' hard work with the residue of my meals, but I try." The disappointment on her face told him two things. One: She *did* hope for an invitation. Two: She knew his habits—and from the hesitant look that followed—probably where he ate.

Should I try eating elsewhere—just in case? But what if Carlie came? The last two weeks would have been a wasted experience. Guilt prompted him to amend that thought. *Well, not wasted. That's not quite accurate. I just want more.*

As usual, Dean sat with papers spread out before him in different piles and, this time, a Bible open on top of two of the piles. A blue— cornflower, according to the sweaters she'd just folded that morning— sport jacket hung from the hook on the edge of the booth. *That is one fabulously nice jacket. How can a professor afford such expensive clothes?*

His hair flopped as he bent to read something closer. *He has some seriously awesome hair, too. Man. I thought Blaine's was nice.*

"Sooo… is it too much to ask—" The menu appeared before she could finish. "—I'll take that as a yes, then. Hi!"

A hint of a smile appeared at the corner of his mouth as he glanced up before taking a bite of his pot pie. He then began clearing the table, leaving only his plate and the Bible where they'd been.

"Wow. That looks good. I've never tried them—well, you know that. You've seen everything I've ever eaten here. That's kind of weird, now that I think of it." She examined the little pie. "That really looks good. Is it?"

Dean fumbled for his unused spoon and dug out a bite, being careful to scoop up a generous piece of the crust. He dropped the paper he held and used that hand to protect the table—and possibly her pants—from drips.

There was a camaraderie to his movements that touched her. The moment she took the bite, Carlie moaned. "Oh, man. That is seriously good stuff. You should stop working and finish before it gets cold."

Janice appeared before she could urge him further, but even as her attention was diverted between choosing roast beef pot pie and chicken pot pie, she saw him lay the paper with the rest and pick up his fork. *That's too cute. I got him to eat. I bet his food gets cold every week. I need to find a way—*

"Miss?"

Carlie blinked and forced her attention back onto the server "Oh, sorry. Drink? Um, I think I'd like the pumpkin latte. That sounds awesome."

"Sure. Would you like the salad…?"

That's what she said! "Um, yeah. I think I'd like that. Can I get balsamic on it?"

"Sure. Bread or…"

When Carlie hesitated, Dean reached for the little basket to his right and passed it across the table. "I think this is his way of saying he doesn't want this bread to go to waste. I'll be fine with this. Thanks." Before Janice could walk away, Carlie stopped her. "Can I be a pain and beg for some water, too? I'm parched."

The moment Janice moved away, Carlie leaned forward. "Can I pay for today? Please? I don't want to just keep showing up and having you pay for my food. I'd like to reciprocate, but if not, please let me pay for my own."

Of course, he didn't respond—not vocally. However, Dean did flip through the Bible for a moment. When he found what he wanted, he merely turned the Bible toward her and went back to eating the last few bites of his pot pie.

"Now I'm just supposed to know which verse you mean, huh? This is the weirdest conversation—or lack thereof—that I've ever had."

There it was again—a smile. *He listens, anyway. That's cool. I just wonder why he doesn't engage. It's like he wants to but can't. Is he that far behind with work that he can't stop to enjoy a conversation at lunch? And even if he can't, can't he say "hi" at least?*

Her salad arrived mid-thought. She poured a little dressing over the top, tossed lightly, and then pulled the Bible closer. "I guess I'll just read the whole thing—or at least until I find what you mean."

Between bites, Carlie read each word, including some verses she'd never seen before. But when she began the thirteenth chapter of Hebrews and got to verse two, she knew she'd found it. Aloud, she read, "'Do not neglect to show hospitality to strangers, for by this some have entertained angels without knowing it.'" Her eyes searched him, waiting for some kind of response, but, as usual, she received none. "I can't decide if you are being serious, flattering, or just teasing me into letting you have your way."

Dean looked up and smiled before picking up his next paper.

"I think it's the last one, but it worked, I guess. It does make me wonder if I should come back, though… Seems like using you if you keep it up and I know it."

Once more, he pulled the Bible close, flipped back toward the center, and found another passage for her. When Carlie took the Bible and began reading, she found herself again in the thirteenth chapter—this time in Matthew. *How am I supposed to understand this? None of it fits. Why is he doing this? I mean, he's sort of communicating—in a weird way. It's—* The thought died as she reached verse fifty-one. She couldn't help but laugh this time. "Oh, that's funny. I just saw the verse about 'Have you understood all these things?' and it was right after I thought to myself, 'How am I supposed to understand this? It doesn't fit.'" Aloud she read, "'They said to Him, 'Yes.' I guess that means I'm supposed to understand... but I still kind of don't."

Though he gave no indication that he heard her, Carlie did think she noticed him relax when she said, "Well, okay. I'll make you a deal. If I get here first, I get to buy lunch. If you get here first, *and you want to,* I won't argue if you take the check."

A crazy thought—one that made absolutely no sense but gripped her in a vice of panic—made her flush. "If somehow you know about my financial issues, you should also know that I put myself on a strict budget in September. I give myself two meals out a week and I have to eat the rest at work—food from home. I do those mason jar salads that are so popular. I make them all on Sunday night—one for each day of the week—and on the days I eat out, I have one for dinner. So, see, it's really not... and yeah." She shook her head and shoved her half-empty salad plate aside. "That was stupid of me. There's no way you could know that I have a boatload of debt to pay off—all credit card, of course. I didn't go to college, and now I'm stuck in this dead-end job. Yeah, someday I'll be manager—but manager at a retail store isn't exactly a fabulous career. Good grades in high school aren't enough if you don't *do* something with them. Now I can't even afford to do online courses or anything. More debt would kill me."

It felt like the floodgates opened, because before she knew it, Carlie was ankle-deep in her personal struggles. "I know it's stupid—even when I'm doing it—but I have a fight with Blaine, and I go buy a new pair of boots." She stuck out her foot to show off her current footwear. "These I got after I told him I wasn't okay with him skipping my friend's wedding. It's just not cool." She sighed. "I won that one, too, so why did I need to spend sixty-bucks—on *clearance*—to console myself?"

Her pot pie appeared and distracted her until the check arrived. She noticed that her order had been added to it instead of put on a separate bill. That prompted another thought, and she rushed to assure him that she could afford her "deal."

"Oh, and I've already set aside my saved lunch money." She dug through her purse and pulled out an envelope. "See?" To her astonishment, he actually looked up. "I've got plenty in here. I add to it each week, so if I beat you, it won't be going on the credit card. Okay?"

Dean flipped the page of the paper he'd been reading and continued as if he hadn't heard her. If she hadn't seen him backtrack and reread a portion of the previous page, she would have been certain he'd ignored her.

He is paying attention. It's so weir—

Carlie's cellphone rang, interrupting her thoughts. "Oh, wha— Teresa! Hi! Just eating lunch with Dean again. Yeah…" True panic filled her as her friend reminded her that she was supposed to have been at a final fitting—twenty minutes earlier. "Sorry! I'll be—" Carlie took a quick bite. "Rwhight dhar. Sorry," she swallowed. "Took a bite. I'm on my way."

She started to apologize to Dean—to thank him for lunch—when he reached across the table, removed the mini-loaf of bread, wrapped it in a napkin, and tucked two pats of butter in with it.

"Wow. Thanks. You seriously must have the world's happiest girlfriend. See you next week—I'm determined to beat you sometimes."

Just as she rounded the corner, Carlie peeked over the top of the frosted glass partition that ran along the tops of the booths and saw Dean sitting back, paper down, smiling.

Rhonda jerked the door of the bridal shop open just as Carlie reached for it. "Well, someone finally decided to show up. Dean get tired of you?" With that, she sauntered down the street, her hips swaying in a way that would have gotten Carlie grounded until she was thirty as a teen. *Who am I kidding? Mom would* still *try to do it if she saw me shake my hips like that.*

At the back, picking at the bodice of her gown, Teresa stood on the dais and spun slowly. "I think it's just right. What do you think, Carlie?"

Something Carlie had read in a magazine made her shake her head. "No, no. Dance."

"What?"

"*Real Bride* had an article about the most common mistakes brides make with their dresses and number eight was not making sure they could move in it. Dance."

Teresa swayed, arms over her head. "Feels fine."

Determined to do her job as bridesmaid to the best of her ability, Carlie jumped up on the dais and grabbed Teresa's hands. "C'mon… *dance!*" She began singing "Twist and Shout" at the top of her lungs. Their laughter drowned out any hope of finishing the song, but she did manage to prove that the dress would allow true freedom of movement.

"Perfect." Teresa hugged her. "Thanks. I never would have

thought of that. Now go get your dress on."

The dress fit perfectly—better than any dress she'd ever worn, better than any*thing* she'd ever worn. "I love this. I love it! Look!" She stepped out of the room. "Isn't it fabulous? Every bridesmaid should be given the opportunity to wear something that actually fits *and* looks good. Seriously, you are a genius."

"That's about the opposite of what Rhonda said."

"Now I would never have imagined…"

Teresa laughed. "Yep. It's too tight, the color is boring, and the fabric is too 'street.'"

She shouldn't have been surprised, but Carlie couldn't help but ask, "Seriously?"

"I thought that it was mild for her. I mean, it took this long to say anything. That shows unusual self-restraint."

"She probably thought you'd change your mind from the million hints she left."

To Carlie's surprise, Teresa didn't respond. Instead, she changed the subject. "So, you were at lunch with Dean. How was that?"

"Weird. I mean, good weird, but weird. He's still not talking, but he kind of did today."

"How do you 'kind of' talk?"

Carlie hurried back into the changing room to change. Part of her insisted that speed was a waste of time. *I'll be late as it is.* But the need to *keep* her job kept her hurrying—hurrying and talking. "Well, I told him that I couldn't just keep coming if he wasn't going to let me pay—at least for my own meal."

"That makes sense. It would be kind of rude just to show up, I guess."

"That's what I thought! But he flipped to some verse in the Bible about showing hospitality and entertaining angels. I almost thought he was flirting with me for a minute, but then when I asked how I was supposed to handle that, he just flipped to another verse that basically said, 'yes'." She rolled her eyes in the mirror. "Whatever that means."

Carlie stepped back out of the room as she pulled on her coat. "Look, I'm super late. I wanted to talk about it, but I'll have to wait until I can call. I really don't want to talk about this around Rhonda. She's too—" Carlie blushed.

"I know. And, you know, it sounds to me like this guy was *asking* you out to lunch with his Bible verses. And if someone invites you, it isn't rude to accept."

"What if he doesn't want to anymore? I would just keep showing up and he could keep paying for a lunch he doesn't want to have."

"Or he could go somewhere else…" Teresa kissed her cheek and shoved her toward the door. "Trust me, if a guy wants to get away from a girl, he'll find a way. Go. Have fun. And who knows, maybe he'll turn out to be someone you *really* like."

"I *really* like Blaine," Carlie insisted. "And this guy is way out of my league. I think he must have like old family money or something. His clothes really seem crazy good quality."

She hadn't made it to the corner when she heard Teresa calling out behind her. "Stop, Carlie!" Seconds later, she stood before Carlie, hands on her knees and gasping for air between words. "You—you have this—stupid idea—that— you just aren't—worthy of good things. Well—it's not—true." Teresa hugged her and whispered. "If you love Blaine for who he is, that's great. I want you to be happy. But if you are with him because he's all you think you deserve, then know this. You're wrong."

Guests mingled, laughed, drank, and well, danced to the tune of "Dancing Queen." Alone at the bridal table, Carlie picked at the half-eaten food on her plate and allowed a server to refill her nearly empty wine glass. Her eyes sought Teresa and Eric, and despite her own funk, she couldn't help but smile at the picture they made, swaying beneath the soft lights of the giant chandelier. *I want that. And not with a guy like Blaine who would just* abandon *me like this.*

Though she worked herself up into an indignant determination to expect better for herself and her relationships, a few more sips of wine and the sight of Rhonda pointing at her and giggling into the ear of a handsome man sent it all crashing down at her feet again. *Yeah, I may think I deserve better, but why? Why should I expect that a really great guy would settle for a girl with no education, no future, no self-control, and a history of choosing the wrong guy? I mean, that's just stupid. That makes* me *the wrong girl. It doesn't take a genius*—the thought of Dean made her smile ever so slightly—*to figure that out.*

As her eyes focused again, she saw a man at the next table watching her. He smiled, and, at first, Carlie wondered at whom or why. However, the memory of her own smile at the thought of Dean made her flush. *Great. He thinks I'm flirting with him.*

The man stood, grabbed his own drink glass, and joined her. "Not a dancer?"

Carlie sighed. "No, actually, I love to dance."

"Then why aren't you out there dancing with your date?"

That was very smooth. Complimentary and inquisitive both. "Well, I would be if he hadn't bailed on me between the ceremony and the reception."

"He left you at the church?"

Sounds almost like I got jilted at the altar. "Not quite. He didn't bother to come to the ceremony either. I got a text about three minutes after the last person made it through the receiving line. I think Vic gave him a heads-up when I got to my phone."

"Usher Vic?"

She nodded. "Yeah. Vic doesn't like me." *Stop whining.* "But anyway. It's all about making sure Teresa's having fun, and I'd say she is."

"She'd have more fun if you were dancing." He held out his hand. "Dance with me?"

While the decision wasn't exactly unconscious, Carlie did, a minute or so later, find herself clapping with the rest of the guests at the DJ's joke between songs. Before she could thank her partner for the dance, the distinct, delightful voice of Louis Armstrong singing "What a Wonderful World" filled the room, and Carlie found herself pulled back into his arms. "We can't walk off on this one," the man protested.

"It's my favorite song," she agreed. "I can't *not* dance to my favorite song."

"See, I already know one of those things guys are supposed to know about girls."

"Oh really?" Carlie murmured. "And what other things are guys supposed to know?"

"Favorite flower?"

"Freesia." She shook her head as he started to ask another question. "Oh, no. I don't know *your* favorite song or *your* favorite flower."

"Song— 'Bohemian Rhapsody.' Favorite flower—whichever one will give my date the most pleasure."

The exaggerated wink he gave her made Carlie laugh. "Okay, that's good."

"So, favorite movie." Torn between a joke and her true favorite, Carlie hesitated. He gave her a small spin before pulling her just a little closer than he had before. "You're one of those people who likes too many things to choose?"

"Fatal Attraction."

The color drained from the man's face. "Oh—"

Carlie couldn't restrain herself any longer. Her laughter echoed around them, and Teresa, dancing past, grinned. "Great. Now Teresa thinks I'm cheating on Blaine."

"Blaine the couldn't-be-bothered-to-come guy?"

She nodded. "Yeah."

"His mistake. Now is that really your favorite movie or did I just fall for a good one?"

"I've never seen it."

"I think I like you. That's genius." The crowd of clapping dancers blocked their path as he tried to lead her back to the table as the song ended. "Drink?"

"Sure."

"Only if you tell me your *real* favorite movie."

And here's where he goes to get me a drink and never returns. "Seriously?"

"That's why I asked."

"*Cinderella.*"

"Disney or Rogers and Hammerstein?" The man stood with his arms over his chest, daring her to make the wrong choice.

"Well, the fact that you know Rogers and Hammerstein even *did* a Cinderella musical, hints that you're a genius of a guy, but, of course, it makes the 'right' answer easy." She rolled her eyes at herself and her "air quotes."

The man didn't get it. "What?"

"Seriously? Air quotes? What next?"

"I'll be right back," the guy promised.

Yeah, sure.

But before she could reach their table, he reappeared with punch in hand. "Favorite book?" He held it just out of reach.

"Um…" Carlie flushed and drained her drink. "Okay, people always roll their eyes, but it's *The No. 1 Ladies' Detective Agency.*" The disbelieving look on the man's face made her giggle. "I know, it sounds silly, but it's really a great book. It usurped my lifetime favorite, *The Secret Garden,* last year."

"Got it. I'll be sure to look it up. I've never heard of it. I was sure you'd say Alexa Hartfield." He thought for a moment. "Hmmm… um, what other questions are guys supposed to be able to answer? Oh, favorite col—"

"Name would be good, don't you think?" Carlie grinned at the sheepish look on his face.

"I'm Beverly Fillmore and you are…"

Talking to one of the Rockland Fillmores? Oh, man. I made fun of him! "Carlie Denham. Right hand to the bride. Nice to meet you."

"No quirky jokes about my name?"

"It's unusual—now…"

He shrugged. "Once upon a time it was a guy's name. And my family hasn't embraced the switch yet."

"Do you go by Lee or…?"

Beverly shook his head. "Unfortunately, no. I tried that in the third grade. I nearly got disowned, and my mother still has palpitations when someone mentions it."

So not just a rich, educated guy—but one with a snobby mother who probably requires college transcripts, blood tests and criminal background checks of any girl her little boy blinks at. Carlie gave him a weak smile. *Yeah, well, I won't pass.* "Bev?"

"Only slightly better than Lee. 'Your name is *Bev-er-lee*, not Bev. Not Er. Not Lee.' I tried to get away with Lee again when I went off to Stanford, but—"

Carlie jumped up. "Sorry. Looks like Teresa needs us. I think they're getting ready to leave. It was nice meeting you." *And nice to get away before you find out that I dropped my one and only community college class before the end of the first week.*

"Hey, can I get…" Beverly's voice faded into the general buzz of the room as she hurried to Teresa's side. A glance over her shoulder showed him staring after her, confused. She saw something else—something that took her a minute to identify. Disappointment.

It's easier this way—for both of us.

Dean shifted again as he heard the sounds of the street filter through the background noise of the restaurant, a signal that the door had opened. The next line seemed disjointed, and only after he'd marked the place did he realize he'd skipped the line above it. *Pay attention.* Despite his internal orders, his eyes slid to the small pumpkin truffle sitting on a lone saucer across from him. *She probably despises pumpkin and white chocolate.*

He felt her presence seconds before her skirt appeared in his peripheral vision. This time, she didn't ask. She simply sat down and curled up in the corner of the booth—smiling. "I thought I'd beat you here today, but I guess not. You must get here really early."

As his answer, he passed her the menu and took a bite of his pastrami on rye.

Carlie moved her silverware out of the way and smiled at the truffle. "Is—is this for me?"

Dean only smiled and continued reading.

"Thank you. That's—that's just really nice of you."

The rattle of flatware as people unrolled their napkins and the clink of forks against plates reminded him that they weren't alone. *Why does it feel as though we are?* He wanted to ask—to insist on knowing what she thought—but of course, he didn't.

She ordered the turkey wrap again. Once Janice left them alone, Carlie began talking—rambling really. "Remember how I said my boyfriend would be ticked off? Well, yeah. He totally flipped out."

I can't really fault the man. I would be disconcerted if my girlfriend informed me that she planned to have lunch with another man—and had already done it twice.

"—jerk about it. I mean he can go out with a ton of girls and that's just fine, but if I dare to eat lunch across from a strange man—well, a man I don't know. I guess I can't say you're actually 'strange'..." She eyed him. "Or are you..."

Acting quite strange right now, in fact. Lord, this is concerning. Someone should inform her that this man sounds dangerous. His conscience slapped a bit of sense into him. *Okay, perhaps that is rash. There could be more to it than she said, but, Lord! I don't care what her faults may be, going out with other women... She implies that he expects monogamy at the same time. Is it a fact, or is she just suspicious about his behavior? I could be misconstruing her words. Not asking questions requires many assumptions, which can lead to errors in judgment...*

When his mouth tried to open—almost of its own accord—determined to tell her that her boyfriend sounded like someone who would leave her heart *and* her arm or neck broken, Dean clenched his jaw shut and willed himself to mind his own business. *She didn't request your opinion. It's the purpose of this little experiment—learn how to allow others to have opinions you don't agree with.*

Carlie's voice broke in again. "—decided that he can just deal with it. It's not like I'm going to run off with you to wherever people go when they run off these days."

She is, as Larry would say, "on a roll" today. Dean took another bite of his sandwich and sipped his coffee as his thoughts wandered all over the place. Once more, Carlie's voice interrupted them.

"—tried to punish me with the whole 'I can't go to the wedding' thing, but I'm ignoring it. Teresa said it's like a little kid throwing a fit for attention. Ignore them and they don't get what they want."

He stared at her, uncomprehending. Her lips moved and words formed, but they made no sense. She must have noticed because she repeated herself. "It's crazy, right? I mean, he's known about Teresa's wedding for months. He went to the couples' shower with me—complained all the time about how I wasn't available because of that dumb wedding,' but once it was here—with an open bar, no less—he just goes parasailing with the worst of the girls." A sigh escaped. "Okay, in *his* eyes, she's probably the best—"

No, he should think you're the best, or he should let you go.

"—I mean; no girl wants to have to compete with someone who should be a super model. I get *why* he wanted to go with her. She probably wore a shirt cut to *there*." Her finger pointed to the general vicinity of her midsection. "And jeans that she airbrushed on that morning, and she probably hung *all* over him, but still..." Carlie sighed. "Pathetic, right?"

Janice brought Carlie's soup and told her to enjoy, but the server's eyes remained on Dean. He read the message loud and clear. *Do something for her. Help her.*

But his conscience objected. *You cannot discern if this is a genuine problem or a matter of perception.*

When, once again, he stared at his hands—his *clenched*—hands, Carlie sighed and said, "Yeah, I know. He sounds like a big jerk. And I don't help that when I get upset about stuff like this. I mean, I'm not good about also telling my friends when he brings me my favorite ice cream or tells me I'm beautiful. I'm more likely to tell them how he brought me the ice cream and joked that he shouldn't because I'm getting chubby."

Dean started at those words. *Chubby is ludicrous. I am confident that you are in the perfect range for your height and bone structure—your* fine *bone structure, I might add.*

Her next words gave him verbal whiplash as he tried to follow the rabbit trails of her thoughts. "You wouldn't be the first to tell me that," Carlie admitted. "Everyone says he's just a jerk, and I should dump him." At his look of disbelief, she shrugged. "Yeah. Everyone. None of my friends like him, and only a couple of his friends dislike me, so sometimes I think they're right. But he's not all bad, like I said. I just get hung up on the negative when it comes in clusters. He does care about me. He is always disappointed if I can't do something with him or if he gets called into work. And it's not like he's *abusive* or anything."

Is he not? In an emotional way, perhaps? No, you've implied that he doesn't physically harm you, but it would be bad enough to hint that you were fat if you really were. To say that when you're not sounds more like some twisted mind game. A new idea struck him. *I suppose he could have a social skills deficit—perhaps Asperger's?*

"—at work thinks that him going out with other girls is just as bad as getting physical, but he just goes out with them because I *won't* get physical." She flushed. "And I can't believe I just told you that." She took a bite of soup before adding. "Yeah, so anyway, it's like everyone's against us. But I think if they really knew him, you know? I mean, they seem to like *me.* And I'm with *him,* so why can't they trust that I know what I'm doing?"

For several bites, Carlie said nothing, but midway through the small bowl of soup, she dropped her spoon, "Man, I'm sorry."

Dean couldn't help it. His head jerked up and he stared at her, trying to understand why she'd apologize. Something in her expression nearly overrode his plans to keep his mouth shut. *She doesn't appear to be truly afraid of this man, but she does seem a little…*jumpy *about him. If he's half as rude as he seems…*

For ten minutes, Dean tried to read his papers and finish his food.

But when he didn't even make it through an entire paper, he glanced at his watch and decided to spend the rest of his time between classes locked in his office where he couldn't be distracted.

Carlie sounded disappointed when she realized that he intended to leave. "Oh, busy day? Yeah. Well, maybe I'll beat you here next week." She fingered the saucer that still held the truffle he'd brought for her. "Thanks for this. I really needed something like it today—something that tells me the world isn't an ugly place."

Those words tore at the fabric of who Dean was as a person. He paused as he pulled on his blazer and grabbed his coat and hat, almost yielding to his desire to tell her to surround herself with people who speak truth. Instead, he gave her a weak smile and hurried away before he lost all self-control.

However, as the hostess rang up his check, he stopped Janice on her way to turn in a check. "You heard her, right? The way she talks about this boyfriend?"

"Sounds like a jerk to me. I don't care what her hidden flaws are; she shouldn't have to put up with that stuff."

Dean glanced over Carlie's way and saw the defeated look on Carlie's face, which sealed his resolve. "Perhaps coming from a 'stranger' it might sink in. If you find a chance, would you consider suggesting that if *all* her friends and family are opposed to this man, that perhaps, just maybe, the problem is in him rather than *everyone* else?"

"I could lose my job, or I would."

"What if you phrased it in a way that implied I asked you to say it? Something like, 'I think Dean wanted to say…' or something of that nature?"

"That I can do." Janice eyed him curiously. "So, what's with you and the silent treatment? It's crazy quiet once she gets here."

He pulled on his hat and moved toward the door. "New experiences, Janice. Have a wonderful day."

After the third person knocked on his door, Dean remembered exactly why he'd given up trying to work through his lunches at the school. *This is insanity. If one more person asks if all is well, I'll do an Irish jig or something.*

At that moment, a student burst into his office without knocking. *I should have locked it as planned.*

"Dr. Sager, my counselor says if I don't get my grades up by the end of this semester, I'll lose my financial aid." He dropped into the chair in front of Dean's desk with an air of defeat.

"Well, then—"

"But it's so easy to say, 'Bring up your grades,'" Trace wailed. "It's not so easy to do—"

"Well, actually, in your case, it is. You're intelligent, you know the material, you are perfectly capable of writing a decent paper if you put forth the effort. But you don't. And no one but you can make you do what you need to do to pass this class."

"But you don't understand, I—"

"Do you remember what you told me the first day of class?" Dean waited half a second before continuing. "You said, 'I'm an A student—never got more than a couple of Bs in my life.' Then you said the same thing the day you earned your first C. 'But I'm an *A* student.' And what did I tell you?"

"'Then do A-level work.'" Trace began to say more, but Dean was on a roll.

"This is the scourge of modern education. Students enter college who previously enjoyed the fruits of mommy micromanaging their schoolwork to ensure they did well. Mommy *did* their schoolwork in the name of 'helping,' or mommy fought the school until the school capitulated. Then these unfortunate students enter higher academics incapable of functioning without mommy looking over their shoulders, and you all expect me to say, 'Oh! I forgot. You're an *A* student. Let me go erase the grade you earned and give you the one you think you *deserve.*'" Dean shook his head. "Not in my class. This is *seminary*, Trace. It's time for you to stop whining and do the work we both know you're capable of doing."

Trace started to say something—to object—but he stood. "Fine. Whatever." The way the young man stormed out reminded Dean of a toddler deprived of his desires.

Dean shook his head and went back to grading papers. *They always come in with such entitled attitudes. Why doesn't* someone *prepare young people for the realities of life outside high school?*

"Dr. Sager?"

Tiff of-the-improved-paper inched her way into the room. "Sorry, I couldn't help but overhear."

"I should not have raised my voice."

"You should have been nicer. He spends all his time here helping everyone else and then has to go home and take care of his mom—dying of cancer, you know. It's not easy to get your own stuff done when everyone else needs or demands something from you."

Guilt kicked him in the gut and left him gasping for air. "I was not aware. Why didn't he—"

Tiff—the girl he had secretly dubbed "the clueless wonder"—interrupted him. "Because you didn't let him. He kept trying to tell you,

41

and you just kept going off on him. It's like you decided you knew what he'd say, and you answered that rather than what he *did* say." She turned to leave, but, at the door, she added, "I thought you were nicer than that. I'm pretty sure Jesus would have listened."

Conviction hit hard and fast. Dean jumped up and grabbed his bag, shoving his papers inside. He hurried out the door, pausing by his classroom only long enough to drop off his bag and write out a quick assignment and a note on the whiteboard. *If I'm late, begin with the vocabulary words. I'll return shortly.*

It took Dean twenty minutes before he finally found Trace in the library—thanks to the librarian's assurance that the young man spent most of his free time there between classes. "Always helping someone," she assured him.

Groups of studying students dotted the room as Dean made his way to the corner where Trace sat alone, hands covering his head and staring at the page before him. "May I speak to you for a moment?"

Trace glanced up and back down again—but not before Dean saw a frown on his face. "I really need—"

"Please." Dean swallowed what was left of his pride and said, "I owe you an apology."

Trace's eyes rose and his expression changed. "You heard. I don't want pity. I just want—"

"Half a chance? Perhaps a suggestion for how you can improve? I'd like to begin with that apology, maybe a bit of prayer, and a plan, if that suits." Two seconds after he'd finished, Dean shook his head. "I do that often, don't I?"

"Finish people's—"

"Senten—oooh boy." He sighed. "People have told me for years, but I didn't quite understand the severity of my flaw. I do now, I suppose."

The Wednesday before Thanksgiving arrived, and with it, a rainstorm that left Carlie dripping as she burst into The Fiddleleaf Café and accepted a towel to wipe off her umbrella. To her astonishment, she had to wait—not only for a place to sit, but an extra few minutes just for *their* booth.

"Wow. In almost two months of Wednesdays, I've never beaten him or had to wait," she told the hostess.

"He's usually here long before now. We held it for about ten minutes on the hour but then we had to let it go. You want to accommodate your regulars, but…"

Janice caught her eye and gave her a thumbs-up. Seconds later, heads appeared over the booth, and a trio of businessmen rounded the corner. The hostess noticed and nodded that direction. "Go ahead. We'll get it cleaned up in just a second."

But, as usual, The Fiddleleaf staff impressed her, and someone was already clearing the dishes from the table. Only once—that first day—had she ever had to wait for anything. *Probably because they were used to his work pattern.* A smile formed as she remembered him sitting there with his hand in the air. *Well, no one can say I don't mix things up.*

"Can you hand me that menu? I'd like to order right away—starved."

The man—one of the holiday hires, if Carlie read him right—handed one to her and said, "Today's kitchen tasting was fabulous. They have a chili size that is out of this world. I've never had chili so good, and the burger patty is so flavorful—comes with a salad that has this spicy dressing—amazing."

"Thanks!" Carlie closed the menu. "I'll have that then. You're new?"

The man nodded. "I'm supposed to be serving, but one of the bussers didn't show up today, so they put me here for 'training.' Don't blame them, but kind of disappointing too. Tomorrow, though."

"Well, your attitude and helpfulness is great. I'll put in a good word for you." Carlie slid into the clean seat and smiled. "And at least you do a good job. Booth looks great."

"Can I tell Janice to get you something to drink? Coffee? Tea?"

"I'll take the pumpkin coffee. Thanks."

"And you're ready to order, right?"

Carlie smiled. "You're gonna be a huge asset here. Yes, I'm ready."

Never had Carlie felt so awkward sitting alone in a booth. *It's just because you're used to using him as a personal therapist-slash-sounding board.* A rifle through her purse showed her Kindle and a small notebook. *I could make a Christmas list... For the sales on Friday. Yeah.*

She stared at the empty seat across from her and back into her purse. *I could also put his card out now. Might be less awkward. But he's probably not coming.* Carlie reached for it and hesitated as her fingers gripped the textured envelope. Janice passed with a pot pie that smelled amazing. Another server brought out what had to be the fajita soup. Her stomach rumbled as she sat there, hand shoved in her purse, and deliberated the earth-rocking decision of whether to remove a card from her purse or not. *I'm just being stupid. Why not?*

Her shopping list, however, she filled without hesitation. With each gift listed, her discomfort grew. *I'm going to end up deeper in debt. This is crazy! Why didn't I shop all year long? I say I will every year, and then I never do.* Six more names and items stared back at her by the time her meal and Dean arrived.

"Hi! You came! I beat you and we have a deal, remember?"

As expected, he didn't respond. Well, he didn't speak. But the smile he tried to repress—and failed in the attempt—told her he both remembered and wouldn't cheat. Dean picked up his card and smiled at the "address" she'd written. A thought occurred to her, and she snatched it back. Several quick lines gave her the look she wanted and she passed it back. "I should have done that. Teachers—especially *professors*—should have apples, right?"

Dean fumbled through the pocket in his blazer, pulled out a little packet tied in jute string, and passed it to her. A tiny tag that read "Happy Thanksgiving" hung from one of the bow loops. She untied it immediately and pulled a stack of sticky-notes from a plastic wrapper. A flourish and a short verse about "redeeming the time" kept a simple gift from being boring.

I need to remember that. This is the kind of gift I need to find—gifts that reflect the person or our friendship rather than the value trying to reflect how I feel about them. Yeah.

After flipping through the little stack of notes, she smiled. "They're all different. Wow. Thank you!"

Twice she saw him finger the edge of the envelope as he perused the day's specials. But when he set the menu aside and reached for the papers in his bag, Carlie reached over and nudged his arm with her index finger. "You going to open that card or not?"

With a smile, he reached for it, turned it over, and started to unfold the flap from inside the envelope. Each movement, in painstaking slowness, was clearly designed to drive her utterly crazy. He succeeded. But when he reached for the card inside and then folded it all back up with speed that needed a slow-motion camera to appreciate, she rolled her eyes. "You are cruel."

The Southside Plaza buzzed with shoppers who didn't seem to realize that the economy hadn't quite recovered from its latest downturn. *Or perhaps they're each single-handedly trying to reverse it. This is unbelievable.* Dean rode the escalators to the third floor where he wove through the throng to the door of The Nuttery. *If I didn't love Larry, I'd inform him that cinnamon almonds are bad for his cholesterol and leave. That looks like a line out the door.*

Before he could thread his way through the shoppers, he heard a voice. *Carlie!* His eyes scanned through the sea of faces and landed on hers. *She's so beautiful. And the best part is that it is if that popular song was written just for her. She doesn't seem to know it.* As her head turned his way, Dean ducked into an accessories store and nearly knocked over an earring turnstile. He fumbled to straighten it and then backed out of view of the doorway. To his dismay, the group of women entered. *Just leave, and if she sees you, smile and wave. This is not an impossible situation. On the other hand, you could say hello. That might be amusing.*

But he didn't. Dean nearly squeaked past, but hearing his name made him duck behind a display of scarves and listen. "—the cutest little sticky notes. It was genius. I mean, there are these little verses on the bottom of each one. It fits him—being a seminary professor and all—but it's something we've talked about—"

"I thought you said he doesn't talk."

Dean knew, even without anyone referring to the woman by name, that she had to be Rhonda. *Your snide reputation precedes you.*

"Okay, *I've* talked about, and *he* has… listened. I told him I wanted to do more Bible memory. Look how awesome." She dug in her purse

45

and pulled out the gift that he'd agonized over for days.

Well, at least she *appreciates it. That is what matters. However, the boyfriend probably has other opinions.*

"Blaine pitched a fit, of course."

"Well, I can't really blame him," Rhonda interjected. "I mean, Blaine is a jerk, but you *are* his girlfriend, and some other guy did give you a present."

"A five-dollar package of Bible verses. Yeah, he's totally in love with me and trying to steal me from Blaine." Carlie rolled her eyes at the other woman. "What do you think, Teresa? Did Blaine overreact or not?"

"I think he did. I mean, he's accepted super-expensive tickets and stuff from girls. Forget that. I've seen him *kissing* other women. For you to accept a little token of the holiday is absolutely fine, and he's one hundred percent wrong. You never pretended you weren't eating lunch with Dean, and you didn't hide it from him. That's more than he can say."

Dean tried to force himself to leave. A straight shot to the door opened, and he started toward it, but Carlie's next words stopped him again. "It's silly, but this is probably the most *thoughtful* gift I've ever had. I mean, even if it jumped off the shelf and into his shopping cart while he was buying toilet paper and shaving cream—he's got killer after-shave, by the way—he still realized that it was a nice way to encourage me to do what I said I needed to do."

Killer aftershave, is it? Nice.

A display of ivy caps produced a snicker. "I bet Dean would *love* these. If I could afford it, and if it wouldn't cause world war three with Blaine, I swear I'd get him this one."

"He actually wears those? What guy wears those?" Rhonda snickered again. "You've got a weird dude. If you go missing, I'm going to send the police to that seminary and have them question him."

Not wanting to hear just how ridiculous she considered his personal style to be, Dean turned to go when he heard her say, "That's just it. It really suits him. I don't know how to explain it, but he's got like this Euro look going for him. Blaine would look totally stupid in the same stuff, but I can't imagine Dean in Blaine's clothes either, so, whatever."

"Defensive, aren't you?"

Okay, I officially do not like you. What makes you such a miserable person? Is rudeness and snark impregnated into your DNA?

"Oh, and here I thought we were just having a conversation. I didn't know you were actually trying to insult him, but now that I do, yeah. I am defensive."

"You have to admit, the stuff you've described is a little out there," Teresa murmured. "So, it's hard to picture it as anything but kind of silly."

Dean could only imagine what Carlie had said about his wardrobe. *I admit that I'm a little... eccentric. Is that such a fashion crime?*

"—know how Prue wears all that hippie stuff—totally out there? It's like that. It works for her, but I'd look totally stupid in her clothes. His works for him when it wouldn't for most people."

"Yeah, but Prue still stands out and looks ridiculous. Yeah, it's attractive on her, but put her in a room full of average dressers, and she just looks awkward."

Though he expected Carlie to protest, she didn't. "Yeah... that's true. Maybe it's because she's more casual looking and Dean is always so polished. I guess—oh! I know. It's like Alexa Hartfield. No one thinks she looks ridiculous when she's walking down the street like she woke up in the wrong decade—"

"Or century," Teresa joked. At Carlie's protest, the woman laughed. "No, really. I get it."

"I don't."

Of course, you don't. You don't want to understand, Rhonda; do you?

As if clueless to Rhonda's deliberate snark, Carlie tried explaining again. "Well, she can look like a flapper in a room full of people with jeans and t-shirts. It's flattering and weird at the same time. Anyone else in the room doing something like that would look out of place, but it just works for her because of who she is as much as what she wears."

That's a fascinating way of putting it. I wonder if it's true.

The conversation shifted just as Dean ducked behind a shelf of purses to avoid being seen. *I must leave. The others are waiting. They'll be merciless if I tell them about this. Regardless, I wonder what Larry thinks of her theory...*

Just as he passed the window, Dean saw Carlie holding up a pair of earrings. The way her head turned, the earring sparkled, the girls laughed at something she said—it all combined into one attractive picture. *Attractive and uncomfortable.*

Minutes later, as he stood in line at The Nuttery, Dean remembered the note she'd written on her Thanksgiving card—the note that he'd read so many times he'd memorized it. *"Thanks for giving (see how I did that??? good, right?) me the opportunity to just 'be' me without any expectations. Having someone to talk to every week is really wonderful. I hope you have a great Thanksgiving."*

Carlie reached for a coffee mug from the dish drainer but dropped it and did a half-jog to the right when a mouse scurried straight toward her. "Aaaaaaaack!"

"What is it, babe? If you spilled—"

"I didn't *spill* anything. There's a mouse!" Movement in her peripheral vision sent her jumping on a chair. "It's gross! Ew! Get him!"

"I'm not chasing all over your kitchen for a stupid mouse. But I do need some more milk. Oreos without milk are disgusting."

"Mice in my *apartment* are disgusting! Do you *want* mouse droppings all over your mug?"

"Just wash one. C'mon, the commercials are almost over."

"Just wash one." Why don't you *just wash it? Seriously, I have* vermin *in my kitchen and all you care about is getting your precious milk. It's like the G-rated version of "Gimme anoddah bee-ah."*

And with a further blow to her self-respect, Carlie did it to keep the peace. But as she sat down beside him, Carlie growled, "I am not taking this lying down. Tomorrow, I get a cat."

"Isn't that overkill? Just get a couple of mouse traps. Call an exterminator. Cats are litter boxes, spilled food, and claws in your back at two o'clock in the morning."

"And they're mouse killers. Twenty-four-seven protection against droppings in my dish drainer. I mean, that was low, even for a mouse."

"I doubt it was personal."

"Well, I'm taking it personally. That mouse will regret ever setting a whisker in my living space. He's going to be food for feline in a matter of hours. Ha!"

Apparently, her indignation sparked Blaine's affectionate side—a testimony to her ability to delight him with her quirkiness. While that usually annoyed her, being still unsettled by the discovery meant she wanted to feel protected from an invasion of scurrying creatures. *I've seen* Ratatouille. *I know that if you see one, there could be hundreds.* She shuddered, which prompted Blaine to pull her even closer.

"It'll go away now. I bet you scared it as much as it scared you. Or maybe a shard of flying glass—"

"Ceramic."

"—right. Ceramic sliced it good and it's bleeding out somewhere." He kissed her cheek. "You're so cute when you're mad."

Why do guys say that? Don't they know it just makes us madder? Carlie realized how ridiculous her thoughts sounded. *I guess they do. It's deliberate.* She crossed her arms over her chest. *Jerks.*

D

ean found himself distracted—unable to concentrate on more than a sentence at a time. Christmas music played in the background—Mannheim Steamroller, he thought. As if percussion to "Deck the Halls," plates rattled just as he got to a complex sentence in the third paragraph. Laughter erupted at the table next to him—loud, raucous guffaws over something he suspected was crass. *Glad I missed the joke anyway.*

The closer it came to her usual time, the more distracted he became. *She likely saw me and has informed the police that I am stalking her. She won't come.*

Janice paused. "Have a good Thanksgiving?"

"Yes, you?"

"Not too bad. We all got a pie to take home, so my family was happy—no pathetic Janice food this year."

"I take it that you are not fond of the culinary arts?" Dean tore off a piece of bread from his bread bowl and sopped it in the stew juice. "Actually, I can see that. Something about you says, 'I'm too busy socializing to babysit a burner.'"

"That's it! That's it exact—oh!" Her voice dropped. "I think your date's here. You sure do torture her with your silence. Gotta tell me about that sometime." Janice turned to Carlie as she appeared. "Hi! Coffee or tea today?"

"Coffee—please. Thanks." Carlie smiled at Dean as she seated herself. "Have a nice Thanksgiving?" As she spoke, she flipped her hair behind her shoulders and the earrings she'd admired in the store dangled from her lobes.

You decided to purchase them. Good decision. They look lovely on you.

"—to Morganfield to see my family. Dad deep-fried a turkey. It's his thing. I wanted to stay all weekend, but the shop needed backup, and I agreed before I knew what day I was agreeing to, so I had to come back early. Missed all the Black Friday hoopla, which is nice. I'm not safe around sales—which, will mess up my Christmas shopping and make it worse. A girl can't win." She waited for Janice to set down her coffee before continuing. Had he not looked up at just the right moment, Dean wouldn't have seen Carlie handing their server a note.

What was that?

"—just hung out at the mall with Teresa and Rhonda. Well, for a while. Rhonda decided I was too much of a downer on her mad shopping skills and took off with another STDer."

Dean couldn't help himself. He raised his eyes from the paper in his hands and stared at her with an unspoken question in them.

"Wha—oh. Shop-till-you-drop-er."

So, isn't that STYDer?

She laughed at the concentrated look of confusion he tried to manufacture. "Yes, we left out the Y. Because shop-till-drop-er still works, and STDer sounds funnier."

Before she had her sugar in her coffee, Carlie's phone rang. She snatched it from her purse with speed that could have been eagerness to answer or to stop the noise. Dean waited for confirmation as to which. "Hey, Sarah! How—"

From the exasperated expression on her face, something had gone wrong. Dean struggled to follow the conversation even as he marked up quiz answers. It sounded like another wedding—like something had gone all wrong.

"—it's *your* day. So, if she doesn't like it, she can just bow out. It's better to have an extra groomsman than to be all stressed out on your wedding day. Want me to call her and tell her to back down?" From the way she pressed on the fork in her hands, Dean began to worry that she'd bend it out of usefulness. "I don't care what she thinks you should have in your bouquet. You call that florist and tell them that you're paying the bill, and if it isn't what you have in your contract, you won't accept delivery."

That will ensure she has no flowers at all. Wouldn't that be worse?

The bride clearly had the same question, because Carlie said, "I'll be on call and go to grocery stores and grab stuff last second. We can make it work, but you shouldn't have to pay hundreds—" She blanched. "Okay, *thousands* of dollars for flowers that aren't what you want or what you ordered! Now go call 'em. Don't back down now!"

As she disconnected the call, Carlie sank against the booth back.

"Whew. People think that if they can push a bride around then they should. I don't know if it's making up for all the bridezillas out there or what, but I'm sick of it. They tried it with Teresa, too, but her mom fielded all the mess for her. Sarah's mom is half the problem."

Janice appeared to take Carlie's order, and behind her stood the owner. While Carlie debated between the French dip and the "leftovers special," Frank clapped a hand on Dean's shoulder. "How've you been? I haven't had time to come talk to you lately. Students treating you well?"

"Hello, Frank. I'm very well, thank you. How are you?"

Frank beamed. "Business grows every week. We're talking to an interior guy to see if we can increase seating without compromising comfort. So far, he wants to pull out these booths, and I've said no."

Dean winced and shook his head. "Please don't." He glanced at Carlie and saw her eyes widen with shock and her jaw drop. *So, you enjoy our Wednesdays as much as I do...* He smiled at the thought. *"Our Wednesdays—it has a nice sound to it.* Another thought assaulted him. *Oooor is that your "I can't believe he's talking in front of me" expression?* Before Frank could reply he added, "I'd be sorry to lose this booth. It's my favorite."

He should have expected it, but Dean's internal monologue, combined with the delight in watching Carlie's reaction left him almost speechless as Frank asked, "So, who is your friend?" Frank offered his hand to Carlie. "Frank Manis."

When Carlie didn't offer her name, Dean capitulated. "Frank, may I introduce Carlie Denham. She works over at Skyline, if I recall correctly."

"Hi! How do you know Dean?"

"I don't—but I'm learning. He's a bit of an enigma."

"Dean?" Frank stared at him and then back at Carlie. "I don't think I've ever heard anyone say that about Dean. Then again, you bring out a different side of him. The whole restaurant is talking about how he's so fascinated by you that he's speechless—not exactly the Dean we know and love. I usually have to remind him that my employees are here to work, not visit."

Perhaps you should "spread it thicker," Frank. Are you aware that this is torturing me? He glanced across the table and sighed. *If I read Carlie's face correctly, she set this up with that note. Well played, Carlie.*

"I'd say he's just struck dumb by my beauty, or my mesmerizing conversation, or something equally fabulous, but let's face it. That's not likely. I can't decide if he just doesn't like me or if he's just that conscientious about his work." Carlie sat back, crossed her arms over her chest, and leveled a "take that" expression on him.

"Isn't she amusing?" Dean heard himself say before he realized what he was doing. "She believes that there's a man alive who could think clearly with a beautiful face like hers across from him." Carlie blinked and scowled at him. *That might have been overkill. Retreat.*

"He has a point," Frank agreed. The man's eyes traveled to the other side of the room. He nodded and turned back to Dean and Carlie. "They need me in the kitchen. Someone is probably trying to smoke the turkey or something equally devastating to my insurance policy. Nice to meet you, Carlie. You keep him in line. This is an interesting Dean we're getting to know here."

Left alone, Dean met her eyes, smiled, and then forced himself to look back at the paper in his hand. *There is no reason not to speak now. You just—* the thought died as a new one surfaced. *Then again, my comments were restricted to Frank, not Carlie. So maybe…*

"Sounds like you're usually chatty enough. It's interesting to try to figure out why you're not with me. Oh," she waited for him to look up at her, but Dean didn't yet trust himself to refrain from talking. She tapped his leg under the table, and this time he looked up at her. "Thanks for the compliment. That was nice. I—" Her phone rang again. "Sorry, Sarah. Wonder what's up."

From the sounds of it, the flower situation had escalated. Dean set aside his paper and ate, shamelessly listening to her side of the conversation. "Okay. Just hang on. Let me see what I can find out before we do this. So help me, if I see Darby, I'm going to slap her into next Tuesday. This is a nightmare. Call you back."

Well, are you going to share, or shall I create my own story?

He needn't have urged. "Can you believe this? So, Darby is like this frustrated bride-wannabe who keeps putting her nose in. Self-appointed maid of honor, no less. First, she called and changed up the flowers—pretended to be Sarah! So, Sarah's order for bouquets and arrangements of chrysanthemums became poinsettias. Darby thinks that chrysanthemums shouldn't be seen after Thanksgiving. Like it matters what she thinks!" As she ranted, Carlie searched through her phone. "Ugh. Can't find—"

Dean pulled out his laptop and passed it across the table. He scribbled the Wi-Fi password on a sticky note and passed it as well.

"Wow! Thanks. Anyway, so Sarah finds out and calls the florist—like I told her, you heard—and the florist can't *get* enough chrysanthemums now. It's too late. I've got to find someone who can supply us with enough in two days. As if."

While she called what seemed like every florist within a four-hour radius, Dean finished his food, pulled out his papers, and managed to get several graded. She worked, moving the laptop to the bench beside her when her food arrived, for a good fifteen minutes before giving up.

"No one can do it on that short of notice. Great." She passed him the laptop. "Thank you anyway."

Wouldn't it be just as effective to purchase them at local stores? Eager as he was to help, Dean decided to assume that she'd already considered and rejected that idea for reasons he couldn't fathom.

She dialed yet another number—Sarah's, if the defeated look on her face meant anything. "Hey, Sarah. Look, no one has chrysanthemums. They just aren't out there. So, this is what you do. You call your florist and tell them that you want them to substitute gerbera daisies for the chrysanthemums. Tell them that the contract explicitly states that all changes have to be made in writing, and they do not have that. So, since they can't provide what they promised, they need to substitute with the daisies at no additional charge." A wail of protest reached Dean's side of the table. He looked up, smiled, and gave her a thumbs-up. Carlie sagged against the bench and her furrowed forehead smoothed. "No way! The contract clearly states that if for any reason your flowers are unavailable, they have the right to substitute something of equal or greater value. Well, they need to exercise that right. Don't back down. Just do it." This time, the protest sounded a bit milder. "This is why you read contracts. You all thought I was stupid for being so 'OCD' about that. Well, this is why. I have it all in my notebook."

Dean raised his eyebrows and folded his arms over his chest. Carlie fought back a snicker and pulled a little spiral bound notebook from her purse and flipped open to a tabbed section marked "Sarah's wedding." *Her handwriting is stunning. It's almost like a trendy, well, not quite calligraphy. Regardless, it is incredible.*

"Okay, Sarah. Let me know how it goes. Talk to you later."

As he passed back the notebook, Dean met her eyes and held them, trying to show her how impressed he was with how she'd handled it. Carlie flushed and Dean smiled. *It seems that you read me well.*

"Bad thing is, I really hated the chrysanthemum idea. I think she chose them because they're cheap and colorful. Gerberas are better. She'll be glad she had them when she sees the pictures."

Her phone rang again. Dean expected another call from Sarah, but Carlie exclaimed, "Hey, Mark! How are you? We're so bummed—what?"

Janice passed by the table and Dean stopped her. "Can you bring us a piece of carrot cake?"

"Sure—one each or…"

Dean hesitated and shook his head. "Your pieces are big. One is fine. Thanks."

"Oh, wow… yeah. I—okay. I can do that. What time? She's going to be so excited! Okay. I'll be there. See you soon!" Call disconnected,

Carlie leaned back against the booth, eyes sparkling. "Mark's coming. He's at the airport in Tampa now. Sarah is going to be so excited." She paused and gave him an inscrutable expression. "Did I hear you mention carrot cake?"

He only smiled in response.

"Man, you are awesome, you know that? It's exactly what I need today. That, and another cup of coffee."

Dean's hand shot up in the air again.

A gentle knock on the door jerked him from his study. He looked up in time to see Amy Westin peer around the door. "Can I come in?"

"Of course. May I help you?"

She nodded, holding her most recent paper in one hand and her backpack in another. "I have a problem with my paper."

"I doubt that. It is no secret that you're my best student. If I recall correctly, you had a perfect paper." Dean accepted it with confidence and smiled at the A at the top. "See."

Amy reached for it and flipped the page twice. There, she'd highlighted a section of a paragraph. "I put that in there deliberately. You missed it."

Dean read the words, confusion filling him. *Therefore, one can clearly see that the book of Proverbs, written by the Apostle Paul, was written to help the New Testament church know how to function in relation to church government and day-to-day living.* He glanced back at the front page and then flipped to the last where he'd written his notes. *Excellent work as usual, Amy. You demonstrate a solid understanding of what a proverb means and show a clear progression of Solomon's life through his proverbs.*

He blinked before looking back up at her. "I don't understand."

"That sentence was in there the whole time. You missed it." She pulled a chair closer to the desk and sat down, dropping her backpack beside her. "Dr. Sager, you've been missing a lot of stuff lately. We're all a bit concerned. Well, and some of the class is relieved, but I don't think they should be. I mean, this is *Bible* we're talking about."

"I've overlooked others?" Dean's heart sank. *I couldn't have.*

"I've read enough of them to know. There's a lot of stuff you usually wouldn't let get past you." She shifted awkwardly. "But I'm really here because we're worried about you—if this is even you." She fidgeted. "Are you okay?"

Oh, no. Now she's "bonding." What do I do?

"Dr. Sager?

He scrambled to respond. "I apologize, Amy. I'm just a bit—well, dumbfounded."

54

"I told everyone you probably had someone grading for you. I just thought you should know." She stood and turned to go. "I hope I wasn't out of line when I wrote that crazy paragraph. I—" Amy flushed. "I just thought I probably could afford the hit to my grades more than some of the others. It was supposed to make you wonder—if you even saw it."

Dean found himself in the unfamiliar and awkward situation of having little to say even when he could speak. He just nodded at first— nodded until he saw the pained look on her face. "No, you were right to show me. I needed to see this. I'll take care of it. Thank you."

Long after the door shut behind her, Amy's words reverberated in his mind and heart. *"...this is* Bible *we're talking about."*

Carlie knocked on the door to the dressing area. "Can I come in?"

"Sure!" Sarah fussed with her necklace. "Did they come? Are they right?"

She pulled out her phone and flipped through pictures. "I have them setting everything up in the sanctuary first and then they'll bring the bouquets and boutonnieres to us after that. They're late, obviously, but considering they had to scramble for flowers, I didn't give them too much grief."

"You are a lifesaver! These are gorgeous—better than the others."

"Well, duh. You ordered *chrysanthemums.* Who does that?"

If Carlie hadn't known that Darby-the-wedding-wrecker had never met Rhonda, she would have sworn they were either twins or out to create a new wedding nightmare—bridesmaidzillas. "Well, she ordered what she wanted, and I'm sorry she couldn't have it. But these do look great."

"Oh, ignore Darby. She's been in a snit all day. Comfort Janet instead. Her dress is too big." Sarah winked at Carlie. "I keep telling her it would be worse if it were too small!"

Carlie eyed the dress and shook her head. "That thing isn't safe. You're totally going to fall out of it if you try to dance."

"See! That's what I said!" Janet crossed her arms over her chest. "I am so not dancing."

"Oh, c'mon. It's not that bad," another bridesmaid—the groom's cousin from Schenectady—insisted.

"No, really." Carlie raised Janet's arms over her head and the dress came dangerously close to ultimate exposure. "Take it off. I'll figure something out."

"Only Janet would have sympathetic nerves badly enough that she *lost* weight before the wedding," Sarah teased.

As Carlie examined the dress with its full lining and boning, she shook her head. "Okay, Janet. You can have comfort, or you can have coverage. What'll it be?"

"Coverage!"

"Got any crunchie mama guests, Sarah?"

"What?"

"People who might use diaper pins?" Carlie frowned as Sarah shook her head.

Sarah's mother stepped forward. "I have an emergency sewing kit…"

"Well, I don't know how to sew, but I'm about to find out. Okay. Let's see it."

Her first attempt failed the minute Janet bent over to strap on her shoes. "I think I just ripped out the stitches."

"Was it too tight?"

"No, it was perfect, but…"

She tried again with smaller, tighter stitches, double threads, and several whips along the top of the seam to finish it off. "If that doesn't hold, nothing will."

"I didn't know you could sew."

"I can't. I told you. But I think it'll hold now." Carlie heard a knock at the door and went to answer it. "Flowers are here. Everyone decent?"

As she pinned a corsage on Sarah's mother's dress, Mrs. Milton asked, "Have you ever considered wedding planning? Sarah says you've been a lifesaver this week."

T
he sight of Dean working hard on his papers brought a smile to her lips as Carlie shrugged out of her coat and hung it. "Hard at work, as usual."

At those words, he marked the paragraph, stacked the papers on the table, and set them all in his bag. That's when she noticed—he either hadn't received his order—or he hadn't even ordered yet. He passed her a menu, his finger tapping the attached daily special, and grabbed one for himself.

"Done already?" The moment she asked, Carlie realized she'd begun to hope—just a little—that he'd eventually interact with her. She also realized that today was not that day.

Janice appeared. "Ready to order now? The special right?"

Dean nodded and pointed to something else. "Will you bring this later as well?"

"Sure." She turned to Carlie. "What can I get you?"

"Dean seems to think I'd like the special, too. So, let's go that way."

"Oh, so his vow of silence is over, is it?"

Carlie snorted. "That would make more sense if he didn't just refuse to talk to me. Unless..." She reached across the table and grabbed his wrist. "You will answer this. Do you have some sort of religious conviction against talking to women? Like some kind of vow or..."

Dean smiled... and shook his head.

"Whew. The last thing I need on my head is guilt because I've been irritated at a guy who's just obeying God."

"Weird god to do that," Janice muttered. "Be back with some

bread and a…coffee?"

"I think I want a Coke, if that's okay."

Not until she went to unfold her napkin did Carlie realize she still held his wrist "Oh, sorry."

His not working changed the dynamic of their lunch. She was used to jabbering at him about whatever was on her mind that day. It had become like a personal therapy session—a chance to unburden all the thoughts that she felt too stupid to say aloud. But with him no longer distracted, his eyes occasionally on her, opening up became harder—more awkward.

The sight of a flower in the vase on the table gave her something to talk about. "The wedding was gorgeous, by the way. The flowers—perfect. I think Sarah was glad that Darby ruined things for her. It was a good lesson for the flower shop, too. Those people could have gotten someone who would sue. I mean, that was a total breach of contract."

Dean listened. Despite the disinterest he tried to feign as he fiddled with a straw wrapper, he listened. And as he did, the initial awkwardness morphed into their usual camaraderie.

"So, the wedding could have been a disaster. Sarah didn't have a bunch of things covered. The ushers didn't know where to go or what to do—started to seat people by walking them down the *aisle!* The flower people were late, and no one was out there to tell them where to put what. I probably got half of it wrong, but at least the flowers were in place." She sighed. "Man, those gerberas are so pretty when arranged well. This florist was really good with that. I mean, she altered the design just enough to ensure that they looked good without doing anything that further risked their contract. Genius."

Her Coke appeared as if out of nowhere, and Carlie watched as Dean just sat. Listening. *He looks upset. What's going on?* When he just sat—waiting—she asked the obvious question. "Are you okay?"

Dean's smile didn't light his face like his quiet, amused smiles had in weeks past. He seemed ready to explode with something. *Or are you ready to bolt?* She shook her head. "I don't believe you. I wish you'd tell me."

An almost imperceptible glance toward his bag prompted a new question. "Student struggling? Maybe with his or her faith? That would be hard as a Bible professor, I suppose."

Her words stung—she could see it in his eyes. She didn't know how close to the mark she was, but Carlie did know something was off. "Sorry. Well, then you'll just have to let me jabber about this wedding, because I have to talk it out." She took a long drink of her Coke and frowned. "I shouldn't use a straw. Just read about how it causes lines around the mouth—premature aging. That prompted a snort from him.

"Glad to make you smile."

A text message appeared, and she smiled at the picture. She passed it to Dean. "That's Sarah and Nate in the Bahamas. Makes a mess of a day all worth it, I guess."

Before she could continue, Janice arrived with their plates. "Two specials, more bread?" She stared at the still-full basket. "Or not... Anything else?"

"I think we're good, thank you, Janice." Dean gave the server a weak smile. "When you see us nearly done..."

"Sure."

"What did you order this time?" Carlie picked up her sandwich and took a bite. "Mmmm... wow."

Without his work to distract him and her conversation to distract her, they ate more quickly than they ever had. Carlie finished first. "So, I wanted to tell you about the rest of the wedding. Why? Who knows? It's not like you know these people or care. Anyway, apparently, they also didn't do a fitting a week before the wedding, because one of the bridesmaids had a dress that literally fell off of her. I had to alter the thing at the last minute." She leaned forward. "I can't sew. But if my friends are going to keep getting married, I might need to learn."

The one thing she'd wanted to talk about became more difficult with each passing second. Finally, in a moment of "do or die," she blurted out, "Sarah's mom said something just before the ceremony started. She said that I was good at organizing the wedding and handling problems—"

Dean's nod surprised her. "You think?" He nodded again, this time with a genuine smile. "Yeah... I think so, too. I wonder what I have to do to learn how to do that. It wouldn't be the dead-end job that I have now." She sighed. "Okay, it's not really. I can advance up to management eventually. I can. But I don't know if I *want* to manage retail for the rest of my life, you know? This sounds fun, but for all I know, you have to have a degree for that, too—hospitality or something."

Janice arrived with The Fiddleleaf's famous brownie a la mode. She set it on the table with two forks and smiled. "This guy is a keeper. Just sayin'."

"Yeah, well, I don't think my boyfriend would like to hear that."

The expression was fleeting—almost nonexistent—but Carlie could have sworn Dean masked disappointment. *All day I've wished he'd talk to me, but maybe it's good he doesn't. That right there—that looked like things could get complicated if he did.*

59

Never had Dean been so nervous before class. Even on his first week he'd been confident and excited. But he half-leaned, half-sat against his desk, hands in his pockets, and waited for the class to file in and take their seats. Nervous faces passed him and grew even more unsettled as they watched. *They expect a pop quiz. Look at their near-terrified faces. And they should be concerned. Most couldn't make a passing grade if I did. I failed them, Lord. Help.*

Once everyone had been seated, and now squirmed in their chairs, Dean laughed. Though a weak, uncomfortable sound, it did relax a few of the students. He took pity on the rest. "First, let me reassure you. There will be no quiz. Take a deep breath and exhale."

A ripple of laughter washed over the room, and a voice from the back called out, "Who died?"

As the room hushed the joker, panic on several faces, Dean laughed—genuine, hearty laughter. "Actually, Trevor's assumption isn't unrealistic. I—well, I have a confession to make, and my pride protesteth." He took a deep breath. "It has come to my attention that I have been doing an inadequate job of grading your work. I've allowed errors to slip through. This is a disservice to you as my students, not only because many of you have received better grades than you earned, but also because it'll hurt you later in the course."

A hand shot up near the front. "So, does this mean we have to bring back our papers?"

"No. Your grades will stand. This class requires enough work without you having to redo any of it. However, I also must make it possible for you to bring up your future grades. To this end, I will increase my office hours—earlier in the day and later at night. I'll also be here on Saturday mornings until the break. You all have the ability to excel in this class, and I hope that the better grades you have gotten will help balance the effect this may have on your final."

Tiff spoke up first. "So, what are your new hours?"

"I will be in my office all day, Monday through Friday, except Wednesday afternoons. Additionally, I'll also be available Saturday mornings. More specifically, if the college is open, my office is open, except between eleven and two-thirty on Wednesdays and when I'm up here for classes."

"So why not Wednesday?"

He should have known the question would be asked, but he cringed inside when he saw Amy watching him with interest and concern. *Help?* "You'll notice that the assignments returned to you on Mondays were graded more carefully than the ones you received Thursdays."

Several more hands shot up as the class asked for more information. Was a friend or someone in his family ill? Chemo treatments?

Was *he* ill? Weekly counseling sessions? They fired questions at him in rapid succession until Dean burst out laughing. "Uncle already!" The class stared at him. "Forgive me; it's something my uncle used to make me do. I think it's some kind of idiom, but I've never looked it up. Returning to the topic at hand, Wednesdays are my day to take myself out to lunch and work on your papers. However, for obvious reasons, I will not be correcting papers during my meal anymore. Well, I may work on them before and after, but..." Curiosity on faces, combined with his natural desire to talk, overrode any reticence he might have had. "I see I owe an explanation." Dean took a quick breath. "A few weeks ago, I was seated in my usual booth and eating—correcting your papers." He zoomed in on Tiff. "I think it was yours, if you really want to know."

The girl blushed. "Covered with pencil marks then."

"Perhaps... I don't remember. The server brought my check, and then a woman came up and requested to sit with me to prevent a long wait for a table..." Dean described the meeting, his focus on the paper, and the inspiration his friend had given him to try *listening* for a time. Before he continued, Dean ducked his head and dug his toe in the carpet. "I doubt it's a secret that I like to talk."

The class laughed, and from the back of the room, a voice called out, "You're a teacher—occupational hazard, right?"

He nodded his approval. "Precisely. It was *difficult*. Embarrassingly one of the most difficult things I've ever done." He shook his head. "She'd ask a question, and I struggled not to answer. After a while, I found myself *really* listening—only occasionally, but I did. It was... illuminating."

"I don't get it. What does that have to do with anything?" Amy sounded annoyed.

"Well..." Dean prepared himself for a further annoyed student. "She returned the next week—and the following. Since the first week in October, I've had lunch with her every Wednesday—"

The class erupted in whistles and jeers. "Ooooh... Professor's got a girlfriend finally!"

Despite his best intentions, Dean's eyes slid over to Amy. Her face, a mask of unintelligible emotions, told him he hadn't been wrong about her. *Put her out of her misery now.* But as he spoke, he realized, if anything, he'd be giving her more hope, not less. "Much as I hate to disappoint your romantic little hearts..." He grinned at a few awkward shuffles. "I still haven't spoken to her. I go, I sit, I listen, and I grade papers—*very poorly*, I might add. So, I'm just removing that from the equation."

"Why? Is she like, you know—not very attractive? Too old? Married? What?" Trace actually took notes on the discussion as he asked.

61

"Quite the contrary. She's young, beautiful, and unmarried. She does have a boyfriend—someone I wish she'd dump. He treats her terribly."

This time Amy piped up. "How do you know?"

"She discusses him—their relationship. He has a series of girlfriends but resents her eating lunch with a stranger who doesn't even talk to her. No decent man treats a woman that way. Who thinks that is acceptable behavior?"

"Someone who can get away with it," Trace muttered.

"Wha—?"

"Sorry."

"No, please," Dean insisted. "What did you say? I think you have something."

"Well, he does it because he can. She's letting him treat her like that. She either really loves this guy, or she's caught in a cycle of some form of abuse. If she marries him, statistics say he'll cheat on her and likely escalate to verbal or even physical abuse. She doesn't respect herself enough to expect it from him, so…"

"Now I *want* to talk to her. Because I believe you are correct. This guy—" Dean choked back what he really thought and nodded at Trace. "Thank you."

Amy's quiet voice hardly reached him, but her words finally made their way into his heart and lodged there. "It's hard to know a person from the little they tell you over lunch—especially when you can't ask leading questions. There're always two sides to a story."

When her phone rang, Blaine snatched it from her and tossed it aside. "It's just your mom."

"Mom never calls me on Monday nights. Gimme the phone."

But he didn't, and when she reached for it, he held her back, pinning her wrists against her couch. "Just leave the stupid phone. She'll leave a message."

Fury flooded her, and Carlie fought him. "Let. go. of. me."

"Oh, c'mon. Give me a break. It's *just* your uptight mom. You can call her back later."

"No, I can call her now. Give me my phone!"

He shoved her back—not hard enough to injure her, but enough to release his pent up irritation. "Fine. Call Mommy."

Carlie expected him to stalk out, but he didn't. He sat on the couch, glaring at her as she scrambled for the phone he tossed in her general direction. Seconds later, her mother's voice filled her with guilt. "I was so worried when you didn't answer."

"Sorry, couldn't get to it in time." *True enough—even if my jerk of a boyfriend is the cause of it.* "So what's up?"

"There's no easy way to tell you this. Aunt Phoebe died about an hour ago."

Tears filled Carlie's eyes. "No… I thought she looked great at Thanksgiving! What happened?"

"She had a heart attack—totally unexpected. We got there just in time to say goodbye. I'm so sorry we didn't call—just didn't have time."

"Oh, Mom…" At Blaine's irritated expression, Carlie whispered, "My aunt died."

"And it couldn't wait?"

"Mom, I gotta go. I'll call you in the morning. Thanks for telling me."

"What's wrong? Carlie!"

"I have a jerk here who needs to be evicted. Then I want to go cry. Talk to you tomorrow." As she spoke, Carlie jumped up and strode to the door, jerking it open with excess force. "Bye, Blaine."

"Oh, what is your problem!?"

She hated herself for it, but Carlie lashed out. "My *aunt* just *died,* and all you can say is 'and it couldn't wait?' Seriously?" The tears she'd tried to repress flowed. "Next to my parents, she's the person I'm closest to in the whole world. *And you know that.* Just get out before I say something I shouldn't."

He tried to kiss her—something that usually worked to get him his way, but Carlie stood resolute. "I mean it, Blaine. I don't want to see you, talk to you, *or* kiss you. Just get out of here." With that, she shoved him out the door and locked it behind him.

He felt her appear before she even stepped around the corner. Carlie shrugged out of her coat, hung it, and she sank into the booth with an air of someone deeply bothered by something. *I can't take this. I should ask—show concern. Look at her, Lord. She looks broken.*

"Hi."

Dean put away his papers—only three to go—and pulled out menus. As he handed her one, he paused and covered her hand with his—a gesture of comfort while his mind and heart wrangled the wisdom of continuing his experiment. His mind argued that she might need to feel free to unburden herself without fear of someone talking—asking questions. His heart insisted that she might just need a word of comfort. As a compromise—at least until he decided what to do—he pulled out his Bible, turned to the book of John, and put his finger next to, *"Do not let your heart be troubled; believe in God, believe also in Me."* It seemed a clear way of assuring her that he sensed her melancholy.

Tears flowed—tears that tore at his heart. *Just ask her if she is in need of anything. You don't have to converse. Just ask.* Dean decided it was necessary. He'd have to if he hoped to be able to help. But just as he opened his mouth, he heard her heartbreaking whisper.

"My aunt died."

Again he reached for her hand and squeezed it. This time, he didn't let it go until Janice appeared, asking about their drinks. The excited look on their server's face cut him. He shook his head and gave his drink order. "I think she'd like some cocoa. Can you get her some of the peppermint chocolate?"

"Sure… You okay, Carlie?"

Carlie just shook her head. When she didn't reply again, Dean explained. "She lost someone close to her this week—an aunt."

"Oh, I'm so sorry." Janice hugged Carlie, and Dean felt an odd sense of loss that he wouldn't—couldn't.

An odd sensation, as well. Why doesn't it bother me?

"Thanks. She was like a grandmother, you know? No one expected it."

"You just get back from the funeral?"

Carlie shook her head. "No. It's on Friday in Morganfield. I've got to go, of course. My boss isn't happy, but she understands."

Dean's eyes pleaded with Janice to ask the obvious question, but Janice didn't notice. The moment she left, he began praying. *Just a name, Lord. Or a church name. Something. I could attend—or send flowers. Her boyfriend will probably be there. Flowers would be better. Or perhaps Bibles. I could donate Bibles in her name. Yes…*

"—won't even go with me." Her voice dropped and took on a tone of a "dumb jock." "'I hate funerals. Dumb things. Boring. What's with people and their obsession with death, anyway?'" Her lip trembled. "He doesn't understand. Mom says it's better if he doesn't come if he's going to be like that, but a girl just wants someone there, you know? Someone to support—you know, give her—me. I can't do this third second—whatever person thing. I just want to know he cares enough to come, put an arm around me, and promise me that it'll be better someday. Is that too much to ask? But noooo… he can't be bothered." As if on a roll, she rambled nearly non-stop. Only sniffles broke her tirade. "I bet if it wasn't on a Friday, he would have gone—Tuesday, Wednesday—any weekday but Friday. Friday means he can't go out with friends—other girlfriends is more like it. So, he makes up this junk about how morbid funerals are and he thinks he's off the hook. Well, he's not. Aunt Phoebe deserves better."

Their drinks arrived before she could continue. Carlie took one drink of hers and sighed. "How did you know this is just what I needed? Seriously, this is awesome. Thank you."

"Dean's a pretty great guy. Everyone here is half in love with him, you know. We keep telling each other that someday he'll ask one of us out, but no… he just waits for his weekly lunches with you. If you weren't so nice, we'd all hate you."

He laughed. How could he help it? The ridiculous faces Janice made to try to cheer up Carlie amused him anyway. She did smile a little. "I'll remember that when Carlie realizes I'm a lousy lunch partner."

"I can't figure out why I put up with him now. I mean, I come here every week, and he doesn't say a word to me. Not a word! It's like

I'm some kind of freak. He buys me lunch, dessert, comes every week. He even puts his papers away now instead of working on them, so it can't be that he is all conscientious about his work. He just doesn't want to talk to *me!*"

Dean caught a glimmer of understanding in Janice's eyes and nodded. She grinned. "Or, maybe, he just really likes listening to you. And you do have a boyfriend, so if he doesn't talk, no one can accuse you of cheating on your guy."

With that, and a few signals from nearby diners, Janice hurried away. Carlie stared back at him. "Is that it? You don't want to make Blaine mad?"

This time, he couldn't stop himself. Dean shook his head.

Carlie didn't speak again—not until after Janice took their orders and left. Carlie, still wiping occasional tears from the corners of her eyes, looked up at him and asked, "So, what is the best cat for mice eradication purposes?"

Carlie slammed the cupboard door shut and burst into excessive and uncontrollable tears. *It's just a mouse! Get a grip.*

But despite her protests, she knew that the mouse only illuminated her true problems. She hesitated—her rational side demanding that she be prudent—but fear, grief, and a bit of loneliness won out over practicality.

Hat, coat, scarf, gloves—Carlie donned them all and grabbed her purse. She hated to do it, but desperation drove her to her car. *It's just a few miles. It's not that much of a waste. Besides, the memorial will kill the gas budget this month anyway.*

She drove past two malls to the nicer side of town, where a large, well-rated pet store sold everything from fish food to actual pets. Inside, she wove through the shoppers, the aisles of gourmet foods, and the maze of aquariums to the pet pens near the back of the store. Puppies yapped, kittens mewed. The squeaks and squeals of guinea pigs drove her nearly insane, but she'd made it her mission to find a cat—tonight.

"May I help you?" The pimple-faced boy seemed eager, but Carlie held little confidence in his ability to pick out a good mouser.

"I'm looking for a cat—preferably one who loves to hunt mice."

"Well... on adoption day we have really wonderful cats and some—"

"I need one tonight."

He stared at her as if she'd lost her mind. "Did you try the pound?"

"No."

"Well, the pound might have cats, but we just have kittens—none of them are very good hunters yet."

Undaunted, she tried a new tact. "Okay, well, which kinds are usually good at catching mice?"

"What?"

Carlie tried again. "I want a cat that'll kill mice. I can start with a kitten and hope he'll learn eventually, but I need to know which kinds of cats are good at that."

"I'd recommend you do some re—"

Whether grief overrode common courtesy, or if sleep deprivation had finally taken its toll, Carlie didn't quite know. But she did know the minute she blew up at the kid. "That's what I have stores for. We pay a lot of money for overpriced animals, food, and accessories so that we can get expert opinions without spending hours of research that all contradicts itself anyway. So, just point me to a kitten that'll take on a mouse, and I'll be out of your hair."

The stunned look on the boy's face was as effective as ice water. Tears filled Carlie's eyes. "I'm so sorry. It's been a bad week, okay? My aunt died, my boyfriend won't go to the funeral, and now I have mice." She frowned. "Okay, so I had the mouse before Aunt Phoebe died, but tonight was the last straw. I *need* a cat."

"A mouse trap might be easier, don't you think?"

She shook her head. "I'd never be able to set a snap trap, and I'd be covered with glue if I tried that kind."

"Well..." the boy glanced around, obviously searching for someone who would help him. "I think you'd have better luck with a snake, but..."

"Ew! No. Okay, fine. I'll pick one out myself. Is there a toy anywhere—preferably one with a string?"

Eager to help with something he *could,* the kid led her down an aisle of cat toys. "These—"

"Oh, good grief." Carlie ripped a mouse on a string from a package, stuffed the packaging in her shopping basket, and carried it to the pens.

"Um, you're not supposed—"

"I'll pay for it when I pay for the cat," she snapped. Again, Carlie apologized. "I'm not usually this nasty. Sorry."

One sweep of the mouse across the pen was all it took. A kitten from the opposite corner saw it and plowed through the others to get to it. "I'll take him."

"Do you have a litter box or..."

"I'll take him and everything he needs to survive in an apartment." As she followed the boy to the cat accessories, she glanced back at the pen. *I wonder if I shouldn't get him a friend—for backup, in case that was a fluke...*

The Congregational Church couldn't have been more picturesque if it had been custom ordered for the memorial service. Set against a backdrop of vivid golds, greens, rusts, and even a few deep purples, the white church with its traditional steeple seemed to scream "Americana." Dean sat in the parking lot, waiting for the attendees to be seated before he stepped from the car. As he waited, he chided himself for his foolishness.

You don't truly know her, nor she you. You will not be of any real comfort, so why are you here? But no matter how silly he felt, he couldn't bring himself to leave. *If her self-absorbed boyfriend would have come, I wouldn't have. But she said herself she wanted someone there...* The arrogance in them stopped his thoughts cold. *Speaking of self-absorbed... Now, because you have arrived, her heartbreak will be lessened? She, of course, has no friends or family to comfort her. Do you remember what comfort she wanted? Are you going to hold her and assure her all will be well?* He squirmed in his seat at the thought. *And you will do all this without uttering a word? Have you learned nothing from your so-called listening experiment?*

Before he could reevaluate his thoughts, the last group entered the building. Dean grabbed his Bible and hurried from his car to the door. It creaked like an ancient mausoleum as he pulled it open. Thankfully, no one seemed to notice. He signed the guest book, accepted a program, and tried to slip into a back pew. Every seat in the back was filled. He couldn't find a spot any closer than halfway up the aisle.

Carlie sat up front, her hair hiding her face as she gripped a program and tried not to cry. Even from his vantage point, that much was evident. He identified her mother, her father, and what had to be a sister or cousin. An elderly woman beside her mother might be a grandmother, but Dean couldn't be certain. On Carlie's other side, a head popped up—short dark hair—almost Carlie's exact shade. Probably a brother.

The pastor rose and led the congregation in "Amazing Grace." Dean sang quietly—a deviation from his usual style. *It seems wrong, somehow, to sing out when I don't even talk to her.* His rational side objected. *And that's absurd. The—our singing—isn't for her!*

He followed the scriptures, sang the songs, and listened to the eulogy. From the sound of it, Phoebe Price had been a remarkable and beloved woman. After a prayer and communion, the pastor requested that friends and family come forward and share memories of Phoebe with others. Carlie rose and took the mic first.

"I didn't think I'd be able to do this—might not get through it either. But I think we all know Aunt Phebes would have something to say about me giving up before I even tried. So here goes." She talked about baking cookies, reading stories, and slumber parties where "Aunt Phebes" told ghost stories and played tricks on her like any teenager might have. "She made memories—lots of great memories. I never missed out on having a grandmother. Mine died before I was born, but Aunt Phoebe was the best grandmother I could have asked for. She kissed my bumps, bandaged my scrapes, and cursed the idiot boys who broke my heart in school—her words, not mine." Carlie laughed with the rest of the room. "Okay, so I agreed with her."

At that moment, her eyes met Dean's and held. She wavered. "I—she—" Her hand shook as she tried to regain her momentum and failed. Dean gave her the most reassuring smile he could manufacture.

When she wavered again, Dean glanced toward her family's pew, silently willing someone to come to her rescue. At that moment, the man—her supposed brother—looked back at him. Glared at him. Dean returned the gaze. *What is your problem?*

Tears flowed. Carlie shook her head, handed the mic over to the pastor, and rushed back to her pew. Her mother held her as they wept together. Still the man glared at him. *Perhaps this was a poor idea. They likely heard about our lunches and suspect that I'm using her for some nefarious deed. Or, perhaps he thinks I'm Blaine.* That idea made the most sense. *That's probably it.*

Dean waited for the rest of the guests to file out before he joined the end of the receiving line. When Carlie saw him, she hugged him. "Thank you so much for coming. I can't believe you did that, but it means a lot."

He smiled and pulled a card from his Bible. He tried to speak—to tell her how sorry he was for her loss—but the words stuck in his throat. *I would freeze when I finally decide to say something.*

To his relief, Carlie patted his arm. "I understand. Are you coming over to the fellowship hall for the meal? I'd like to introduce you to my parents—and Blaine."

"Nice that you remember I'm here." The "brother" glared at Dean. "So, you're the jerk who won't leave her alone. You know, this is probably legally equivalent to stalking," he growled.

"Blaine!" Carlie pushed him toward the door. "Go get something to eat. I'll be there in a minute."

But Blaine dragged her with him, his hand wrapped around her wrist in a grip that had to hurt. Dean started to protest and changed his mind. *Her family can and should take care of her. I'll just make it worse.* His eyes caught hers as she looked back at him. He smiled and waved before turning to go. *Lord, please bring her back on Wednesday.* After one last glance over his shoulder, he added, *And please help her see that this man is not what she needs. She deserves better than that kind of treatment.*

As the clock wound down to her lunch break, Carlie grew increasingly agitated. Chandra waited for the customer to leave the store before pouncing. "Okay, give it up. What is going on with you?"

"I—" Her teeth chomped shut and her lips pursed. *How do I answer that? I don't even know myself.*

"C'mon…" A change came over Chandra. "Oh, sorry. Your aunt—"

"It's not that—not really. I just…" she sighed.

Chandra checked her watch. "Hey, why don't you duck out for lunch now? Meeting with your professor always cheers you up."

"I didn't know if I should go. I mean—"

"The guy drives two hours to your aunt's funeral, gets blasted by your boyfriend for being a nice guy, and you can't go have lunch and say thanks for that and a nice card?"

"And a hundred Bibles. Don't forget that. He donated a hundred Bibles in Aunt Phebs's name." But Chandra's words broke through her remaining resistance. "I guess you're right. Blaine just gets so mad—"

"Well, he can deal with it. I swear, I think he only went because you mentioned the professor one too many times. You have him scared." Chandra moved closer and hugged her. "Look, sometimes the way you let Blaine push you around scares me. I'm not going to bother you about it, but I thought you should know."

Those words followed Carlie through the store, out the door, and down the street to The Fiddleleaf. A bit of uncertainty reappeared as

Janice grinned and waved, but when she saw Dean sitting there, nearly done with his work, all hesitation vanished. "Hey there!"

Dean set his papers aside and smiled as he handed her the menu. But the smile seemed more of a question than a reassurance—as if he wanted to be sure she was doing well. That small gesture of kindness opened a floodgate of self-doubts, explanations, apologies, and appreciation for the odd friendship they'd forged.

"So, first I want to thank you for coming—"

Janice interrupted with a request for their drink order. Something about the unselfconsciousness of Dean's request for pomegranate and lemon tea amused Carlie. "I'll try that too."

"Got it. Ready to order or…"

Before she could respond, Dean answered for them. "We'll need a minute."

The moment Janice left, Carlie tried again. "I couldn't believe it when I saw you there. I told my mom about it, and she said it was probably because I told you Blaine wasn't coming."

The way he stared at the table, listening and yet obviously aching to speak gave her hope. *Maybe now…*

But despite giving him time, Carlie gave up and continued with her weekly unburdening session. "Anyway, Blaine decided to come last minute. Mom thinks his date fell through, so he tried to look like the good boyfriend. Whatever. I was glad to have him until he went off on you like that. That was just so not cool." A menu item distracted her. "Have you had the ham and potato combo? That sounds good."

Dean, of course, didn't answer. For just a moment, she felt like blasting him. *What is so wrong with me that you can't even be civil?* Conscience struck. *Okay, so you're not uncivil. Or dis-civil. Or whatever it is. You've never pretended that you'd talk to me. And you do buy my lunch. What kind of moocher am I anyway?*

His laughter jerked her from her self-flagellative thoughts. "What?"

An odd quirk to the corner of his eye looked like a combination single eyebrow raise-slash-wink.

Dismay flooded her and her breath quickened in a moment of embarrassed panic. "I spoke out loud."

A slight shake of the head relieved her until Carlie realized what it meant. "It's that obvious?" Groaning, Carlie tried to explain. "I just wonder sometimes why you won't talk to me. And then I felt guilty because I got all worked up about that, like you were some kind of rude guy and you're not. I mean, I'm the moocher here."

To her delight, he pulled out his Bible again. He flipped through pages, frowned, and flipped again. When he didn't find the verse he needed, he pulled out his phone—the first time she'd ever seen it—and did a search on it. Seconds later, he pushed the Bible across the table with the satin ribbon marker underlining a verse.

"'In everything I showed you that by working hard in this manner you must help the weak and remember the words of the Lord Jesus, that He Himself said, 'It is more blessed to give than to receive.'" Carlie smiled. "I think you mean that too. Thanks."

Janice appeared again, waiting for their orders. "I'd like the ham and Swiss sandwich with the potato soup and mini salad. I think Carlie wants the nasty ham and potato combo plate."

"No!" *Very cute.* "I want what he's having." The moment Janice left, she leaned back and grinned. "That was good. Funny."

As she pushed the Bible back, Carlie racked her brains to find something less depressing to talk about than Blaine's poor manners. Dean sat—waiting. She could sense it in the way he stirred his tea, pausing each time she opened her mouth. *It's like a cat and mouse game—but a weird one.*

That worked. "So, did I tell you about the mouse who has taken up residence in my apartment?" Without waiting for the reply she knew wouldn't come, Carlie rushed on. "Yeah. I'm now overrun by at least one if not two or two hundred rodents. Blaine is just ticked that I don't get him his milk fast enough to satisfy his Oreo craving. I mean, who does that?"

The half-hidden expression on Dean's face stopped her story mid-track. *He looks ticked.* Dean's eyes rose to meet hers, and she could have sworn he urged her to continue. "Anyway, so here I am with this mouse who thinks he owns the apartment, right? I got fed up the second time he showed up—*under my clean dishes in the drainer, no less*—so I went out to get a cat. Did you know pet stores don't sell adult cats? What's up with that? I mean, not everyone wants a kitten! Anyway, I gave a pen of kittens a 'chase it' test and one dove for the fake mouse like from across the other side. So, I took him home. Named him Pouncer. I wanted to call him the Executioner, but my mom said that since he's a cat, he'd turn out to be afraid of mice if I did that. She thinks cats are deliberately difficult."

Before she could continue, Janice plunked down a basket of bread and a small bowl of whipped butter. "Eat up. Just had a fire on the grill, so orders are backed up for a couple of minutes. Sorry."

Dean caught Janice's sleeve. "I'm not in a rush, so if Carlie has time…"

"Yeah, put us at the back of the line. I'm taking a long lunch anyway." Carlie waited until Janice left and reached across to squeeze Dean's hand. "You're a good guy, you know?"

He shrugged, and Carlie imagined it to mean, "It's just a few minutes for me, but it might be a difference for someone else."

"And that's why I said it. It's just neat. Anyway—cat. Where was I? Oh, so I bring home this kitten that isn't much bigger than a rat herself, and I put her in the bathroom first. All the books say to do that—give them a little bitty area and then slowly let them have run of the house. So, I get up in the middle of the night…" She couldn't repress a giggle. "And when I open the bathroom door, this fur ball runs between my feet. Now, I'm thinking mouse, right? I mean, I've totally forgotten that I had the kitten at that point. So, I scream. Grab my brush from the counter, and go after the 'mouse.' Oh, em, geeness! That kitten nearly scared me to death. I almost whacked it. Ended up hitting my hand instead. *Ouch!*"

As she told the story, Carlie watched Dean's face closely. He sat, hands wrapped around his cup, staring into it as if tea leaves at the bottom held the answer to his fate, and just listened. He smiled at all the right places, and then laughed as she squealed her "ouch." Then a shift came and he reached across the table. She didn't quite know why until his hand pulled hers close. The yellowish-green bruise—the one she'd almost forgotten about—captured his attention.

"Isn't it ugly? Who knew a hairbrush could do so much damage? Then again, I was out for blood."

He almost spoke. She saw his lips part twice, and he leaned forward as if propelled by the words he wanted to say or the question he wanted to ask. But he pressed his lips together, and after a quick brush of his thumb over the bruise, leaned back and continued to stare into his cup.

"Yeah. It's gross. But the story gets better. So, I got this kitten to kill mice, right? Well, now I see two for sure in my apartment. It's like they're flaunting their presence now that I have a mouse eradication plan. But I have the memorial, so I put Pouncer in his crate and off we go. I figured I could cry into his fur if Blaine took up with some girl at the fellowship dinner."

There it was again—that… *disapproval! He's ticked at Blaine. Well, who isn't? Everyone is ticked at Blaine these days.*

"But when I got to Mom's house, she has this cat there. Aunt Phoebe's. Guess what the cat's name is?" At his quizzical look, she said, "Moros—you know, like the 'spirit of doom' in Greek mythology. Come to find out—she's a great mouser. I wasn't home fifteen minutes before she had one of the little beasts lying in Pouncer's bowl. I expect the other one dead when I get home. Blaine says the kitten will have its entrails spread across the whole place, which would be revolting," she added quickly. "But I'll take that over running through my cupboards."

Carlie could have sworn Dean snickered as he took a sip of his tea.

Conference attendees milled through the convention center—some leaving for nearby restaurants, while others, like Dean, waited in line for a table at the hotel restaurant. The group he waited with stood near the entrance and discussed the previous workshop—*Addressing the Worldview Crisis.*

But what do we plan to do about it? he argued to himself. *Few dispute the fact that too many Christians today are not cognizant of a Biblical worldview, but that defines the problem rather than the solution. Students arrive in my classrooms without any concept of how to make decisions based upon a Biblical mindset rather than a psychological, logical, or humanistic one.* That *is the real problem.*

"You feeling okay, Dean?"

Jerked from his reverie, Dean stared at his mentor, Dr. John Ehman. "Pardon me, what did you say?"

"You're just awfully quiet about this. You deal with first year seminary students. What do you think?"

"I…" He cleared his throat. "I agree that there's a problem. I see it daily. I can't count how many times students spout 'proverbs' that are cultural rather than Biblical. But the true problem comes in when you tell them. They can't seem to comprehend why it's important to base their beliefs on Scripture over conventional wisdom."

"I still think the answer is to deal with this in the youth groups," one woman argued. "We need to get them while they're forming their own identities as individuals. Those are the years when most kids are trying to spread their wings."

"And by that point, they have had years of undermining of basic core Biblical beliefs every day in the classroom," Dr. Ehman argued. "We need to make Sunday School less about being kind to kittens and more about honoring a holy God by aligning every decision with His Word."

"But that's how four-year-olds *do* that," the woman argued. She turned to Dean. "Don't you think? How can we expect kids who are almost toddlers to turn to the Bible when they don't know what to do about a cookie thief at preschool?"

Dr. Ehman turned to Dean. "I would be interested to know your opinion as well."

"I think the proposed solutions are an over-complication of the issue. Why must it be either/or? Why shouldn't we teach them that Scripture says to go to their authorities when they don't know what to do and to ask for what the Bible says? And," he added, before the woman could protest, "the Bible does imply that we should be kind to kittens. So, definitely teach that. But they don't need fifty-two lessons on the value and importance of kitten kindness." Once on a roll, Dean found it impossible to stop. "And *please*, may we stop using 'be kind to kittens' as the moral of stories like the Samaritan or the woman at the well? Seriously?"

"Dean's back!" Dr. Ehman shouted with a grin. He pointed to the hostess stand. "I think they're calling our name."

But, at the hostess station, the woman apologized. "It's taking longer than expected. We can seat you all in the lounge, or we can give you a booth for two next to a table for two. Or you can wait another ten... fifteen..."

The group agreed to the split, and Dean found himself across the table from the one man he hoped to speak to most. But as they looked over their menus, suddenly, he found it hard to ask the questions that burned in his heart. Dr. Ehman spoke first. "Is everything okay? You haven't said much at all since you arrived. We practically had to drag you into that mini-debate."

"I'm good. How about you?"

The man laughed. "Okay, what's going on? Since when do you ask how someone is doing?"

"I don't?" Dean's heart sank. *I knew I became engrossed in discussions, but when did I quit showing basic courtesy?*

"Don't take it so personally. You're a bit more serious than polite chit-chat. Everyone knows it. Everyone gets it. It's you. There's nothing wrong with that."

"Seems rude to me." He took a sip of the water the server brought and tried to act nonchalant. "But you still didn't answer the question. How are you?"

"Curious about you." The man laughed as Dean dropped his roll of silverware in exasperation. "Yes... something is most certainly different. So, talk to me."

"I still don't—"

"Dean, I've known you for twelve years. This weekend, you've talked about as much as you've listened the other twelve years combined. So, I want to know. What is going on with you?"

"I—" He sagged in relief as the server appeared, ready to take their orders. "Know what you want?"

Dr. Ehman ordered his usual conference fare—green salad with a small piece of grilled chicken on the side. Dean opted for soup and a sandwich—one that reminded him of Carlie. And that thought prompted a smile.

"Okay, that's it. What's going on, Dean? First, we can't get you to talk when we usually can't get you to shut up, and then you act like you have a secret over a roast beef sandwich—oh, my word. You're in love."

"No."

The man eyed him with evident suspicion. "You act like it—in a sense."

"There is a young woman—"

Delight filled the man's face. "I knew it," Ehman interjected.

"It isn't how it appears. It's... complicated." The old Dean kicked in gear and then into overdrive. He began with the first day and his decision to listen and told his story through the present. "I have learned a great deal about people—understanding them better."

"That happens when you allow people to contribute to a conversation."

Embarrassment and a tinge of anger burned in Dean's ears. *I believe I just admitted that, didn't I?* But he tried to be gracious. "I have become an ad hoc therapist for her. She talks, I listen, and because I don't respond, it seems as if she opens up in an interesting way. Sometimes, it is quite difficult for me, but as I said, she has responded well to it. She shares things that I doubt her family knows. I know she tells me things she won't tell her boyfriend."

"Tell me about this guy."

Dean read between Dr. Ehman's words and nodded. "You are correct. As I overheard a student say last week, he's a 'creep of the first order.' I truly cannot comprehend why she is willing to endure what is near abuse if not true abuse. He expects her to remain monogamous, from what I gather, but he dates multiple women—even canceling dates with her if he receives a better invitation. He does *not* like that she has lunch with me." He sighed. "I don't think she's aware of it, but some of the things she has said imply that he is controlling in other ways. I don't think he's ever physically harmed her, but it feels like such an abusive relationship." Almost unable to stop once he'd begun, Dean added, "She talks about 'making him' lash out by doing or saying the wrong thing without thinking. That sort of thing."

As Dean spoke, Dr. Ehman nodded, until the last bit. "Well, that could be perception rather than reality. Sometimes we think the oddest things. I remember my daughter, when she was about fifteen. That girl was convinced that if she told me she failed her math test, I'd beat her to a pulp. I'd never even spanked her as a kid. Lora spanked the girls and I spanked the boys—on the rare occasion it happened—but she got the idea in her head and nothing would change it, until one day she kind of snapped out of it and told me. And, it could be phrasing," he added. "She could word things badly."

"Could..."

77

"But you don't think so." Dr. Ehman's statement hung between them.

"No," Dean said at last. "I don't."

The older man nodded as he said, "Yeah, I don't either."

"I considered discussing it with her. I mean, I think—or at least, I hope—I would be a better listener now that I've had some practice. So, I think I'm capable of it now. But then…" Dean gripped the water glass until it shook, splashing water all over his hands. "I just imagine her stuck—" He swallowed. "Do you remember the Froelichs?"

"Overbearing jerk of a husband and his broken wife—yes. I remember them. Did you know she committed suicide last year?"

Grief choked Dean at the idea of the sweet, gentle woman driven to desperation by a man who strangled the life out of her. "It sickens me to realize that I wouldn't be stunned if this relationship went that way. I already see flashes of it. At the funeral, Carlie was so broken, and he didn't show any kind of comfort at all until he knew I was there. Even then, it was more proprietary rather than genuine concern." Dean sighed. "I don't know. Perhaps I *should* talk to her."

Dr. Ehman listened but said nothing. Dean couldn't help but feel a sense of what Carlie went through as he wondered what the man thought and would say. But the server brought their food before he could ask, and when she did, Dr. Ehman offered to pray. The prayer soothed Dean's unease as his friend prayed for strength and wisdom for Carlie and for Blaine to treat her with honor and respect. As their heads rose, Dean murmured, "Thank you."

"You won't."

Dean frowned and scooped soup from his bowl. "Why?"

"Because I'm going to tell you what I don't think you want to hear." Dr. Ehman waited a moment and said, "Look, I don't think you should discuss this—well, anything with her. Right now, you're the only one just listening. I bet, assuming this guy is really as bad as he sounds, that she has people all over the place telling her to dump him. And it's probably the only reason she's still with him. Dumping him means she was stupid, and well…" He shrugged.

He had to admit that Ehman made a good point. "There is a certain level of insecurity in her. I see your point."

"And even if she does keep talking to you, she could transfer her loyalty and affection to you. Neither of you are ready for that. She's going to be in a needy place. If you change your dynamic, she'll see you as her rescuer—her protector. Even if you do decide you want a relationship—"

"No!" Dean shook his head emphatically. "I understand why you might think it, but that is *not* where my interest lies. I can't even imagine

78

having any kind of—no!"

Dr. Ehman raised his hands in surrender. "Okay. That's fine. But if that changes, make sure it's been a while after she's decided against this guy, okay? It sounds ripe for trouble."

Though he nodded in agreement, Dean protested in his heart. *The idea is preposterous—almost as inappropriate as dating a sister or close cousin.*

The TV blared with the fevered pitch of a sportscaster as he gave a play-by-play of a touchdown in progress. *"Touchdown! Broncos!"*

Yippie doodle for you.

Riding high from his team's success, Blaine pulled her closer. "So, what are you doing?"

"Thank you notes—for the service."

"You send thank-you notes to people who attended a funeral?"

"No…" Why she bothered to explain, Carlie didn't know. "But we thank the church for the facility, the pastor for performing the service, the women who made the food, the people who sent flowers. Stuff like that."

"Can't your mom do that? I mean—"

"I offered to help. Mom shouldn't have to do it all, so I took the ones from my friends and stuff."

He frowned and took the stack of cards. "Your friends sent flowers? Why? They didn't know her."

"The flowers aren't for the dead. They're to comfort the living—us."

"Oh. So, I should have bought flowers. Great."

Carlie tried to throw him a bone. "You came—even when you didn't want to. That mattered."

As Blaine flipped through the stack of cards, Carlie grew nervous. *Don't keep—ugh.*

"What the—*Why* are you sending a card to this jerk? You have his *address?*"

Her temper flared. "Just who are you calling a jerk, Mr. I-Will-Only-Support-My-Girlfriend-in-Her-Time-of-Grief-Since-My-Other-Girlfriend-Was-Busy? Dean came all the way to Morganfield just because he knew you wouldn't be there. He just wanted me to know that someone cared enough to come."

Carlie shrank back into the cushions as rage filled his eyes. Blaine gripped the couch on each side of her head, and with his face centimeters from hers, blasted Carlie with accusations of the vilest nature. "—are not going to disrespect me! You are *mine!* How *dare* you!"

Though she hated herself for it, Carlie cowered, covering her head with her hands. "Go away." It came out as barely a gasped whisper.

"Why? So, you can call for your stupid preacher to come tell you what an evil man I am? I don't *think* so. You're going to promise me that you'll never see him again!"

Despite the fear that tried to drive her to her room and lock the door behind her, Carlie wrestled free of him and hurried to the door. She flung it open and demanded he leave. "If you even look wrong at me again, I'll scream for help. I'll call the police."

"Oh, don't be so dramatic."

She jerked her finger toward the corridor, not saying a word. Her hand shook, but she held it there until he grabbed his coat and raged, "You'll regret this, Carlie. No one orders me around and gets away with it. We're done unless you apologize *right now!*"

With more courage than she knew she possessed, Carlie shoved him through the door and slammed it shut behind him. She slid the deadbolt in place just as he tried to reopen it. "Leave. Me. Alone!" For good measure, she hooked the chain as well.

Tears—angry and anguished—flowed as she curled into a ball on the couch, cats on either side of her, and sobbed out her grief and fears. *How can he do this to me one day and swear he loves me the next? And he does! I can see it. It's not all in my head, he really does. But, c'mon! I can't deal with this.*

Her phone buzzed. Like the naive girl in a horror film, mesmerized by the danger before her, Carlie pulled the phone closer and stared at the screen. Her heart twisted. YOU CAN'T GET AWAY WITH TREATING ME LIKE THIS. NO ONE ELSE WOULD PUT UP WITH YOUR STUPID DRAMA. IF I DIDN'T LOVE YOU, I'D BE SO OUT OF YOUR LIFE.

Her hands shook as she sent a quick text to Teresa. Three simple words. CAN YOU CALL?

Fifteen seconds—it took fifteen seconds for Teresa's ringtone to blast through the apartment—or so it seemed. "Hey."

"What's wrong, sweetie? You sound—oh, Aunt Phoebe. I'm so sorry."

"It's not that—not really. I just had a fight with Blaine."

"I'm sorry. What's up?"

She heard it—that wary tone in Teresa's voice that always signaled her friend's attempts at civility. "I was just writing thank-you notes, you know? And Blaine thought it was stupid. He actually said he didn't send anything because he didn't know Aunt Phoebe—like she cares about the flowers. The guy just doesn't get it. But then I was stupid and let him have the stack—or didn't stop him anyway. So then he was all ticked off when he saw Dean's name. I should have waited to do Dean's after he left, but—"

"No, Carlie. You should be able to extend basic courtesy

anytime."

"But I know he gets upset about stuff like this, I provoked him by saying how great Dean was to come to the memorial and stuff. I was mean, and then he just got all crazy." Once on a roll, Carlie couldn't stop. She described every second of the fight in precise detail. "I know he loves me. He texted right away and told me. Of course, then he had to point out that no one else would put up—"

"Okay," Teresa interrupted. "I really try not to bash Blaine. I know you don't like it, and I know I wouldn't want people telling me what to think about Eric. *But* right now, I'm more freaked out about your reaction to this than I am by what Blaine did! Did you hear yourself? Carlie, you just blamed yourself for triggering your boyfriend? You are exhibiting typical abused wife-slash-girlfriend behavior. Carlie! I'm scared for you. You don't deserve this."

"He was just mad. It's not like he hit me or anything. You know I wouldn't put up with that."

"But why will you put up with him treating you like his personal verbal whipping post? I mean, c'mon! I don't get why."

"Yeah, you said that." A nervous giggle followed. "Look, he's right, okay? No great guy is going to put up with me when I get all bent out of shape over stupid stuff. Blaine cares enough to stick around even when I blow it. Shouldn't I do the same for him?"

"I guess you have to ask yourself if you want to spend the rest of your life with nights like this in regular intervals. Because that's what's going to happen." She sighed. "I know you like Blaine—care about him even. But do you love him enough to endure this forever?"

When Carlie didn't answer, Teresa said goodbye. "—and I love you, Carls. There's a man out there who will treat you well because he loves *you*—not just how you make *him* feel. Don't you want a man who will treat you the way you want to be treated?"

The words pounded through her heart and into her mind. *"Don't you want a man who will treat you the way you want to be treated?"*

Moros climbed up in her lap, purring. "Of course, I do," she sniffled. "But who is going to love *me* like that?"

The drive from the airport left him exhausted and anxious, creating several "near misses" along the way. "She will arrive long before me. It's almost noon now." Dean zipped through a couple of back streets, and though it was several blocks out of the way, decided that he'd managed to shave ten minutes off his trip. "I believe I have just proven that should they ever trim my department, I could make a living—of sorts, anyway—driving taxis," he muttered as he grabbed his messenger bag and sprinted from the car and down the street.

Amber, the hostess, smiled as he burst in the door. She beckoned him close and murmured, "Someone is going to be happy you're here. I know she made Janice promise that the check was hers, but then I don't know if she really thought you'd come." She glanced around to make sure no one noticed. "She's sitting on your side and she looks a little lost. Like I said; she's convinced you aren't coming."

"Would you request that Janice bring us cheesecake or something similar for dessert? I'd prefer to pay for that now, if I may."

"We'll get it from you next week if you lose the coin toss. No worries."

"I appreciate it."

At the table, he gestured his request to sit with her, but she hesitated. *Please don't insist...* he pleaded.

"I should make you ask," Carlie said with an enigmatic look on her face. "This is just kind of sad."

Yes! Again, he gestured, and she nodded. He'd never sat on that side of the table and couldn't help but notice that a change in view also changed his perception of the restaurant. Where he had always considered it a quiet place that was popular with diners, he'd never seen the hustle and bustle around him. With a line of sight that led directly to the kitchen doors, his entire dining experience changed.

But amid his adjusted change of scene, Dean also watched Carlie—and she noticed. "Okay, I know it's stupid, but I just didn't want to sit and stare at an empty spot where you should be." She flushed. "Or that's what they'd say in some romantic comedy." Her flush deepened. "But, obviously, that's not what we are. We don't even talk."

At the discouragement in her tone, Dean gripped the menu and tried desperately not to respond. *Is it wrong, Lord? Is it time to invest more personally?* Honesty forced himself to add, *I truly enjoy what we have now. I would hate to lose it, despite its being a bit... odd.*

Carlie's voice interrupted his prayer. "So, today officially sucked, until you came. I mean, I got chewed out at work because I didn't notice that a sale item wasn't ringing up properly and a customer flipped out on us about it. At least ten people bought one at full price before we noticed—all my fault, of course. Then I get here, and you weren't, and I thought I missed you because I was a little late. I was sure you'd just given up and left, and then I felt guilty because I thought maybe you stay later just because you can't get enough of me yakking at you about the stupid stuff I do."

You are beautiful, intelligent, and interesting. How is it possible that you are so insecure?

"—and I got here first, so I get the ticket. The first to arrive gets it, remember? That's how it works."

Am I foolish and more than a little ridiculous because I enjoy knowing we have a "thing?" Our unspoken agreement—and this is it.

Before Dean could find a way to acknowledge her, a four-hour flight and a dash through the airport without stopping for a restroom break hit him hard and fast. He gave her a weak smile and bolted from the table. In his haste, Dean nearly bumped into two servers carrying trays but managed to avoid creating a catastrophe.

The restroom mirror showed evidence of his exhaustion. His hair flopped to the proper side—but looked a little wild and untamed. His shirt was rumpled, his tie creased. "Well, looking like this, I'll never have to be concerned she'd be tempted to cheat on him, will I?"

"What?" A man exiting a stall startled him.

"Just talking to myself."

"Date going bad?"

There was no way to explain without making him look like a bigger fool than he felt. "No, but thank you. Just noting that my friend isn't likely to get 'other ideas' with me looking like this."

"Just get back from the airport?"

Dean grinned. "You know your travelers. Yes." As he left the restroom, Dean called back, "Have a nice day."

A familiar ringtone greeted him just before he reached the table. Carlie answered and rolled her eyes at Dean as he seated himself. "Hello, Blaine." Her face contorted into an unrecognizable expression. Carlie held up one finger and winked. "So, what you're telling me is that you need a date for your work party, and you want to take me—see where we want to take our relationship?"

He couldn't hide it—didn't even try. Dismay washed over him, and Dean began praying. *She's his girlfriend. He has every right to expect—*

"Didn't I just throw your sorry backside out of my apartment for *scaring* me? I—" Fury flashed in her eyes. "I don't care what you didn't 'mean' to do, you scared me. I'm done, Blaine. I—"

The fire and anger within her fizzled with his next words. Dean leaned forward, trying to offer whatever comfort and support he could. Carlie appeared to take it as curiosity. Her hands and voice shook as she said, "I don't care if you think that no guy is going to put up with my so-called stupidity and clinginess; I'm not going to be screamed at like that—ever again. Just don't call me—" She hesitated, tossed Dean an apologetic look, and added, "Look, 'Father Dean' here is about ready to leap through the phone and strangle you, so just go away. At least someone agrees with me that I don't have to take it—not from anyone, and especially not from you. Goodbye. We're done. Don't forget it."

The phone clattered to the table as Carlie's eyes closed. "Sorry for bringing you into it. I figured it might drive him away if—" Her eyes widened as a man appeared—as *Blaine* appeared—beside them. "You were out there? All this time?"

"I just wanted to see how much interference this guy would try to cause. He didn't, Carlie," the man almost yelled. "He didn't say a word. Do you even realize that?" The way Blaine moved too close to Carlie, and the way she backed away—cowering—unnerved Dean. Torn between defending her and solving the problem in the quickest and least disruptive manner, Dean bolted from the table and rushed for the kitchen. Blaine's laughter, followed along with a, "He's such a wuss! Seriously..." But Dean heard no more.

Frank saw him enter and frowned. "Dean, you can't—"

"There's a man accosting Carlie at our table. She acts threatened by him, but I know if I try to eject him, it'll become loud and ugly."

"I'll handle it. Thanks."

The scene blew up far beyond Dean's imagination. Carlie sat shrunken into the corner of the booth, shaking, while Blaine leaned over her and spewed out the vilest ugliness. The quiet in the room testified to everyone's shock and interest in the scene playing out. But when Dean arrived with Frank, Blaine laughed, not even trying to remain quiet any longer. "Had to go get Daddy to fight your battles? You religious nuts—"

"I have to ask you to leave," Frank said, quietly. "You're disturbing my customers."

"I'll leave when I'm good—"

Frank pulled out his phone and called before Blaine could finish. "Yes, I am requesting police assistance at The Fiddleleaf Café. I have a patron who refuses to leave and is intimidating a customer—"

Blaine threw up his hands. "Fine! I'm going!" He leaned over her once more and growled, "I am *done* with you—so done. You are not worth this."

To Dean's dismay, Carlie followed the retreating Blaine. He turned to Frank. "Do you think I should—?"

"She's an adult. You can't force her to make smart decisions. I'll have Amber keep an eye out, but otherwise…" Frank shrugged and sauntered away, pausing by tables and booths to apologize for the disruption as he went.

Dean slid back into his seat and stared at the table. *Why do you allow him to do this to you? You are worth so much more than this. He called you unworthy to be his girlfriend. That's preposterous…* That thought sparked a new one— and another. Dean pulled out his Bible and a highlighter. After several flips through Isaiah, he stopped at chapter forty-three, pulled the cap off the marker with his teeth, and highlighted the words he wanted her to read. *I can't force a search—not this time. She needs comfort, Lord. Give her comfort.* "…*Since you are precious in My sight, Since you are honored and I love you…*"

Carlie plopped in the seat across from him, pale but calm. "I just told him to butt out of my life or I'd get a restraining order." She shivered, and Dean realized she'd gone outside without her coat. He shrugged out of his blazer and offered it to her, but Carlie shook her head. "I—"

He slid the Bible across the table as well. *I feel ridiculous now. If I'm going to try to communicate, then why shouldn't I just talk to her?* He opened his mouth to urge her to take it—to remind her that it was warmer than hers would be—when James chapter one came to mind. "—*everyone must be quick to hear, slow to speak and slow to anger…*" It rocked him. *Is this Your doing, Lord? It felt so me oriented, but if it's Your will…*

"Thanks. You're right. I am cold." She took the coat from his hands. "I'm sorry Blaine did that. People kept telling me he scared them—for me, I mean—and I didn't listen. I kept thinking that I

85

provoked him, or I didn't deserve nicer guys."

Dean couldn't contain his shock.

"I know, I know. I'm fearfully and wonderfully made—yadda yadda, bling, bling."

That you are. And don't allow anyone to tell you otherwise.

"—realized that even if I don't—even if the great guys aren't going to be interested—I don't need to settle for a creep. No guy is better than a bad guy."

Janice's voice interrupted her words and his thoughts. "I can name ten guys who would kill for a nice, gorgeous girl like you to notice them. Don't sell yourself short. Now, what do you want to eat, or did Jerk-Face ruin everyone's appetite?"

Dean pointed to the mini chalkboard hanging on the wall next to their booth. "I've been anticipating the return of Frank's famous prime rib grinders." He almost forgot to keep his eyes on Janice as he added, "They're my favorite."

"I'll have it, too." Carlie waited until Janice left before she leaned back and smiled at him. "I wonder what you do on weekends. Do you, like, row on a rowing team? I could totally see you doing that. What about lacrosse? That seems kind of… you. Or, or! Cricket! You'd be fabulous on a cricket team. I bet you're into that, aren't you? I went to a game once in New Cheltenham… totally confusing. I had no idea what was going on. They kept talking about the pitch but never when someone actually pitched. And then there were the bats… they were *huge*—like clubs."

You are amazing. Just moments ago, you were verbally accosted and threatened—sat there trembling with fear and anger. Now you're discussing cricket. By way of reply, he just paused, waiting. Thankfully, she took the hint.

"Fine. I don't know how I'll be spending weekends now that I don't have to wait around for Blaine to tell me if I'll see him or not—oh-my-goodness-I-am-such-an-idiot. I really did that. I became *that* girl." She dropped her head into her hands for a second or three before jerking it up again. "Well, no more! Besides, this weekend I actually have plans. I always sing with a group of carolers in New Cheltenham the last two weekends before Christmas. We dress up in costume and everything. It's a lot of fun."

And now I know what I'm doing this weekend.

The chime rang as the last customer of the day finally escaped from the store, her credit card definitely worse for the wear. Carlie collapsed over the end of the counter, her arms draped over the sides, and pressed her warm cheeks to the cool surface. "Another day gone."

Chandra called from the changing rooms, "At least we didn't have any kids with accidents—no puking either. A bodily fluid-free day."

"What every woman aspires to—except nurses, I suppose." The words struck a pang in her heart. *Don't go there. You do not have what it takes to be a nurse. Just let it go.*

"Yeah, that'd be a waste of time. I mean, c'mon, nurses probably never have a day without catheters, bedpans, and those—what are they called? The kidney-shaped—"

"Emesis basins."

"You totally should have gone to nursing school," Chandra insisted. "You always know this stuff."

"Who has the time or the money? You have to eat. Besides the guidance counselor in high school, the junior college counselor, not to mention my parents all told me I couldn't hack it—not grade-wise, not personality-wise, not at all. So, there you have it."

"I bet you could get financial aid. You're a woman. You're white—strike against you—but you're a woman. So, why not try it?"

Instead of saying the words she wanted to most—something about being left alone and minding own business—Carlie forced a bit of civility into her words and tone. "Because you need more than dollars, okay?"

"You're grumpy since you dumped Blaine's sorry butt."

Defensiveness rose up within her, but before she could launch and load her retaliation, the truth of Chandra's words hit hard and fast. "Yeah. I probably am. I still feel guilty. He was so hurt—"

Chandra appeared at the register and snapped her hands to her hips. "Ummm-uhhhh… you don't get to go there. No way. He totally flipped out on you. You said it, he almost shoved you. If your professor—"

"Dean was great, okay? I know that. But Blaine was just embarrassed. He wouldn't have hurt me. And I overreacted, okay?"

"No, you've had time to let old thought patterns override your common sense. You totally…"

The truth of Chandra's words stung, but Carlie refused to listen. She hurried to the entry way and pulled the security gates closed. By the time she returned, Chandra had restored order to the front and wiped down the counter. "You can go if you want," Carlie offered. "I'll get the drawer in the safe and be right behind you."

The woman stood, watching as Carlie printed out the day's receipts to add to the drawer. "You know, you should apply for the assistant manager's position. You've worked here long enough—do all the work of one anyway. Might as well get paid for it, right?"

"I don't know. They probably want at least an AA for that. I've got nuthin'. So—"

"I overheard Marissa talking about it. They're looking for someone with experience and confidence. You've got both—or you do when you're actually working. You sure don't when you're talking about it."

"I'm realistic."

"You're cynical about yourself. It's not healthy. You're a fabulous person, but it's like you're the only one who can't see it." Chandra gave Carlie a quick hug. "Just think about it, okay? But think fast or they'll hire someone that none of us want to work with, like last time. Remember Rachel? Oh, man. Ugh."

Carlie waved as Chandra left and then carried the register drawer into the office. *She has a point. They already trust me with the key and the cash. Why not get paid for it?* The applications—both filled and blank—sat on the desk top. *I could so do this. I mean, what's the worst that could happen? They say no, and I keep doing what I'm doing. Is that so bad?*

Her hand reached for the paper. She slid one from the pile and stared at it. Perspiration beaded on her upper lip as a wave of panic washed over her. She crumpled it into a ball and dropped it in the wastepaper basket. "If they wanted me, they would have offered it to me."

Boutique Row—Lynn Rivers' favorite shopping area. Dean, on the other hand, considered his mother half-crazy for preferring the wet and cold to the convenience and warmth of the local mall. Add to it the overpriced merchandise from stores usually frequented by people with a budget far beyond his, and it became a logistical nightmare. However, the annual trip remained one of the few traditions the Rivers-Sager family still observed, and Dean refused to miss it.

"So, who is first on the list?"

"Well, I need something for my travel agent. She's into scarves this year, so I'll be looking at those. Do you have anyone that needs a scarf, Dean?"

"No one I can think of. I could purchase one for Carlie, but it seems a bit personal."

"Carlie. She sounds like a nice girl. Why haven't you asked her out? I'm sure you've told me, but—"

But you don't really listen unless you're interested. I suppose she intrigues you now? "Well, until this week she had a boyfriend, so that would have stopped me, regardless. However, I find I'm more interested in *understanding* her. I have discovered an entirely new person in her—just by listening."

"Well, if you found a woman who can make you listen, then you need to do everything—oh! Look at that jacket. It is perfect for you!"

Dean stared at the window display, nodding, until he realized that his mother meant the leather motorcycle jacket rather than the leather blazer that had caught his interest. "I do like the brown…"

"You would. Come in. Let's try it on."

"Just because I like it doesn't mean I want or need it." Why he bothered, Dean couldn't say. *Habit, I suppose. Larry will tease me on Sunday.*

"There's so little that you do like, that I can't afford to pass it up when I know." Lynn wrapped her arm around his and tugged him inside the store. "Besides, maybe a nice leather sport coat will open this Carlie's eyes." She smoothed his hair. "Maybe a new haircut…"

"I was at the salon two days ago, Mim. This is my preferred style, as you well know."

"It's a little outdated, don't you think?"

Yet we both know it suits me. So I'm outdated. Who cares? "Probably, but you have always insisted that everyone should have a signature style. This is mine, and you know that the last style change Drew attempted was a disaster. Now where's this jacket?"

As she went to pay for her most recent addition to his wardrobe, Dean excused himself. "I'm going to pop into the bookstore down the street. Please stop in on your way to The Antiquarium. I wanted to browse there, and perhaps I will find a suggestion for Larry for your Christmas present." *And I might find something for you too, but we'll both pretend that isn't my intention.*

"Okay. Just keep an ear out for me. I'd rather not have an allergy attack from all those musty old books."

His favorite store in Rockland boasted more out-of-print used books than he'd ever found anywhere. The old theology books in the religious section gave such rich insight into how the church had evolved—sometimes devolved—over the past century and a half. As he passed the comedy section, Dean saw Garfield comic books and wondered if perhaps something along those lines would be appropriate for Carlie. "She might like something lighter and amusing—particularly with her cats…"

"I'm sorry, can I help you?"

The woman behind him made Dean jump. "Oh, I apologize. I didn't see you. I had planned to peruse the religious section before Garfield distracted me."

"Cat lover?"

He shook his head. "Not particularly. I have a friend who recently acquired a pair of cats. I thought perhaps it might be a good gift…"

When the little bell over the door jingled, and a whoosh of cold air followed, the woman turned. "Well, if you need anything, just call for me. I'm pretty familiar with the theology section—my favorite."

"Student or hobby?"

"Both? I'm studying so I'll be prepared for Logos Theological next semester."

Dean dug out a business card. "Well, I hope to see you in my classes when you go. I'll watch for you…" He waited expectantly for her to share her name.

"Gabby." She held out her hand. "Gabby Marceanu," she said as she stared at the card. "Nice to meet you, Professor—Dr. Sager. Th.D. Wow. You look kind of young for that."

The question—one so familiar that he often answered without thinking. "I am."

"Wow. Do you tell your students that story, or do I have to hound you during office hours for it?"

Dean opened his mouth—ready to tell her all about every bit of his childhood, and how it had spurred him to greater heights of scholastic achievement—and suddenly heard himself say, "Zip me an email. I'd be happy to share." He glanced over his shoulder. "My mother will be here before I've had a chance to peruse. I should hurry…" *Wow, I'm learning. That's interesting, isn't it?*

"I'll do that—email, I mean. Thanks. And hope you find something fabulous. We just got a book by Alexander Campbell in the other day. Haven't had a chance to read it, but I thought it looked interesting when I put it into inventory."

The book was displayed—face first. *Easy to find.* Dean pulled it from the shelf, flipped through it, and held it. *Must see more of this…* A Bonhoeffer that he didn't own in hardback called to him. Dean answered. But then, tucked away in the very corner of a high bookshelf, he found a beautiful book designed in the style of the 1920's with an oval inlaid picture on the cover. *"Fearfully and Wonderfully Made."* A glance inside showed a subtitle: *"Embracing the Master's View of His Workmanship"*.

"That's incredibly modern for the time. Interesting, not to mention timely, considering her comment this week."

A few minutes later, his mother tapped his arm. "I'll need a ride to the ER soon, if you want to drive me."

"Translation: 'I've arrived and would like to leave.' I'll be done in a moment, Mim."

"What has you so engrossed?"

"I think I'm going to get this for Carlie. It appears to be an excellent book. It works through the issue of people's misperceptions of themselves and apparently, without delving into near self-worship. I hope she reads it."

"She really is insecure, isn't she?" Lynn flipped through the book as she followed Dean to the counter. "Sounds… interesting."

The curiosity on Gabby's face prompted Dean to encourage his mother to go to The Antiquarium. "I'll be there as soon as possible, but these old books will have you wheezing like an emphysemic octogenarian. Larry will be seriously displeased with me."

She kissed him and beamed at Gabby. "Isn't my son the most thoughtful young man? I can't imagine why he's still single, can you?"

Gabby stammered, but Dean opened the door for his mother and promised to follow in just a minute or two. "I apologize," he murmured as he pulled out his wallet. "She has become obsessed with the idea of grandchildren. I'm afraid I'll be forced to ask what she'll want to be called when I'm blessed with children—Grandma? Nana? Grammy? That ought to give her perspective." He winked. "My bet is on 'GiGi.'"

"You're cruel—hilarious, but cruel. What if she says, 'Oh, I've waited to be Mee Maw my whole life!'?"

"I'll begin a search for discount strait jackets?"

Her laughter filled the front room of the store. "That's it. I'm taking your classes first. Even if I fail, you'll probably make me laugh about it."

He waited until his books were safely stowed in a shopping bag in his hand before he turned to go and said, "Well, that will be a first. I usually get tears."

T he cold burned his nose and prompted Dean to turn up his coat collar while he wandered the streets of New Cheltenham. As he rounded a corner, he heard them—the carolers. The voices grew stronger with each step, until he found them, a half a block away, tucked under the overhang of a store. *She didn't exaggerate. The costumes are amazing. That rich green is a beautiful color on her.*

"Angels We Have Heard on High" filled the air as the group moved away from the corner to cross the street. They shifted on every verse change, slowly moving up and down the street. Dean followed. Twice, he could have sworn that she saw him, but Dean ducked into nearby stores and waited for her to become distracted again.

She has an excellent voice, he decided. *It may not be solo material—not like her friend—but the ensemble loses its richness when her part doesn't sing. Her voice is likely perfect for a quiet ballad. Standing near her in church would be amazing.*

Another glance his way prompted Dean to pull his ivy cap lower and bend down to tie his shoe. *Would it be such a foolish decision to say hello— offer to buy her a warm drink? Perhaps hearing a compliment from someone who does know her, but not well enough to be inordinately biased, would mean something.*

Her voice broke into his thoughts. "—do you say to getting a drink at the pub?"

"I'm driving. Can't."

"I didn't mean a *real* drink, Ann!" Carlie insisted. "That'd be stupid with the roads the way they are. But the pub here has a cool virgin hot toddy that is delicious and warming."

"Ann" paused, nearly making Dean bump into them. *Not too close, or they'll see you.*

"Which one? I've never seen that."

"It's that new one two streets over—The Grouse and Thistle."

"Where do they get these names?" Ann laughed. "Then again, my sister went to one in the north country of England— 'The Hind's Hind.' I guess Grouse and Thistle sounds almost normal in comparison."

Carlie glanced at her watch. "Twenty minutes to go and then you, me, and the thistle it is." She leaned closer. "I wonder if I'll see Dean there."

"Dea—the lunch guy? Why would he be there?"

The group began singing again, drowning out Carlie's reply, but Dean suspected he knew the answer. *Because I am a dismal failure at evasion. I should go.*

Halfway to his car, Dean did an about-face and hurried down streets until he found The Grouse and Thistle. Inside, he waited for the bartender to have a moment and said, "Pardon me. I wonder if you could help."

"Happy to try. What can I get you?"

Dean glanced over his shoulder and back again. "A group of carolers will be arriving—two in particular—and order the virgin hot toddies." He pulled out his wallet and fished out a twenty-dollar bill. "I'd like to pay for them now."

"I'd love to help, but I can't guarantee that I'll get the right people. Sorry."

Undaunted, Dean pushed the bill across the bar. "One of the women has long dark hair—gorgeous—wearing a dark green coat—the old-fashioned kind, of course."

"Of course," the man agreed. "This is New Cheltenham. God forbid people wear anything, oh, I don't know, current?"

Laughing, Dean nodded. "Precisely. The other lady is wearing a white coat. She's blond. Regardless, I'd be obliged if you'd try. If you don't see the right ladies, I'll never know. But if you can, tell her that the person who paid for her drinks thinks she has a beautiful voice."

"Sure you don't want to do it yourself? Might get a date out of it…"

"I have no doubt she'll know I am responsible," Dean admitted. "But I'd rather not interfere with her outing with a friend. Have a wonderful evening."

Stepping into the restaurant and out of the snow became an event rather than an action. Weaving her way through the throng waiting for

a table earned her several complaints, one cursing, and an accidental bruised rib. That man apologized profusely and, if she were honest with herself, flirted. *Don't respond. Don't respond. Don't respond. This is exactly what gets you into trouble. No guys—for a year. Maybe two. Get your life together.*

"No problem. Just need to get to my table."

"Oh, did they call you?"

She smiled back as she broke through the crowd and into the main restaurant. "No, a friend is waiting for me." Carlie shrugged out of her coat as she hurried around the corner to their "regular table" and bumped into Dean. "Oh, sorry—wait. You just got here?"

Dean pushed his messenger bag to the other side and took her coat for her, hanging it on the hook. When he sat, he reached for the menu without touching his bag. *He has to do his work. He can't just ignore it because I'm here. Wonder why he doesn't work anymore...*

In an attempt to encourage him to concentrate on his papers, Carlie retrieved the Kindle she read on her subway rides and pulled up her current book. Dean hesitated and reached for papers. *Whew. That worked. Still, I wonder why he's late...*

She tried to read—to follow the storyline, but more often than not, when she reached the bottom of the page, Carlie found herself starting over again. Janice appeared for their drink order and laughed when Carlie said, "I think I want another peppermint mocha. Those things are seriously addicting."

Dean placed his thumb to mark where he'd been reading and looked up. His eyes met hers, sending a kaleidoscope of butterflies fluttering in her heart. *No! You will not get all weak over another guy—not now. You made the decision to embrace singleness, now stick to it.*

"—try one, too. She likes it so much."

Aw, now you're just making it hard. I mean, I don't really even know you, but everything you show me says you're awesome. You probably have a girlfriend. I mean, what guy like you wouldn't. And even if you don't, c'mon. Me? Yeah, right.

Carlie tried to go back to her book, but words swam on the page. After the third attempt to reread the same page, a menu covered the screen. She looked up and saw Dean smiling at her. The butterflies fluttered with renewed vigor. "Wha—" Before she could ask the question, Carlie stopped herself. *Why be dishonest? He knows I'm not reading. Aaand there go his papers. Maybe...*

"So, since you were late, and since you didn't get any work done, I submit that I should get the check today."

That same smile—the one that meant she'd lost—appeared on the corners of his lips. He glanced at the menu one more time before setting it aside. A second later, his laptop followed the papers into the messenger bag and out of sight.

Unsure what else to do, she slid back into the corner and propped her legs up on the bench. When her coffee arrived, she still hadn't spoken. But, once Janice took their orders, she leveled a look at him. "If I didn't know better, I would have sworn you were in New Cheltenham Saturday night. It was hard to tell, of course—your style tends to blend with the store owners who get into the whole 'England in America' kind of thing."

The smirk on his face gave it away. "So, you sort of admit it. Should I be concerned that I traded an almost abusive boyfriend for a stalker lunch partner?"

Dean's laughter rang out across the restaurant, earning them a few curious looks. Carlie cocked her head, waiting. A moment later, he studied his cup with decided amusement.

"And thanks for the drink, although it might have been nice if you sat with us." She waited, hoping. *Just tell me that you're shy or... something. You don't act shy, but what else would you call this silent thing?* When he didn't— not that Carlie expected he would—she sighed. "And the compliment was nice, but you got the wrong girl. Ann's the one with the amazing voice. The bartender told me what you said, and I went back to Ann and said, 'Dean was here. He paid for our drinks. He also thinks I have your voice.'" She gave him an odd look. "Ann thinks I have a weakness for dangerous men. When I pointed out that you are practically a preacher, she said, 'Great. He just wants to induct you into some cult. That's so much better. Have you ever heard of Jim Jones?'"

Dean's upper lip twitched, and Carlie sighed to herself. *If you had a mustache, you'd be like a little old man from like ages ago.*

Janice appeared, out of breath and looking a little harried. "Texas Trio for Carlie..." She glanced at Carlie's cup. "And another peppermint coffee?"

Carlie shook her head. "No, how about a Coke or something. I think peppermint chili would be gross."

"Great." Janice plopped Dean's turkey wrap in front of him. "And for you..." she stared at him. "Did you get anything done today?"

Before Carlie could comment, Dean nodded. "I arrived before her—barely. Today, that's an accomplishment in itself."

As he took his first bite of turkey wrap, Carlie pulled out her Kindle again. "You know, I think I can concentrate now. I just wanted to thank you and tell you about Ann and..." She flushed. "I swear; you're like my own personal therapist. Once I'm talked out, I'm good."

She powered up her Kindle, chose the book she'd abandoned the previous week, and began reading. Only when a brownie a la mode appeared did she realize that Dean was gone—with the check, of course— and she truly had lost herself in the story. "When did he leave?"

"About five minutes ago." Janice smiled. "He got a lot done, too. I saw him finish the last paper before he got up from the table."

"Oh, good. I felt bad."

"He knows," the woman assured her. "He also had a good five or ten minutes where he just finished his meal and watched you."

"Creepy, huh?" It didn't feel creepy to her, but Carlie had begun to accept that her creep-o-meter didn't function properly.

"Maybe if it was anyone else, but from Dean, I'd say it's just nice." Janice took Dean's empty dishes and waved a few free fingers. "Have a good day."

As Carlie dug into the small brownie with its dollop of ice cream melting in the bottom of the bowl, her thoughts went to Dean and the realization that she knew nothing of him. *Okay. Time for parental input— much as it hurts to admit it. Ugh.*

A Sunday morning with nothing to do—Carlie woke to the realization that it hadn't happened in months. Pouncer clawed at her arm while Moros yowled for morning kibble. "All right, all right. You're almost as bad as Blaine calling to talk me into taking him out for breakfast." The words stuck in her throat. "I did not just say that. I did not— oh man."

She ignored the way the cat with a kitten shadow tried to butt her away from the bathroom and into the kitchen. Instead, Carlie stood before the mirror and stared at her reflection. "Dropping him was the best thing you could have ever done. You put your whole life on hold in case he'd call, and for what? So, he could send you deeper into debt? How pathetic is that?"

The cats only meowed in response.

"This is it. I'm not waiting for New Year's. I'm starting over— today. A new me. Starting with the important things. Food for the kitties…" She shook the kibble into each bowl—one for older cats, one for kittens—and rinsed out the water basin.

"Now, what else—I know! Church!" Shame hit her full force as she realized that the idea of attending worship with other Christians shouldn't exactly be a novel idea. *Inspired one, perhaps,* she thought to herself. *But I shouldn't feel like I've created a genius idea! C'mon!*

Pouncer rubbed against her ankle. "Right? I'm going to go get dressed and then figure out what church to go to." Another slug of guilt hit her in the gut. "I've lived here for three years. I shouldn't have to try to figure out *where* to go!"

Moros just purred.

"You guys are no help."

Shower, hair, makeup, clothes—changed twice, of course—and a mad scramble to find where she'd stashed her Bible. The next hour flew past, making it nearly impossible for her to go anywhere of any distance at all. "I'm just going to walk, and the first church I come to, I'll go in— even if it's a synagogue that started half an hour ago." Something about that statement seemed off, but Carlie couldn't pinpoint what.

At the corner, she asked a man if he'd seen a church nearby. He pointed behind him. "About three blocks back that way—little church in a storefront. The writing was in English, so…"

"Good enough for me. Thanks."

She almost passed it—a little, unassuming building with a hand-lettered sign on poster board taped to a recessed door. Rockland Christian Assembly. A man near the door saw her and opened it for her. "Would you like to come in?"

"Yes… sorry. I wasn't sure if I was in the right place."

"If you're looking for Christian fellowship, I'd say you are anyway." He stuck out his hand. "Jared Schepp."

"Carlie Denham. Nice to meet you."

He grabbed a chair from a stack leaning against the wall and led her to the group. "Hey, everyone. This is Carlie. She's from—" he frowned. "I didn't ask."

"Just a few blocks over," she said. Several questions flew at her until one woman stood, a toddler on her hip, and came to greet her.

"Give Carlie some room. Just because we don't get a lot of visitors doesn't mean that we need to smother her. Sheesh, people!" The woman stuck out her hand. "I'm Natalie. Nice to have you here. Why don't you bring your chair up and sit with us? I've got a few kids to distract you enough, so you don't notice how rude we all are in gawking at you."

The moment she sat, a little girl climbed up on her lap. "You're pretty." Wide eyes never left Carlie's face, but the little girl spoke to her mother. "Isn't she pretty, Mommy?"

"She is."

Carlie's face flamed. "Thank you. What's your name?"

"Sarah." She pointed to her siblings. "That's David and that's Daniel."

A woman plopped into the seat ahead of them and turned to say something to Natalie. "I got the bottle uncorked—finally. Juice is ready. Bread is in the oven." Her eyes moved to Carlie. "Hi! I'm Kate. Nice to meet you. Are you a friend of Nat's?"

"No…" Carlie's eyes moved sideways. "Not yet anyway."

"I like her!" Natalie's eyes swept the room. "She knows good friend material when she sees it."

"No one is friendlier than Natalie," a voice called out from behind a partition. "That's for sure."

Kate didn't turn around. Instead, she asked the question apparently burning on everyone's heart. "So, how'd you find us? The phone rings at our house, and as far as I know, we didn't get a call…"

"I was late getting up and just thought I'd walk to the first church I found. A guy on the corner pointed me this way—how he knew this was a church, though, I'll never know. I mean, I almost missed it. You could use a better sign."

"This is just temporary until we figure out how to split up. Jared owns the building and it's empty, so he's letting us use it free."

Great. I just walked into a church split. That's the last *thing I need!* "Sorry to hear about the split, but it must be nice to have free rent."

Laughter erupted around her and Natalie patted her shoulder. "We're not splitting like that—just that there's too many of us for one house now, so we're branching out into two. But no one has decided that they're ready to commit to it at their home yet."

Double great. They're home churchers. Just what I need. A bunch of fanatics telling me how messed up I am. Truth hit her hard. *Then again, who am I kidding? I'm pretty messed up.*

Jared seated himself behind her and passed her an iPad. "For the words," he murmured. On the other side of the room, a guitar picked a few notes before the group joined in singing. Carlie had never heard such an odd combination of contemporary and hymn in one song—a song she'd never heard yet somehow seemed familiar. Various parts and harmonies joined, confusing her, but Jared just pointed to the screen. "Stick with the melody for now. Nat sings melody," he whispered.

By the fourth song, third Scripture reading, and second prayer, Carlie was confused, fascinated, and touched. Bibles appeared as if by mutual agreement, as an older man pulled his chair to the front of the semi-circle. "I fully expected to continue our study of Daniel this week, but with the big Facebook blowup of that actress coming out without her makeup, my daughter and I had some interesting discussions. We spent a lot of time examining Psalm 139—particularly the 'fearfully and wonderfully made' part. I don't want to take things out of context or presume to add to what the Lord meant by that, but I couldn't help but think it might be an apropos topic while it's fresh in our minds. Jared, can you read the chapter for us?"

It's like a Bible study—but not. I've never seen anything like it. I wonder if they have a website or a statement of faith or—something. So close to home would be great.

Absolute silence filled the room at the end of the study of Psalm 139. Three women stood and disappeared behind the partition while Jared leaned forward and whispered, "If you can take communion with a clear conscience before God, you are welcome, but if you are just seeking—"

"I'm a Christian," Carlie whispered back. "I've been neglecting the Lord these past few years, but..."

Jared smiled. "Tell Him. He'll forgive—always. Just tell Him. Get it right with Jesus, and let His communion refresh you."

J anice laughed as he pulled a bubble-wrapped package from his messenger bag, removed the protective covering and a ring of cardboard that protected a bow before he slid the package across the table to where Carlie would sit—he hoped. "You are so weird, Dean. What guy protects a package like that? It's crazy."

"A 'guy' whose mother considers the packaging to be as important as the gift. 'If you don't care enough to protect the outside, do you really care about what you put *inside?*" He groaned. "It's been a birthday and holiday mantra throughout my life. So, I learned, at a very young age, how to transport packages without getting scuffed corners or crushed bows."

She picked up the package and weighed it. "I thought maybe a DVD—it's the right size—but this is too heavy. It's a book? Only a professor would get a girl a book for Christmas."

Dean pulled out a tiny plastic container and removed a truffle box from it before setting it on the table as well. "It's just chocolate. Don't allow your fluttering heart to get too excited."

The woman snorted. "I know it's chocolate. You can't be that ignorant."

"Ignorant of what?" Dean reached for his papers. "I'm confused."

"To think that a girl you've never talked to could possibly know you well enough for *that.*" Janice suggested the cordial cherry coffee and turned to go. "But seriously, if you could see how cute you two are…"

Cute is irrelevant. My silence serves as a conduit for her to express herself—to allow her to share her thoughts without burdening her with my opinion. Difficult as it is to admit, I would have attempted to "fix" her before this. And that probably would have driven her away.

He nearly made it through the stack of papers—convinced by that point that being Christmas Eve, she wasn't coming—before Carlie appeared at his side. He felt her presence before she even entered his peripheral vision. "Hey! You're still here. Great. I was so a—oh!" She shrugged out of her coat, hung it, and tried unwrapping her scarf as she sat opposite him. "That's so pretty." Her finger traced the ribbons that crisscrossed the present before her.

On his side of the table, Dean gripped the papers in his hand so tightly they began to crumple. He found it impossible to look at her— to watch her as she slid the gift in slow circles, examining it from all sides. *Have you lost your senses? It's just a gift. Common place enough occurrence.* But the answer refused to illuminate his confusion.

A card slid beneath the papers in his hand, and he heard Carlie say, "I got you something, too—decided to stick with tradition. Card for Thanksgiving... card for Christmas. Who knows, if you're a good boy, I might even get you one for Valentine's Day."

His throat went dry. *Surely by then we'll be conversing.*

"—open it this time? I..."

She looks so eager—excited. Watch how her eyes sparkle. Don't douse her excitement simply because you are uncomfortable with opening gifts. It will be an improvement to your character to be able to do so without rambling to cover your discomfort.

He slid his finger under the flap and popped it out. The card had to have come from Hallmark. Dean forced himself not to glance at the back to prove himself right. *They do make beautiful cards,* he mused as he read the outside greeting. When he opened it, a gift card fell out—a card to The Fiddleleaf, no less. Dean looked up and gave her a deliberate smile.

"I thought, 'What could I give him that shows him how much I enjoy coming here? What would say 'thanks' in a way that was still personal?' Then I realized that something to make keeping it up easier would be best." His heart blasted him as he watched her wait for him to speak. "Anyway, Merry Christmas."

Her fingers fiddled with the bow on her package, but she didn't open it. Ignoring the side of him that demanded he thank her and urge her to open his, Dean opted for something more personal—even if it wasn't what she hoped for—what she expected. He reached across and squeezed her hand. *Thank you,* his eyes said for him. Carlie squeezed him back before pulling the present closer.

"So, my turn, eh? I had a friend in high school—her family used to open their gifts on Christmas Eve. I kind of feel like I'm cheating."

Her fingers slipped the ribbons off the edges and pushed them aside. "I know it's a book—that's obvious. But I'm curious what kind of book *you'd* get *me*." She pulled the wrappings from the book, and Dean held his breath.

Will she understand? Will she see it as beautiful and practical, or will she be insulted? Inexplicable panic knocked the breath from him. *This was a terrible idea.* As much as he wanted to rip the book from her hands and rush out to buy flowers or perfume—anything girly and, in his opinion, less personal—Dean leaned back and waited.

"Oh..."

She hates it.

"This is so beautiful..." Her fingers traced the oval. "They used to make books so pretty. And the title! How did you find something with that? I just mentioned it last week, wasn't it? Also, I went to this church on Sunday, and they are usually studying Daniel—I think it was Daniel, anyway. Whatever. The guy did Psalm 139 instead—all about the fearfully and wonderfully made stuff. He said that we're different from inanimate objects like rocks and trees and water—even from the animals. He said that the more people understand how humans were designed, how our minds work, how delicate we are even in our physical strength, the more we will understand what the psalm means."

An excellent explanation of the passage. Where was this? What church? And why did you go there instead of your usual assembly?

"How can we know things—like all of our lives—but not really 'get' it until we are broken and feel worthless?"

You're worth everything to the One who created you—to the One who gave up everything to save you from yourself. How can that not be the most beautiful thing?

"But the idea that if I'm God's workmanship—I'm *His* creation. The idea that He called mankind 'good' and that includes me... I don't quite know how to handle it. I've reread that chapter three or four times since Sunday." She ducked her head. "Okay, more like three or four times a day. Pathetic, isn't it?" Tears filled her eyes and slid down her cheeks. "Maybe this book will make it all make sense. That would be nice."

Dean found himself praying for her in a way he'd never prayed for anything—ever. *Help her, Lord. Show her how precious she is to You.*

"—almost didn't come today. I got off early and was going to go home, but I got halfway to the Loop and turned back." She ducked her head. "It just seemed like something was missing."

His nod seemed to spur her on.

"So, I'll just say it. These weekly lunches are the highlight of my week, okay? Although..." Her lip twisted oddly. "I think Sundays might trump that someday. I really liked that church, and I've got a meeting with the elders next Sunday night—to talk about what they really believe. It's just so weird. They're like this home church, but they meet in this empty store now…"

Dean grinned. *And that trumps gift cards and beautiful books. Your excitement over things of the Lord is the best Christmas present you could give anyone. It's breathtakingly beautiful, isn't it, Lord?*

The Rivers-Sager family had few traditions, but sleeping in as late as each person liked was one. Dean staggered out at nine-thirty, after a late night working at the Rockland Relief Center, to find an empty living room. "Foiled again," he muttered to himself. "They will likely appear the moment they hear me reach for the first bowl." He clattered the bowl on the counter, and less than a minute later, Larry appeared.

"Merry Christmas, Dean. Need help?"

The temptation to ask for ingredients while he mixed the batter tempted him, but Dean shook his head. "Not at all, thank you." A glance at Larry's sleep-wrinkled face prompted him to add, "But you should pour yourself some coffee. Oh, and Merry Christmas to you too." As Larry moved to pull out his mug, Dean noticed something glinting on his t-shirt. "Larry… did you turn vampire overnight?"

"Huh?"

He picked it off. "You're sparkling." Dean rolled the piece in a ball. "Interesting aside… Carlie told me an amusing story about tinsel yesterday."

"You're still having lunch with her, eh?"

"Yes…" Dean counted through his ingredients, trying to discover what he'd missed. "Almond! I almost forgot my 'secret' ingredient."

Larry sat sipping coffee for a minute or so before he said, "So, the tinsel…"

"Oh! Yes, tinsel. Just before her aunt died, Carlie discovered a mouse in her apartment. The solution: a cat. So, late one evening, she drove across town and purchased a kitten—to kill her mouse problem."

"Seriously?" Larry took too big a sip of his coffee and yowled. "Ouch! I didn't know people actually did that."

"Well, Carlie apparently does. Then her aunt died and bequeathed her beloved… cat. At this point she owned a cat—Moros, no less—and a kitten. Oh, and let's not forget the mouse, although Moros has proven somewhat efficient in the vermin eradication department. Backstory complete. Now yesterday, Carlie regaled me with an amusing story. She found a nest—full of tinsel from her tree. You will," Dean insisted, "show proper appreciation for my self-restraint in not informing her that cat owners should never use tinsel. They swallow it and horrible things happen."

"Really? I didn't know that. How did you know that?" Before Dean could respond, Larry shook his head. "Never mind. You read it somewhere. You know everything. Why should I be surprised?"

The words kicked him in the gut. *Am I truly that much of showy know-it-all?* The question didn't need to be asked—or answered. Dean knew it was true.

"Anyway, tell me about the tinsel. What happened with the Christmas nest? She has some pretty talented mice. HGTV should consider a design show—'The Mice Before Christmas.'"

Dean chuckled at the image Larry's words conjured in his mind. "I wish I would have thought of that. She would have been amus—then again, since I wouldn't have told her anyway, perhaps it's best." Dean swallowed hard and pulled out a fork to start stirring the batter. "Regardless, she discovered the festive nest and, as she put it, 'freaked out.' She dragged the cats into her kitchen—and has scratches to prove it—to demonstrate the evidence of their shirked duty." His voice rose just a little into a falsetto. "'I think they thought I was crazy. Kept fighting to get away, and then the next thing I realize, I'm sobbing in bed and my cats are purring next to me. I'm just hoping I scared the mouse off with our freak-out.'"

"I wish I would have seen that. It belongs in a movie."

"She has shared several of her cat tales with me. She also jokes now about being a 'crazy cat lady at the ripe old age of twenty-four.'"

Larry buried his face in his cup and murmured, "When are you going to ask her out?"

"Considering I couldn't if I wanted to—which, I confess I am not certain of—the answer is maybe someday or possibly never."

"Why not?"

Had anyone else asked, Dean might have frozen him out. But Larry never meant to pry—even when he did. "I won't deny that I've considered it, but I'm not sure I see the point. We have a strange friendship, Larry. In one sense, it isn't real. She only knows what she can presume from what little I share, and my silence seems to prompt a therapist-inspired—well, more of a confidant relationship. For all I know, she's the true psychopa—" He cut himself off. "And I don't believe that myself. Regardless, we don't have enough of a foundation for a genuine friendship for me to be confident that it would be an advisable idea."

Lynn entered the kitchen looking perfect—as usual. "Good morning, my handsome men. Merry Christmas." She blew kisses on her way to the coffee maker. "Are those pancakes done yet?"

"First one is going in now."

"Good." With cup in hand, she slid onto the barstool next to

Larry and watched Dean work. "So, what time do you have to be at the Relief Center?"

"Three-thirty. I assure you that there will be sufficient time for our festivities. Will you be attending the Delmonts' annual party, or is there something more exciting under the tree that I should be aware of?"

"You'll have to wait and see," Larry insisted. "I cannot affirm or deny anything without getting into trouble."

Lynn kissed his cheek and jumped from the stool. "Oooh! I'll go finish packing. Just save mine until last, Dean. Be back in a minute."

Over the top of his cup, Larry muttered, "In a Lynn-minute—the ones that last an hour each."

Dean turned back to the stove and flipped a pancake. "And you love every 'Lynn-minute' you have with her." *And that is the best gift you've given both of us.*

The annual "whose job is most stressful" debate raged in the Denham household. Carlie's brother, James, lobbed a wadded-up ball of paper through the kiddie basketball hoop his son got for Christmas and said, "The travel for my job alone trumps your night shifts any day."

Carole shook her head. "So a few flights in *business class* and quality hotels—oh, and fine dining, I might add—is sooo much worse than being puked on, peed on, and cussed out in languages you've never heard of."

"At least Carlie was smart," James muttered. "She just has to scan tags all day and smile. No student loans, no mortgage—she knew the way to go."

Why she allowed herself to get sucked into the debate, Carlie never knew. But it happened every year like clockwork. "Yeah, because having a dead-end job is so cool. It's great to get yelled at on a continual basis because you have to stop people from stealing from you or you can't give them their order for half off because we didn't have any more of the sale items in stock. It's great to have managers who flip out at you for not doing their job for them before they have a chance to. Yeah... great to live in apartments that have crack busts on a semi-regular basis and *mice*."

She jumped up and started to leave, ignoring protests. But another dig from her sister made her pause and add, "You can whine about your horrible jobs all you want, but you're not fooling anyone. You wouldn't change them for anything. Me, I'd change mine for *almost* anything that paid better and had better working conditions, so just stop with the fake first-world problems. You don't even have *real* first-world problems.

105

They're just another way to one-up everyone, and it's sick."

Her old room provided its usual solace. She flopped on the bed and stared up at the ceiling, willing herself to go talk the kids into building their annual snowman. Instead, she reached into her purse and pulled out the book Dean had given her. "They can be all condescending if they want. God values me. That *should* be enough. I need to learn how to accept that as enough," she whispered.

Though she opened the book and stared at the page, Carlie read nothing. The screeches of children squabbling drove her from the room. "Okay, guys. Let's go make the snowman! Coats, gloves, and hats please. I'll get Dylan…" She grabbed the toddler's coat and chased down the little guy. "I'm gonna getcha!"

By the time a three-foot snowman stood perched out by the mailbox, that nice warm-with-work and cold-from-snow feeling filled her. "Hot chocolate? Marshmallows?"

Squeals of agreement streaked toward the house as fast as little feet could propel the children who made them. They tracked snow through the mudroom and into the kitchen, stopping just shy of the living room before Carlie's mom blocked the way. "No, no… go get those boots off before you ruin the carpet. Come on… hurry, hurry! I've got water hot already."

A minute later, Gina pulled Carlie into a hug and murmured, "Don't let their competitiveness drag you down. They were born trying to outdo each other and forget that their words can hurt others."

"It's like I'm the middle child—but I'm not!"

"I thought you were smart to point out that they are just being ridiculous and then leave before they could drag you into it."

Carlie shook her head. "No, I did. I got defensive, like *always,* so now they won't listen—won't even *think* about what I said. I do it every time." She hesitated and then, before she could talk herself out of it, Carlie said, "Can I talk to you guys tonight—like after they're gone? I need some advice…"

"Sure. You just give me until I've got them out the door, and we're all yours."

For the next six hours, Carlie endured teasing for being "oversensitive," assurances that she really had it "too easy," and jabs that she finally "got smart and dumped Blaine before it was too late." By the time the house emptied, she was physically and emotionally spent. She and her parents waved until her sibling and their families drove off into the night. Once the taillights disappeared from sight, they turned back inside and all collapsed in weary heaps on the furniture.

"Whew! Christmas gets more hectic every year," Gina exclaimed as she closed her eyes.

"It's a good hectic."

Carlie glanced at her dad. "Sometimes."

Doug reached over and patted her hand. "I know you feel picked on, but it's just lifelong habits. Maybe we shouldn't have encouraged the teasing—became a habit and now…"

"If you didn't react, they—" Gina began.

"—wouldn't keep doing it," Carlie finished. "I know. But it's hard not to when you feel judged for everything you do."

"You know they love you, right?" Gina watched her reaction closely.

"I know. But love isn't like that, okay? And they make me feel like I'm just worthless, in the way, and there for their personal amusement." She swallowed hard. "They're no different from Blaine sometimes."

"I don't think—"

"I can see why she thinks that," Doug said. "I've felt that way at times. It'll never quit until she puts a stop to it. At this point, only she can." He stretched out and nudged her knee with his toe. "Sorry, Carlie Charlie."

Her mother's discomfort with the direction of the conversation became readily apparent when she asked, "So, Carlie. What did you want to talk about?"

Now that the moment had arrived, Carlie didn't know if she *wanted* to discuss it after all. "I don't know… maybe…"

"C'mon. You wouldn't have mentioned it if you didn't want to make yourself talk. So talk." Her father grinned. "I know you well."

"Okay…" She took a deep breath. "You know how I broke up with Blaine?"

"Best thing you've done for yourself in a very long time," her mother agreed.

"Yeah, well, I didn't tell you all of it." Her hands shook as she tried to explain. "It was bad—horrible, really. I mean, he really scared me. I don't know if he ever would have hit me, but he made me feel like he might. And that's almost as scary."

"I knew it. Didn't I tell you that, Doug? Didn't I say that he was too protective and demanding and… aggressive? I'm so glad—"

"Part of it was over another guy…"

"Another guy?" Understanding dawned. "You're dating the guy who came up for Aunt Phoebe's funeral?"

"No… but I do have lunch with Dean every week, and Blaine hates it. I mean, seriously hates it."

Both parents stared at her. Carlie's father spoke first. "You always complained how Blaine demanded that you remain exclusive to him while he dated other women. Why did you think it was right to do to him what he didn't like—?"

"It's not a date, Dad. It's the weirdest thing. I don't know what to think about it. Hang on." She rushed to her room to retrieve the book and returned, passing it to her father. "This is what he got me for Christmas. This guy knows me better than anyone in my life, almost, and he's never actually spoken to me."

As expected, her parents reacted with one unified exclamation. "What!?"

"We're…he…I…" Carlie's throat went dry. "Okay, I sat down at his booth one day, ate lunch with him—he even paid for it—and he never said a word." She licked her lips before she gave a weak smile. "I've gone back every week since late September. He…"

"And he doesn't talk to you? He just sits there?"

Okay, so they think I'm nuts. Great. I walked into that one. Carlie tried again. "I know it sounds crazy—"

"It sounds," her mother blurted, "like you've traded one unhealthy relationship for another."

"Mom!"

Doug shrugged when she looked to him for support. "You have to admit, it does seem like it…"

"Why would you keep going if he doesn't even talk to you? It seems… creepy."

Carlie chewed her lip and fought back unreasonable tears. "I know why you'd think that, but remember how he came when he heard that Blaine wasn't coming to Aunt Phoebe's funeral? He bought those Bibles. He's a theology professor. I think he's just used to people confiding in him… or maybe he's shy. I don't know. All I know is when I talk to him, I don't feel stupid. I don't feel like a loser."

"So, what do you want from us?"

She frowned. "Help? I mean, I want to talk to him. Get to know who *he* is, too, y'know? I just don't know how. I thought about asking him if he wants to go to that new church I found, but if he doesn't even talk to me…"

"—how would that even work? Right?" Gina looked to Doug for input. "Well, a little help here? You're the one with the genius ideas in cases like this."

"Because we have lots of experience with daughters making one-sided friendships." Despite the unintentional cut to his words, Doug winked. Carlie just managed to hide the pain that followed.

And that's how they got away with it—Carole and James. They learned it from you. How did I never know that? And does that mean they don't mean to be harsh either? 'Cause I know you don't.

"I have it." Her father leaned forward. "I recommend you go

listen in on one of his classes—sustained talking for an hour or two ought to break that ice. What other profession offers such a perfect chance to observe *and* listen?"

Dean arrived well over an hour before Carlie possibly could. The week after Christmas had been the most miserable lunch of his life. With nothing pressing to occupy him—no papers to grade over Christmas break—he'd found himself staring at his book unseeing for an hour. Now, a week later, the memory still unsettled him. *I shouldn't have. She said she couldn't come.* Self-recriminations notwithstanding, Dean now waited with an eagerness that, in a moment of raw honesty, disturbed him.

Again, he held his book before him, and again he saw nothing but incomprehensible hieroglyphics on the page. Her seat remained empty. *She said she couldn't come last week, but she didn't hint about not coming at all...*

Janice appeared. "Want more coffee?"

"I don't know... maybe cocoa. Why get even more jittery?" He glanced around at the half-empty place. "Amazing how the first of the year changes everything. Even last week this was a bustling place, and now look at it."

"Yeah...Frank had to let a few people go today—later hires. They knew it was probably coming, but you know it had to be hard."

He heard the door open and stiffened in anticipation.

"It's her." Janice put a hand on his arm and leaned down to murmur, "Relax. Seriously, you've got to get over this weird shyness with her."

"I'm not shy. I just enjoy listening to her talk," he objected.

"Well, that's a first—for you. We're usually the ones listening to you talk, but not the last few months." She stood to greet Carlie. "We have raspberry hot chocolate—want some? Or salted caramel hot chocolate?"

"That! Definitely *that*. I *love* salted caramel." She shrugged out of her coat. "Sorry I'm late—sort of. I didn't know they'd change my hours until I got in on Monday, and well, I didn't have any way to tell you. I thought it might be weird to call the seminary and say, 'Hey, can you tell Dr. Sager that I won't be at the restaurant until after one-thirty?'"

Dean just leaned back, relaxed, and smiled. *Well, now I won't need to find a way to inform her that I'll be arriving a bit later myself. I'll still have time to grade papers after my morning class—even with the time change.* His heart lifted prayerful hands to the Lord. *You orchestrated this. That's amazing.*

She beamed as she removed gloves and shoved them in her purse. At his quirked eyebrow, she shrugged. "Fine! I admit it. I couldn't wait to get here. I missed you last week. Isn't that weird? It is weird, isn't it?" Her eyebrows drew together, and not for the first time, Dean noticed the incongruity of lips that naturally turned up into a smile even when she tried to frown.

Despite his attempt to wear the deadpan expression he had spent the last couple of months trying to perfect, Dean knew the exact moment when she realized he'd missed her too. "Did you come last week, or what? I mean, you can't have had papers to correct, and you knew I wasn't coming—wait." She chewed her lip and stared at the table. "That sounds so full of myself. That's not what I meant. I just wondered if you came on days like that anyway or—"

Janice appeared with coffee and hot chocolate. "Oh, he was here. Frank finally kicked him out when he let his food get cold—twice. He looked a bit lost." Janice winked and added, "Check the menu. It's been updated for the new year. I'll be back in five..." Dean's frown prompted her to amend that. "Maybe ten minutes. Yeah. Ten sounds good."

Even without looking, Dean felt her eyes watching him. He spent the better part of a minute debating asking how her Christmas went. However, just as he decided it wasn't a good idea quite yet, she spoke again. "I like that sweater—looks kind of Irish. Did you get it for Christmas?" At the smile he couldn't repress, she nodded. "Yeah, I thought so. It's cool. I wonder what your Christmas is like. Ours is so loud and chaotic. I love it—until the sibs start in on their horrible lives. Then I get all defensive, and my feelings get hurt, and it's just so predictable. I know better, but, I'm pathe—no." Her eyes bored into him until Dean looked up at her and met her gaze. "My New Year's Resolution: Live Philippians 4:8."

Yes! Yes, yes, yes! That's the spirit! Or, rather, perhaps I should say-slash-think, 'That's the Spirit!'

His reaction must have shown because as she reached for the

menu, she smiled. "I thought you might like that. It's your 'fault,' you know. That book is so great. I keep reading it, over and over, and then I feel guilty for reading the book about the Bible verse instead of reading the verses themselves, so I go back and read them a few times."

Just keep doing that. Let the Word saturate you.

Carlie studied him, indecision plainly written on every feature of her face. She gathered courage—every emotion that she used to do it overwriting the indecision—and then stared at the open menu before her as she said, "So, you're not married, right?" Her eyes rose to his hand, and she frowned. She reached for it, examining it closely. "No... you're not just not wearing a ring. You never have. But then, you're a theology professor. Maybe you don't believe in wearing jewelry..."

Dean pulled a chain out from within his shirt and let it lay against the cabled sweater he wore before tucking it inside again. *Now what might that do to your theory?*

"So not married. Girlfriend?"

With timing too impeccable to be coincidence, Janice appeared. "Like any woman would put up with a guy who doesn't speak to her. I don't *think* so." She leveled a look on Dean that could mean anything from, "Prove me wrong," to "You disgust me."

Carlie seemed to misread his amusement for discomfort and pointed to her menu. "I think I want the curry pita." She looked up at him. "With that sweater, you totally need to have the shepherd's pie."

"It appears that I am to have the shepherd's pie," Dean said as he replaced the menu. "May we also have the chocolate stack when we've finished?"

"Good deal. I'll get this in."

The moment Janice disappeared, Carlie leaned forward. "I wanted to ask you to do something for me." She pulled a sticky note—one of the ones he'd given her at Thanksgiving—and stuck it to the table in front of him. "That's my email. Can you check out the church, 'Rockland Christian Assembly,' and see if you can find anything about what they believe? I really liked their church, but the whole home church thing kind of freaks me out."

Dean nodded slowly as he stared at the email address. Ideas swirled in his mind as he watched Carlie observe his reaction. Her eyes swept the room as he processed her words and a frown creased her forehead. "Wow, they're empty compared to usual. I don't see Steve. Did you know he has four kids? I saw him showing off their pictures to the hostess on Christmas Eve. All little guys. So cute." Her features relaxed. "Oh, there he—" She reached across the table and grabbed Dean's hand just as he heard a shot ring out. "He's got a gun!"

Without thinking, Dean jumped to his feet and shoved her under the table, whacking her head on the corner in the process. When he could still see her foot, he pushed it under and turned. Fear pummeled him until he felt like he'd drop. The screams that filled the restaurant with that first shot intensified as several more rang out. The man's back was to Dean as he shouted maniacal threats against anyone who interfered with his ability to feed his family. Dean advanced with one thought in mind. *Stop him before he kills someone.*

He almost made it. The 1.7 seconds it took him to come within tackling range passed in cinematic-worthy slow-motion. Just as he leapt, Steve turned and fired. Dean nearly landed on the guy, but instead he crashed to the ground, landing on his burning chest. Amid the screams of terror and panic, he heard one voice cry out, "Dean!"

She'll come out now. She'll be shot. With that thought, he lunged, ignoring the pain that demanded he lie writhing instead of tackling, and jerked one leg. The man fell. Dean scrambled for the gun and flung it out of reach before trying to pin down the shooter.

As if the shock that had frozen everyone momentarily vanished, three other men tackled Steve and held him. In her haste to get a dig in, a nearby woman kicked at Steve and landed it squarely in Dean's wound. This time he screamed, and everything faded from view.

Carlie's boss let her off half an hour early. Unwilling to waste time walking in the cold or riding odd subway routes to get to St. Vincent's Hospital, she ignored the accusations of her conscience and called a cab. *I'll learn how to make rice and beans every other night until I pay it off.* The ridiculousness of her thoughts caught up to her seconds before the scene replayed itself in her mind—again.

"—He's got a gun!"

As soon as the words left her lips, Carlie regretted them. He'll look this way now, stupid! *Concern filled Dean's eyes before he jumped up and jerked her under the table. Her head whacked against the corner, and for an irrational moment, she wondered if she actually saw cartoon stars. A second later, she felt him shove her foot against her, his silent command clear.* Get all of you out of sight now!

What about you? *She ached to scream the words, but another spray of gunshot sent her quivering into a puddle of tears.* Blaine would make fun of me. Stupid, stupid, stupid! Why is Steve doing this?

Dean charged, and the shooter fired. Carlie screamed as the bullet clearly hit Dean somewhere in the chest. How, she didn't know, but Dean managed to shove the gun out of the way before lunging at Steve. C'mon, people! Help him. He's injured! Give me a break! What is wrong with you— *Even as she thought it, three men piled on the shooter, and then Dean collapsed, unmoving.*

Carlie's heart stopped as she watched him lie there. As heartbeats restarted and kicked into overdrive, she ignored the flood of people who bolted from the restaurant, and who would likely trample her if she got in their way and crawled across the floor to Dean's side. "Hey... hey. Look at me." She patted his cheek, but he didn't move. Blood oozed from the wound, soaking his sweater. She glanced around her. "Should I put pressure on this? Anyone?"

Sirens wailed as she attempted to jerk a tablecloth from a table without flinging everything everywhere. She failed. The silverware rolls, condiment caddies, and menus spilled all over the floor, making her glad it hadn't been occupied. But the worst of it came as she pressed the cloth against Dean's wound. She braced herself for his reaction, but there was none.

"—ffic is horrible right now. I can skirt around and get you there faster, but it'll cost a bit more mile wise. What do you think?"

"Do it. I just want to get there."

"Boyfriend?" The man hesitated. "Family?"

"Just a friend—got shot today in that thing at The Fiddleleaf."

"Oh, man. I heard about that. Some laid-off worker goes on a rampage. What kind of creep does that?"

She shook her head. "He's a dad with four kids—always been so nice to us. I can't imagine what must be going on for him to freak-out like that." Carlie's voice trembled as she added, "Dean wasn't moving when they took him out of the restaurant. He was so pale—didn't even flinch when I put pressure on it."

"Wait, you were *there?*"

Carlie nodded. "Yeah... see this cut—no, don't. Keep your eyes on the road. Anyway, I got that when he shoved me under a table to protect me."

"Sounds like a good—oh, perfect. Look, the alley's not blocked. I might be able to shave off a little distance and time now. Shh... don't tell."

"I won't. Thanks."

Eight o'clock came and went before she found her way in and out of the gift shop, to the right floor, and through an odd-shaped hallway to Dean's room. Just outside the door, she heard him talking with someone. "—remember much about it. I just heard the gun and reacted. I think I hurt Carlie when I shoved her under the table."

"You might have saved her life," a woman suggested.

"No... the officer who took my statement a bit ago said I was the only one actually hurt."

The same woman's voice pressed her opinion further. "No, I think you did. I mean, he was probably turning to keep shooting. You just got in the path! There are news people out there who want to talk to you!"

Carlie looked around her at the empty corridor, confused. *What news people?*

A man's voice interrupted. "Now, Lynn. They've been gone for hours."

"Well, they *were!* They probably got pushed out into the lobby or on the street or something."

The voices grew low—as if murmured. Carlie couldn't hear what they said, but she thought she heard Dean's again and realized she'd been eavesdropping. She knocked. "Hello?"

Her heart sank when she saw how pale Dean still was. In a hospital gown, with just a thin blanket covering him, he looked hopelessly ordinary. "I thought I'd come see how you are. I didn't know if you had family here or..."

The woman stepped forward. "I'm Lynn—Rivers. This is my husband Larry..." Lynn waited for Larry to extend his hand before she continued. "I'm Dean's mother, of course. And you are..."

"That's Carlie, Mim."

"Oh, your lunch date!" The woman hurried over and hugged her. "I'm so glad you're okay."

Though she tried not to be too obvious, Carlie couldn't help but watch Dean. "Thanks to him." *And surely you haven't had time to tell her my name today... so she knows about me. That's interesting.* Another thought nearly made her miss his mother's next words. *And why does he call her "Mim"?*

"Dean has told us so much about you. Did you like the book? I really—"

"Lynn, you haven't eaten in hours. I can hear your blood sugar plummeting with each word."

The woman nodded. "Would you be a dear and bring me up a sandwich from across the street? The food here—not so good. I wish—"

"Why don't you come with me? We both know you'll be here all night as it is. Carlie will stay until we get back, won't you?"

Okay, I seriously love this man. She mouthed the words, "Thank you" before she spoke aloud. "I'd be happy to. And you can't be coherent enough to follow all the crazy hospital orders without something to keep up your strength..."

"But I—oooh... certainly. We'll be back soon, but..." Lynn fished a notepad and pen from her purse and scribbled a number on it. "Call us if he or you need anything."

"I will."

"I could have given it to her, Mim."

Both women snickered. "The way he never talks to me, I'm tempted to give it back. Then I can figure out a way to make him need you. Maybe describe the juicy steak sandwich…"

"I still can't believe *my* Dean sits through lunch, every week, and doesn't talk. I would have said such a thing was impossible. I used to pay him to be quiet when he was little. His father would get so mad, but I needed just *five* minutes of silence. And then to think—"

"And she wonders where he gets it," Larry muttered as he steered his wife from the room.

Carlie sat, clutching the stuffed cat she'd purchased in the gift shop. When her eyes rested on it, she shoved it at him. "This is for you—obviously. I thought maybe he'd scare mice away from your house, too. I mean, it is probably the ugliest stuffed animal of any kind I've ever seen, so maybe…"

In a move that told much about Dean, he picked up the toy, smiled at the lopsided face with its crumpled whiskers, and tucked it under one arm.

"It's been all over the news—and with your picture. It looks like a staff picture from work or something. I was watching it on my phone, look…"

With one eye on him, Carlie searched for a news clip and then leaned close to share it. "See?"

As the announcer droned on about the laid off employee and father of four who went on a shooting spree at a "popular local restaurant," Carlie watched Dean's face. *He has amazing skin—hardly any stubble for this time of day. Blaine would have been all sandpapery. And why am I even…*

Piercing blue eyes met hers as he passed her phone back to her. They held and Carlie's breath held with them. *Just ask him to say something. He probably would if you* asked. *You're contributing to this silent thing you're always complaining about.*

His eyes closed, and her thoughts changed directions. *He's tired. I have no business pushing him. I'll just wait for whenever he decides that he is willing to give me the time of day—literally.*

She sat back on the hard, uncomfortable excuse for a chair the hospital had and watched as he lay there. His body slowly relaxed until she decided he'd drifted off to sleep. *Probably the pain killers. I didn't even get to ask about his chest.*

It didn't seem possible when she finally heard Lynn and Larry's voices in the hall, but well over an hour passed with her just watching him sleep. Carlie stood, whispered, "Good night," and turned to go, but an impulse overtook her. She leaned down to kiss his cheek, but at the last second, he turned. Their lips met. Just as she started to pull away, she felt the tug of Dean's own lips for a brief moment.

A little shaken, she hurried to the door and met Lynn there. "I think he's sleeping," she whispered. "I heard you coming, so I thought

116

I'd warn you." *And thought I'd get out of here so I can think. What was that, anyway?*

Lynn thanked her, squeezed her hand, and hurried to the side of the bed where she could keep an eye on her son. Carlie waved at his father—*or is it stepfather? Wasn't her last name different?* But at the elevator, he caught up to her.

"May I ride down with you?"

"Um, sure…"

Larry stuffed his hands in his pockets. "Are you okay?"

"I think so… I wasn't until I got here, but once I saw him—" She flushed. "That sounds ridiculous."

Larry watched her as she rambled but didn't show any response until she called herself ridiculous. "I don't know about that. A man quite possibly saves your life—what is so foolish about being concerned about him? What is so foolish about that kind of trauma unsettling you?"

"Yeah… I guess."

"Dean talks to me about a lot of things—"

"That kind of surprised me. I mean, I know he talks to other people—that's obvious. But the owner mentioned something once about Dean talking too much to the staff at The Fiddleleaf, and then his mom says she used to pay him not to talk. That's not the Dean I know. He's like communication-phobic or something. At first, I thought he was shy, but…"

Larry stepped out of the elevator with her and followed her to the door. "I know Dean doesn't converse with you, but I suspect he communicates somehow. It's who he is."

Mid-protest, Carlie clamped her mouth shut and nodded. "I guess you're right. He does. Wow." She looked at Larry curiously. "I was surprised to hear he'd talked about me. That, I didn't expect."

"He's talked more to me about it than his mother. He opens up to me in a way he never did with her. You'll have to ask him about it sometime."

Her laughter rang out in the lobby. "That's funny. I don't think he'll ever talk to me."

Larry didn't respond—not at first. He pulled out his phone, called for a taxi, and arranged to pay for it—despite Carlie's attempts to stop him. When he finished, Larry leaned against the wall and smiled at her. "They're just around the corner. Be here in a minute."

"Thank you. It wasn't nece—"

"It's my pleasure."

The taxi pulled under the portico a minute later. As Carlie reached for the door, she found Larry holding it for her. He smiled as he said,

"It was nice to meet you. Thanks for coming. And as for Dean, I guarantee you that if you keep coming, someday he'll be ready to talk. I just can't say when."

After he finally convinced his mother to leave, Dean turned on the TV and listened to the late night news. "—thanks to the heroic efforts of one of the regular diners. Frank Presario, the restaurant's owner, had this to say about it:"

"Dean is a great guy—here every week. It doesn't surprise me at all that he did this. I just wish someone would have gotten to Steve before he shot anyone. Our thoughts and best wishes go out to the families of the injured and the two people who didn't make it."

What? I thought I was the only—Mim! His thoughts drowned out much of the rest of Frank's interview, but Dean managed to concentrate as the reporter continued.

"—at first thought that only the theology professor from Logos Theological Seminary was injured, but when police began to process the crime scene, they found one employee in the back—possibly someone who tried to stop the shooter—and a customer crumpled in a booth. While it hasn't been confirmed, there is some speculation that this man was not actually shot but died of a panic-induced heart attack or stroke. Witnesses at the scene said they saw no blood when paramedics wheeled the man out. He arrived at St. Vincent's, where Dean Sager was taken, and was pronounced dead upon arrival. In other news…"

Dean snapped off the set. "I didn't even stop it. I got shot for nothing."

A nurse entered to check Dean's monitors. "That's a lie. You probably saved more lives than we want to think about."

"May I go home tomorrow?"

The nurse checked his chart and shrugged. "It's possible. It looks like they primarily kept you because you had such a hard time coming out of the anesthesia. How you managed to get shot while avoiding all major organs…" He glanced around him. "Are you tired, or do you want to do a little walking. We like you up and walking if you're up to it."

"I'm allowed out of bed?" Dean jerked himself up and nearly screamed from the pain.

"Take it easy. You need to favor it a bit. Just grab the IV pole, and I'll keep an ear out for you." The man offered his hand. "Need a steadying arm?"

As much as he hated it, Dean forced himself to accept the help. "Thank you."

To his astonishment, he barely made it to the end of the hall before he realized he'd be wiped out by the time he made it back to his bed. The nurse, Javier, grinned as if he'd run a marathon. "You did great! Most people don't make it to the end, or if they do, they don't make it back again."

"I feel... dead."

"You feel. That means you're not." Javier refilled Dean's water cup. "We're keeping you hydrated, so you might not remember to drink, but try. It'll help you avoid cracked lips and bad breath. Just sayin'."

With lights dimmed and the room empty of all save him, Dean slowly relaxed and relived the day. Emotions cycled through him at dizzying speeds. Panic as fear filled Carlie's face. Fear as he saw the gun swing his way. Terror when he didn't think he'd make it to the gun. Blackness when the pain and the sight of his blood-stained sweater assaulted him at once—confusion when he awoke hours later in a recovery room with a nurse standing over him that looked like every nightmarish caricature of Nurse Ratched. *At least she was better tempered. Oooh, she unnerved me at first.*

But the memory of hearing Carlie's voice, seeing her enter, and her dismay at the sight of him overshadowed it all. *I must look horrible. But she stayed. Perhaps, I should have spoken to her. It would have been the right time, I think.* Dean felt the slow smile spread across his face. *That kiss though... That, I couldn't have planned if I tried.* He closed his eyes again. *What was I thinking? She'll never come back now. Not that I blame her. I was a bit idiotic.* Dean's thoughts stopped in their tracks and stood at attention as he examined each one. *You sound like Carlie now. Stop it. Readdress it tomorrow.*

Monday, Carlie called and learned that the restaurant would be open again by Tuesday evening. The next day, she called at four and learned it would likely open by six. Wednesday morning, she called and heard the bustle of diners in the background. Hearing they were open lightened her mood, which provided her boss much teasing fodder.

Pulling open the door, Carlie braced herself against an onslaught of emotions. However, the hustle-bustle of patrons coming and going, the familiar sounds of plates rattling and staff taking orders, and the entryway packed with people waiting for a table assaulted her with twice the force she'd expected. *Man, I hope Dean's here. I don't think I can wait otherwise.*

She picked her way through the crowd, ignoring the grumbles and complaints of people who didn't appreciate someone pushing through the line, and hurried to the booth—*their booth. Please let him be here and be okay.*

The sight of the top of his head sent a wave of relief over her. Without thinking, she scurried around the corner and gave him a quick hug. "I am so glad to see you. I've been so worried—almost called your mom—oh, did I hurt your bad side—I—"

His chuckles stopped her mid-sentence. "Okay, so yeah. I'm being ridiculou—" Again she stopped. "You're wearing *glasses!* How did I not realize you usually wear contacts?" *And how did I not realize that you'd look dangerously cute with nerd glasses? Wow.*

Janice appeared, and Carlie's throat went dry at the black armband she wore. "What can I get you?"

"Tea," Dean croaked. "I'd really like some tea with honey and lemon."

"Want me to doctor it for you or bring it out for you to handle?" Janice winked at Carlie as she spoke.

Dean just nodded.

"I think he wants you to do it." As he nodded, Carlie relaxed, hinting to herself that perhaps she'd been a little less confident of her assessment than she'd intended. "And I'll have the same."

Her eyes traveled to his chest, just below his right shoulder. *What, like it's going to randomly start bleeding? What is wrong with me?*

To her astonishment, he opened his mouth to speak. She watched—never more fascinated by the first movement of lips—and then crashed into utter frustration as he leaned back, closed his eyes, and appeared to try to steady himself. When a second or ten passed without any change, Carlie grew nervous. When a dozen more passed, she grew positively panicked.

"Are you okay?"

He nodded.

"You don't look okay," she began. Then the realization that he'd answered her hit. Before she could mention it, Carlie watched as his face drooped with defeat. *Yeah, and you realized it, too. Okay, God. What do I do?* She didn't wait for an answer before plowing onward. "Thanks. I know you're not a big talker—to me anyway—but I'd be freaking out if you didn't answer that one."

"He spoke?" Janice set their cups down and pulled out her order pad. "Know what you want to eat?"

Just the idea of making a decision overwhelmed her. "Um, why don't you surprise me? I can't think—don't want to."

"Dean?"

He looked up at Janice with weary eyes and shrugged. "Surprise me too?"

The moment Janice left, their eyes met—met and held. Carlie felt thoughts jumble into a pile of nonsensical jibberish as she watched Dean grow paler—seemingly by the second. "Are you sure you should be here? I could get a taxi—take you home. Or if you brought a car, I could drive you home and take the subway back or..."

Dean reached for his cup of tea and took a sip, but he almost dropped his cup as he set it back down. Frustration masked his face. *It must have hit a muscle that isn't happy with him or something.* "I'm sorry. You didn't have to come—wait. That sounds wrong." Exasperation prompted her to add, "Oh, you know what I mean. I was hoping you'd come. I—well, I was worried about you. You looked so pale in the hospital, and you don't have much more color now. Are you *sure* they got it all out or it didn't hit an odd organ or something? Is your heart on the other side of your chest or…aaaand you're not going to tell me, so why am I asking? I don't know. I just feel like if I don't talk, I'll cry, okay? So I'm going to talk about a lot of stupid stuff. Like, did you know I saw Blaine at the New Year's party?" The way he stiffened told Carlie he didn't like the sound of that.

"Yeah! I saw him. He was there with some girl—probably one of the ones he dated while he was dating me. Tried to make me jealous with how great he treated her, but I—" Carlie bit her lip. When her eyes rose, she saw the tension in Dean's face. *You want to hear it but you don't. Interesting.* "Anyway, I felt stupid, okay? I mean, why did I stick with him for so long? He's *still* trying to prove how pathetic I am, but now it's all because I'm too stupid to see how stupid I was to let him go."

Dean's hands balled into fists as he leaned against the table.

"So, I told Teresa that being single is so much better than having a guy like him. I said, 'I'm better off without that loser. He'll figure out how good he had it, and then he'll regret treating me like nothing,' and do you know what she said?" Carlie didn't even wait for a reaction this time. "She said that I sound like I'm trying to convince myself. *As if!* I'm not quite that ridiculous—"

His reaction spoke more than words could have. *He agrees with her.* Carlie swallowed the emotion that threatened to choke her and leaned back just as Janice brought pot pies.

"We have roast beef pot pies today—from last night's prime rib sandwiches. Seriously good stuff."

Carlie hardly heard her. Instead, she stared at the armband on Janice's arm. "Did anyone ever find out why Steve did it? It doesn't seem like him."

"I guess I can tell you…" Janice hunkered on her heels, gave a quick glance around the room, and focused back on Carlie. "It'll be on the news tonight—special report. I guess he'd been out of work for so long the unemployment ran out. Then he got this job, and got laid off too soon to qualify…"

"Oh! That's terrible." At Dean's amused look, she added, "I mean, that doesn't make it okay for him to shoot up the place and *kill* people, but that's just awful for his family. Now he'll be in jail and how will that get them fed? What was he thinking?"

Janice leaned forward and murmured, "The kitchen gossip is that he planned to get the police to shoot him—life insurance. It won't pay out for suicide, but it also probably doesn't have a 'won't pay if you get shot by cops while on a shooting spree' clause." She wiped at her eyes. "I don't think he really meant to hit anyone. I think that was an accident.

Something I heard one of the staff say—office manager says she heard a cop say that the bullet patterns indicated they couldn't have hit seated customers. Either that or the guy was just really lucky. He'll face two counts instead of dozens. So only two consecutive life sentences." Janice's lips twisted in a grimace. "Like that'll comfort his family."

"Can we help them?" Carlie felt Dean's eyes on her as she spoke, but Carlie couldn't stand to see the impatience she imagined she'd see in them. "Does Frank have a phone num—no, he couldn't give that. Maybe he would give them our number? Or—" She forced herself to look at Dean. "Or Dean's? Maybe they'd trust the theology professor over the retail 'associate.'"

Dean, despite the slow motion in which he moved, pulled a stack of sticky notes from his messenger bag and fumbled for a pen. Janice passed hers over. Dean wrote the number slowly—so slowly, in fact, that Carlie had it memorized before he peeled it from the stack and passed it to Janice. "Please have Frank try to convince them to call."

"You're the real thing—religious, I mean. Both of you." Janice hugged Carlie and squeezed Dean's good shoulder. "I'll do it."

Before Dean could put away the sticky notes, Carlie reached across the table and stole the pad from him. She rolled the pen toward Janice and reached for her own. "Okay, so we need to figure out what this family is going to need, because they're not going to get any help from the community—whatever community that is…"

Wednesday evening, after a long, exhausting afternoon getting his drain lines checked, Dean collapsed on his stepfather's couch. "I may fall asleep. If I do, please let me sleep. I'm exhausted—squared."

"Did you go to the coffee shop?"

"Yes…"

Larry brought a glass of water and Dean's pain killers. "Take one tonight. And you need to inform your mother of that. I just won dinner at *my* favorite restaurant. She's convinced you'll 'never want to darken the door of that place again.'"

"Will she ever learn," Dean groaned, "that I am not her? There are reasons she never skates, never rides a bicycle—or a horse—never *swims!* And it's not because she is incapable. She failed the first try. Am I not an only child because she didn't like labor? They failed to anticipate when contractions would begin and medicate her to prevent her ever feeling one. No more children."

Larry's laughter held that note of camaraderie of someone who understands *and* loves despite the faults that annoy and irritate. A moment later he asked, "So, did she come?"

"Carlie?" At Larry's nod, he said, "Yes. It appears she was uncertain of my ability or willingness to come. She almost called Mim to inquire about my condition…"

"I don't know if I told you, but I really enjoyed talking to her."

"You didn't. I enjoy listening to her. I would never have imagined *listening* to be so intriguing. I learned something about myself through all this, and I'm not particularly proud of it."

"What's that?"

It took a moment for the question to register. Dean blinked. "Forgive me. I am either more weary than I thought, or the narcotics are taking affect quicker than usual." He closed his eyes. "In the beginning, I missed much of what she said. Now I know why. I have a deplorable habit of not truly listening to people. While I stay partially attuned to the discussion, most of my time is spent planning my response."

"I've been telling you that for years."

Dean closed his eyes and sighed. "It took an inordinate amount of time, but at last I understand. I'm incapable of preventing it in every situation. For example, while you spoke, I prepared my response because I anticipated yours. Regardless," Dean sighed once more. "I have not yet learned to control it consistently—not yet," he added with a firmness that unnerved him a little. "But I consistently and *truly* listen to *her*. She breaks my heart, but I listen."

"You need to watch your heart, Dean. She's a broken woman in some respects. You have the potential to keep her that way."

Dean's carefully orchestrated speech fizzled at those words. "Why thank you! I can't—"

"By that I mean," Larry explained, "that she will not grow beyond her identity being wrapped up in a man who controls her if she transfers loyalty so quickly."

"And this means that you do not recommend I break my silence."

Larry nodded. "I really think a few more weeks at the least would be best. Maybe you can tell by how she talks about things or something. I just think…"

What Larry said next, Dean didn't hear. All the plans he'd made for conspiring with her to help Steve's family fizzled. "I understand your position, but I don't understand how we'll do it, then."

"Do what?"

"We have planned to help the shooter's family. From what we understand, he was out of work, unemployment ran out, then he was hired at The Fiddleleaf, only to lose that position as well. I made a few calls and spoke to their landlord. His family is on the verge of eviction. How we'll raise twenty-four hundred dollars in less than a week, I don't know."

"It's twenty-four hundred a month? Maybe they *should* move."

You are so far removed from the reality of average lives, Larry. It's almost amusing—almost. Dean shook his head. "No, they're two months in arrears, and next month's rent is due in a week. When they don't pay that, he'll be forced to evict. I tried to pay one of the back months, but he is required to collect all of it for reasons he didn't make clear—probably related to the eviction process."

Larry left the room without a word. Dean, resting on the couch, didn't notice until he heard a drawer shut in the other room. *Wha—*

"Do you have the landlord's name?"

"I do, why…" His eyes opened, and his gaze fell on a checkbook on the coffee table. "Oh, Larry, I didn't mean—"

"I know, but I can do it, so let me. What's the exact amount and to whom?" The moment Larry passed the check, he began scribbling another one. This one was made out to Dean, in the amount of five hundred dollars, with a note on the memo line. *For groceries or utilities.*

Dean grabbed Larry's arm and managed *not* to wince when his wound protested. "Thank you. I suspect you just helped keep Carlie from plunging deeper into debt. I hadn't yet decided how I could prevent it—or if I should. Is it any of my concern—truly?"

"Let me know if I can do anything else. I have friends who might like a chance to help." Larry stood. "You look beat. I'm going to go read a book or something while you rest. See you in the morning if you stay."

Dean shifted, wincing. "I will stay, definitely. Thank you, Larry. I love you."

"Love you, too, son."

Best words ever arranged into a sentence—well, a fragment that it is.

Armed with decorated donation cans featuring the faces of four small and quite adorable children, Carlie walked the blocks surrounding The Fiddleleaf Café in search of businesses willing to allow the donation cans at their cash registers. She struck out with an impressive 100% rate of failure. One man berated her for trying to exploit the misfortunes of others. "Bad enough that these things happen, but for people to use it to try to extort money from sympathetic people—"

"But I'm not! Here's a letter from Frank at The Fiddleleaf Café, assuring that he will collect all cans himself and distribute the money."

"Which brings me to my next point. How many people are going to want to give money to the guy who killed two people? That's crazy!"

"He has *four* children who will be out on the street soon if someone doesn't help. It's not *their* fault that their dad did something wrong! Look at those faces!" She shoved the can at the man. "Those kids now have no way to eat, no way to pay the back rent—three months almost. The mother is trying to keep her family together, but with Steve's crime, you know child services is going to get involved, and if she can't keep things going, she'll lose her husband *and* her kids. This isn't *their* fault."

"Yeah, well, tell it to the two people who died. Tell it to the guy who got shot trying to stop this lunatic."

Yes! That's just what I needed. She smiled. "I don't have to. He's trying to raise money elsewhere—for them. He doesn't blame them for Steve's mistakes."

"Oh, right. So, the fabulous 'Dean' rides again."

Her heart chilled at the words—the voice. Without turning around, Carlie said, "Just go away, Blaine. I'm not in the mood."

"Do you see what he did to you? He nearly got you killed."

Carlie blinked slowly—twice. She stared at the man before her, unwilling to meet Blaine's eyes. "Did you hear that? Did he really just say that the guy who shoved me under a table to protect me nearly got me killed?"

"Sounds like it to me."

"I don't believe this." She set the can down. "Can I just leave it—twenty-four hours? That's all I ask. If no one donates in that time, I'll come get it myself, and I won't bother you again. Deal?"

She felt Blaine's hand on her elbow and the pressure that was meant to guide her out of the store. Before she could respond or resist, he'd led her halfway to the door. "I'll get her out of here for you. I'm sure she's dealing with some PTSD from the trauma of it all. Sorry for your trouble."

Dumbfounded, Carlie found herself out the door and turning her collar up to the wind before she found her voice. "What do you think you're doing?"

"I'm saving you from further humiliation. That guy was about to call the cops! Didn't you see his hand on his phone?"

Her heart sank. She hadn't. "No—I…"

"C'mon. I'll get you a coffee. You could use a break. I bet you've been trying to get every business on this street to put those cans up. Looks like a lot of cans left…"

Once more, her heart tumbled to the pit of her stomach. *Yeah. That's true. Maybe he's right. And here I thought he was just being his usual jerk self. Not fair, Carlie. Don't be like that.* "Yeah… maybe. Thanks."

How it happened, she spent the rest of the evening trying to discover, but Carlie found herself sitting in a coffee shop and listening to Blaine plan out their lives.

As if a testimony to the strange morbidity that compels people to flock to accident sites or houses where people have died, The Fiddleleaf buzzed with activity that third Wednesday in January. Several people moved ahead of Dean as he waited on a bench, his pen and a student's paper in hand, and tried to work. Anxiety made concentration more difficult than usual—almost as difficult as working while listening to Carlie.

She entered at precisely the moment Dean decided they'd never get a seat. *We'll have to accept an alternate booth,* he grumbled to himself as Carlie began to weave through the waiting patrons.

"Carlie…" The hostess beckoned her to the stand. Pointing to where Dean sat seated against the front wall, she said, "He's still waiting for the booth. Let me know if you want the next table instead. It's long past his turn."

"I—" Dean's eyes met hers and he waited to see how she'd respond. To his relief, she gave him a wink before turning back to the hostess. "We'll wait."

Dean scrambled to stand and give her his seat, but the hostess called out another name and the two women next to him jumped up. Instead, he began packing away his papers and the book he used for a lap desk. Carlie stopped him. "Might as well get them done while we wait. I can pull out my Kindle—unless you're just looking for grammar stuff. I'm pretty good at catching little nit-picky things."

Though he knew he shouldn't, Dean passed the next paper in his stack to her and watched as she read the exposition on Hebrew poetry.

The way she wrinkled her nose told him the author was either a poor writer, had used an abundance of Hebrew as evidence, or failed to capture Carlie's interest. Her question answered the one he ached to ask.

"So, how do they know all this Hebrew? Is it like a prerequisite to your class? I mean, this guy—Mark—is writing like everyone knows what all these words mean, but I know I don't." She passed it back. "I think I'll stick with my novel." She pulled out a Kindle and turned the screen so he could see it.

So, she likes cozies. That genre suits her. While he pondered the books they might have in common, thanks to his mother's propensity to insist he pre-read everything she thought might be interesting, Carlie read. His mother's words mocked him as he wondered, not for the first time, why he let her get away with it. *"But I can't just start reading,"* she always insisted. *"Because I don't want to be disappointed, you know."*

Another minute passed in wasted study of yet another sub-par paper as they waited for a table. Carlie shifted, and her proximity did unexpected and unsettling things to his emotions. *This is Mim and Larry's fault—particularly Larry's. He speaks as if I'll develop feelings for her. Now that we're in such close proximity, my emotions respond to that suggestion. I feel like a hormone-riddled teenager.*

"Dean, your table is ready…"

He jumped up with speed that could only make Carlie feel as if he wanted to get away from her, but Dean almost didn't care. He shoved papers in the messenger bag with such haste that he nearly crushed the top one. And before he could stop himself, he offered his hand. Carlie, shoving her Kindle into her purse, almost missed the gesture, but her fingers closed over his just in time. Again, he felt that spark of something he knew he needed to ignore. *Then again, why must I? If we conversed, we might find common interest. She seems to be doing well, and she's reading the Bible. It'll speak truth to her.* His thoughts were interrupted by Carlie's words.

"—believe how busy they are. I mean, this is as bad as Christmas week!" She paused outside the booth to remove her coat, and Dean found himself reaching for the red wool as she shrugged out of it.

Janice greeted them—even as they stood—with a breathless, "Good… afternoon—right? Yeah, thanks. Anyway, I recommend the hazelnut mochas."

"We'll take 'em," Carlie said. She slid into her seat and allowed her eyes to meet Dean's. "Unless he doesn't want it." At his nod, she smiled. "There you have it."

Dean hung her coat, removed his, and hung it on a hook as well. He hadn't seated himself before her eyes met his. "That's a cool coat. I mean, it's really *you*. I love that military type collar thing. It kind of looks

Russian—or maybe like the ones on those British guards or something. But it's cool, and somehow it looks great with that sweater." She frowned, and Dean opted to slide into the seat while she seemed distracted. "How *does* that sweater work with that coat? It should look stupid. Then again, I don't know any other man who could wear that without looking ridiculous. You always make it look like—" The full impact of her trains of thoughts and speech must have hit her hard and fast, because she closed her mouth and returned her attention to her Kindle.

They ordered minutes later, each pointing at what they wanted on the menu. Dean considered the ramifications of suggesting to Janice that they order for each other the following week—in particular, how it might be perceived as too personal for a friendship that had remained most definitely impersonal. *And yet, has it? Are our mutual concerns for each other anything other than personal?*

Carlie's embarrassment didn't last long. Once more, she eyed the sweater he'd bought to replace one his pen had destroyed over the holiday break. "That really is a great color for you—brings out your eyes. Like I said, not many guys could get away with it. Blaine—" Her face froze as she worked through whatever emotions the name created, but a moment later, Carlie shrugged. "Well, he'd look stupid." Her voice dropped a bit. "Maybe I should get him one. Maybe then he'd see how it hurts when people tell you how stupid you are."

Despite his internal speech, demanding he not respond when Dean heard her mention Blaine, his head snapped up and his eyes searched her face.

"Yeah... saw him while I was trying to distribute the donation cans. I hate how he can take something I'm enthusiastic about and convince me that I'm just an idiot for even thinking about it. He had me agreeing to go to Mexico with him for Valentine's Day before Teresa talked me out of it." She dropped her eyes. "And, of course, now I feel even stupider than ever."

Well, nothing could make it more obvious. She is definitely not ready for me even to consider if I'm interested in a more personal relationship. She's clearly not out of the cycle. Lord, help...

Dean's hope that the new semester would be free of students teasing him about his weekly lunch dates deflated in the first week. As much as he'd taken the good-natured ribbing with grace, he'd looked forward to having a class who didn't want weekly updates on his "half-dates," as they'd called his lunches with Carlie. Alas, it was not to be. The first day of class, he'd found a printout of The Fiddleleaf's menu on his desk. That afternoon, a Fiddleleaf "signature mug" had appeared in his office.

But the overt teasing during his Wednesday afternoon class began with a simple question about the shooting: "Were you scared?" Dean hadn't minded answering, but when they asked him to tell the story he'd forgotten to leave out the part about Carlie seeing the shooter first. Two seconds after he mentioned shoving her under the table, the room erupted in "ooo-oo-ooohs" and a wolf whistle or three. Only his evident weariness during the discussion had moved the students beyond their fascination with his weekly dates and back to the basics of Hebrew poetry.

Monday had been a little better, Wednesday, acceptable, but the Friday morning group held the promise of a tease-free zone—and the chance to talk with Gabby Marceanu again. As he strolled to his classroom, one thought repeated itself in perfect synchronization with each step. *She's such an interesting woman—she's such an interesting woman—she's such—*

As he entered the class, half a dozen seats were already occupied. Gabby, up front to the left of the room, a few people sprinkled throughout the middle and a trio clustered to one side—but behind them, half-hidden by the tallest young man Dean had ever met, Carlie sat alone. *Why is she here? This will prove to be utter mortification if anyone discovers who she is. Perhaps I should ask...* That thought fizzled as more people entered the room. The class "Samson," as Dean had begun to think of him, headed her way and plopped into the desk next to her, his hair shining nearly as beautifully as hers as he flopped a lock over the top of his head.

Don't respond, he pleaded

Carlie smiled at the young man, murmuring something that made him laugh. Dean stood there, gut clenching, and racked his brains for some way to interrupt the conversation. His lesson plan lay in ruins on the floor of his subconscious, and trying to open that door to retrieve it proved impossible. So, when the final student entered the room, he pulled out the attendance clipboard and began checking off names as he went through the room. "Abbot, Arvide, Burma, Calvin, Cooper, Cygnet, Denham—"

In his peripheral vision, a hand shot into the air. Dean continued as if he didn't see it. When he finished, the girl with the raised hand spoke. "Who's the new girl? I didn't know you could join this late."

Dean ordered himself to assume an air of nonchalance as he said, "Carlie, would you mind standing?"

The shock on her face amused him, but he managed to keep from smiling. She eased herself out of the chair. "Yes, Professor—I mean, Dr. Sager?"

"Class, I'd like to introduce Carlie Denham—my weekly lunch partner."

The collection of oohs and a couple of whistles brought a blush of embarrassment and possibly confusion to her cheeks. Carlie gave a half wave, sat down, and said, "Nice to meet you. If you know we meet every week, maybe you know he doesn't actually talk to me, so I thought I'd come here and listen in on a class—figure out just who the guy is who buys me lunch every Wednesday and serves as my personal therapist."

"As is evident, I have a lovely and lively lunch partner. Holding my tongue isn't as simple as it might appear, but I do enjoy listening and getting to know her." Dean shifted and reached for his notes. However, as fascinating as Ms. Denham is, our lunches do not offer much insight into the parallelisms in Hebrew poetry. So, let's continue the discussion from Wednesday. Who can tell me which parallelism was next?"

Gabby's hand shot up as she called out, "Emblematic Parallelisms."

"Can someone give me the definition of an emblematic parallelism?"

"Samson" spoke up. "It's when the first line is literal and is followed by a figurative statement."

"Excellent," Dean praised as he continued, almost without hesitation. "Can someone give me an example from one of the books of poetry?" *And please, no one offer the one I added into the class notes!* When Stella Zimmerman's hand shot into the air, his heart sank. *Ugh! She'll use it. She never deviates from the notes.*

"'Your oils have a pleasing fragrance, Your name is like purified oil; Therefore the maidens love you.'" The older woman smiled. "It's one of the better Song of Songs quotes, don't you think? So many are almost risqué or worse—a western turn-off!"

The classroom erupted in laughter. Dean nodded, waited for the room to settle, and leaned against his desk, his notes in one hand as his eyes scanned the room. "Try to imagine my own discomfort. I sat in those very seats when I was *fourteen!* My voice hadn't yet *begun* cracking on a regular basis. I had a particularly nasty case of acne—one no insecure young person should ever have to endure—and my glasses—"

Carlie piped up and interjected, "Have you seen him with his glasses on?" A low murmur of negative responses rippled over the room. "Let's just say, there's something totally adorable about a professor in nerd glasses—particularly with his sense of style." She leaned back in the chair, crossed her arms over her chest, and leveled a "Smoke that pipe" look at him.

As much as he tried to be smooth about it, Dean fumbled. "Well, I'm pleased to hear it. Regardless, my point is that our professor, Dr. Jainof, used to require we read Song of Solomon aloud to the class. So, there I was, a *young* teenager, and reading aloud about how the Shulamite woman viewed Solomon as a packet of myrrh lying between her breasts. I don't know how I ever made it through it."

Though he spoke to the right side of the room, Dean watched Carlie's reaction from the other side. Not surprisingly, her hand shot up. "I thought that Song of Solomon was about Christ and the church. What does myrrh between the breasts have to do with that?"

His notes demanded that he stick to the topic of parallelisms, but Dean ignored them. Excited about the parallels between Christ and the church and a decided love poem from a man to his bride, Dean couldn't resist explaining. The class listened with eyes fixated on him as he spoke.

Within half a minute, his dry erase marker squeaked across the white board, showing step by step parallels in the first verses of chapter one. "As you will notice," he concluded, "the book describes more than *just* that relationship. They're *parallels,* but they're not strict metaphors where one phrase *only* refers to *one* particular meaning. If I say, 'You are my sun'—as in a fiery star in the sky that provides us heat and light, not my male offspring—it cannot mean both that you are literally on fire to give me light and heat as well as warming and illuminating my heart. It's *only* a metaphor. But Song of Solomon has the distinction of meaning both. Solomon's love for his bride and hers for him is genuine and beautiful. It has taken me years to manage to say that without my ears growing red, but it's true. And Dr. Jainof ensured that we learned not to dismiss the literal because we were uncomfortable with it. I recommend that as well."

A discussion—more like a debate—took up the rest of class time. As he saw the clock tick past the five o'clock mark, he dropped the marker and wiped off his hands. "Don't forget that your papers on three of the types of parallelisms found in Hebrew poetry are due on Monday! Have a delightful weekend, and I *will* be in my office until eight tonight, as well as all morning on Monday, if you have a draft to submit for critique. *Use* this opportunity. I won't be lenient simply because we deviated slightly from our coursework today."

"Should have taken this class last semester," the girl closest to his desk quipped. "I heard that a few people got great grades on some pretty sloppy papers." Her eyes flitted to the back of the room.

Please don't...

"Don't you think you can distract him a bit better during lunch again? That was seriously awesome for my cousin Tiffany."

Carlie stood and shook her head. "He doesn't grade papers after I arrive anymore." Her eyes shifted to him. "Now I know why."

Dean's face flamed as the class filed out. A few talked in clusters, but Carlie waited until most had gone before she stepped up to the desk where he, in his usual relaxed position, half-sat half-stood. "So, your class knows about me—about our lunches. You've actually talked to *them* about me. But you don't talk *to* me." Her eyebrows drew together as she frowned. "I don't get you." With that, she left—no word on if she enjoyed the class. No assurance that she'd see him on Wednesday. Dean's heart sank.

That... that was a dismal experience.

"Your girlfriend is nice."

His eyes snapped to where Gabby stood. "She isn't my girlfriend, but yes. She is nice." *This wouldn't be an appropriate time to invite you for coffee in May.* He gave her a weak smile and ordered his mouth to remain silent. *Additionally, the professor-student ethics rules have never adversely affected me... until now.*

"Well... have a good weekend." Gabby paused at the door. "Oh, and we got in this tiny little devotional-type book from the late nineteenth century. Really cool. Thought you might like to take a look at it sometime."

As her mom's phone rang, Carlie struggled against the desire to terminate the call. *I feel so stupid. I don't even know why!*

"Carlie? You there?"

She swallowed, took a deep breath, and blurted, "Yeah. Sort of. How are you?"

"I'm fine and you obviously aren't. So, was he upset you went? I spent all night last night trying *not* to call you. Dad finally hid my phone from me, and then, of course, forgot to pull it back out. Took forever to figure out it was in Aunt Phoebe's old teapot."

It sounded so familiar—so homelike—that Carlie nearly cried. "I don't know. I—it was awesome. I wish I could afford to take classes there. I'd probably bomb them, but I'd learn so much. I finally *get* what makes Job, Psalms, Proverbs, Song of Solomon—all those. I get what makes them poetry now. It's totally different from Western poetry."

"Buuuut..."

She dangled a piece of leftover Christmas ribbon and smiled as Pouncer batted at it. "Mom, the class knew about me."

"What?"

"Right? They *knew*. It was so weird. They *all* knew about me. And... and... Dean apparently stopped correcting papers while we—well, I—talked because he was missing stuff. He comes *early* now to get it done and then sits there just to listen to me. I can't decide if it's really sweet or totally creepy."

"Did he say *anything* specifically to you this time?"

Her brain rewound the class, and she started to say no. "Oh, yeah. He did. He asked me to stand and then he introduced me to the class. So, technically, yeah."

"Did he seem put out, or—what's wrong?"

"Did you not hear me? Mom, the class *knew* about it."

Gina made dismissive sounds. "No, listen. You said that he was missing things in the papers he corrected, right? He probably got 'caught' in a way, and if he's the guy he sounds like he might be, then he probably confessed to the class and apologized. So of course—"

"But that was *last* semester! How—"

"Well, I guess the students could have spread the word through the college, but that seems a bit much. Maybe they asked about what happened at the restaurant and it came out then."

The idea made sense. It sounded like Dean, somehow. "I suppose..."

"So, why didn't you call me last night? I was going crazy." When Carlie didn't answer immediately, Gina growled. "Noooo... don't tell me you were with *Blaine!* I thought he was history!"

"He is!" she protested. Truth won out, however. "Well, I think so. I don't know. I saw him when I was passing out donation cans for Steve's family, and he was nice. He took me for coffee and tried to make me feel better about no one wanting to donate." She giggled. "But he *was* wrong. The store owner that didn't want to take the can had a ton of donations when I went back for it the next day. That guy is even helping me get them passed out to other store owners. I don't think Blaine liked it when I told him that last night." The moment the words left her lips, Carlie nearly bit off the end of her tongue in frustration. "No! Don't say it, Mom."

"I'm confused. He consoled you after the owner said no and then got mad later when the owner said yes. So that means you've seen him twice?"

"Yeah... he came over last night for a bit, but I didn't let him stay, okay?"

"Did you tell him that if he was really interested," Gina asked, "that he would be willing to prove it before expecting to pick up where you left off?"

Carlie flushed. "Not exactly. But I didn't like how panicked I felt, so I told him I didn't feel good. He's probably going to try to come back tonight, so I think I'm going out with Teresa and a couple of the others. Maybe I'll get them to go to the Grouse and Thistle. He'd never find us there."

"You're hiding from an ex-boyfriend! Doesn't that bother you at least a little?"

I was trying to ignore that little tidbit, thankyouverymuch! She sighed. "Mom…"

"Look, just think about something for me. I'm not saying this Dean guy is date material, okay? I wouldn't go that far. But you have to admit that an almost stranger treats you better—without even speaking to you—than your *boyfriend* ever has. Just take that into consideration, okay?"

"But he's a *professor,* Mom. It's probably part of the training. Blaine is a personal trainer. He's used to pushing people to get what's best for them."

"Then you need to look for more professors and fewer jocks, because the only thing separating jock from jerk is a vowel."

She couldn't help it. Carlie erupted in laughter seconds before her mother followed. "Mom, that was—"

"Pathetic, I know. But the point remains. You deserve someone who will treat you well—not like his little lovey."

Carlie started to respond, but her mother's words halted her thought processes. "What *are* you talking about?"

Gina sighed. "Blaine has always treated you like Carole's kids and their lovies. They want them there when *they* want 'em, but they get trampled, dragged through the mud, and slobbered all over in the process. And they don't care. It's all about *them* and *their* needs."

"They're toddlers, Mom!"

Silence filled the phone until Gina said. "Yes, yes they are. But Blaine isn't. He shouldn't be treating someone he pretends to care about like a toddler treats his stuffed bear."

Panic welled up in Carlie and she scrambled to go. "Yeah, well. I'll think about it. I better get ready and call to see if everyone can go. Talk to you later. Love you, Mom. Bye."

Carlie punched the "end" button on her phone and pocketed it. Pouncer scrambled up her leg and over her chest, nestling himself in her neck. He purred. "I wish you could tell me what to do. You can't even catch a stupid mouse! If it wasn't for Moros, we'd be overrun. But two in the dish last night was a bit too much. It's like it's prophetic or something. Eradicate both men from my life and become a nun. Can non-Catholics even do that? I wonder what Catholics believe. Maybe I should consider converting…"

Carlie burst into The Fiddleleaf and a cloud of snow blew in behind her. "I tried," she muttered to the girl manning the hostess station. "It's coming down hard."

"I'll get it. Don't worry. It's been that way all morning. I'm kind of glad we're not that busy."

As she hung her coat, Carlie eyed the woman. "I don't know you, do I? Where's Amber?"

"She got a new job as a manager in Marshfield."

The woman's defeated tone prompted Carlie to add, "Well, she'll be missed, but it's nice to meet you."

"Thank you. Just one…"

"Actually, I should have someone waiting for me."

She started to go, but the woman leaned close and said, "Oh, are you Carlie?"

"Yeah…"

"You guys were the first—"

Janice interrupted. "He's looking a little panicked over there. You're later than usual. Put the poor guy out of his misery, will you?"

With a wave at the new woman and a smile at Janice, Carlie hurried toward the booth, her heart warming at Janice's words. *This may be weird and totally bizarre, but it's* our *weird and totally bizarre thing. And that's just fine with me.*

Dean's eyes met hers the moment she slid across the booth. She settled back into the cushion-and brushed melted snow from her hair. "Whew! It's nasty out there. I need coffee." She blinked as she saw Dean arrest Janice's attention and sign for something. "Was that a coffee grinder motion? Is it real sign language or yours?"

To her astonishment, Dean waggled an eyebrow and smirked. A coffee cup appeared a moment later. Janice grinned. "I recommend the Tuscan chili. It's amazing and comes with a stuffed baguette. To die for. Amazing, seriously."

"We'll take it," Carlie agreed. "Right?"

Dean nodded. The moment Janice left, he slid an envelope across the table. A mixture of excitement and disappointment settled over her as she opened it to find a receipt. It took a moment to decipher the scratchy scrawl, but the realization that rent was paid through the month of February on Steve's family's apartment nearly overrode the letdown of not having a personal note in there.

"This is awesome! I can't believe you did this for them—" He shook his head, stopping her effusive praise. "—or arranged it anyway. That's so awesome." Carlie frowned. "I said that already. I don't care. It is. It's amazing."

The coffee cup warmed her hands almost as effectively as Dean's smile warmed her heart. A glance around her brought a chilling reminder that life goes on—even when death visits. "The black bands are gone. I wonder why—"

Janice passed with steaming bowls of spicy soup just as Carlie spoke and murmured, "I'll be right back." Once she'd served the dishes, Janice returned and hunkered down, whispering. "They made us remove them. Customers were complaining."

"That's ri—" Carlie lowered her voice at Janice's panicked look. "—diculous. I don't know what people's problems are, but seriously. People died!"

"I know. But people don't want to think about sitting where someone died, and the bands reminded them." Janice hurried away before Carlie could respond.

Carlie reached for the breadbasket and wondered when Janice had left it. *Probably before I arrived—to keep him from starving.* Dean watched her with evident concern. "Want to know the worst of it?" Carlie ducked her head. "I think I'd be the same way. I totally get it, too. You know," she said impulsively, "I'm going to go visit her and the kids—see if they need anything else. Maybe figure out what I could do for little Valentine gifts or something. It's just a couple of weeks away, so…"

The way Dean's face relaxed told her he approved—or that's how she interpreted it. A new idea occurred to her, and Carlie leaned forward. "Would they let you visit Steve? I mean, maybe not because he shot you, but being a minister and all…"

Dean's amused smile unnerved her. *Does he think it's a stupid idea, or does he like that I thought of it? Maybe it's just some law that everyone but me knows. That's probably it.* "Well, I think you should if you can." She passed the receipt envelope back and nearly jumped as their fingers touched. "You should probably give that to Hannah. She needs it, doesn't she?"

As he tucked the envelope back in his pocket, Dean leaned back and watched her. Seconds ticked into minutes as they waited for food, unspeaking but observing. Carlie's mind rambled and jerked into odd, *This is weird—cool, but weird,* thoughts. *I wonder what he's thinking. That Nordic sweater is scary attractive on him. He's better looking now than when I first met him. You'd think it would be the other way around after the whole getting shot thing. Surgery ages people.* That thought sparked a new one. *Then again, he's probably one of those guys who looks better with age—like Harrison Ford or Frank Sinatra. Yeah. That's probably it.*

Janice arrived with their bowls and sandwiches. "It's perfect, Janice. Thanks." Carlie eyed Dean and said, "I am so tempted to ask you to pray…"

Without hesitation, Dean bowed his head and, again without hesitation, prayed aloud. Her eyes widened and then snapped shut as she listened to him thank the Lord for their food and ask for wisdom in how best to help Steve's family. Just as he said, "Amen," and raised his head, her eyes flew open. "I should have known you'd pray. It's not talking to *me*. Maybe I should consider asking you to pray more often."

She knew he didn't say it—not really—but for a moment, it felt like he'd muttered, "Maybe you should."

The apartment building could have been fabulous. An old brick office building had been broken up into tiny apartments sometime in the sixties and, if Carlie's guess was correct, hadn't been updated since. The halls were trash-free but coated with grime. The elevator rattled enough on the way down that Carlie decided to take the stairs—even if her destination was three flights up. *How does Hannah do it with four little kids? I mean, I couldn't put my kids in a death trap like that thing, but there's no way they can go up and down with anything in their hands.*

A couple of teenagers jogged down the stairs above her, and Carlie had to flatten herself against the dirty wall to avoid being mowed over. A string of lewd comments followed, but Carlie ignored them. She did, however, pull out her phone. *I will so call the cops if you come back. You freak me out.*

Screeches radiated from Apartment #309. Carlie hesitated before knocking. *If this is bad timing, I'll cry.*

A woman—approximately Carlie's age—opened the door. Dark circles under her eyes told a story of overwork and sleepless nights. "The rent's paid. I have a receipt..."

"Oh, I'm not here—"

"I talked to Social Services. They said if I had my rent paid, they'd close the case—"

Carlie shook her head. "No, no. I just came to see you—to see if I could help." She stuck out her hand and willed herself not to wince if the woman's hands were dirty. They weren't. "I'm Carlie Denham—"

"Wait—from the restaurant? I saw you on the news. That's where I recognized you from. You were there—"

"Yeah... Steve was always nice to us. I—well, I was worried about you."

Tears coursed down Hannah Pierce's cheeks. "I can't believe you came here. He shot your boyfriend!"

The door across the hall banged open and a woman stuck her head out. "It's bad enough that we have drug dealers and third generation welfare bums in this place. Now I have to live across the hall from a murderer. Just go away—"

"Go inside, Hannah. You don't have to listen to it." Carlie shot the woman a nasty look. "She's a victim here, too. She didn't pull that trigger. She did nothing."

"She married the louse. Here he seemed all nice and normal—"

"Her *children* can hear you screaming at her," Carlie hissed. "Do you want them to grow up thinking that there is no hope for them, or do you want to show the kind of compassion you'd want if you were them? Really?"

Carlie crept into the apartment after Hannah and shut the door behind her. "Mind if I come in? I didn't want—"

"No. Thanks." Hannah tried to shove the laundry that covered the couch to one side. "The super let me use the laundry room—free—so I could get caught up. We just didn't have—"

"It's fine. I left a huge pile on my couch when I left this morning. It'll be covered in cat hair when I get home and then I'll have to wash them all over again. It's life."

Hannah gestured for her to sit. "I only have water and some lemon in a bottle I could squirt in it..."

She wanted to decline—to assure the woman that she didn't need a drink—but Carlie could see the woman's pride shattering before her eyes. "That would be great. Lemon makes everything good, don't you think? My favorite treats are all lemon-flavored."

"Mine too. Steve used to bring home these lemon pastry things from the restaurant. They were so good—and the lemon chicken soup. Man..."

"I've never had either. I'll have to try them next week." Carlie

139

looked around her and her heart broke a little at the sight of four young children seated huddled in the corner, shrinking from her. "Are any of your kids in school yet?"

"Just Stevie. He's six. Bailey could have gone to head start this year, but we didn't have the money for better clothes with Steve out of work, so we didn't do it. Kids can be so awful about things like that."

From the looks of the pile of laundry beside her, they hadn't managed to improve the clothing situation. Everything looked faded and worn. *Clothes for the kids. But how?* An idea presented itself. "Look, I don't know if she's taken them to Goodwill yet, but my sister just cleaned out her kids' closets after Christmas. Her kids seem about the same ages as yours. I could bring what she has if you can use them." The hesitation in Hannah's face prompted her to add, "Look, they're all like new. Carol's a bit... um... well, she likes to shop. There's seriously gobs of hardly worn—if ever—stuff."

"I want to say we'll be fine, but we won't. I don't know when we'll ever be able to get anything on our own again. Steve won't be a—round to be able to help, and welfare is already demanding I put the kids in daycare and find a job." Her head drooped. "I married him two weeks after I graduated from high school. I was pregnant before we got back from our weekend honeymoon. Minimum wage won't pay daycare, much less anything else."

Carlie's forehead furrowed. "Then you can't work. They'll have to deal with it."

"But I have to."

"But you *can't* if you can't pay the daycare." *This isn't rocket science, Hannah.*

Hannah shook her head. "Oh, no. They'll pay what I can't. So, they'll pay for the apartment, food stamps, monthly assistance, and daycare to cover what my job won't. But I have to have the job—or appeal."

"So we'll appeal. This is a waste of taxpayer dollars. I get wanting people to work for their money, but wasting money to make that happen is just stupid." Carlie pulled a notepad out of her purse. "Meanwhile, let's get sizes and things so I don't fill up your house with stuff you can't use. I'll see if my brother's wife has anything from her boys, too. They might be Stevie's size."

She didn't know how she managed it, but by the time Carlie left, she had a list of clothing and shoe sizes, as well as specific needs. She knew the kids' favorite foods, what utilities needed to be paid, and how much laundry they generated each week. She hurried down the street and to the subway, marveling at how much people would talk with a few leading questions. *Now, if Carole will just meet me halfway to pick up clothes, that would help. But the kids need their own shoes. I'll have to get those—maybe tomorrow on the way home from work.*

The enormous TV screen froze, and a timer was set on the shelf beside it. "Our half-time show begins now! Who volunteers to delight us first?" Dean scanned the room. "I must warn you, if someone doesn't step up to the mic and give us an improv or karaoke show, I'll be forced to begin a lecture on why Job qualifies as Biblical poetry…"

A voice from the kitchen cried out, "Coming! I'll do a dozen imitations, but then someone else has to take over."

"And you may all cheer now. Ray is taking donations of gratitude to use as a down-payment on a vehicle that actually operates." Dean handed over the karaoke mic and bowed as the group of men from his stepfather's church all cheered his departure.

Larry brought him a half-frozen bottle of root beer and met him in the doorway to the kitchen. "Good one—Job as a poem. Almost had me."

His throat went dry for a moment, until Dean realized that Larry was joking. "Amusing."

"Almost had *you*, though…"

"Succeeded, actually." Dean pulled a receipt from his pocket. "I brought you a copy of the receipt for the Pierce's rent."

Larry didn't even look at it as he pocketed the paper. "They doing okay?"

"Struggling, of course. I visited Steve yesterday. Hannah had just left—Hannah is his wife—and she told him about the rent, food, clothes, utilities…"

"Food—what?"

Still stunned about it himself, Dean said, "Apparently, Carlie visited yesterday morning. It appears to be a reconnaissance mission. Last night, she returned with bags of food, several bags of clothes and shoes, and a coin purse filled with quarters for the laundry."

"Seems generous…"

Dean sighed. "Yes. It was. However, I am aware that she has a shopping problem that has resulted in excess debt. She had a reduction plan in place, but now I'm afraid she's 'back on the wagon,' so to speak."

"She's an adult, Dean. Let her make her own decisions—"

"Or mistakes, I suppose? I would have enjoyed assisting had she asked."

The "halftime" show switched to a pathetic rendition of "The Star Spangled Banner," which required Dean to be silent as Larry's Sunday School teacher butchered the song so badly that it sounded more like a parody than an anthem. As the room erupted in cheers—likely that the massacre of every cardrum in the room had ended—Dean muttered, "It's a pity that Carlie isn't present. She would have made it enjoyable."

"How do you know?"

And this is when his romantic ideas sprout proof. "I saw her with a group of carolers in New Cheltenham a few weeks ago. I must have neglected to tell you about it."

"You did."

Larry's subsequent silence nearly drove Dean crazy, but he was determined not to say a word. That determination failed after exactly twenty-three and a half seconds. "So, yes. I was aware that she would be present and singing. I was curious about it, so I went."

"And she's good?"

"She has a lovely voice—truly wonderful. She'd never be considered solo material, her voice is too quiet for that, but she is an excellent addition to an ensemble. I also believe she could break hearts singing bittersweet ballads around a campfire—preferably accompanied by a guitar."

"And you're a bit too intrigued by her for my taste," Larry murmured. "She's still just out of what sounds to me like an abusive relationship. This isn't a healthy idea, Dean."

Why must he continually confuse friendship for something deeper? He punctuates nearly every conversation with a reminder of her fragile, broken state. Frustration welled up in him. *I doubt he'd recognize her if he spent a little while conversing. His perception is far from her reality.*

"—get defensive. I just know that these things don't work if the timing isn't right."

"That isn't…" Dean grabbed a handful of Chex mix and stared at it for a moment. *Tell him about Gabby. Maybe that will divert his attention.* "Larry, you should know that I am waiting—with eager anticipation, I might add—for the end of the semester. There is a student I very much would like to get to know better. Mim met her at Christmas." He sighed. "She enrolled in my class before I could get back to the bookstore."

"Just promise me you'll consider what I've said."

"Of course. I always do. However, since there is no true concern that I'll lose my heart to Carlie—I make no promises on Gabby—I don't think you have any cause for concern."

Larry pointed to the all-male cheerleaders, complete with pom-poms. "Just indulge an old man, will ya?"

"If Mim overheard you call yourself old, she would pull out an arsenal of torture devices that drug cartels in Columbia consider cruel and unusual punishment."

The lure of books pulled Carlie further and further inside Price & Bradbury Booksellers—farther from the door where she'd promised to meet Jared Schepp from church. *It happens every time I walk into a bookstore. I see all kinds of things I want to read about—and never do.* The memory of her last visit to the store with Blaine—of his mockery of the idea that she could make it through anything of substance—soured her. *I'm not stupid. Not that stupid anyway.*

Carlie's eyes slid toward the door, up to the clock above it, and back to the door again. *I've got another ten minutes before he's supposed to be here. I could look a little...*

Ornately bound discount classics drew her to a center table. Dickens, Austen, Bronte, Thackery, Wilde, Emerson, Elliot—names swam before her eyes and taunted her. *I read Bronte in high school—Wuthering Heights. It was okay. Kind of depressing.* Her eyes caught sight of a book of classic poetry. *Five Hundred Years of Verse.* Carlie picked it up and picked at the shrink wrap. "How am I supposed to know if I want it if I can't see what's inside?"

Jared's voice at her elbow startled her as he said, "That's how they sell so many. If you knew what was in it, you might not like it."

She jumped, spun in place, and fought the temptation to whack Jared with the book when she saw him standing there. "You scared me."

"Sorry—couldn't resist."

With a shake of the book, Carlie asked, "So, why wouldn't I like what's in it?"

"They're five hundred years old. Nowhere does it even hint that

143

they're good. They could have been buried in a publisher's reject pile for the last five centuries."

"Or they could be the best poems of all time!" Carlie stared at the cover as though looking hard enough might allow her eyes to burn through the pages to read the words inside.

"They could." He took the book and turned it over. "They don't even have any of the poets on the back. Hang on." He disappeared to the information desk and returned a minute later with the wrapping removed. "They took it off for me. There you go."

Her finger slid over the table of contents. "Browning... Byron...Keats...Lowell..." Carlie looked up at Jared. "Those are good names, right? They seem familiar."

"Sure. I remember them from lit classes, why?"

"Well, then maybe they won't be junk. I think I'll get it." She steeled herself against his reaction.

"You'll have to let me know your favorite." He pointed toward the left side of the store. "I think the language dictionaries are over here. Should we go see what they have, or..."

Carlie stared, blinking but uncomprehending.

"Carlie?"

"Sorry, what?"

"I suggested we go see what they have in the way of a dictionary for you." He looked closer. "Are you okay?"

What prompted her to say it, Carlie didn't know. Even as her pride screamed for her to stop, she heard herself admit, "I was waiting for you to say it was stupid to want to buy it."

"Why would that be stupid?"

She followed him—almost as if on auto-pilot. And as they walked, she again found herself explaining things she didn't mean to share. "It's just that my ex-boyfriend would have really made me feel stupid for wanting to read something like that—poetry, I mean."

"Not a big poetry fan, eh?" Jared pulled a book from the shelf and flipped through it. "No good. That's impossible to follow." He shoved it back. "We want something that won't have you saying something inappropriate because you don't know which way to move your hands."

Laughter bubbled over—part amusement, part embarrassment for his assumptions about Blaine. "That would be nice..." *You brought it up. Now admit that he doesn't think you can understand anything deeper than a nursery rhyme and get it over with.* She took a quick, cleansing breath and blurted it out. "I don't know if Blaine ever read poetry or cared. He just didn't think I was smart enough to understand it."

"I can see why he's an ex."

"How do you know I dumped *him*? It could be the other way

around."

Jared leaned one arm against the bookshelf and gazed at her. "Look, either you got sick of him not appreciating you and dumped him—making him your ex, of course—or he was too stupid to see what he had and he dumped you." He ducked his head at her blush. "So, see, either way, I can see why he's an ex. Because either way, he's an idiot."

"Thanks… I think."

"You think?" Jared turned back to the shelf and pulled out another book. As he examined it, he muttered, "It was definitely a compliment."

"Except that he *was* my boyfriend—by my choice. Doesn't say much for my taste in men if I chose a guy that you think is an idiot…"

The book snapped closed and slid into place almost before she saw him do it. "Because you would have gone out with him if you'd known he would insult your intelligence or your taste in reading material?"

She started to protest—to assure him she would not have. But Blaine's pick-up line replayed in her memory at blaring levels. *"You obviously have no taste in movies. Let me get your tickets for you. You won't regret it."*

Carlie's voice cracked as she admitted the truth. "Yeah, he even insulted me when he introduced himself. I never noticed until now." Loyalty forced her to add, "But it's just his way. Blaine's just really blunt. You never have to wonder where you stand with him. He's forthright, you know?"

"Blaine?" Jared pulled another book from the shelf. "The guy who insulted you when he met you and told you that you weren't intelligent enough to read poetry—his name is Blaine?"

"Do you know him?"

Jarod passed the book to her. "This one might be good. And no, I don't. So when did you break up with *Blaine?*"

"Few weeks back." She passed the open book to him and tried to sign "thank you."

"You're welcome." Jared passed the book back and signed the words. "See?"

Just ask him. The worst he can do is say no. She stacked the book atop her book of poetry and jerked her head toward the registers. "I'm going to go pay for this. If I buy you a coffee, will you show me a few other signs?"

"I'll get the coffee. You go get your books. What do you like?"

"Just a mocha is fine. Thanks." Carlie started to turn and decided to ask for a cookie while he was at it, but she looked back just in time to see Jared pump his fist. *Oooh… that's awkward.* A smile appeared. *And kind of cool. Totally cool, actually.*

Just as Dean flipped to the last page of the last paper, Carlie's coat appeared beside him. A smile formed before he could stop it. The realization that he'd skimmed most of a paragraph hit just as he moved to the next. With a sigh, he fumbled for a sticky note flag, stuck it on the paragraph, and slid it into his messenger bag. That's when he noticed. *She hasn't spoken.*

His eyes rose and met hers. She signed "hello."

Why is—oh no... she's under the mistaken assumption that I know and "speak" ASL. How awkward.

It took less than a minute for understanding to sink in. He'd have to watch her to *listen* to her this week. *This is contrary to my carefully orchestrated plan. I only succeed in remaining silent because I don't watch her much. Lord, help?*

She signed a few things—one being something about eating. Dean raised an eyebrow. She pulled out a three-inch book and consulted an index before flipping to the page. Her fingers moved as she used her elbows to hold the pages open. Once satisfied, she set it down and smiled as she signed a response.

This bodes for a long meal. He started to speak—to give up and just tell her he didn't understand—when another idea hit him. Dean pulled out his phone and held it, ready to record. Once more, he raised his eyebrows.

This time, she spoke before she thought. "I shouldn't do this—drat." A determined expression replaced the frustrated one. "I will not speak," she muttered to herself.

Dean readied the camera and began recording. A few signs he recognized—signs they used in worship at his church and ones he had learned as a youth at camp. Others were obvious. Most, he just shook his head, smiled, and recorded away. *This is entertaining, at least. I must ask Merlinda to interpret for me.* His heart sank as he imagined the scene. *Explaining, however, will be awkward.*

A server—one whose name escaped him at first—appeared. "Hi! I'm Marie. Janice had to take her mother to the doctor this morning. She told Dawn and me to be good to you guys, so here I am to provide excellent service. Are you ready to order?"

Carlie spoke up. "Well, I'd *love* a Coke. I'm totally in the mood for carbonation today..."

One could say that you have a... bubbly *personality.* He stopped the recording and reached for the menu.

"—and I think I want to try the Fiesta Meal. Mexican sounds fabulous. I haven't had *albondigas* in a long time."

"Cilantro or no…" At Carlie's confused expression, Dean snickered, and the server said, "Some people don't like it, so we ask before we sprinkle it on top of the soup and the rice."

"Oh! Sure. Love cilantro. I keep trying to learn to cook with it, but everything I make is just meh. I'll figure it out."

"Stir lime juice in the rice first," the server suggested. "Then sprinkle some on top. It's delicious that way—especially if you cook it in a frying pan first." Marie grinned at Dean. "And you?"

"I'll have the same—double cilantro, please."

Marie pointed to his cup. "More coffee? Oh, and since you're both doing the Fiesta, would you like chips and salsa?"

Before Dean could answer, Carlie squealed. "Yes! That's perfect. Thanks!"

"She's easy to please." Marie hesitated, her eyes darting back and forth. "You guys have this whole restaurant so confused about what's going on with you. So, I'm going to ask. Are you dating or not?"

Carlie started to speak, but Dean couldn't help but tease the woman. "That would depend upon your definition of 'dating.' We share our lunchtime once a week every week. Is that a date, or is it something more nebulous?"

The server glanced at Carlie and back at him, but she addressed her question to Carlie. "So, do you concur? It's a date?"

She choked, sputtered, and finally said, "Well, I do call it my Wednesday lunch date…"

Exasperation manifested in hands thrown up. "I give up. You guys are hopeless," Marie grumbled as she hurried off with their order.

Their eyes met. Carlie smiled, and Dean's heart warmed. *We have a wonderful friendship. I enjoy it. Why would we risk changing something as special as this? She has someone to discuss her troubles with—er…* He rephrased his thoughts. *To, anyway. And I am blessed with the opportunity to learn how to be "slow to speak." We both benefit.*

Her signing resumed. Dean punched the button and recorded. He caught finger spelling, thanks to her slow process. *A man named… Jared taught her a few signs…* After a few more seconds, Dean got the gist of her explanation. *And helped her choose a signing book… translation?* Carlie held it up for emphasis. *Oh, dictionary. I see.* Her fingers flew over the pages, searching for just the right ones before signing again. *I think she is saying that he is a church or invited her to—oh. Did this Jared ask her "out"? Lord, I would appreciate the arrival of our meals. I'd like to ask Merlinda to interpret for me—as soon as possible.* He stared at her fingers, trying to decipher what words she signed, but the realization that Carlie had implied she had a date with someone new drowned out all else. *This could be a wonderful thing for her—perhaps.*

As if she'd heard his thoughts, Marie appeared with their tray.

Wednesday found Merlinda out of her office. Thursday she was swamped with students seeking help on their Deaf Evangelism class papers. But Friday morning—just as he'd lost all nerve, of course—Merlinda stepped out into the hall as he entered the building. "Hey, Dean. I've got time to look over that video now, if you like."

I should not have succumbed to the temptation to ask her for help. I should have purchased my own dictionary. But, despite his disconcerting thoughts, Dean stepped into the office and pulled out his phone. "She isn't a fluent signer. For all I know, the signs will be half-wrong from following an illustrated dictionary."

"Well, that's often good for a laugh. Let's see what we've got here…" She sat down and watched, her lips twitching a time or two. After a minute or so she started over. "Okay. I got a feel for her, I think."

"A feel?" *What does that mean?*

"Well, there are exact signs for each word, okay? But people can't help but put their own flourish or twist on things sometimes—especially new signers. So, it's kind of like learning any new language. There are odd mispronunciations, but usually they follow a pattern—like when people can't roll their Rs or something similar."

"Oh, I understand. So, are you able to translate?"

Merlinda leaned back in the chair and stared at the screen. "'I was at church and saw that this guy, Jared, was teaching some of the kids how to sign a song, so I asked him if he could teach me…'" Merlinda hesitated. "I think maybe she says get a DVD to teach me. I think she used movie, but I can't be sure. The phone moved. Anyway. 'Decided to go to the bookstore and buy a dictionary. We talked for hours. I learned a lot about their church. I wasn't so sure about them—the home church idea—but Jared talked—' No '—explained about it. They started as small groups from bigger churches and decided to just *be* the church instead.'"

For a moment, Merlinda didn't translate. Dean leaned forward. "Did I move the phone out of sight?"

"Someone in—oh, there it is. 'I told him about Blaine and everything. I tried to be fair—' She used fair like a carnival," Merlinda snickered. "If you tell anyone I laughed at that, I'll deny it. Totally unprofessional. Anyway, 'Jared agrees with everyone. Blaine is a jerk who treated me wrong. I tried to explain that I—' I think she's looking for a word for antagonize. She's trying to say, 'egged him on' or something like that."

"She always says things like that—as if she doesn't deserve anything better. I've never talked to a more insecure woman in my life."

"I heard you don't talk to her at all."

"Correction," Dean growled. "*Listened* to. Regardless, she's gorgeous—" Dean pointed at the screen. "Look at her! She's one of the most beautiful women I've ever seen. She's interesting and intelligent, but she believes herself to be worthless."

"Maybe it's just a habit. Some women are so desperate for affirmation that they—"

"—trawl for it. I know. I don't think that is the case with her. She's so matter of fact about it. It is evident that she isn't even cognizant of it sometimes, because when she is, it's almost as if she's embarrassed to admit it but won't let herself *not* admit it."

As Merlinda watched the next part, she started laughing. "Oh, I think I like this Jared. If you're interested in this girl, I suggest you do something fast, because if I were her, I'd fall for him just for his sense of humor."

"Why? What did she—he—whoever, say?"

"Well, remember that she just mentioned Jared's opinion of how this guy Blaine treated her. Then she says, 'Jared says he was the Blaine of my existence.'"

"Well put," Dean muttered. "Excellent joke and true as well. He sounds like a good man. Maybe he can help her see what. I—" Merlinda's laughter stopped him again. "What?"

"She just said that he invited her to the chocolate Valentine's dinner. I think she meant church's. They're similar signs."

And now I know what to do for next week. Genius.

A head popped in the door. "Dean. I was just on my way to your office. Come see me when you're done here?"

"We are done, actually," Merlinda said as she stood. She passed him his phone. "Thanks for sharing. That was fun."

Dean thanked her and left the office in a bit of a daze. *What did I do to warrant Dr. Purcell searching me out to relay a message? He could have called.*

Inside the Dean of Students' office, Dean sat when indicated and tried *not* to talk. He failed. "How can I help you, Dr. Purcell? I've obviously made some grievous error, but I can't imagine what."

"Nothing—yet. But we did have an interesting conversation with one of your students that we felt warranted a discussion."

Amy Westin. It must be with regard to her. Dean stifled a sigh and nodded. "I'm listening."

"One of your students, Gabriella Marceanu, asked her advisor what the school policy is on professors and students being friends."

He sagged in relief, even as his heart did a quick Irish jig. "Oh."

"As you know, we have a strict non-fraternization policy between students and professors."

"Of course. That is why I haven't even returned to the bookstore where she is employed. I felt it best to be above reproach."

Dr. Purcell nodded. "I know—we all do, really. You're quite conscientious. But, you are also quite personable and gregarious, so I felt it good to remind you. I've confirmed with her advisor that she won't have any other classes with you, so after this May, you're free to do as you please, but—"

"—until then, keep it strictly professional. I will." At the knowing look the man gave him, Dean shook his head. "It won't be a problem, I assure you. She just works at a bookstore I enjoy visiting, and I suspect she wanted to ensure it wasn't against any rules for her to stop by my office for non-coursework related discussions. She likely wishes to share books they've acquired that she thinks might interest me. She seems like the kind of person who strives to stay above reproach. We could use—"

Dr. Purcell stood and waited by the door. "As long as we understand each other. Have a good day, Dean."

As Dean wandered down the hall to his own office, his mind swirled with ideas. *And our good dean of students still finds "Professor Dean" annoying.*

A small pink box with a silver bow sat in Carlie's place the next week. She hung her coat, slid into the seat, and stared at the box. A moment later, she pulled a card from her purse and passed it to Dean. "I was afraid this would be awkward. I should have known you'd find a way to make me feel like I'm normal."

She fingered the bow. "I always hate opening. Isn't that silly? It's just that it's all gone then, you know? The anticipation…" She grabbed it. "But something in your face tells me I need to open it. What…" She ripped the bow from the box and tore the paper off. The confectioner's box didn't surprise her, nor did the chocolate hearts inside. *They're almost cliché.* But the chocolate knife, fork, and spoon left her scratching her head. A little slip of paper tied to the fork read: *Enjoy your chocolate Valentine dinner.*

"What does it mean?"

Dean just smiled—just sat in his seat, holding her card in his hand, and smiled.

"What? How am I supposed to understand what you're talking about?"

Again, Dean smiled, but Janice arrived before she could ask again. "So, what'll you two have today? I'm guessing coffee for Dean and an Italian soda for Carlie."

Dean shook his head. "I would appreciate an Italian soda—orange."

"Guess that leaves the coffee for me." Carlie winked. "But I'm totally stealing a sip of his, so he'll need two straws."

151

"And what'll you have to eat?" Janice hunkered on her heels and leaned against the table. "With that soda, I recommend the BLT with lemon chicken soup."

"I'll take it. What's she having with that coffee?"

Janice glanced at Carlie before saying, "Clam chowder and a spinach linguine."

"This place is the highlight of my week," Carlie said as she leaned back in the booth. "I really need to learn how to cook. I'm horrible. But I come here, and it makes me want to learn. This stuff is so good."

"I'll get right on that. Do you want dark or sourdough bread today?"

They spoke in unison. "Sourdough."

For the first time, Carlie didn't feel like talking—not because she was upset or bored. This time, she pulled out her Kindle, propped her feet up on the bench, and began reading. Only once did she look up—when Dean pulled out a stack of papers and began reading. *It's nice just sitting here with a friend—really nice.*

His favorite song from the *Yeshua's Logos* album filled his kitchen as Dean pulled baked salmon from his oven. A glass of wine sat beside his place at the table and leaning against it, Carlie's card stood waiting. *I hope she's having a wonderful time at the "chocolate Valentine's dinner..."*

Salmon and asparagus with a nice Chablis—what more could he want for a Valentine's dinner? *What an inane question. Of course, I desire more in my life.* A rebellious side of him welled up in his heart. *I could have taken someone out to dinner—Felicia would have enjoyed that. We always have a delightful time, but to what purpose? I'm not interested, and if I'm honest with myself, she isn't either.*

He sat his plate on the table and rolled down his sleeves, buttoning them in turn. His prayer of gratitude for the Lord's provision turned into a plea for a different kind of provision until he felt a nudge—a reminder that the meal he'd worked hard on would be ruined if he didn't eat. "Thank you, Lord."

Between bites, he stared at the card and wondered at its contents. "I feel transported back to the second grade—this time I am the one who received a real Valentine." He swallowed hard. "And this time it isn't from the teacher." The memory overtook him as he recalled the small pile of tiny envelopes—the valentines that every student brought for every other student—and the single red envelope with his name printed carefully in his teacher's perfect penmanship. Dean saw his childish hand pat the little white envelopes—no candy hearts. *Not one larger envelope or handmade construction paper card—nothing to show that I mattered to anyone.* Only the red pity envelope from Miss Fielding. "She was a kind teacher," he mused.

In a moment that felt eerily like a Hallmark commercial, Dean pulled the flap from inside the envelope and slid out the card. "'Friendship warms the heart.' There's truth in that," Dean mused. He opened the card and grinned as he saw words filling the left side.

Dean,

I don't know why you still come each week. You could eat anywhere, with anyone. But I thought you should know how much it means to me that you let me come and eat with you. I don't know you really, but I have learned some things about you. You're a kind man and a generous one. You're an excellent listener and an interesting professor as well.

I hope you spend Valentine's Day with someone really special, and I hope she finds a way to tell you just how special you are.

Thank you for being the most unusual and also one of the best friends I've ever had,

Carlie

The music swelled as he stared at the words. Letters swam before his eyes as the words of the song—the words of Jesus put to music—filled his ears, his heart. *"There is no greater love than for a man to lay down his life for his friends…'"*

The doorbell interrupted his impromptu worship. With a rueful glance at the meal that grew more and more inedible with each passing second, he shoved his chair back and hurried to the door. Larry stood there with a maroon and silver gift bag. "Lynn sent me with your gift. She has one of her headaches."

"Did you have dinner?"

"Not yet. I was going to suggest we go get something, but it smells like you've been cooking."

"I have salmon that might still be hot."

Larry watched as Dean filled a plate. As he accepted it, he asked, "So, why did you make so much extra?"

"Two reasons—first, I forgot to cut it in half before I froze it, and second—since I messed up the first—because I'd planned to turn it into salmon salad for lunch tomorrow."

At the table, Larry pointed to Dean's card. "So we're not the first. Who—"

Dean passed the card. "Feel free."

"I wasn't trying to hint," Larry protested.

"I know, but it isn't so personal that I cannot share."

Larry pointed to the signature. "I'm almost disappointed that it isn't."

The words crept into Dean's mind and settled in a corner that

153

promised to revisit them later. "I don't know how to respond to that."

"You know what I mean. Sometimes I think the advanced track we put you on affected your ability to form peer relationships."

Despite valiant attempts to control himself, Dean's laughter filled the room. "Who are my peers? The people I work with? I have relationships with them. The people at church? I have relationships with them, too. For that matter, I have relationships with former students since many of them are in my age bracket. I think what you really mean is, 'I'm afraid we made you a misfit with the ladies.'"

Larry set down his fork, leaned back in his chair, folded his arms over his chest, and leveled an inscrutable look on Dean. "That'll work."

"I *had* a girlfriend."

"Yeah... one that lasted two months and was back when you were seventeen." Larry leaned forward again. "Why *did* you break up? You never told me."

"I was too embarrassed." He speared a piece of lukewarm salmon and forced himself to chew it. After a sip of wine that he didn't even taste, and a glance at his stepfather that told him he'd not be able to dodge it this time, he sighed. "I surrender! She enjoyed bragging rights regarding her 'college boyfriend' but found it galling, when they met me, having to admit that he was two months younger than she was."

"Ouch."

Yes, and now I am relieved that I never told you about the classmate who considered depriving me of my virginity to be a personal challenge. I almost failed that test of my self-control.

Dean stared at his plate, trying to decide which tasted worse, reheated salmon or lukewarm to almost-cold food. He jumped up. "I'm going to reheat mine. Do you need a nuke?"

"Mine's still warm. Probably from staying in the pan longer." As the microwave kicked on, Larry said, "By the way, your mother loved the roses. Packing them into that heart-shaped vase was perfect."

"Excellent. It seemed a little...*sweetheartish,* but the effect was too lovely to resist."

"I believe her words were, 'My son isn't ashamed to show he loves me.'" Larry jumped up and poured himself a glass of wine. "I appreciate you doing things to make her feel special. Your wife—when you have her—will be a blessed woman."

As Dean carried his plate back to the table, he pondered those words. He made it through the rest of his meal before he spoke. "If I ever have a wife. I'm not confident that'll happen."

The little storefront had been rearranged to mimic an elegant restaurant. Each table had been draped with pink, burgundy, or gold cloths and runners, and bowls of flowers, candles, and small knick-knacks had been grouped on each one in a setting that reminded Carlie of a Pinterest-worthy wedding reception. Large tables filled the center of the room, but in three of the corners, smaller tables had been set as well. "Who—"

"The girls planned it—Hopkins, Zanderberg, Adcocks…"

"It's gorgeous. Look at all the white lights." Carlie turned and signed, *A perfect church Valentine's dinner.* "See, I've been practicing."

"Might need a *little* more practice," Jared teased. "You just said a *chocolate* Valentine dinner." His right hand formed a C and moved up and down, gently striking his other fist. "You swirled it like this—stirring chocolate."

"Oh. Oh, I see. Like church on a rock. That makes—" Her eyes widened. "*That's* why he gave me a chocolate fork, spoon, and knife."

"Who—oh, Dr. Dean?"

Carlie explained her conversation and the gift she'd received. "I should have known it would be something like that." She glanced around. "Who do we sit with?"

Bethany Zanderberg appeared, as if on cue. "We made your table over here. Follow me." The table, set for two, sat a little apart from the rest of the room. "Danielle will be out to pour you drinks…" She pointed to a little basket on the floor beside the table. "There are games and things in there if you'd like to play. Have a good night, and God bless you."

No sooner had she turned to go, then several of the women in the room began to sing, "'Love one another for love is of God…'"

Carlie glanced around, waiting for others to sing—but not all of the women joined. "Wha—"

"Are you alto or soprano?"

"Alto is best, but I can do soprano if necessary."

He pulled out the basket and grabbed a pen and began scribbling on the back of a note pad. "This is the alto part." he whispered, "Sing these with the others." A second later, he broke in with "'…*bears all things… believes all things…*'"

Four-part harmony—four distinct verses blended together simultaneously. Scripture sung as praise, though something she'd grown used to in the little church, sounded different—intensely passionate—sung on a "romantic holiday." Carlie tried to follow the other altos, but found herself sitting, listening, worshiping. *Lord… it's beautiful. Wow.*

Jared's hand covered hers on the final stanza. Once more, she tried to sing but couldn't. The richness of the voices, the depth of the words—pure scripture arranged as a song—all overwhelmed her with their combined beauty. A hush fell over the room and then Alex, the minister, said, "In Jesus name, amen."

Four teens stepped from behind the screen, carrying plates. Bethany arrived with a small plate holding two fried wontons. "They're delicious," she whispered. "I tested just to make sure you wouldn't get icky food."

"The sacrifices you make to serve your fellow Christians," Jared teased.

"Right? I tell you, it's a thankless job." With a grin at Carlie, the girl hurried off again.

"I suspect they'll be bringing soup immediately. They're working with a makeshift kitchen, so..."

"Eat up?" Carlie laughed. "You are hungry."

"Guilty as charged." Jared nearly inhaled his wonton before asking, "So, should we take a look at their activities or are we good?"

Carlie's eyes swept the room and noticed that few of the adults had touched the baskets. "Maybe we should. I feel like the girls went to a lot of work and we're kind of ignoring that."

Jared pulled an envelope from the basket even as he watched her. "You're pretty amazing, you know that?"

A smile tried to form, despite her best attempts to squash it. "Well, I—" She could almost see him wince even before she finished speaking. "Thanks."

"That's a great word. Love it. Okay, this says we're supposed to name three things about the other person that are a blessing."

"It does no—" Carlie cut off her own words as the card was thrust under her nose. "Okay, so it does. What kind of crazy—"

"Most of the people here are married," Jared mused. "I've noticed that married couples tend to forget to say the things that are essential. They're more consumed with the urgent. It's a good idea."

"Not sure I follow, but..." Carlie stared at the card. "I can say that you made me feel welcome when I first came and haven't stopped since."

"Your thirst for the Word totally blesses me." Before she could think of another one, Jared continued his musings on marriage. "Never having been married, I could be all wrong, but what I mean is that sometimes stuff that feels like it can't wait—like backed up toilets, overdue bills, or misbehaving children—crowd out conversations that revolve on their spouse's faith or service. This kind of forces people to remember that there are more eternal things to discuss and appreciate."

Her laughter sent curious and amused glances their way, but Carlie ignored them. "So, what you're saying is that this was your idea."

"See! Maybe that should be my next blessing. Your intelligence—

it's amazing."

"Oh, no. It's my turn. Um… the way you are so committed to this church and the people in it—giving them this building and everything—that blesses me, too. Because you did it, I finally found a church I look forward to being with."

Though articulate enough, Jared hadn't appeared to be a very emotional or sensitive man, but her words seemed to strike some kind of chord within him. His jaw tensed, intensified by candlelight, and his eyes glistened. "That is probably the best compliment I've ever gotten. Thank you."

Carlie gave a seated mock curtsy. "Your turn."

"Just your friendship. The way you asked for help and let me in—that blesses me."

He started to say something else. What if he likes me? Wow. That would be amazing. Someone like him. Just—wow.

"It's your turn… tell me I'm not just a two-trick pony."

"Ha. Ha." Unsure if she should say what she wanted to, and unsure *how* to say it even if she did, Carlie hesitated longer than was comfortable.

Jared shook his head. "No pressure. It's supposed to be fun. I'll just—"

"The-way-you-are-so-nice-to-me." Carlie closed her eyes and took a deep, steadying breath. "You're nice to me, okay? You treat me like… I don't know. I'm just blessed by how you do. It kind of reminds me of Dean."

The quietly delighted expression that grew with each word deflated at the mention of Dean. She saw Jared swallow before he said, "I think that's probably another great compliment. I'm just sorry that common courtesy makes such a deep impression on you."

Oh, boy. Yeah. He likes me.

D ean's phone rang while in the middle of scanning a student's draft. His eyes flitted to the dock where it charged before returning to the paper. He froze. "I think I should answer this. Would you mind?"

The middle-aged woman, who struggled with every aspect of her reentry into academic life, nodded. "Sure."

"Frank... wha—"

At that moment, Dean felt and finally understood what it meant for "color to drain" from someone's face. He felt it even as he listened. "No...*no!*"

Mrs. Valli eyed him with concern. "I can go," she whispered.

But Dean shook his head and held up a finger. "Yes. I'll go. I should arrive in approximately..." he flipped through the two remaining pages. "Forty minutes. Thank you for calling me. My condolences." As he disconnected the call, he closed his eyes. His fingers fumbled with his phone as he tried to set it back in the charging dock.

"Everything's not okay. I won't ask that. But if you need to go, we can do this tomorrow."

Dean shook his head and opened his eyes to smile at her. "It should only take me a few more minutes to finish our session. I'd hoped to show you an easier way to transition with quotes. I feel like you're spending an excess—"

"I am! How'd you know?"

"It shows in your writing."

The woman's face fell. "I knew I wasn't doing it right."

"But you are." At her confused look, Dean explained. "The time you spend on those is evident because they're perfect. However, you can achieve similar results with a little less effort. I'll compose a few examples and email them to you. Meanwhile, why don't you plan on about twenty minutes with me tomorrow before class? Will that work for you?"

"Sure, but…" Her words trailed off into nothingness as he flagged a few more items and flipped the page. Two minutes later, he passed it back. "You have a solid beginning. You need to review the Hebrew vocabulary words and some of the other vocabulary words as well. They will help you provide better support for your content." He gathered a few things, shoved them into his messenger bag, and inched toward the office door. "I'll see you tomorrow…"

"I'll be praying. I don't know what for, but God does, and that's all—"

Dean interrupted, his voice choking on the words. "The man who shot me?"

Mrs. Valli nodded.

"He was just found dead in his cell at the jail. I'm on my way to visit his wife."

"Oh—oh, wow. I'll be praying." Just as he stepped out of the door to wait for her to follow, the woman hugged him. "Thank you for teaching me what it means to live what Jesus said."

With his mind focused on the drive to the other side of Rockland, Dean didn't follow her words. "About…"

"I don't remember the exact words, but it was something about treating people who are mean to you well—being nice to them and helping them even though they tried to hurt you."

Dean patted her arm and shook his head. "That's kind of you to say, but Steve Pierce's wife didn't do anything to me." With that, he hurried down the hall and burst through the closest exit. His shoes slid on slick patches, but he hardly noticed. The parking lot lay in sight, and he pushed himself to run faster.

His speed in getting *to* the car, however, seemed wasted in the craziness that became pre-rush hour in Rockland that February afternoon. Cars crawled at speeds that would disgust the most slothful of snails. The few short miles stretched out before him until Dean found himself pounding the steering wheel in frustration. The depth of his anger shocked him into switching from attacks on his vehicle to prayer, but he doubted the effectiveness of those prayers.

By the time he pulled up in front of Hannah Pierce's apartment building, more than an hour had passed. He locked the car and prayed for its safekeeping as he dashed up the walk, into the lobby, and stared at what seemed like a perpetual "out of order" sign on the elevator. *Of all the times not to have an elevator.*

A child answered the door—one too young to do so safely, in his opinion. Dean stepped into the dingy apartment and noted that it was less cluttered than on his last visit. *She is already adjusting to the new norm. It's amazing how humans do that when our world is shatter—*

The thought froze in his mind as he stepped around the shabby photo screen that created a tiny partition into the room. Carlie, with the youngest Pierce child on her lap, sat on the couch, passing tissue after tissue to a weeping Hannah. The sight stirred his heart. *She's here. I can't believe it. And just sitting there holding that baby and praying—is she really praying?* That thought arrested all others. He listened, straining to hear the half-choked, half-whispered words.

"—just don't know what to say. I don't know how to pray. Just please help us understand." Once more, the same words tumbled out, still choked, still heartbroken.

His heart constricted until he gasped at the pain of it. *I've decided, Lord. It's time for me to speak—to remind her that the Holy Spirit prays for her when she cannot find the words. It's time to invest in her on a more personal level.* But, as he crossed the room and sat on the arm of the couch, he felt a check in his spirit—one that he hadn't felt in much too long. *Well, Lord, we know that I have not arrived at a spiritual level that requires no prompting from Your Spirit. This must mean I've ignored the conviction of the Word in my heart. I assume this is You advising me to wait?* But the same impression—the same, "be slow to speak" pressed itself on him, and no other answer to his repeated petitions on what to do emerged.

When she noticed he'd arrived, Dean didn't know for certain. Her eyes met his, pleaded for help, and then dropped to her lap as she reached for yet another tissue from a near-empty box and passed it to Hannah. Determined not to leave her floundering, Dean placed one hand on her back and began praying. "Lord, I ask that you comfort everyone in this house tonight, but especially Hannah…" The prayer—simple in every way—continued longer than he'd ever prayed for anything. Twice, Hannah got up to help a little one. Once, Carlie got up and fished a fresh box of Kleenex from a plastic sack on the counter. Still he prayed. "—such a difficult time to trust in Your goodness, so please give Hannah the faith to do it…" *And please provide for them in a way that blesses the Pierce family and strengthens Carlie's faith.*

Several more minutes passed—each one wrapped in a blanket of prayer. *Lord, I don't know what to do next. I'm lost.*

Each word she spoke felt more inane and less helpful than the last. Still, Carlie prayed. *Why did I think I could be any help?* she grumbled to herself. Another sniffle prompted her to pass another tissue to Hannah. "I don't know if it's really okay to pray like this, but can You speak to our hearts, so we'll *feel* comforted? I think it would help Hannah because I'm failing in the comfort department here."

She felt a presence beside her as someone settled on the arm of the couch, and Carlie steeled herself against the heart-wrenching pain of another child melting down as the confusing words about daddy being "gone" and "in heaven" sent the child into fear-induced histrionics. *And does she know what she's saying when she says that Steve's in heaven? Does that mean he was Yours, or does she mean it like "everyone who dies goes to heaven"?*

The body shifted and Carlie forced herself to look up. Dean gave her a weak smile. *Oh, thank You, Jesus!* Before she dropped her eyes, she pleaded silently with him. *Help her. Pray for her.*

Dean's hand rested on her back, and he began praying. Each word filled her heart, soothing, comforting, strengthening. *He has a nice voice. Is that wrong to think of—probably is right now, isn't it? I don't care. It's true. Hannah needs it now.* The box of Kleenex emptied at her next pass of tissue. Carlie jumped up to retrieve another one, grateful for the prompting that encouraged her to bring them in the first place.

She settled back into her seat and passed yet another tissue to Hannah. *Between the five of them plus me, we're going to use up at least two of these boxes. I should have gotten the stuff with lotion in it.*

"...strength in days to come and the rest of us the wisdom to know when to offer help and know when to give her space."

The rest of Dean's prayer faded as she heard one of the Pierce children whine for something to eat. "I'll get it," she whispered.

Hannah tried to protest, but when Carlie insisted and Dean urged her to sit with her children, she nodded and said, "Thanks. I was just going to do tacos. It's all in the fridge."

Navigating a strange kitchen was more uncomfortable, not to mention difficult, than she'd expected. Twice, Hannah noticed and tried to help, but Dean stopped her by simply asking where Carlie could find the item. *How does he know what I need?* The obvious answer stunned her. *He's paying attention. Why am I surprised? He always pays close attention.*

By the time she started assembling tacos, Dean appeared at her side, scooping meat into shells, sprinkling with shredded lettuce, topping with cheese and tomatoes, and, for two of the children, adding a little salsa as well. He found a jar of baby food, a clean kitchen towel, and a spoon and carried them to Hannah. "I doubt she'd like to try to munch on taco shells with no teeth. But maybe apricots would tempt her."

Carlie listened from the kitchen as she arranged plates at the table and filled sippy cups and plastic tumblers with milk. Before she could call the kids to the table, Dean had them rounded up and seated in their chairs and booster seats. He hunkered down on his heels and prayed with them, thanking the Lord for the food that, from what Carlie had seen, was almost the last in the little apartment. *Where will they get tomorrow's dinner from? There's hardly enough milk for breakfast, not enough for breakfast* and *lunch, much less dinner, and what'll they actually* eat?

As she tried to clean up the dinner mess, Dean interrupted, filling several taco shells and setting them on two plates. He carried one to Hannah, and Carlie strained to hear as he murmured, "You may not feel like it, but you really need to make yourself eat."

Her heart squeezed at the pleading in Hannah's eyes. But Dean shook his head and took the baby. "I'll feed her. You eat. Trust me."

Before he could raise his eyes and see her watching, Carlie turned to wipe down the stove. A moment later, a gentle nudge told her he'd returned. *Don't talk—not now. I don't think I can take it right now. Just... don't.*

When she turned again, Carlie found him standing there holding a plate. He didn't say a word, but the order was plain. *Eat.*

"There's not enough food," she hissed as she took the plate from him.

Dean didn't hesitate. He offered the baby a bite of food, and the moment her little lips closed over the spoon, he set down the jar, plopped the empty spoon in it, and fished out his wallet—all while managing *not* to drop the baby. The ease with which he moved looked incongruous with the ineptitude and discomfort that permeated his expressions. *He's miserable. He thinks he's useless, but look at him. He's holding the baby, handing me food, pulling out his wallet. It's like he's had kids for years, but he also looks like he's about ready to vomit.*

Dean didn't even look as he pulled out the contents of his billfold and set it on the counter. Her heart constricted as she stared at the plate and the money. "I'll go as soon as I eat. You're right. This is something we *can* do."

Twenty minutes later, to her surprise, he followed her down the stairs, out the front entrance, and to her car. The moment she was safely ensconced in her vehicle, he walked back inside, his hands shoved in pockets. *He looks cold. He should have put on a coat. But how nice to walk me out like that. I should go get his number so I can call him to help me when I get back.* Her hand gripped the door handle, but she paused and shook her head. *I can do this without his help. Sheesh. Pathetic.*

The trip took twice as long as expected and cost her twice as much as Dean had given, but Carlie stocked up on every staple she could think of. Flour, sugar—brown and white—spices, butter, oil, eggs, cheese, and condiments. She piled all the frozen produce she thought would fit in the tiny freezer into her cart—then she pulled half back out again. *They need protein, too. Duh.* Two chickens, a roast, a couple of chubs of ground beef, and half of a small turkey ham. Potatoes—she dashed back through the store and grabbed rice and beans before hurrying back to produce—lettuce, tomatoes, celery, carrots, and onions. The cart filled at an alarming rate, but Carlie resigned herself to more debt and kept buying. Crackers, cookies, bread, tortillas, and two tubs of ice cream. The memory of that freezer forced her to put one back.

If they have to eat it all tonight, then so be it. They're getting ice cream.

At the register, Carlie sighed in relief as she unrolled the bills Dean had given her. *Two of them are fifties. That'll help. Wow, Lord. I'm learning that I can really trust You. I think I can afford the rest—if my mental calculations are right—on my debit card. That would be fabulous.*

"That'll be $357.19."

Carlie passed the bills across. "I'd like to pay cash first and use my debit for the rest."

The cashier counted the bills and typed the total into the register. "That leaves $180.19. You can swipe your card now."

Boy, aren't we cheerful today. Carlie winced as she typed in her PIN number. *I can make it, but, man, I can't get to the restaurant before him tomorrow or I'll be putting lunch on credit.*

"Have a nice night." The monotonal quality of the woman's voice sounded empty and pained at the same time.

Carlie met the woman's bored gaze. "You too. I hope you have a line full of happy people who don't expect you to be superwoman."

Relief washed over the woman's face but was replaced a second later with a scowl. "That's not a nice night. That's a recipe for a miracle."

Snow began to fall as she loaded the bags into her car. With each mile, the flakes fell faster—thicker. By the time she unloaded the first bags and hurried up the walk to the apartment building, it had grown heavy enough to be concerning. *I have to go home. I won't make it otherwise, and the cats...*

Dean met her at the bottom of the stairs and held out his hand for her keys. She fumbled for them. "Thanks. I'll get these up and be right back," she started to say. But he'd already gone, the big glass doors banging oddly behind him. She eyed the elevator, not relishing carrying four plastic bags of heavy groceries up three flights of stairs. The "out of order" sign stopped her. "Probably not true either. Probably just the super's idea of a way to save on utilities." At the second floor landing, she groaned. "Wish I had the guts to just use it."

By the time she dumped the bags on the kitchen floor, hurried back down the hall, and jogged halfway down the stairs, Dean arrived with what looked like the rest of the bags on his arms and her key chain bouncing outside his front coat pocket. "Wow! Let me take—"

He shook his head and opened his mouth, but Carlie preempted him. "Are there more?"

Dean nodded.

She grabbed the keys and patted his arm before hurrying back out into the cold. *Stupid of me, but I don't want now to be when he talks to me. It's just—ugh.*

The man had to be faster than lightning. By the time she made it to the apartment with the final bags, he'd separated pantry items from cold items and had separated refrigerated from frozen. Carlie began separating boxes from cans and looking for the proper cupboards.

Hannah led freshly bathed little ones from the bathroom, through the kitchen, and to their bedroom. Her eyes bugged. "I can't—"

"No one said you could. We can't do much, but we can stock the cupboards so you don't have to go shopping right now," Carlie assured her.

Fresh tears coursed down Hannah's cheeks. "Okay. Um, thanks. But—"

Carlie reached for each of the kids, hugging them one by one. "You guys get some sleep, okay? No goofing off. Mommy needs to rest too. Got that?"

Three wide-eyed little faces nodded. The oldest spoke up. "We will."

Dean spoke before Hannah could leave. "Once we have our mess cleared, we must go. It's snowing again. I'll leave my card on your refrigerator. Don't hesitate to call if you need anything." Carlie watched as he stepped forward and grasped Hannah's hand. "I mean it—anything."

"Thank you. I just don't know how I'll—"

"God will get you through it. Sometimes we get to help Him. Please don't allow your pride to prevent us from helping. We already feel helpless as it is."

Surely, he knows she's talking about paying for the food. Is he just that good, or is he really that clueless? Who knows? It's nice. But as he turned to finish the arranging of the perishables, Dean winked at her. *He's just that good.*

Squeals and giggles erupted the moment the children entered the bedroom. *That's not what she was hoping for tonight. Help her, Lord? Please?*

While Carlie piled cans and boxes into empty cupboards, Dean fought to fit everything in the freezer. At last, he pulled out a chub of ground beef and a package of chicken legs and put them in the fridge. Finally, the remaining bag of chicken nuggets squeezed into place. Veggies, milk, butter, yogurt—every other perishable item, including the ground beef and chicken legs—he crammed in the fridge. With a grand swoop, he gathered all the empty plastic bags and shoved them all in one, leaving them on the counter. Then, he just disappeared.

Where—

He reappeared a moment later, with her coat and purse in one hand and his coat slung over his arm.

"Are you sure we should go—" Dean held out the coat for her, waiting to help her into it. "I'll take that as a yes. Oh, and—" Part of her screamed not to say it, but a stronger side of herself insisted. "Thanks for not talking now—this isn't the time, you know?"

Without a word—and that somehow felt like the world's most eloquent silence—Dean led her out the door, locking it behind him, and down the stairs. How she hadn't noticed the umbrella on his arm, she didn't know, but Carlie grinned as he pulled it out and opened the door. "Some New Yorkers would have your hide for that, but I, for one, am grateful." At her car, she turned and hugged him. "Thank you. When I saw you sitting there, somehow, I knew I'd get through it." She winced. "Ugh. Like I have anything to endure compared to Hannah. Good night."

Dean stood there long after she'd gotten in her car, long after she finally turned on the engine, and, for all she knew, long after she pulled out of the parking space and drove off into the night.

Dean hailed Janice as he arrived and ordered coffee. "Would you please bring Carlie the caramel coffee she likes when she arrives? We visited Steve's family last night. I think…she'd appreciate it."

"Got it. By the way, we've got a grilled fish sandwich and a gnocchi soup today—fabulous."

"I would like that." As much as he hated to do it, Dean added. "I must leave early today so…"

"I'll put it in now." She started to walk away but hesitated. "Thanks for going. Frank said he wanted to, but you know…"

Left alone, Dean pondered her words. *Though unfortunate, it also makes sense. Hannah might consider Frank responsible for driving her husband to desperate measures, however unintentionally.*

After reading the same page of the same paper for the fourth time and still not finding anything to mark—on his worst student's paper, no less—Dean put it away and wrapped his hands around the hot mug Janice brought him. *I wonder if Carlie received word regarding the memorial service. Such an odd day—a Sunday. It also feels a bit… rushed.*

He'd made it halfway through his fish sandwich and soup before Carlie arrived. Janice paused on her way past and whispered, "She just got here, and she looks terrible. I think she's been crying."

Though Dean expected Janice's words to be somewhat exaggerated, he had to admit, it was true. Carlie looked truly terrible. She dragged herself into the booth and stared at her sleeves before stepping out again and removing her coat. Once more, she sank down on the bench, and this time, she stared at the floor instead of sliding into place. "It's just so horrible."

Before Dean could decide if he should ask what she meant or let her talk, Janice arrived with the caramel coffee. "Here… he said you'd need it."

Tears poured down her cheeks. "Isn't—" Carlie sniffed, "—he just the nicest guy?"

"Yeah… Do you need to eat? Can I bring you some bread?"

"That'd be great," she agreed. "I don't care what I eat, but I need to. I don't think I had breakfast."

Janice hurried off with a "coming right up" promise.

Dean waited for something—a sign, a sigh—anything. Carlie just stared into the mug and inhaled the scent. "It smells so good."

I have been told—by you, no less—that it tastes even better. Why don't you take a sip?

A basket of sourdough rolls and two plates appeared as Janice rushed past with another table's order. When Carlie didn't reach for it, Dean pulled one out, buttered it, and set it in front of her. Carlie didn't touch it. He pushed the plate closer, nudging her hand with it. This time, she sighed. "You're right. I need to eat. I actually am hungry, I think." The first bite seemed to open her up to him. "So, Hannah called twice last night—sobbing. I should have just stayed. It was awful. Then, of course, she called back each time and apologized for bugging me." Her eyes met his and she took another bite. The moment she washed it down with a gulp of coffee that had to burn, she choked and said, "Did you know she has family here? They aren't speaking to her since Steve's…" Her eyes closed. "Incident."

Why do people hold to the mistaken notion that the silent treatment will somehow remove the problems of their lives? I do not understand the logic that says, "Our daughter's husband committed a crime; therefore, we'll cut her off and let her flounder alone when she needs help the most."

"The insurance company is requesting the coroner's report and an investigation into the incident. They don't want to pay."

What insurance company does? Their job is to avoid compensation wherever legally permissible. Unsure what else to do, Dean reached for her hand and squeezed it. *Please let her "hear" me. Furthermore, if she wishes me to speak now…*

"Are you going to the memorial service?" Without waiting for a response, she continued—a testimony to how used to his silence she

166

had become. "I don't want to go. I don't want to hear a preacher try to make sense of something so senseless. I don't want to hear how he's better off, when his family isn't. I know that's probably all kinds of horrible, but I don't care." Tears splashed down her cheeks again. "I hate this. I don't want to go. I don't know how I'm going to get through it."

Dean started to offer to pick her up—to go with her, but Carlie's next words stopped him. "I got ahold of Jared, though. He said he'd go with me. Wasn't that nice?"

Her phone buzzed. Carlie dug her hand into her coat pocket and pulled it out with little interest. She held it until the screen flashed and announced a voice message. *Jared. Should've picked up.*

The message was brief but exciting. "Got tickets to that concert we were talking about at the memorial service. They're for tomorrow night, though. I don't like leaving an invite on voice message, but if you can't or don't want to go, I'd like to give them to someone who would. Please call as soon as you can."

She waited until she got off the subway and onto the streets. Cold, icy air blasted her, but Carlie hardly noticed as she dialed Jared's number. "You called?"

"Oh, you got the message. Good."

"Yeah—something about tickets? I was on the subway..." *God, forgive me for being evasive. It's embarrassing.*

Jared perked up. "Well, you know that concert with the three new indie groups we were talking about? I was looking on Craig's List for folding chairs for the church, and I saw tickets. So, I met the guy down at the mall and bought them. Want to go? We could get dinner maybe..."

Internally, she squealed, but aloud, she just said, "That sounds great. What time?"

Carlie spent Saturday choosing and rejecting outfit after outfit. Curious, she plopped Pouncer and Moros on the bed, one at a time, and ordered them to pick for her. Each cat showed minor preferences for different options—opposing really—and in the end, she chose neither.

A trip to the mall produced nothing that she could justify or afford. By the time she arrived home again, Carlie nearly returned to buy an overpriced outfit designed to inspire self-confidence. "It's stupid," she announced to Pouncer as she stepped in the door. "I've wasted a whole day trying to find something remotely attractive, and for nothing."

In a frenetic scramble to clean up the disaster created by her fashion failure, Carlie swept the room free of discarded outfits and replaced all of them in their drawers and closet. She stood before the wide closet doors, stared inside, and willed the tops and bottoms to give her some kind of hint as to what she should do. With eyes closed, she reached out and pulled out the first thing she touched. "Great. It would be the shirt Carole gave me." With only one pair of pants in her entire—much too large—wardrobe that matched, the decision was made for her.

Straight hair, curled hair, simple makeup, no-holds-barred makeup—the decisions choked the life out of her excitement until she stood before the mirror, ready to go, and tried to see herself through an objective lens. "Not too—"

A knock startled her out of her excessive preparations and into panic mode. "He is so going to regret inviting me," Carlie muttered to Moros as she passed. But when she opened the door, even Carlie could see his appreciation.

"Wow. You look awesome."

"I need to grab my purse and get my coat. Want to come in?" The minute she asked, Carlie flushed. *That was stupid. Of course he'd rather stand in the hall and wait out there.* A new thought hit her almost simultaneously. *Then again, maybe it's a religious thing—stay out of temptation's way or whatever.*

"—happy to, but I don't want to run you over or anything."

"What?" Carlie blinked just as she realized what he'd said. "Oh, sorry. I'm kind of out of it, and I have to keep the door mostly shut or the cats try to make a run for it."

Jared stepped in and glanced around him. "I like it—modern without being too sterile. Comfortable but not contemporary."

She couldn't help it, despite a valiant effort not to correct him. "Technically it is contemporary. I like some Modern design elements, but I also like comfortable upholstery and a few other contemporary things." She slid her arms into her coat. "It's a common mistake, though."

"So contemporary can include Modern, but Modern can't include contemporary?"

"Exactly!" She grabbed her purse and gave him a smile. "Ready?"

By the time Jared opened her car door for her—something Blaine never would have done—Carlie realized what she'd done. She waited for him to start the engine and said, "Sorry about that. I get excited, think I'm being helpful, but it's just rude. You didn't ask what it was. I just—"

"It's fine, Carlie. Really. I hear people using these terms, and I never know what they mean. I try to pick up meaning by context, but obviously I got things a bit backwards. You helped. That's a good thing." When she didn't respond, he nudged her arm and added, "I didn't mean to make you feel—"

Her head whipped to the side as she stared at him and interrupted. "You didn't—really. I just." *You just know that Blaine would have blasted you for correcting him and can't get out of the habit of apologizing for any potential annoyance.* Her eyes closed as the thoughts washed over her. "Wow. That was a bit of a revelation."

"What was?"

"I just realized how often I try to avoid annoying people because almost everything I did would have annoyed Blaine."

Jared didn't respond at first, and the seconds that passed as she frantically tried to find a way to backtrack created a torturous cycle of self-recrimination. Just as she started to suggest he take her home again, Jared said, "I don't know Blaine, obviously, so I don't know how to say what I want to."

"And that is…"

"I want to say that he was an idiot—which is redundant. I believe I already expressed that opinion." A glance at Jared showed his hands gripping the steering wheel with excess force. "I guess I just don't know what you mean when you say everything you did annoyed him. I can't imagine you annoying people. Everyone at church thinks you are a lovely woman with a kind heart and a teachable spirit. I agree and would add beautiful, inside and out."

"Um…"

"No, listen, Carlie. The guy has to have some redeeming qualities. I mean, you went out with him for quite a long time, right?"

"A little over a year, yeah." Her mind tried to do the math and still came up with just past twelve months. *Seems like longer than that. We didn't even celebrate our "anniversary." Shocker.*

"So, I know he's not all bad."

She winced. "I do talk bad about him all the time, don't I? Ugh. I'm one of *those* women. I hate that."

"That's the thing. You don't—not intentionally anyway. I was talking to Natalie about it the other day." His eyes slid her way for a moment. "Hope you don't mind. We weren't trying to gossip or anything. We were actually complimenting you about something, and it just came up."

Something in the back of her mind told her she should be annoyed at the idea of people talking about her, but Carlie just shook her head. "So, what were you talking about?"

"Well, she said something really insightful. She said, 'One thing that bothers me about Carlie is something she isn't even aware of. She mentions things about her ex-boyfriend in such casual tones—things that, if another woman said them, would be intended to run the guy down. Carlie says it like it's totally normal.'"

"I don't know what that means."

Jared pulled into a parking lot and put the car in gear. He turned to face her and gave her a reassuring smile when hers failed to materialize. "It means that some girls will say their jerk boyfriend didn't even care enough to come over and hold their hand when their goldfish died. And they mean it. They're ticked off and want the world to know how misused and under-appreciated they are. But you'll say things in passing that everyone can tell you don't even realize aren't good—like having other women in his life."

"Well, I didn't like it! I'm not this martyr or anything. But I knew it when I agreed to go out with him. It was my choice."

When she started to open the door, Jared stopped her. "Give me a second."

Midway through dinner, Carlie was near tears. Jared had asked what she wanted to eat—asked her opinion on whether he'd prefer the shrimp or the chicken. He'd sent the server away when she ordered the least expensive thing on the menu and asked her point blank if it was what she really wanted or if she was trying to be considerate of his wallet. He asked about her week, about Hannah and the Pierce children. He apologized for not being able to stay after the memorial service and for not calling later to assure that she'd made it home safely. But, more than anything, he listened as if what she had to say meant something. He asked questions to keep her talking.

However, when he set down his fork, leaned back in his chair, gazed at her for a moment, and said, "Carlie, thank you for coming," she almost cried.

"I can't do this—I don't know how." Carlie stared at the plate in front of her as if it would give her answers.

Jared leaned forward, reached for her hand, and pulled back again. "What? What did I say—do? What can't you do?"

"I don't..." She swallowed the lump that filled her throat. "You're too nice, okay? It's just—it's too much. I don't—" Her voice broke.

As she spoke, he nodded. But when she couldn't continue, Jared just pointed to her plate. "Maybe you should eat. I can tell you're hungry. We can talk about it on the way to the concert, okay?"

Those words only compounded her confusion and dismay. *Is this guy for real? He's just so* nice—*hasn't told me I'm ridiculous even once. He moved when the air vent was blowing hot air in my face. It's weird. Nice, but weird. I swear, how is he still single?*

That thought blurted out as a question. "So, how are you still single?"

After staring at her, shock and confusion in his eyes mixing into what seemed to be amusement, Jared laughed. "I could ask the same question."

The longer she thought about it, the more determined Carlie was to inveigle an answer out of him. "No, seriously. How is it even possible?"

"I never met the right girl—the one who liked me how I am."

All attempts to hide her growing admiration for him fizzled at those words. "That's exactly what I mean. Who wouldn't? You have done nothing but try to make me comfortable, make me feel special. You're *nice* to me, and it's not just an act. It's real. I can see it. Man, you opened *my door!"* At the glances some of the fellow diners gave them, Carlie dropped her voice a little. "I hardly think I'm the only girl you've ever been out with and treated this way. So, how are you still single?"

Food forgotten, Carlie and Jared agreed to leave. With an hour to spare before they needed to get in line for the concert, Jared drove out of town and onto the Loop. Cars whizzed past them, but he didn't seem to mind. Mile after mile passed until they reached the other side of the city. Unable to stand the silence any longer, Carlie repeated the question in her heart. "So, how?"

"I'm still single because I'm just as flawed as the rest of humanity, and I haven't met anyone who can stand to put up with me."

Though delivered as a joke, Carlie heard a note of truth in Jared's words. "I don't believe that. You're awesome—seriously amazing. Any girl would—oh, my goodness. I sound like I'm throwing myself at you. That's not what I—" Carlie nearly cried with the frustration of it all.

"I know what you mean. Really." He sighed as he changed lanes behind a car going ten miles under the speed limit in the middle lane. "I want to take credit for being the amazing man you're describing, but I'm not doing anything that any guy wouldn't do."

"Not any—"

"Fine," he agreed. "Any guy *I* know. Obviously, you've known a few that wouldn't. How you meet them, I don't know." At her disbelieving silence, Jared added, "Look, it's just basic dating stuff. I always feel bad because I'm not a good date—not really. I'm pretty bland. I'm not romantic. I don't know how to be."

"Excrement."

Jared's eyes bugged, his jaw dropped, and he nearly plowed into the car in front of them. "What?"

Carlie waited until he glanced her way before she repeated herself. "I know you probably hate 'bad words' so I'm using my better vocabulary. It's the same thing. Excrement."

He snickered. "Okay, I knew I was just your basic date, but I didn't think I was *that* bad."

She folded her arms over her chest and glared at him.

"Are you seriously mad at me? Because I'm not the guy you made me out to be in your head?"

Shaking her head, Carlie leveled one last indignant glance at him and said, "No. You're just full of it. You *are* everything I said. It's a compliment. You're supposed to say thank you or something."

"Thank you. I just wish you knew how absolutely ordinary—"

"Now who isn't listening?" Frustration boiled over. "Jared, you haven't been on other dates with me, maybe, but I've been on lots of dates with lots of guys. I mean it when I say that you're different. And it's amazing. I just don't know how to handle it. I never thought I'd say it, but you're *too* nice."

"Thank you. Seriously," he added when she tossed him another indignant scowl. "I mean it. I'm glad you can see something worth complimenting in me, okay? What I want you to understand, though, is that it *shouldn't* be that 'amazing' to you. Because I don't know any girls who would be impressed by it. Okay?"

"Whatever."

In one fluid motion, Carlie dropped her coat onto the hook at the edge of the booth and slid into the seat. Without hesitation, she blew on her hands to warm them as she exclaimed, "It's nasty out there!" She shivered. "I want a huge, steaming—" before she could finish, his hand rose in the air—just like that first day. "—cup of hot chocolate." She smiled at him as he tried to shove his papers in his messenger bag one-handed. "Thanks. Here... let me hold that for—"

"You thirsty?" Janice winked at Carlie and nodded at Dean. "You can put that down now."

Dean's hand dropped and he managed to shove his papers in the bag without further complication. Carlie clasped her hands together and blew on them once more. "Can I get the biggest, hottest hot chocolate ever made?"

"Well, I can't promise it'll be the biggest or the hottest, but it will be the *best,* and I can refill it until you slosh your way out of here and back to work."

"Deal."

Janice paused. "Know what you want to eat?"

"No… got any ideas?" A smile played around Dean's lips. *You know what she'll suggest. Do you agree or not…*

"I'm a huge fan of the chicken pot pie soup and spinach bread."

Carlie waited for some response from Dean and nodded as he did. "If Dean says yes, then I'll take it."

"Two pot pie soup lunches coming up. You won't regret it."

Left alone, Carlie fidgeted as she rubbed her hands together. "So… I went out with Jared on Saturday…"

Dean's eyes snapped into focus. He leaned his elbows on the table and rested his chin on his hands. For just a moment, Carlie thought he'd speak.

"We went on this date, and it was great—really great. I've never had a guy treat me so amazing—or is it amazingly? Is that a word?" Carlie frowned. "Irrelevant. Anyway, he made me feel like I was the greatest thing alive. You know; asking me what I liked to do, what kinds of things *I* like—stuff like that."

In one of his rare interactive moments, Dean gave her a look that clearly said, "So?"

"What? It was cool, okay? He—" Carlie chewed her lip as she struggled to speak. "He listened to me—really listened, you know? I've never had that."

Dean's expression changed again, but this time she couldn't read it. "What? I can't tell if you're shocked or sad. And why would you be either one?" When he didn't answer, she continued describing the date. She expected to struggle to explain herself, but instead, the words tumbled from her faster than she could think. "Another amazing thing is that I said a couple of really stupid things—I mean really stupid—and he just smiled." Her lip trembled. "When I said how stupid it was— what I said—he just said, 'Well, we all do or say silly things sometimes. Innocent things can come out all wrong.'"

Hot chocolate appeared, and Janice paused. "Who is *he?* Sounds like a keeper."

"Just a guy I went out with. It was so weird. Great, but weird… I tried to make him understand, but—"

"Make him understand what? He sounds like a good date."

Carlie nodded. "That's what I was telling Dean. I told Jared that, too. I told him how awe—"

Janice nodded, smiled, and hurried off to help another customer.

"—some the date was. But he kept trying to convince me that it was just normal." Carlie sipped at her chocolate as she remembered Jared's words. "I don't understand."

With that, her eyes rose, met Dean's, and held them. His opinion proved easy to read. *You think it's normal, too. It's not normal to me.* She didn't move her eyes. *Okay, maybe it is normal, or maybe you're just being nice. After all, you really didn't like Blaine.* Another thought formed. *Not even my family treats me like Jared does.*

Their plates arrived before she could say any more. She tore bites of spinach bread and dropped them into the bowl as she ate. Dean's movements mirrored hers. Then, as if she hadn't taken a break to inhale half her meal, Carlie said, "The worst part is that it was a great date. I had such a wonderful time with him, but there's nothing there." She felt her lips twist in that way that always made her sister snap at her for being insensitive to something. "I kept trying to feel something, but I couldn't—I can't."

Janice stopped close and whispered, "I think that was because you were out with the wrong guy." Carlie closed her eyes, took a deep breath, and opened them again. At that moment, Dean looked up from his soup, apparently unaware of Janice's words. But the woman's next question definitely sparked interest. "So, are you going out with him again?"

"I know I'd have fun if he asked me out again, but…"

Janice inched away as she asked, "But what?"

"I just know I won't be disappointed if he doesn't." She gripped the spoon with excess force and tried to fill it with the creamy soup. Once Janice was out of earshot she added, "I've already had that—a lot. If I'm going to *be* with a guy again, I want to be with someone I *want* to go out with. Does that even make sense?"

Her jaw hung open as Dean met her gaze and nodded. *I don't know or understand. Dean has no personal investment here. Jared might think that being modest is spiritual or a way to get me to think he's great, but Dean…*

Lost in thought, she stared at her bowl and tried to reason through the turmoil in her heart. *Why can't I just like Jared?* That prompted a new question. "Do you think it's wrong to go out with someone knowing you aren't interested now but hoping that it might change?"

It took several seconds for her to look up, but this time Dean's head didn't move. He just gazed at her. His expression: inconclusive. "You're a lot of help."

He laughed, and that laughter relaxed her.

Ten minutes later, she sat munching on her spinach bread and lost in a world of intrigue, courtesy of her smartphone and a favorite author. Her foot slid up and down the pole that supported the table as the main character crept through a dark alleyway. Just as headlights flashed against the woman's face, Carlie hooked her foot around the pole and braced herself. The pole moved. Her eyes widened, and she forced herself to look at Dean. He sat, smirking at her and visibly resisting the urge to laugh.

Oh, God, why? Why would you let me—oh, this is mortifying! "Um…" She jumped up, grabbed her purse, phone, and coat and fled. "Bye!"

Late Friday afternoon, Dean sat in his office going over some of the papers from his online classes and enjoying the "deadness" that Friday afternoons brought to campus. His Friday night poker game had been rescheduled for Saturday, so he took his time, allowing email and a few text messages from his mother to interrupt the flow of his work.

A knock interrupted his quest to play all seven letters in a game of online Scrabble against his stepfather. "Oh! Gabby. Did we have an appointment?"

"No, I had one with Dr. Lovelace and thought I'd see if you were in. I finally chose a topic for my research paper and wondered if you'd take a look and see if you notice any pitfalls."

"Come in, come in. Your 'finally' amuses me. As much as you may consider yourself a procrastinator, as far as I know, only one other from your class has narrowed down a topic. Two weeks before the end of the semester, you will see a line of students out that door and down the corridor waiting for their turn to beg for help because they chose poor topics and didn't get my input."

"Then I rephrase." She slid the single paper across his desk and pulled up the chair. "This is my chosen topic—the poetry of prophesy."

Dean tried not to let his excitement show. He pulled the sheet closer and read. "I like this. While it is implied, I'd state directly that you mean messianic prophesies."

Gabby reached for her paper, and the brush of her fingers against his hand nearly drove him to distraction. *Do not forget that she is your student.*

"So… why is the professor who is half the school's crush sitting alone grading papers on a Friday night? Inquiring minds want to know, and I was delegated the inquisitor."

"Do I get strapped to the rack if I don't answer to everyone's satisfaction?" She hesitated, and in that hesitation, he saw the reason. *Is she second-guessing the appropriateness of her teasing me, or the joke itself? It must be one or the other.*

"I don't think anyone would accuse you of being 'on the rack,' but to say you're 'off the rack' is equally incorrect. I leave the answer to you."

Flirting. That was overt flirting and yet it wasn't. Well played, Ms. Marceanu. His conscience warned him to stay out of murky waters, but Dean found himself wading in. "I agree that grading papers on a Friday night isn't all it's *racked* up to be, but…"

"Ooooh… bad one—really smelly-socks-bad-one." Gabby folded the paper and stuffed it in her backpack. "C'mon, I need more than that, though. If I go out there with, 'He's just sitting in there making punny jokes,' no one is going to believe me."

"Well, this week it's true. Our poker game was postponed until tomorrow night, so—"

"Wait—wait. So, what you're telling me is that the most eligible professor in Rockland first was going to spend his Friday night playing *poker* with a bunch of guys—"

Dean interrupted. "Almost evenly split between men and women—charity poker. We gamble freely, but the pot goes to the winner's charity of choice."

"Cool. But now your Saturday night is ruined, too? You'll have girls weeping into their facial masks all night long." There was a moment of hesitation—so brief he almost missed it—before she said, "You know, if there weren't rules against it, you'd have a couple dozen invites to dinner or a movie instead of a couple dozen papers to read on the influence of Song of Solomon on modern romance."

"That isn't an assignment I've ever considered giving." He leaned forward. "And what would your conclusion be?"

"Considering we haven't dissected the Song of Songs, I can't say. I suspect I'd compare modern sensuality in prose and poetry with eastern poetry—possibly taking in his vast personal experience with almost a myriad of women." She frowned. "No, that's ten thousand. I was thinking one."

"That you knew the difference is enough to make any professor's—" He choked back the words *heart pound* and said, "—impressed."

"Right…" She rose and backed slowly toward the door. "I'll go break a few dozen hearts now. Friday night with papers. Saturday night with cards and chips. One can only imagine the heart-fluttering things you'll do on Sunday…"

Dean stared down at the paper before him and let his mind think what he'd never allow himself to say. *If I'm not careful, it will be spent devising ways to become better acquainted with you once you are no longer one of my students.*

That thought drove him to pick up his phone. "Hello, Larry? Yes. Do you have time for a visit? I think I just flirted with a student."

"You think?"

"Fine," he grumbled. "I know I did. Help."

The rest of Wednesday and all day on Thursday and Friday, Carlie considered Dean's eloquent silence on the topic of her date with Jared. By the time she arrived home from work on Friday, she found herself curled up on the couch with a bowl of tomato soup and a grilled cheese sandwich—the ultimate in comfort food—and waiting for their date.

"I sure hope I made the right decision. Seems like one date isn't really enough to know, though." She took another bite of her sandwich and sighed. "Smart guy, too—not doing dinner first. Then it's not such a big deal. I like Jared."

She stared at the kitten at her feet. "Why can't I *like* him? Or can I? Maybe attraction can come later? I mean the deeper stuff. I'm superficially attracted to him, but that's not enough for more than a fun date. He just doesn't seem like the 'just a fun date' kind of guy."

A sigh escaped as she loaded her spoon with more soup and slurped it with the abandon of a child. "And I know better than to try to get serious. That means all kinds of trouble."

Pouncer played with a dangling thread from her sock, while Moros looked on with what could only be seen as a parental eye. Outside, snow fell in soft flakes—the kind that would last only until wind or rain drove it away. "Moros, what do you think? Are Dean and Jared just trying to get me to be pickier about who I go out with, or are they right?" The answer seemed ridiculously obvious. "No, they're just being nice. I mean, c'mon! Even my own brother says I'm pathetic and funny looking."

After dinner, Carlie unfolded herself from the couch and went to put on the outfit she'd already chosen. "He'll like it. I think he'd like it if I wore a gunny sack. The guy has issues."

The doorbell rang as she considered whether the question was that of a male versus female opinion, or if people outside her family could be more objective. *Or both,* she mused as she hurried to open it. "Hey, Jared! Come in. I haven't finished brushing my hair—took too long eating dinner."

Jared stepped into the room and nodded at the coffee table. "Tomato soup and grilled cheese?"

"How did you guess?"

"Favorite meal when I was ten. Now I just save it for nights like this—smart move." He gave her an appreciative smile and said, "You look great—as usual. But still…" He winked. "So, how's your week been?"

"Good… really good, actually. Well, aside from mortifying myself on Wednesday, anyway."

Jared's laughter and the way he smiled at her should have sent butterflies fluttering through her heart. It only made her feel even more foolish. "C'mon, you've got to spill it now. And then I'll tell you how I was so lost in my book that I sat on a woman on the subway—completely missed the seat I was going for and landed right on her lap."

"Oooh! That—" she choked, "that is so funny—and kind of like me. I was just sitting in the booth with Dean, reading my book, and my foot…" Carlie flushed again, just at the thought. "I was rubbing my foot on what I thought was the table pedestal—that metal pole down the middle, you know? Then the scene got all tense and I hooked it to brace myself…"

"This is gonna be good."

"You guessed it. The 'pedestal' moved. Dean was just sitting there trying not to laugh at me. I bolted."

Silence—well, mostly silence—preceded a quiet question. Jared leaned against the back of her couch and folded his arms over his chest. "Why leave? Anyone could have done it. I doubt he was offended."

"No, but it was embarrassing! I mean, even *Dean* was laughing at me." Just the memory of it made her want to crawl into a hole. *Why did I tell him about this again? It's like I can't keep my mouth shut. I'm always making myself look stupid.*

Jared chuckled again, and Carlie nearly threw a couch pillow at him in frustration. "Carlie, he was laughing *with* you. You don't think he was embarrassed with you? A gorgeous girl is playing footsie with him in a restaurant—without even realizing it. It's just one of those things that happens."

Several failed attempts to reply ended in a stammered. "I—well—yeah."

Taking pity on her, Jared reached for her coat. "You ready?"

Just she opened the door, Carlie shut it again. She searched his face for a moment—for what, she didn't quite know—and then asked, "Why did you ask me out again?"

"Why wouldn't I? I like you. I have fun with you. You're nice to be around." Jared reached for the doorknob again as he added, "And who knows, something might come of it."

Jared's words clouded their conversation all the way to the cinema. They jerked her from the story half a dozen times as she watched the movie. They taunted her as he drove her home. Several times she started to say something, but Carlie didn't quite trust herself anymore. *This was fun, but still—nothing. What do I do? If I keep going out with him, I'm no better than Blaine. And they think Blaine is awful.*

That thought sent her into a panicked interruption of Jared's story about a little boy who shared his ice cream with a homeless man. "I think you should know..." Carlie chewed her lip.

"I should know..."

"It's coming out all blunt and rude, but I can't stop thinking about what you said."

Jared pulled into a parking lot and parked the car before asking, "What did I say?"

"That you asked me out again because 'something might come of it.'"

"Oh."

Jared's silence and awkwardness nearly stopped her, but Carlie couldn't let it happen. "I just think you should know that I don't really think anything *will* come of whatever this is. I mean, I like you!" She added with almost excessive haste. "I have a lot of fun with you, and I like to spend time with you, buuuut..."

"Just tell me, Carlie. It's okay."

"It's just that I don't have the 'Can't wait to go out with you again' thing." She hesitated, wondering if saying more would be wise, and then added, "Although, I was happy when you asked. I don't even know what that means. But I just needed to be honest with you. So, if you're expecting... *more*...I think you should know that I don't think it'll happen."

Jared put the car in reverse and backed out of the parking spot. Though he didn't speak until they were a block down the road, Carlie sensed that everything would be okay. *His pride is hurt, I think. It seems like it. But he's not seething over there. His ego is still intact. Or maybe it's not his pride but his feelings. Maybe he does care a little more than he thought.* The idea that she might be letting him down harder than she'd expected hurt. Carlie almost asked if he was willing to go out again—to see if maybe she just wasn't ready after her breakup with Blaine—but Jared spoke first.

"You know what? That was just a really good let down." He glanced at her with a wry smirk. "That sounds weird, huh? But it's true. You're really good at telling people the truth without hurting their feelings or embarrassing them." He reached over and squeezed her hand. "I just thought you should know that."

He kissed her cheek at her door and turned to go, but seconds after she closed it behind him and hooked the chain in place, he knocked. "Carlie?"

Steeling herself against the awkwardness she expected to follow, Carlie twisted the knob and jerked it. The chain rattled in its place. "Oh, duh. Sorry. Stupid—"

"Stop it. Easy mistake that we all make. Doesn't reflect on our intelligence or our common sense. It's just something that happens." As she relaxed, he added, "I might ask you out again sometime—maybe in two months, maybe in six. I'm not sure. I want to be a friend, regardless."

"In my experience, guys can't be 'just' friends with girls." The words erupted from her before she could stop them.

"Then maybe I won't ask you out again." Jared grinned at the look of incredulity she leveled on him. "I want to prove to you that it *can* be done. So, let's put it this way. You ask me. Even if it's just for someone to have fun with on a weekend or even weeknight. If you want to go out for any reason, you ask me—or at least give me a strong hint that you'd like me to ask you. Meanwhile, stop stressing about it."

Incredulity morphed into shock. "How'd you—"

"You're a lot more readable than you think. Just enjoy life. That's all you need to do. Enjoy life." With a quick wave, he turned and disappeared down her hallway.

Carlie grabbed her favorite mini-tub of Ben and Jerry's and curled up on the couch with it. Pouncer arrived seconds later, followed by Moros. She refused to share, citing the animals' health, and then beat herself up for eating what she wouldn't let a cat touch. "You're seriously more pathetic than you thought." Jared's words brought a smile. "Then again, I know how to let a guy down. That's got to be worth something. Maybe I'm not so pathetic after all."

But the words of her siblings, the teasing of her father—they mocked that idea. The thought of how Blaine would have reacted to those same words nearly made her shake with repressed anxiety. Part of her insisted it was him—Blaine's fault, not hers. But Carlie knew better.

With ice cream dribbling down her fingers and pooling into her palm, she stroked Moros with the back of her hand and mused, "But I've had a lot of boyfriends—too many, maybe. None of them would have thanked me for a nice let down. They'd have let me have it for being too stupid to appreciate them. So, either I can't pick a good guy at all—seems statistically improbable, don't you think?" When the cat didn't respond, Carlie sighed. "Or Jared is just really the amazing guy I thought." Moros purred. "Yeah. That's what I thought." She licked the back of her spoon as she mused, "He's probably the most amazing guy I've ever met, and I basically told him to get lost. Well done, Carlie."

The constant clink of glasses and rattle of plates as tables were cleared, combined with the drone of constant conversation and made concentration difficult. The scent of chili, chicken noodle soup, and minestrone mingled as they passed his table. Dean reread the same paragraphs on the same page until he could quote them, but still he had no idea of the quality of the content or if it even was accurate. Once more, he read the words, his lips moving as he whispered them under his breath, and this time he caught the first error. With a pencil, he underlined a few words and scrawled a note in the margin.

"She's late."

Dean looked up at Janice and pulled out his phone. "The store must have had a sale on something irresistible," he murmured. "Would you bring her a lemonade when she arrives? I think the weather is nice enough for something a little lighter for a change."

"You're a good guy, Dean. But you'd be a better one if you'd just give up and ask her out already."

He'd started to read the next sentence, but Janice's words stopped him. "What?"

"C'mon. Anyone can see you're in love with her. So why don't you just ask her out?"

"Perhaps you were unaware, but Carlie has a new boyfriend—a good man this time." He glanced around him before leaning forward and adding, "And as soon as the semester ends, I plan to ask out one of my students."

Janice looked over the tops of the booths as the café doors opened and then back down at him. "You think that, but you're wrong. Anyone in this place will tell you that you know when she enters even without looking. You anticipate her needs, you listen to her troubles, and you bring out something beautiful in her."

"I appreciate that you recognize my attempts to be a good friend to Carlie," Dean began. As he heard the defensiveness in his tone, he tried again. "I truly am. Perhaps you've forgotten something important."

"What's that?"

"I don't talk to her. She knows nothing about me."

This time, Janice snickered. "Yeah. You've fallen for her."

"I just *said*—"

But Janice interrupted him. "Yeah. You said. Who cares? No one said she loved *you*. I just said you—"

The door opened again out front, but before Janice could comment, customers from across the aisle beckoned her. Dean sat there waiting, watching, and disappointed with each shaft of light and cooler air that blew into the restaurant as patrons entered and exited. He sat through the lunch rush and into the afternoon. With one eye on his watch and the other on the paper that he hadn't even glanced at in over an hour, Dean waited, and as he did, he prayed.

Is she coming? Did I not encourage her enough with Jared? Perhaps it was too much? Did she go out again? Perhaps Jared is just another creep? She could be dead somewhere.

That thought brought his internal questioning to an end. *Don't be ridiculous.*

Twice he picked up his phone to call her store. Both times he put it down as he realized they couldn't give out her number if they wanted to. He actually dialed Hannah, but when she answered, Dean only asked how the woman was doing and if she needed anything. Though she assured him that everything was fine, he heard what the woman didn't say and made a note to make sure her utilities and rent were paid. Then, of course, he fought the urge to bang his head on the table for not asking the question he'd called about in the first place. As if a consolation prize, Dean assured himself that if Carlie had wanted him to be able to call her, she would have given him her number.

The longer he waited, watched, prayed, considered—the more curiosity morphed into concern and then true worry. He hated to leave. Each minute that sped toward his afternoon class left him even more ragged emotionally, until he almost felt nauseous at the idea of leaving. At last, he pulled out his business card and handed it to Janice as he dragged himself away from the table. "If she does arrive later for some reason, will you ask her to call me or send me an email—something? Carlie has missed our lunch before, but she told me she would."

"She's probably fine—dentist appointment changed, or maybe she has that flu that's going around."

"That's likely, but I would appreciate the reassurance." At the knowing look she gave him, Dean shook his head. "I'd be equally concerned if you hadn't arrived for your scheduled shift."

"You think that if it makes you feel better."

The keynote speaker ended his session with a call for believers to hold fast to Scriptural authority in their lives. A round of applause filled the auditorium, but Dean sat staring at an empty notebook—not a single word written on the page. Others around him stood, and a man asked to pass. Dean looked up. "Oh, I apologize."

"Good session, wasn't it?"

"Yes—no—I don't know." He stood and shuffled out behind the others. Once in the main aisle, he wove his way in and out of other conference attendees and into the lobby. The elevator began to close just as he neared it, and Dean leapt forward, catching it just before the doors shut. He squeezed in and apologized to the confused group in the car.

In his room, he stripped out of his slacks, shirt, tie, and jacket and pulled on gym clothes. A Facetime message from his mother appeared, but he ignored it. Dean set his phone on the dresser, grabbed his trainers, card key, and a bottle of water and left the room. *Mim and Facetime with me in gym clothes equals relational disaster. Must remember to call before I go down to dinner.*

After a few stretches, Dean jumped on the elliptical and tried to work himself into mental oblivion. Blood coursed through his veins. Perspiration poured down his temples and soaked his shirt. But the turmoil in his mind and heart did not respond to his numbing techniques. His mind zipped in a dozen directions, his heart heavier than ever. *Only a run will help,* he finally admitted to himself. And with that thought, he allowed the elliptical to rock to a stop before stepping off and moving to the treadmill.

The fitness room door opened as he began a brisk walk. A familiar voice—one that usually he looked forward to—asked a question Dean didn't know how to answer. "Hey, Dean. What's wrong?"

"Wrong? I don't understand" He kicked up the pace a notch. Thirty seconds later, he added another couple of bumps of speed and began jogging—slow, but steady.

"You've been brooding all weekend. What's up?"

Brooding? What does he mean? Dean just shrugged. "Don't. know. didn't. realize. I. was—" He exaggerated his breathlessness as his feet pounded the treadmill.

"Come off it, bro. You're talking to *me* here—which alone makes me feel a bit better. At least you're talking. You've hardly said more than 'excuse me' all weekend."

"Ex—huh?"

Nate Lanski stepped onto the treadmill next to his and leaned against the handrails. "You're kidding me, right?"

To Dean's credit, he tried. His mind attempted to scan the events of the weekend, but only a blurry, blank canvas appeared. "I apologize, Nate. I don't understand."

"The life of the party is dead. How about that? So, what's wrong?" Before Dean could open his mouth to answer, Nate punched the on button and began walking. "And don't even pretend that it's nothing, because I know you too well. Something's off. Tell me about it. Let's work it out."

There's nothing to say? How can I possibly explain? Should I mortify myself and say, "My weekly lunch date didn't arrive this week, nor did she inform me she wouldn't be there. Now, I am worried and confused." That? I don't think so! But despite rational *thought,* Dean's mouth assumed a mind of its own and spilled everything. "I feel foolish even discussing it, Nate." When Nate didn't respond, he continued. "I have a… lunch buddy. We've eaten together every week since October? September? I can't recall."

"Yeah…"

"She never arrived this Wednesday."

"So, you're all worked—wait. She?" Nate hit the red stop button and nearly walked into the control panel. "*She?* Your lunch 'buddy' is a *she* and you are just now telling me about her? Whoa…"

"It's just lunch, Nate. Just lunch."

But Nate knew how to get to the core of the issue. "And who pays for that lunch?"

Dean hesitated before saying, "If she leaves first, she does." The memory of Carlie bolting from the restaurant after sliding her foot up and down his calf forced him to add, "—usually." That image blasted his memory again, and this time he groaned. "Oh, no. I may know why she didn't come. Why didn't I think of it?"

At Nate's urging, Dean told all—his silence during their lunches and the reason for it; what he'd learned about himself in the process; how she shared her life, her struggles, and her relationships with him; and even his trip to Morganfield. "Perhaps if I hadn't urged her—"

"Without talking, no less. Man, you can persuade anyone to any-thing. You just proved it. It's not your eloquence—fabulous as that is," he insisted. "It's *you.*"

"Her relationship with Blaine was… unfortunate. Toxic. I ex-pected to have to put myself between them to keep him from assaulting her. The revolting and cruel things he said." Dean punched off the treadmill and tripped the handrails. "Nate, she responds as if that kind of ugliness is normal!"

"Mmm… hmm…"

There remained no doubt as to what Nate thought of the whole thing. *He's another Janice—or Larry. It's as if a man cannot have a female friend anymore without people making rash assumptions. I am interested in* Gabby! In an attempt not to be defensive, Dean homed in on the facts. "Nate, she's dating someone new, and from what I've seen of him, Jared will be good for her." Honesty demanded he add, "However, she seems uncertain. I don't think she knows how to appreciate someone who treats her as a person instead of an object."

"You know, Dean…" Nate lay back on a bench and began doing sit ups. "You don't talk like someone who is glad she's got a guy who is 'good for her' in her life. You talk like someone who doesn't *want* her to go out with this guy."

"What? I don't—"

But Nate interrupted before he could protest further. "Look, you are bothered by her not coming this week—not just curious—bothered. For someone who is 'just a lunch buddy' you're actually *worried* about her. Are you *sure* you're not more personally invested in this woman than you think? I know you. You haven't exactly had a lot of experience with women."

"That is flattering," he joked, trying desperately to hide his chagrin. A new idea occurred to him, and Dean ran with it. "Look, Nate. I shared the kind of man her ex-boyfriend is. She begins dating someone new and then doesn't arrive for our lunch. This man has threatened her in my presence—for eating lunch with me. While I don't think he has physically harmed her yet, I am not confident he never would. So, yes. I am concerned." He looked up and smiled at his friend. "Thanks, Nate. I think your questions helped me discover my true concern. Perhaps I *will* call Hannah Pierce."

"What? Another woman? Are you kidding me? I've never seen you with anyone, and now two?"

He almost missed Nate's joke. But he covered himself just in time. "Let's not be overly optimistic. We both know I'd never survive two."

Dean mopped up the lingering perspiration from his neck and dropped the towel in the bin by the door. "I'll meet you downstairs for dinner, and thanks again."

"Sure—but, Dean?"

"Yes?"

Silence hung between them before Nate sat up and spun around on the bench. "You remind me a little bit of that guy in some play Shakespeare wrote—the one where he says, 'he doth protest too much, methinks.' Think about it."

He did. All the way to his room, throughout his shower, and then down to the banquet hall, Dean mulled his friend's words. And though complete impartiality might be impossible, he convinced himself that anyone might see the situation the same as Nate had—from the outside. But they couldn't see his heart—couldn't know that friendship alone and concern for Carlie's safety drove his thoughts. *This is all about Blaine. Had I realized that before I left, I would have found her to reassure myself of her safety. I can do that this week if she doesn't arrive. She has other friends—people who would report her missing if Blaine became dangerous.*

But Sunday morning, as he rolled his suitcase toward the lobby desk, he overheard someone say his name. With a pillar blocking the group from his line of sight—hiding him from the others as well—he listened as they spoke. "—not himself. I'm worried about him."

"Yeah. Nate said he'd talk to Dean, but I think it just made everything worse." Dean recognized the voice as that of a colleague from Rockland. "He was weird this week at work, too. One of his students complained that they couldn't follow him in class on Wednesday. *That* never happens—not with Dean."

Someone else spoke up—a low female voice that he recognized as that of one of the women on his dissertation committee. "There's been a silver lining in it, I have to say. We have had a reprieve from his know-it-all-ness."

Quiet laughter rippled through the group, reached his heart, and squeezed it. *I knew—but I didn't. I seriously need to take James to heart—the whole "slow to speak" part in particular. I think I'm a walking example of Lincoln's twist of Proverbs. I have "removed all doubt" from people's minds. They do think I'm a fool.*

A younger voice that belonged to a grad student, if Dean identified it correctly, spoke up and soothed his pride a little. "—but I kind of miss the knowledge. The guy knows everything. He's smart. I miss that, I just don't miss the nonstop verbiage."

Dean froze—his heart racing and perspiration beading on his forehead and upper lip. The suitcase slipped from his hand as he heard the woman from his dissertation committee say, "Dean acts a little like my brother did when he found out his ex-girlfriend was going out with another guy. Does anyone know if he has a girlfriend? Maybe they had a fight."

At that moment, for the first time, Dean wondered if his "platonic" friendship didn't mean more to him than he'd realized.

Fidgeting, jumpy, unsettled. Dean sat in the booth, hands clasped together, waiting. Twice Janice commented on the dark circles under his eyes and the way he jumped at every sound. She'd brought him coffee at first, but after his second cup, she switched to chamomile tea and a loaf of sourdough bread with honey butter. "Eat up. It'll settle your nerves."

"She's late." His eyes met hers. "Again."

"No... you're crazy early. She won't be here for at least another half hour. Why don't you correct some papers or something to keep your mind off it?"

Dean shook his head and stared into his cup. *I often see Carlie's reflection in hers. Odd how I never realized that until now.*

"Come on. Those students need to know whatever it is you teach them."

"I didn't assign a paper last week. I was a bit out of it."

Janice sank down into the booth and stared at him. "Now, look, I won't pretend that I don't think you assign way too many papers, but, c'mon! It's who you are. Snap out of it!"

"The papers are a way of breaking their final papers into manageable snippets. They combine it all at the end and flesh it out."

"So why didn't you assign one last week?"

He fidgeted again, his fingers nearly shredding his napkin. "Wasn't concentrating. I was worried about Carlie."

"Worried? About her? Why!"

Dean shoved the napkin aside and took a long drink of his tea.

"Blaine—the ex-boyfriend. He might have hurt her. She might not return if it happened and she became embarrassed. We'd never know."

"So, why didn't you just go down to her store and see?"

Movement from the corner of the room, combined with Janice jumping out of the booth, hinted that Frank wanted her to work. "My 'it's none of my business side' trumped my nosy side."

"Well, she'll be here soon, you'll see she's okay, and you guys can go back to your bizarre flirtation."

Dean, weary from concern and still worried, didn't even try to argue the insinuation. Instead, he prayed—beseeching the Lord for every bit of wisdom he could squeeze from the Almighty. He questioned every thought, every discussion, every conclusion. He buried himself so deeply in prayer that he jumped when Carlie breezed in, dumped her coat on the bench and dropped to the seat.

"Hi!"

His eyes searched her face for any sign of turmoil or injury. But she seemed fine—happy even. *Perhaps the second date with Jared was so perfect that they eloped.* Despite the foolishness of the thought, Dean couldn't help but glance at her left hand. *No ring.*

"Hey, sorry I wasn't here last week. I was *so* sick. I mean, down-for-the-count, dead sick." She gave him an apologetic smile. "I meant to call when they opened—you know, let you know I couldn't make it so you wouldn't wonder, but I slept through. Then I thought about calling the seminary, but I decided that was kind of stupid. 'Hey, I have lunch with one of your professors every week and I can't come this week. I'm sick. So can you give him my excuse?'"

While Dean allowed himself a moment of grateful relaxation, Janice appeared. "Glad to see you. This one's been worried sick about you. I think he had decided that jerk of an ex-boyfriend of yours murdered you or kidnapped you to some god-forsaken place. Tea or coffee?"

"Coke?"

"Coke it is." Janice patted Dean's shoulder. "You can have coffee again if you want it." At his nod, she took the cup and hurried off.

Carlie leaned forward and squeezed his hand. "Sorry. I should have called—or emailed. I thought of that last night. Your email is on the school website, surely. I could have done that. I just didn't think of it." She rambled about how sick she'd been, how fast it came and went, and about her date with Jared. "It was nice again—really. But I don't see us having a real relationship. Oh, and get this. He said I was really good at letting a guy down." Carlie rolled her eyes and winked. "What a talent to have, right?"

She reached for the menu, but Dean wrapped his hand around

hers. As her eyes met his, he swallowed hard, ordered his heart to slow to a reasonable beat, and asked, "Will you go out with me?"

He'd expected her to be surprised, hoped for happy. But her utterly flabbergasted response worked as well. In fact, he found it somewhat charming and delightful. Her eyes lit up and, for a moment, he actually thought she'd squeal. However, just as quickly, emotion vanished from her face. She gazed at him, not moving her hand or engaging at all. Carlie swallowed twice and nodded. "Yeah. I'd like that."

Her calm, cool demeanor unsettled him again. Determined not to give up now, Dean smiled. "Thank you. Would Friday suit? I have a commitment on Saturday night, but Sunday..."

"Friday night is good."

There it was again—a flicker of something, but what? Dean couldn't decide. Carlie still sat there, her arm outstretched across the table, her hand and wrist covered by his. Something about it seemed off to Dean, but he couldn't decide what. *Focus. You must focus.* With a mini-pep talk behind him, Dean tried again. "Would you like me to pick you up, or perhaps I should meet you somewhere? What suits you best?"

Janice appeared with drinks and grinned at the sight of Dean essentially holding Carlie's hand. "Well, it's about time. What'll you guys have?"

"Bring me whatever you want, Janice."

Carlie nodded. "Me, too." She beckoned for Janice to come closer and whispered something.

"Double that—it's *really* about time. And here I thought he was just worried about your ex." As Janice hurried off, Dean almost groaned. *The entire restaurant will know inside five minutes.*

"—at work."

Dean blinked. "Pardon me, what did you say?"

"Why don't you just pick me up at work? I take the subway, so if you could take me home after..."

"Excellent."

Carlie slowly sat back and folded both hands in her lap. At that moment, Dean felt the change. *Her hand. I was still holding it. Ugh. Well, not ugh—no, no. Focus.*

"What do I wear?"

"Huh?"

She picked at her sleeve. "On this date. What do I wear? Dressy or casual? Something in between?" She gave him a smile that sent his heart into overdrive. "I have to keep you talking while I can, you know. I had decided you would *never* do that."

At that moment, Dean realized that he'd only thought through *asking* her out. He hadn't actually decided what to do or where. "What would you enjoy? Would you prefer to dress up or down? Would casual be best since you'll be at work, or..."

Her hesitation lasted longer than he'd expected. In fact, Dean began to be concerned that she might change her mind. But before he could suggest options, she grabbed her Coke, took a sip, and blurted out, "I want to dress up. I don't get to do that very much, so if you're okay with it—"

"Delighted. What time is your shift over?"

This time, she relaxed a little. "Six. Give me until six-thirty though. I'll have to change."

Two Turkish wrap plates and bowls of red lentil soup arrived before Dean could reply. Janice winked at Carlie and said, "This meal started it, if I remember right. Seemed perfect."

Dean had expected to talk—to try to interact a little—but he found himself eating, listening to her describe the crazy morning at work, tell about her cats' latest antics, and bemoan the state of her credit card. *I wonder if I'll think those cats are as funny as she describes.*

His phone buzzed just as he was about to ask a question. Dean glanced at it and sighed. "A colleague needs me to take his class in..." He glanced at his watch. "Twenty minutes. I must leave now, or I'll be late. I'll see you Friday?"

Carlie nodded. "Six-thirty."

"I'll be there."

Outside, as he fumbled for his keys, Dean stopped short. "But did she *want* to accept? She was uncharacteristically mellow. Then again, she did appear to be excited—for a moment."

A woman passed him, giving him a wide berth, as if a man talking to himself as he patted his pockets somehow meant danger.

"Who cares?" he muttered to himself as he slid behind the steering wheel. Dean pulled out his phone and sent a three worded message to his stepfather. SHE SAID YES.

Carlie burst into her apartment, tossed her keys into her purse and dumped it all on her couch. She grabbed salad fixings from the fridge and dumped them on the counter. While she worked, she pulled out her phone and dialed Teresa. "Hey! I've got news!"

"I—"

"You will not believe what happened at the restaurant today." Carlie tore lettuce into shreds as she spoke. Teresa tried to talk, but once Carlie got going, she couldn't stop. "So, I get there today, and I should have been prepared for something. I mean, Janice kept hinting that he was worried about me—"

"Why?"

The tomato slipped from her fingers and flung itself across the counter and into the sink. She hesitated as she tried to decide if it was worth it to dig out another one or if she should just skip it. "Well, I was so sick last week. I didn't go, remember?"

"That's right. You were going to call him at the seminary, though." Teresa mumbled ingredients under her breath for a second. "I take it you didn't?"

"No. I decided that was kind of weird. But then I realized that I could have sent an email to his work—too late, of course."

"Of course."

Carlie slid Pouncer out of her way with her foot and reached into the fridge for a replacement tomato. "Right. Well, so I get there, and I'm telling him about this stuff—like about my date with Jared. Everything. But I'm hungry, right? So I reach for the menu and he grabbed my hand."

"Nice grab like..." Teresa's voice took on a falsetto as she sang a line from the Beetles' "I Wanna Hold Your Hand." After a giggle she added, "Or was it more of a Hannibal Lecter kind of thing?"

"You tell me. He just looked at me—"

"Which is all he ever does. Definitely Lecter."

Carlie laughed. "Yeah, well, this time he spoke."

"What! Shut whatever the phrase is this week. Front door, back door, phone box spaceship—who cares! Spill it!"

"I'm trying, but *someone* keeps interrupting me. So, anyway," Carlie tossed everything into her bowl, grabbed a bottle of salad dressing, and carried it to the couch. "He said, 'Will you go out with me?'" She squealed. "I mean, I was so excited, which totally shocked me. I mean, I guess it shouldn't have. I go every week. It only makes sense that I'd be interested, you know? But it just didn't translate."

A voice—the last one Carlie wanted to hear at that particular moment—broke through the airwaves. "Tell me you said no and left. I *told* you this guy was creepy! Besides, you can do better than him. He's no different from Blaine—just a different kind of abuse."

Teresa's voice broke in, sounding as indignant as Carlie felt. "When did you get here?"

"Well, you didn't open the door..."

So, that explains the lack of warning. Rhonda probably walked in without even trying to knock—again, and Teresa obviously had me on speakerphone.

"Carlie!"

Jerked from her thoughts, Carlie stammered, "Sorry, what?"

"I *said,* I disagree with Rhonda. I think it's great. I always wanted you to go out with him—just to see what you thought. I mean, if you did, surely, he'd talk, you know? And *he* asked *you!* That's even better. You know he's not feeling obligated or anything."

"I know, right?"

Rhonda's protest gave Carlie an excuse to get off the phone. "Hey, I know Rhonda's there. I don't want to cut into your time with her. I just wanted to tell you. I'll call on Saturday and update you."

"You better! Talk to you then. Call Friday if it's before midnight. I'll wait up." With that, Teresa disconnected the call, and Carlie speared her salad with her fork.

A purring cat hopped up next to her. Carlie used her toe to scratch behind Moros's ear and said, "At least you can be happy for me. Rhonda is never happy unless she's trying to make someone else miserable." For a moment, she had a crazy temptation to call Jared and see what he thought, but she resisted. "Seriously, cat. It's like I lost my mind when he spoke or something!"

Dean circled the block for fifteen minutes before a space became available near the entrance to Carlie's store. The waiting game began. With one eye on his watch and another on the door, he continued the running pep talk he'd engaged in since leaving the restaurant Wednesday afternoon. "Don't monopolize the conversation. Encourage and facilitate *her* conversation. People enjoy talking about themselves."

Things he'd always wanted to say to her bombarded his thoughts. *But she needs to know that she's an amazing woman—beautiful, intelligent, caring. Blaine didn't tell her that. Jared did, but she didn't listen. If I tell her, perhaps she'll begin to see it as truth.*

The side of him that was determined *not* to blow it demanded that he take it slower. "I'm not required to say everything at once. Slow. Steady." He inhaled deeply and exhaled in one long, slow breath. "Listen, Cecil Dean Sager—" Those words prompted a groan. "Lord, opening up to a woman may be a mistake. I'll be forced to admit my full name *sometime*, and we both know what happened last time I did that. A name change would have been advisable."

His watch distracted Dean from his prayerful aside. "It's time." He hurried from the car, locked it, and strode toward the store. His tie, his jacket, his coat—he adjusted each item with infinite care until he reached the entrance and pushed open the door.

A woman in her forties—or sixties, if she spent what his mother did on youth creams and cosmetic surgery—greeted him with the warmth and affability that makes for a good saleswoman. "How are you today? Nice weather for this time of year, isn't it? Can I help you with something, or would you like to browse?"

"Thank you, but I'm here to pick up—"

A cry from the corner of the store arrested both Dean's and the older woman's attention. "You—you're *him!* I think she's convinced you won't show up. Hang on. I'll get Carlie."

The woman's eyes took him in—assessing him, he assumed—and she gave a short nod. "You look okay, but Carlie is probably the best girl I've ever had. If you're another Blech, you can just leave now before she gets hurt again."

But Dean didn't reply. Carlie stepped out, coat over one arm, and his heart lodged in his throat. *I thought she was beautiful—but she's truly exquisite.* "Hello...are you ready?" As he led her to the door, Dean turned and assured the woman, "It won't happen if I can prevent it."

Carlie's eyes slid back and forth for a second before asking, "What won't?"

"Oh, get out of here. Liz is just getting all maternal on us. Have fun. Call me!"

He offered to help her into her coat, but Carlie hesitated. "How far is your car?"

Dean pointed. "Right there."

"Oh! Wow, great car. Sixties?"

Despite ordering himself not to rhapsodize about his classic Mercedes, Dean couldn't help but correct her. "It's a '53. Graduation gift."

"High school?" Carlie pushed open the door and crossed the sidewalk in seconds. "Nice..."

"Grad school," he answered as he opened the door.

Dean jogged around to his side of the car, and as he did, gave himself a stern lecture. *Listen. Remember "slow to speak." It's* her *time.*

Once he climbed in behind the wheel, Dean turned to Carlie. "Ready? You look amazing." He started to mention that her dress looked like something from his mother's favorite designer but stopped himself just in time.

Carlie didn't seem to notice. "Yep. Thanks. Where are we going?"

"Um—I made reservations at two restaurants—just in case."

"In case... what?"

What had originally seemed like a good idea, now felt excessive. "I first planned for Thai but was concerned it might be too spicy. I then decided to make another reservation at The Stockyard. Which would you prefer?"

When she didn't answer, he gripped the steering wheel and prayed for strength, self-control, and half a chance to prove to himself *and* to Carlie that he wasn't a hopeless case. Just as he started to offer something else—Chinese or even The Fiddleleaf—she sighed. "Whichever you want. I'm good."

His heart sank as he realized she already felt uncomfortable. *We both are! What do I do? I've made a mess of nearly every date I've ever had. But this time it truly matters that things go well.* The memory of his dates with Felicia buoyed his spirits a little. *Those aren't miserable. Perhaps...*

When the silence became unbearable, Dean, in a fit of desperation, said, "Were you aware that Thai food didn't become popular in America until the nineties."

"Really? I don't remember anyone eating Thai until I got to Rockland. Interesting. So, do you eat here often?"

Dean turned onto the street where the restaurant was located and pulled up to the valet ropes. "Whenever my mother requests it. It's the only place she considers authe—" His inner self forced himself to stop. *She isn't interested in stories about your mommy. Ask her about* her *favorite food! That would facilitate rather than dominate the conversation...*

But before he could do it, the valet opened her door and helped Carlie out of the car. Dean stepped out, tossed his keys to the young man, and led her to the restaurant door. As they waited for their table, he sent a text to the other restaurant to cancel their reservation. Carlie stood there, rocking on her heels and fussing with her coat, while Dean tried to think of ways to engage her.

Their server had them in stitches, the food arrived at perfect intervals, the quiet music and soft atmosphere set a perfect stage. Yet, with everything, Dean felt the evening slipping from his grasp. *She's bored. I've already failed. What do I do?*

"So... how is work going? Are your classes as, um... involved... as last time?"

Dean took a sip of his drink, and as he did, took a moment to remind himself not to get too carried away. *Answer the question and then turn it back on her.* "I have excellent students this semester. After some of the awkward momen—yes. So, you mentioned a promotion at work a few months back. How did that go?"

Her face fell. "I didn't apply. I decided I wasn't up for it."

Aaand... you knew that. She told you. Dean's mind argued with her while he sat there unspeaking. *But you are perfect for the position. I believe you have that enviable talent for success at anything you give your full attention to. You only lack confidence.*

As he watched her try to mask her disappointment, Dean's hopes shattered on the floor of his heart. *I finally meet someone, don't recognize how deeply I care about her, and then I destroy all hope of a relationship. This is why I should avoid dating. Even without monopolizing the conversation, it's still a disaster.*

"So, you said you're busy tomorrow—anything you can share or..."

"Moderating a debate on old earth versus young earth in

creationism. Had I been able to decline—"

Carlie shoved her plate back and shook her head. "I wasn't complaining. I just—" Her eyes met his and the exasperation she'd shown dissolved. "Sorry. I..."

His own food no longer looked appetizing either. He tried to think of something—anything, that might salvage the evening—but the look of pure misery on Carlie's face clinched it. *Take her home now before she decides never to return to the restaurant. You can work up to this slowly.*

"Shall we go? I'm sure they'd like the table if you're—"

"Great. Sure. That's really thoughtful of you." Carlie's smile, while genuine, seemed conflicted. They stood outside the restaurant waiting for Dean's car and still, the conversation stagnated.

Why are you so quiet? You appear uncomfortable, yet you talk at the café...

"Oh, here's your car. Nice color. I like the gray. Or is it silver?"

Dean pounced—anything to kill the awkwardness. "I believe the official color was 'Dove Gray.' In full sunlight, it has a warm tone to it—just a hint of brown."

Just as he pulled away from the curb, Dean realized that he couldn't remember if she said she had a car or not. "Should I take you to retrieve your car—?"

"No, you said you'd take me home..." He felt her gaze on him. "I can catch a bus or the subway if you—"

"No, no. I just didn't remember. I am a bit flustered, I—" *Don't discuss it. She might be insulted that she is out with such a dating failure.*

Carlie cleared her throat, shifted, and folded her hands over her purse before adding, "Subway's cheaper on gas—and parking. I don't get free parking at Skyline, so..."

"I would have assumed parking access would be provided. Where do you live?"

Her address discouraged him. The area of town didn't bode well for a safe living environment. While infinitely better than Hannah Pierce's place, Dean still expected a rundown building with a superintendent who cared more about time in front of the TV than a safe and clean place for his tenants. His expectations weren't too far off the mark.

The building loomed ahead just twenty minutes later—twenty minutes in which he'd barely managed to get her to give her opinion on her meal. As he pulled into a parking space, Carlie giggled. "No worries. Your car is safe."

"I—"

"You have a very expressive face when you aren't trying to hide your thoughts." She reached for the door handle, but Dean jumped out. She still waited for him by the time he opened the door for her.

She reads cues so well. I mistakenly assumed I'd learned almost everything about her, but she keeps dropping crumbs.

At her door, Carlie hesitated. "Do you want to come in? I could make us some cocoa…"

Say yes, say yes!!! Just do it! But Dean forced himself to shake his head. "I really shouldn't." He shoved his hands in his coat pockets and gave her a weak smile. "So… would it be possible to convince you to do something with me again? Perhaps Sunday? We could go to the park or…"

His heart sank as Carlie shook her head. "Sunday won't work for me."

"Would next weekend work?" Even as he spoke, Dean knew the chance was slim. *You sound desperate.*

"Yeah… maybe. Can I tell you on Wednesday?"

She wouldn't say Wednesday if she wasn't coming. That's better than, "Get lost, loser." Dean nodded. "I'll look forward to that. I'll see you then." He took a step back, gave her a smile, and waved. "Thank you for your company. It was great." *For me, anyway. You looked like you were trapped in a dentist's waiting room.*

"Wednesday," she agreed. "Thanks for dinner. It was good—delicious."

As the door closed behind her, Dean shoved his hands back in his pockets and shuffled down the hall. He heard her door open, and his heart pounded as Carlie called out to him. Dean waited until he'd reached her door before answering, "Yes?"

"Do you *really* want to go out with me again, or were you just being polite?"

"I absolutely would love to spend more time with you." *Look at me. Doesn't it show?*

Her eyes searched his face as she tried to find something—what, he could only imagine—that would satisfy her. "Look, I've wanted to ask you this all night, but I didn't. I just have to know. Why did you ask me out—why now?"

Dean swallowed hard. "It's difficult to explain—overwhelming."

She crossed her arms over her chest and leaned against the doorjamb. "Try."

Your feistiness is particularly attractive. You—oh…. Dean swallowed hard and attempted to explain himself. "Well, when you were absent last week, it… *unsettled* me. I thought it was—" *Don't ramble.* The moment the thought formed, another followed. *Don't say too much too soon. She'll be unnerved at best.*

"Seriously, Dean. I need you to talk to me, because I can't figure out why you asked, and I'm certainly not going out again if this is your way of trying to make up for Blaine or something."

"Wha—no!" He inched a little closer, his hands itching to touch her face, hold her hand—show her in some way what his heart felt. Instead, he tried to explain—again. Taking a deep breath, he exhaled slowly and said, "When you weren't there, I realized that if I never saw you again, I… I wouldn't be okay with it. The more I thought about it…" *Just say it. She has a right to know.* "Well, I realized that over the past five or so months, I've started falling in love with you."

"Oh!—oh." With a quick nod, she backed into the apartment. "Thanks—you know, for ex—yeah. Thanks. Goodnight." The door shut quietly but firmly in his face.

And that's an end of it. There's no hope now. I tell her I'm in love with her and I get a, "that's nice." She's not interested.

He knocked before he knew what he'd done. Dean stared at his knuckles as if they'd betrayed him. The door opened and he blurted out, "May I give you my number? That way, if you wish to send a text or—"

"Yes! That's great. Genius—brilliant." She reached for something and her purse appeared as she dug through it for her phone. "Just give me a second…"

"I could write it down if you'd prefer. Then if you decide you'd rather I not have your numb—"

"Of course, I don't care if I give it to you." Her hand pulled out the phone. "Got it. Let's have that number…"

Five minutes later, he still sat in his car, staring up at her building and wondering if she'd ever call or send a text. Just as he put the car in gear, the first one arrived. I DON'T KNOW IF I SAID THANKS OR NOT. SO THANKS.

A t the commercial break, Larry punched the pause button. "Are you going to tell me what happened?"

"Mid-game? Since when does Larry Rivers pause basketball to hear about a date?" Dean tried to sound nonchalant and knew he failed.

"Do you really want to play this game?"

Dean couldn't help but pounce. "So, you can watch *your* game?" When he saw it wouldn't work, he sighed. "Obviously it was dismal."

"Obviously."

"However, I don't understand why. We went to Mim's favorite Thai restaurant, I told how beautiful she is, and I didn't monopolize the conversation. It was difficult, but I resisted."

As he described the date, Dean realized afresh just how horrible it had been. Larry listened with that unnerving silence that always meant he would have something to say, and what he said would be spot on— and hard to hear. Dean finished with, "An obvious mistake in hindsight, but I told her I was falling in love with her." His head dropped in his hands. "Foolish, I know, but she asked! I weighed the probability of her preference of honesty over discomfort, and I think I chose the wrong variable." He stared at the floor. "Larry, her response was akin to, 'Oh, wow. Okay. Thanks, bye.'" Hands covering his head, Dean sighed. "I didn't expect her to fling herself at me with utter abandon and joy, but she almost couldn't have been less..." He fumbled for the right word.

"I can tell you exactly why she wasn't enthusiastic about your... *declaration*."

"So amusing," Dean muttered. "*Why?* Tell me. I'm listening with an open mind and a bleeding heart." The moment the words were out of his mouth, he groaned. "My profession's emphasis on poetry is a nightmare. That was—"

"Endearing to the right woman," Larry interjected. "You'll have to tell her about it sometime. She'll enjoy it."

"If I ever have another opportunity. She'll say no to the next date. I'm confident of that point."

Larry leaned back into the couch, hands behind his head, and grinned. "No, she won't. She's going to go. For the same reason she didn't swoon when you *declared* your undying love."

"Not amusing. Tell me!"

Dean nearly threw his Coke bottle in frustration as he waited for Larry to speak. At last, the man said, "I can't believe you can't see it. Look, Dean. This girl—you know all about her, right? She's spilled her whole life to you over the past half-year. You know about her family, her personal life—even her talent for wedding planning. She told you about her cats and the aunt she misses. She told you about her fears, her—"

"Yes, I am aware that I've assumed the role of therapist. So you are implying that she feels it would be unethical for her to date her 'therapist.' Wonderful."

"Very funny. No...the entire time she talked, you listened. Normally, considering your proclivity for verbosity—your words, not mine—that wouldn't be so bad, but you know all about her. She knows nothing about you—nothing."

"Please rephrase in practical terms."

Larry turned off the TV, and dread filled Dean's heart. *The case is hopeless if Larry chooses to ignore the game for a discussion regarding "girls."*

"Look, Dean. She was expecting more from you, and you didn't deliver."

"What was I supposed to *give?*"

"In not dominating the conversation, you gave her a huge gift, okay?" Larry leaned forward, arms resting on his knees and hands clasped before him. "But she doesn't know you were exhibiting self-restraint. From her perspective, you were flat and uninvolved."

His heart sank. "Flat."

"Yes, flat. You gave her nothing. The only reason for her to go out with you would be to get to know you better, but in your attempt at self-control, you left her with nothing. You didn't *let* her get to know you." Dean tried to interject, but Larry talked over him—something his stepfather never did. "You kept your mouth shut, and that effectively shut *her* out—out of *you.*"

200

"Oh. In other words, I'm doomed to failure. I wanted so much to avoid my usual mistakes. It destroys my relationships. Only a few people understand and relate to me. I know this now." He gripped his hands together until they grew cold from repressed circulation. "I didn't want to make the same mistake with her—drive *her* away before we had a chance."

From the corner of his eye, Dean saw Larry nodding. But when Dean finished, he spoke. "You went to the other extreme, son. You didn't talk at all—and at a time when you *needed* to do it. You need balance."

Carlie rounded the corner, and a blast of cool wind rippled her coat and skirt. She shivered and adjusted her purse strap higher on her shoulder. A man smiled as he walked past. "Beautiful day, isn't it?"

Her heart lightened a bit, and she returned his smile as she called back, "It is!"

Nerves still wrestled within her and nearly stretched to the snapping point. With each step that brought her closer to the restaurant, her indecision grew. *To date or not to date: that is the question du jour.*

Why she even wanted to go, Carlie hadn't been able to determine. Her mother and Teresa had both talked her through pros and cons. Not one pro seemed high enough to drown out the cons, and not one con seemed bad enough to give up altogether. Instead, they weighed equally heavy on her heart until she thought she'd go crazy trying to decide. *What's the point? We have more in common when he's not trying to interact with me. I didn't realize he was so horribly shy. Then again, if it's just shyness, he got past it enough to ask me out. Maybe it just takes time…*

Up to the moment she opened the door and stepped into the restaurant, Carlie still couldn't decide what she'd say to him. But when she saw Dean's head bent over his work, her heart fluttered. She stood there, blocking the door, and stared as her thoughts raced through new channels. *I've been looking forward to Wednesdays for months. It's my favorite day of the week, and even after that disaster of a date, I didn't dread today. That's gotta mean something.*

The door opened and a man murmured, "Excuse me."

"Oh, sorry…" She stepped aside, still semi-lost in her thoughts. *I look forward to these lunches more than I ever looked forward to anything with Blaine—more than Jared.* Carlie sucked in air and tried to steady herself as the next thought blasted her mind. *There is something there. That's it. I'm going—wherever he decides we're going. Was it a park? I can't even remember.*

As she strolled to the booth, she shrugged out of her coat and had it ready to hang when she arrived. A smile formed in her heart as she saw Dean stack his papers and shove them in his messenger bag. *At least some things didn't change.*

She tossed her purse into the corner of the booth and slid onto the bench. With her elbows propped on the table, she rested her head in her hands, gazed at him, and grinned. "So… Friday? Saturday? Sunday…? What day are we going, and where are we going? I can't even remember what you invited me to."

The relief in his eyes tugged her heartstrings. "I had suggested the park, but I have a new idea if you're up for a surprise."

"Still casual?"

"Definitely." He pressed his lips together and gripped his hands in front of him. "Carlie, I—"

"Don't worry about it," she hastened to say, but Dean shook his head.

"No, listen. I…" A self-conscious shrug suggested she give him time to talk, but the wait made her fidget with nervous anticipation. "Friday—disaster. I sincerely apologize. It will not happen again."

This time, Carlie didn't know what to say. Pretending it hadn't been miserable would be wrong, but she didn't want to make him feel worse than he obviously did. After a moment, she leaned back against the back of the booth and nodded—nodded and waited. Only then did she realize that he'd made an apology. "I understand, Dean. No apology necessary."

"I doubt that you can understand, but I appreciate that you're willing to. Thank you." He took a steadying breath. "I spoke to my stepfather about it. Larry is so wise. I look forward to introducing you. He's—" Dean took a sip of what must have been lukewarm coffee if the disgusted expression on his face meant anything. "I know I didn't share *me* on Friday. I'm truly sorry about that. My lunches with you have taught me much, and in my attempt to practice what I've learned, I went overboard. Larry showed me that you don't know me the way I know you, and in my attempt not to dominate the conversation—my besetting sin—I left you bereft of any interaction."

What is he talking about? Dominate the conversation? Not hardly. And do I even bother to mention that I have met Larry? She frowned. "Sorry, I'm lost."

"I know—also my responsibility. I am, however, relieved that you're willing to give me another chance. It'll probably take me a while to find a good balance, but I'll improve."

"Get to dominate the conversation? That would have been preferable, but…"

His laughter—never had he let it go like that, and once more, her heart flopped at the sound. "No, that is my usual fault and also why I

202

didn't talk to you that first day" He explained that she'd inspired him to attempt listening as an experiment, and Carlie tried to follow the rambling jumble of words. "You opened up to me in a way that no one ever has before. I assumed it was because I was silent." He gave her a sheepish smile. "I later learned that *listening* was the true secret. What an astounding concept. Listening. Who knew?"

"So you really are a talker?" Carlie gave herself a little shake. "I've heard that, but still having a hard time believing—"

"*I'm* having a hard time believing what I'm seeing."

They both looked up and saw Janice standing there with her order pad and a delighted expression on her face. "You two are *talking!* Like actual conversing talking." She blinked. "That made no sense. Whatever. So the date went well?"

Carlie and Dean shook their heads and said in unison, "Awful."

Janice propped one hand on her hip and glared at them. "Yeah. I don't believe it."

"You should," Carlie insisted. "I didn't know if I'd even go out with him again. It was *that* bad."

"So, why are you? I mean, it sounds like you are…"

Dean grinned. "Yes, Carlie. Why are you?"

Do I answer that? Kind of awkward, but it's less than if we were alone… sort of. Her eyes flitted back and forth until she threw up her hands and said, "Fine! When I saw him, I just realized that I look forward to Wednesdays every week. And I still did—even after that really awkward, never-want-to-repeat-again, sorry excuse for a date." Carlie winked to soften her words.

"Don't hold back, honey. Tell him how you really feel," Janice quipped. She pointed to the menu. "So… do either of you know what you want, or should I come back and let you start planning a do-over?"

"I want the St. Paddy's Day special." Dean grimaced, but Carlie urged him to join her. "C'mon. You don't like corned beef?"

"I do, actually. But…"

"It's tradition," she insisted. "Okay, so it's an *American* St. Patrick's Day tradition. It's not even served in Ireland, you know. But still…"

Dean threw up his hands in mock resignation and nodded. "I'm intrigued about how you know that, but Janice is waiting, so I'll agree only if *you* agree to split a mint shake with me afterward."

Now this is more natural. If— The realization that he hadn't given her a day yet interrupted her thoughts. "What day are we going out again?" She turned to Janice. "Two St. Paddy's specials and a mint shake—hold the shake until we're done eating?"

"Deal."

As Janice walked away, Dean leaned back in the booth and

relaxed, smiling. It was the first time she'd seen him relax since she'd arrived. She started to mention it when he asked, "Which day would *you* prefer?"

All of 'em? Why not? We've got to catch up sometime. As she deliberated, Dean's smile grew larger.

"I warn you. If you delay too long, I may just insist on two—or even three days. Just to teach you a lesson, you understand."

Two can play at that game. Carlie just smiled. After a few seconds she said, "You know, my family is from Ireland. My grandfather came over when he was twenty—from County Donegal. I can't say the name of the place—too Gaelic for me."

"I assume you are aware that I now wish to learn a little Gaelic," he teased. "Inspired by a reference to chocolate dinner and…"

Man, he's cute when he flirts. "That was so funny. You did good on that one." She raised her eyebrows and added, "And I noticed that you ignored the question. I may have to insist on Friday *and* Saturday now."

"I triple-dog-dare you to try for Sunday, too."

Try as she might, she couldn't repress the smile that formed. "Deal. Sunday too. You're going to be sick of me."

Her heart did clumsy flip-flops at the look he gave her when he murmured, "Impossible."

Where she got the courage, Carlie didn't know, but she found herself asking, "You know what you said when I asked why you asked me out?"

Dean's face drained of color. "Yes." The word came out strangled.

"Not trying to make things awkward or put you on the spot. I don't even want to talk about it, really. I just have one question."

His only reply was a tentative nod.

"Did you mean it? How it sounded, I mean." She rolled her eyes and shook her head. "How would you know how it sounded? Forget it. So… where's lunch? I'm famished."

"Carlie?" Dean waited until she looked back at him. "I meant it—and if I said it today, I'd mean it more."

As she changed in a dressing room, Carlie listened to Chandra chatting with a customer. An idea occurred to her, and she zipped a quick text to Dean. MY COWORKER IS CHANDRA. SHOCK HER BY CALLING HER BY NAME. IT'LL BE GREAT.

A moment later, Dean replied. HERE NOW. WILL DO.

Carlie pulled a sweater over her head and strained to hear Dean's voice, but a few seconds later, it reached her quite clearly. "Hello, Chandra. Busy day?"

"Um, hi. Oookay. I lost that bet."

Oh, that was good. C'mon, Chandra. Tell him it wasn't a bet. And his voice—it's amazing. I could listen to him talk all day. She snickered. *Wouldn't that be a role reversal?*

Lost in thought, she almost missed Chandra's reply. "—n't *really* a bet. I just—figure of speech, you know?"

Listen to him apologize for interrupting, she mused as she wiggled into jeans that shouldn't have been as snug as they were. *What's wrong with these things? How embarrassing.* A few squats stretched them out enough to reduce the embarrassment factor. *Okay... fresh powder... a little lipstick...*

Carlie stepped out a couple of minutes later and giggled. "Chandra, look at this guy." She led him over to where the two women stood and gave their customer an apologetic look. "Sorry, but seriously, you have to see this. We're going on a 'casual' date. This is Dean's idea of casual. Chinos, button down shirt, cardigan..." her fingers picked at it. "Boiled *wool* cardigan, no less. That collar—makes me think of a mixture of Richard Gere and C.S. Lewis."

Her stomach did awkward, fumbling somersaults as he asked, "Would that be positive or negative, in your perception?"

Carlie locked her eyes on him, smiled, leaned close, and murmured, "Definitely positive. Tell me you have a cat named Italics, and..." It worked. His eyes lit up and a smile appeared.

But before he could respond, Chandra growled in mock irritation, "Go flirt with him where the rest of us don't have to watch and be jealous," She turned to their customer and sighed. "Sorry, Mona. Let's find you those tops and see which works best for you."

But the woman didn't even try to hide her interest. "Are you kidding? This is the best shopping trip I've ever had—better than afternoon programming any day."

Carlie flushed and tugged Dean's arm. "Let's go before someone calls for cameras to start the 'Dean and Carlie' show."

A degree of trepidation did strike her as she waited for Dean to come around to his side of the car. *Will it be like last week or like Wednesday? Wednesday was fun.* She gave him a sidelong glance as he slid behind the wheel. *And will he flirt...?*

"Are you ready for an adventure?" Dean waited for her nod before turning the key in the engine.

"Yeeesss... but you're making me nervous. What crazy scheme do you have in mind?"

"I suggest sustenance first. I'm famished—a bit too nervous to eat today."

Oh, really? Interesting. Carlie picked at her cuticles as she said, "I went to The Fiddleleaf and ate alone."

At the light, he turned and gave her a curious look. "And how was that?"

"I was bored stiff—and I usually like eating alone. I don't know how you did it before I came." As her words reached her own ears, Carlie choked. "Oh, ugh. That came out wrong."

"You spoke my thoughts perfectly. I've wondered that myself."

When Dean turned into the mall parking lot, Carlie laughed. "You're taking me to the movies, aren't you?" Her laughter turned to giggles as he gave her an inquisitive glance. "You're taking me to a movie—so you won't have to talk. I can't blame you for that."

"Excellent idea," Dean agreed. "But we can both anticipate the result. My usual tendency to excessive speech would take me captive and everyone in the theater would miss the movie in their attempts to silence me."

The food court offered a smorgasbord of culinary delights—corn dogs, pseudo-Mexican food, greasy burgers, hoagie sandwiches—almost two dozen establishments serving nearly as many different cuisines. While Dean munched on a Philly Cheese Steak sandwich, Carlie enjoyed a supreme pizza. They spoke little—observed much.

What does he see when he looks at me? Am I silly and pathetic? Am I oversensitive and stupid? Though her inclination led in those directions, her more rational, intelligent side wouldn't allow her to consider it for long. *No... he can't. He's too smart for that. I mean, he's a professor! He can't be more than thirty-five.* She stared at him and found herself asking, "Just how old are you? How long have you been teaching at Logos?"

"Six years." He gave her a bemused smile before adding, "I'm twenty-eight."

"You—" She frowned. "Grad school at twenty-two?"

Aside from a short shake of the head, Dean didn't answer at first. He finished his sandwich, tossed their trash, and seated himself again, his hands folded in front of him. "Graduated high school at fourteen. Bachelor of Theology at seventeen, Master of Theology at nineteen, and Doctor of Divinity at twenty-four." He sank back against the hard plastic seats and grinned at her confusion. "I began teaching before I got my doctorate, Carlie. And yes," he added with another snicker. "I was a child prodigy. I could pretend it isn't true, but why? Though I'm not very athletic or very handy, I can learn." He stood. "Are you ready? Let's go talk about something less boring than my mother's trophy wall."

"Trophy wall?" Carlie stood, slung her purse over her shoulder and grinned back at him. "Let's go then. If we're not going to a movie, my next guess is an arcade."

"Closer, but no." His eyes slid down to her hand and back up at her.

206

Carlie tossed him a challenging look and laughed when he took it. "I wondered if you'd accept. Lead the way. You've intrigued me."

They walked through crowds and past stores, until they stood before Build-a-Bear. Dean grinned at her. "How do you feel about rediscovering your inner child? My mother says I was never much of one. Which is likely why we're so close. She doesn't do well with children. Regardless, I thought we could 'build' stuffed animals."

"So... I make one for you and you make one for me?" The idea grew on her as she spoke. "I always wanted to take my nieces and nephews to do this. Now I'll know if it's a good idea or not."

"I saw them—a couple of them anyway—at your aunt's memorial service. They seemed to love you very much." Dean squeezed her hand. "You haven't spoken of it much since then. I always wanted to assure you that I've prayed for you and your family."

Carlie didn't know how to answer. Her throat swelled and irrational tears smarted. Desperate to hide the emotion that confused and frustrated her, Carlie tugged him inside. "Okay. Let's do this."

But Dean stopped her. "Are you sure? We can do it another time. I didn't mean—"

"No, really. Let's go. And I'm making you a bear—a nice, cuddly bear."

Dean found his animal first. He teased her about pink and purple cats to add to her feline menagerie, but in the end, chose a long-eared puppy. "You need animal balance in your life—a dog to keep your cats in line."

"For them to torture, you mean." Carlie reached for a brown bear. "I promised you a bear, and this one is perfect—traditional, with kind eyes." She winked. "Besides, I already got you a cat."

"Which I named Hestia—the closest I could get to a Greek goddess of comfort, since your aunt began that tradition." He winked and added, "Kind eyes... I didn't know that." Dean handed his animal to the young girl who stepped forward to assist them. "We'd like these, please. What do we do?"

The girl pulled unstuffed equivalents from bins and handed them over. "Let's get started. You'll need to name your pets..."

Dean seemed to consider the idea of a name quite carefully, but Carlie spoke up immediately. "The bear is Hero—because," she added under her breath, "I never really thanked you for being *my* hero."

"Oh?" The girl's eyes widened as they darted back and forth between them. "I'm curious now."

"He saved my life," Carlie murmured. "Pushed me out of the way and got shot trying to protect a bunch of us."

Dean leaned close and whispered, "Yes, but I do remember a

certain... *token*... of thanks."

Oh... we need to talk about that, mister. You moved... and then kissed me back!

At the machine, he asked to type in the animal's name himself. "A surprise," Dean murmured.

The sales associate moved them to another machine—this one to record something on a "heart" for their animals. This time, Carlie shooed him away. "I'm not going to let you hear it until it's done." She turned to the associate and asked, "How long of a recording?"

"Twenty-seconds."

It took six tries before the recording worked. Dean pretended to sneak closer and closer to hear, and each time she stumbled. "Go away or I'll record for posterity just how obnoxious you are!"

With their "hearts" recorded, the associate led them to the stuffing machine, and as it blew fluff into the little furry bodies, she gave them instructions. "Okay, now you need to rub your little hearts between your hands so your animals will always be warm."

Carlie nearly choked at the awkward way Dean half-heartedly rubbed the little plastic heart. "You clearly want me to have a cold-hearted dog."

He rubbed harder.

"Now rub the heart on your cheeks for smiles and on your head for no bad fur days." Carlie barely contained her laughter as Dean winced and rubbed. "Okay, now rub it on your back so your pets will always have your back..." Dean's eyes closed as he swiped the plastic piece over his upper shoulder blades. "Now your funny bone so he'll make you laugh..."

"Oh, please..."

By now, Carlie choked and chortled as she tried to suppress irrepressible giggles. *I can feel it... I know what's coming. Oh, man, I can't wait.*

This time, the girl laughed—her eyes sparkling. "On your tummy so they don't go hungry, and your knees so they'll always need you."

Dean groaned.

"Now put it on your heart and make a great big wish..."

This time, he smiled and acquiesced with almost eagerness. "That I can do—definitely."

"Give it a kiss..." Either he'd managed to overcome his embarrassment, or Dean meant something as he kissed it while gazing at her. They pushed the little hearts in the animals and handed them to the associate.

"Now I'll just sew it up..." The girl sewed each animal with record speed. When complete, she passed the little animals back and grinned. "I don't suppose you want to give them baths at the table..." She pointed to a "tub" with "shower heads."

"I don't think so," Carlie snickered. "Dean might melt himself if he has to do that." She elbowed him. "I don't think he knew what he was getting into when he brought me here."

Carlie could have sworn the girl gave a swooning sigh. "If my boy-friend did something like this, I swear…"

She couldn't help putting an arm around him. "It is pretty sweet, isn't it?" When he flushed at the attention, she couldn't help but kiss his cheek and whisper, "Thanks."

"May we please clothe these things? If I must play dress up with my dollies, I'm going all out."

"Would you like your boxes now? Surprise each other with the outfits you choose?"

Dean and Carlie exchanged glances before turning back and nodding. Carlie turned away and began picking through outfits until she found the perfect little business suit. *It's so you.*

Within minutes, they strolled from the mall, each carrying the animal they'd "made." Cold, bitter wind that threatened a snowstorm wormed its way through her coat as they pushed through to his car. Dean winced as he unlocked her door. "I'm sorry. Had I known the temperature would drop—"

"Just get in before you freeze! Your sweater isn't *that* warm."

The awkwardness returned on the way to Carlie's apartment. She sat there, unsure of what to say or how to say it. *Give me back this week's Dean! I don't want the weird one.*

"Oh! I apologize, Carlie. That was… strange."

Her eyes slid sideways as he turned onto her street. "What was?"

"I—well, I was wondering how I'd offended you—why you weren't talking." He threw her a sheepish glance that Carlie would have missed had they not driven under a streetlight at that moment. "I apologize—again. It's hard to imagine that listening to you has become such second-nature to me. Larry will find it amusing as well—likely laugh at me."

"No…" She grinned at his one-eye-on-the-road double-take. "I'm going to laugh at you. I was *just* sitting here thinking, 'Don't do this to me! I don't want the weird Dean,' and then you said you were weird."

"And I was. I'll have to stretch even further. Growth is good for us, though." He pulled up to her building, and had she not been wishing that the date wouldn't have to end, she might have jumped out before he could reach her.

Gotta get used to that. Yeah. Carlie couldn't help but grin as he offered her a hand. *Not going to be hard, though… not at all.*

Dean reached behind the seat and pulled out the box with his stuffed dog. "This one's yours now. Take good care of her."

"Only if you promise to take good care of Hero." She frowned and shook the carrying box. "Do I get to know her name yet?"

"When you open it—I named her after me, remember?"

"Poor girl…"

He shook his head. "I disagree—poor me. She's named for *me*, after all."

The words tumbled in her mind as he led her up the steps, through the doors, and to her apartment door. "I can't decide what that means."

"It means that you will have much to absorb tonight—all alone. I'll be waiting for your, 'I never want to see you again' text." He stopped her before she could push open the door and turned her to face him. "I have a question."

"Yeah…"

"How *me* do you want me to be?"

"I want—what?" Carlie searched his face for some hint of what he might mean but found only uncertainty there. "I don't know what that means, but I do know I just want you to be you—all of you. The old you, the new you, the you who isn't sure who he is because he's blending those—all of it."

A troupe of circus performers took up residence in her stomach as she watched emotions flicker across his face. *Whoa… he really does like me. I mean, you can't fake that—or at least,* he *can't. Wow.*

"Good to know. And I sincerely hope you don't decide to send that text."

A kiss on her cheek—one so light and quick that she almost doubted it had happened—a smile, and he was gone. Carlie pushed the door shut behind her. With both arms wrapped around the box with her new "dog," she leaned against it, smiling. "Now *that*, Pouncer, was a great date. I wish I'd recorded some of it. You should have seen him rubbing that heart on his knees and hair and—" the memory of him kissing it sent her to the couch. She pulled open the box and removed the dog and its "birth certificate."

"Cecil Marie." Moros jumped up and sniffed the stuffed pooch. "So is his name C—EE-cil or C-EH-cil? Maybe Marion? Is that his first or middle name? Which is it?"

The cat nudged her, rubbing its head along her wrist.

"I'll send a text just as soon as I listen to the message. The words, in Dean's mellow voice, sent her heart fluttering. "You make the command, 'love one another,' so very easy. Thanks for not coming that day."

She sent a text immediately.

I LOVE CECIL. IS THAT YOUR FIRST NAME, MIDDLE NAME, OR ARE YOU MARION? OH, AND I LOVE YOUR MESSAGE. MINE SEEMS

The box sat on the island in Dean's kitchen, unopened—a silent testament to insecurity he didn't know he had. "Time to be a man and look at a bear. How ridiculous. I'm intimidated by a bear."

He pulled the sides of the box open and peered inside. A paper lay atop the bear. Dean smiled at the name on the "birth certificate" for his new toy. "Professor Hero. I like it. It's certainly better than Cecil Marie." As he pulled out the bear, laughter bubbled over. "You dressed him like me—or as much as you could. Glasses too…"

Dean's finger hovered over the bear's heart as he worked up the nerve to press it. "You are making too much of this. It was just a date— a good one, maybe, but a date. She still doesn't know you. She doesn't care about you—not yet. Not enough." Those words, "not yet," buoyed his spirits. He pressed.

"I always wondered if I'd like you *outside* the restaurant. Well, I thought you should know; I do—very much."

A silly grin plastered itself on his face while Dean pressed the heart again—and again. A text message arrived from his mother, which reminded him that he'd received one from Carlie on the way home. Carlie's words appeared on his screen and the grin twisted into a grimace. "There's always something to shake us off cloud nine and onto the cold, hard earth."

Of all the dates she could have imagined, babysitting Hannah's kids to give the woman a break wouldn't have hit Carlie's radar. Still, watching Dean crawling on a less-than-clean floor with children riding his back did offer insight into the kind of man he was. *That's got to count for something,* she mused. *He's a good guy. Blaine would never do this.* Carlie started to reproach herself for the constant comparisons to Blaine when a new thought struck her. *No one I've ever dated would. Well, Jared probably, but that wasn't technically* dating. *We just went out a few times.*

Lost in her thoughts as she was, Carlie missed the shift in play. The others ran off—for what, she couldn't say—and Dean came to sit beside her. "That is one adorable little snoozing girl."

"Isn't she?" Carlie allowed herself to rest her cheek on the baby's head. "How is it that babies smell so good?"

Dean didn't answer, but the back of his hand brushed the baby's cheeks. "Skin so soft..." His finger slipped under the baby's hand, and he sighed as tiny fingers wrapped around it. "I've always had a fondness for baby hands—feet too."

"It's the eyelashes for me," she murmured. "Look at those things. I don't know any woman who wouldn't pay a small fortune for eyelashes like that."

"Why?" Before she could state the obvious, he added, "You have beautiful eyes just the way they are."

A protest formed on her lips. No one who compared eyelashes could say hers were anywhere near as lovely as little Chrissy's were. But

212

a glance his way stopped her. *He means it. Who cares if he's wrong? He likes your eyes. Don't argue.* "Thanks."

"See... that didn't hurt."

Hannah burst through the door just as the others appeared with blankets and pillows. "Whew! That was great. Thank you!"

"—read the story now?"

Carlie watched as Dean silently asked for permission and then nodded. "I'll read one short story each. So choose carefully." He crawled down to the floor and allowed the children to pile themselves on and around him.

Hannah reached for the baby and carried her out of the room. A moment later, Carlie saw Chrissy's pacifier and carried it to Hannah. The overworked mother sat on the end of her bed, rocking her little one with tears coursing down her face. Dread washed over her. *I don't know how to make her feel better. What do I do?*

"I'm sorry..."

"It's not you. I just had so much fun, you know? Steve—" Hannah choked back more tears and continued. "He used to make me go out by myself or with a friend now and then. 'Once in a while, mothers need a chance to do *something* without being interrupted.' That's what he used to say. It felt great to just sit and watch a movie—and not be able to finish the popcorn instead of reaching into an empty bowl—again."

"I hear a but coming," Carlie murmured.

"But I used to come home to my husband and my kids. Now I come home to kids who don't understand why Mommy is sad—who don't really get why *they're* sad. They miss a man they don't really understand is gone."

"I'm sorry..." *What else can I say?*

"Can you go? I'm really grateful and everything, but can you just go?" Hannah's eyes looked wild—half-crazed with pain and grief.

Carlie nodded. "Yeah. Can he finish the books?"

The woman almost said no. Carlie could see it in her eyes. Pain radiated from Hannah until it nearly filled the room. "Fine. Just..." She winced. "Go." In a desperate whisper, she added, "*Please!*"

Dean stacked a book atop another and reached for the last one as Carlie entered the living room. Knowing she'd cry if she met his eyes, Carlie began picking up some of the mess they'd made. She ran water in the kitchen sink and soaked dishes, wiped down the stove and counter, and fished out a twenty-dollar bill from her purse. This she affixed to the fridge with a magnet obviously made in a school craft session.

She'd just bagged up the kitchen trash when Dean arrived at her side. "Carlie..."

"Not talking about it." Each word she spoke with careful

precision, determined *not* to lose her self-control in front of the children. "Let's go."

"Shouldn't we—?"

"Go," Carlie interjected. "She wants us to go."

"Wha—oh, Carlie." He tried to lead her out quickly, but the children clung to her, asking when she'd return and begging for just *one* more story.

Hannah's voice called to them from the bedroom, and to her relief, they obeyed. Carlie made it down to the first floor, but the trash bag sagged in her hands as she realized that she didn't know where to take it. "Oh, forget it. I'll just take it home."

"I'll just—"

"Just put it in the trunk, okay? I want to get out of here."

He unlocked the trunk—such an old-fashioned move. *The car suits him,* she thought. *He's so modern and so traditional. It's a neat combination.*

As Dean slid into the seat beside her, he turned to face her. "You know it's the grief talking, right? She's feeling guilty that the people Steve tried to hurt are helping them. It's not you."

"I know." A tear splashed down her cheek. "But it hurts. She's all alone. What was he *thinking?*"

Rather than answer or reassure her—her preferred options, of course—he started the car and drove down the half-lit street. Only when she saw his hands gripping the steering wheel with excess force did Carlie see that he too was hurt. *But by what? What is hurting him? Is it Hannah's rejection or Steve's death? Both? What?*

Two cats attacked the moment Dean opened Carlie's door for her. Moros purred as she circled Carlie's legs, rubbing against them with an affection that suggested the animal might have a hidden agenda. Pouncer leapt from the couch arm into Dean's. "Whoa, kitty. I could have missed."

Carlie's sniffle ripped a new hole in his already leaky heart. "No worries," she choked out. "You might miss, but he never would."

Dean tried to distract her—to take her coat. But still, Carlie moved in an emotionally pain-filled fog. *I'll have to rethink leaving. She's still hurt.* Dean removed his coat and hung it as well. "Carlie, let's talk."

She blinked. "What?"

"You're upset. Let's talk."

Once more, her lip quivered. "I don't know how to do that."

"Hmm… I would have assumed that, 'I don't know how to do that' is what is generally understood to be talking."

Carlie continued to gape, her hands stroking Moros' fur as she

214

picked up the animal and allowed herself to be led to the couch. But once she sat, the cat bolted for places unknown. "Traitor," she muttered.

"I'd offer to let you stroke *my* fur, but I don't have any." The joke flopped. Carlie stared at him with empty, confused eyes until Dean added, "I apologize. Appalling excuse for a joke." When she didn't move, he plopped Pouncer on her lap in the hopes of distracting her. That cat left, too.

Tears splashed from her eyes. Dean started to assure Carlie that Hannah would understand—would be back to her old self in a day or two and feel bad about her outburst, but Carlie shook her head. "It's not that—not really. Yeah, it hurts. But it hurts more *for* her, you know? She's all alone now. No relief."

"But you *gave* her relief tonight."

"It's not the same, Dean. It's not. She needs that relief that says, "I'm here *with* you. Not I'm here *for* you."

His hands fidgeted as he struggled against the urge to touch her— to comfort. But when she covered her face and grew rigid in an evident attempt to avoid breaking down completely, he gave up and put an arm around her. "It's kind to hurt for her. It's a blessing."

Apparently, that was the right move, he mused as she turned and buried her head in his shoulder. Small, ever-increasing, and steady twinges of guilt tried to chill the warm glow of joy that filled his heart as she relaxed into him and allowed him to try to comfort her. Dean chose not to pay any attention—*not now. I can examine that later.*

"Why are you still here?"

The chill broke through his defenses. "I—well, I can leave if you'd rather. I didn't like to leave you alone and upset, but I—"

"That's what I mean. Why aren't you halfway to your house by now?" She punctuated her sentences with sniffles, and when that failed, she reached for Kleenex on her end table. "So glad I bought new ones for Hannah. I almost brought mine."

His mind couldn't connect the dots between Kleenex, Hannah, and his presence, so he focused on the one that confused him most. "Carlie, why wouldn't I be here? Do you want me to go? Stay? Neither?"

"My dad and brother would have been out of here. Blaine—every boyfriend I've ever had—would tell me I'm being stupid, or worse, try to make me feel better by getting all physical on me."

And yet, I sit here and hold you. Where is the difference? He had to ask. "I'd say I'm not exactly distant, Carlie…"

"But you're not trying to make out with me like it's some solution to pain."

I think many men would disagree with you, but I doubt it's the proper time to explain that. Dean just held her and waited for an explanation that made sense. It never came. "But why should I leave?"

"You shouldn't—but I've never met a guy who wouldn't want to get away from me right now."

"Obviously you have," Dean murmured. "Carlie, I don't *like* tears, but the Bible tells us that there is a time for weeping. Who am I to deny what the Lord gives?"

Her next words made his own throat swell with repressed emotion. "You can't be this nice to me. I don't know how to handle it."

The sermon—both good and theologically sound. The singing—relevant and Scriptural. Communion—rich and meaningful. The fellowship—couldn't be better. But despite finding no real flaw with Carlie's fellowship of believers, Dean sat uncomfortable in the chair beside her and listened as the closing prayer moved from man to man—and occasionally boy—to the back of the room. He let it skip him out of respect, but Jared nudged him from behind and whispered, "You're welcome to join."

Dean shook his head.

Two more men, including Jared, prayed before a moment of silence overtook the room. Dean tried to concentrate, but he'd made the foolish mistake of looking up after the man at the far back of the room had finished praying. Every head stayed bowed, and beside him, Carlie's hands sat clasped together in what appeared to be earnest prayer.

Once he saw those hands, his mind refused to focus again. Twice he started to reach for them, but his conscience told him to wait. *After the prayer.* His justification processing center, however, insisted now would be the perfect time. *It won't appear self-serving now. It'll be a natural response to corporate prayer. Don't be ridiculous.*

Conscience won out over justification—barely. The moment the first person spoke, he reached for her. The smile she gave him as her fingers wrapped around his hand sent tendrils of hope wrapping around his heart. *Lord, I knew I was falling in love with her. That doesn't surprise me. But I had no idea I was falling so hard or fast. Keep me patient, or I'm going to destroy any chance of a* true *relationship! She needs time and to develop a new norm in her life.*

"—nice to have you. Carlie speaks well of you." The woman, Natalie, held out her hand.

"I was glad of a chance to see what church had Carlie so happy and eager to learn."

Carlie stepped a bit closer and half-ducked her head. "I'm still pretty much ignorant when it comes to the Bible, but these guys have really helped me figure out how to learn more. I think I overcomplicated the idea of Bible study."

Dean's laughter sent several odd looks their way, but Jared asked first. "What's so funny?"

"Well, we all do that, don't we?" He thought for a moment before adding, "Of course, in a sense it's my *job* to excavate every morsel of truth and examine it. But our natural propensity of turning every tryst in the Word into a theological course of study is a bit excessive, don't you think? The Bible was written to and by many undereducated men. That alone should be sufficient proof that it shouldn't be difficult to understand. However, we devise systems and rules about how often we read, what we read, and what we *do* when we read. It's madness." As he finished, Dean winced. "Sorry. Occupational hazard. I'm still learning verbal self-control."

"Told you he can talk—if he wants to. Apparently my beauty and intelligence strike him speechless at times."

Dean couldn't resist responding to that one. "You have no idea…"

His heart raced at the expression she gave him. "And on that note, I think we should go. He'll say something sweet, and I'll be a puddle of emotions fluttering to the floor."

At the door, Jared stopped Dean and murmured, "Thanks for being what she needs. I couldn't be—knew it, but I hoped. But I can see that you're *exactly* what she needs."

"You were there for her when she needed you," Dean insisted. "She appreciates it. She *wanted* you to be…"

Jared's next words stripped all conversational ability from Dean. "I knew she was already half in love with you—she doesn't, of course. Can't blame a guy for trying, though."

217

P aper after paper moved from the stack in front of him to the one beside as Dean worked through the week's assignments. He worked swiftly, decisively, and completely distracted. When he finished in record time, he glanced up over the bench tops to the door, glanced at his watch, and moved the "finished" pile in front of him once more. Dean pulled the first paper—Gabby's—toward him and tried reading again.

"So you're talking now. Going to start dating—really dating?"

Janice's voice made him jump, and his pen flew across the page. "Ugh."

"Sorry. You're usually more aware of your surroundings. Which means, either your last date was another flop and you're not eagerly watching for her, or you *really* want to be done when she comes." At his flush, she nodded. "That one. Good. It's about time. We all wondered what took you so long."

"To do what?"

"Ask her out!" Janice leaned forward, eying him. "You don't get it, do you?" she said at last. "You really think you just fell for her. You didn't. We've seen it for weeks—months. Christmas at least."

Dean couldn't respond. He just stared at the table and tried to keep his jaw from connecting with it.

"She likes you, too, you know." He hated himself for it, but Dean found himself staring at Janice—searching for some sign that what she said was true. "Yeah—really. Not as much as you like her maybe, but…"

"Well, we haven't talked that much. She doesn't know me as well as I know her."

She patted his shoulder. "Well, at least she's got a nice guy, finally. That other creep—ugh."

Although he knew Carlie had rejected the idea of a relationship with Jared, he couldn't help but interject, "There's another man, though. He's everything I would have chosen for her...a couple of weeks ago, anyway." He shrugged at her raised eyebrows. "Janice, I'm not going to pretend that I think she's going to decide I'm 'the one.' She can't when she doesn't truly know me and does know someone else much better."

"And yet, she still comes here every week. This guy may be a great guy, but he's not you."

Dean found himself speaking the words that had been plaguing him for days. "The best description for Jared is 'a good guy.' She seems immune to him. I've begun to wonder if she has a 'bad boy' complex, because she did say she's not interested in Jared."

"So, what's the problem? She's not interested in him because maybe she's interested in you."

His protest erupted almost compulsively. "But she really likes him and enjoyed going out with him." Dean shook his head. "I think the 'bad boy' idea might win."

As another server passed, Janice stopped the guy and whispered something to him. She took off her apron and slid into the booth. "Listen, Dean. Girls like Carlie don't have bad boy complexes. They have self-image issues. It's not really a traditional inferiority complex, because she does know that she has good qualities. I can see that in her."

"Then what is it? Enlighten me and prove that you should be elevated to bartender."

Janice snickered. "Not sure that's much of an elevation—particularly in a café that doesn't serve alcohol." She winked. "But look. It's like this. Carlie really seems to think she isn't good enough for a better guy—in that area she seems stuck in a dysfunctional rut. You've heard the things she says. It's like she's been beaten down so much that she actually believes the things people tell her about herself."

As Janice spoke, Dean listened—listened and nodded. "I see. That's my responsibility now, isn't it? I need to demonstrate to her just how amazing she is. I need to help her see it before I attempt to show her *me*. Before I try to win her heart, I need to try to build up her self-confidence."

"Can I just say, '*Swoon*'? Seriously, if I had heard you say that before you met Carlie, I totally would have flirted with you." She jumped up and pointed to his empty cup. "Coffee? Plain or..."

"Salted caramel. I'm in the mood to celebrate, thanks to you."

"What are we celebrating?" Carlie hung her jacket on the end of the booth and grinned at Janice. "Hey! Can I get whatever he's having, too?"

Dean fumbled with his papers as he tried to clear the table. If he wanted her to get to know him, he needed to talk. But if he hoped to bolster her self-confidence, Dean needed to find a way to get *Carlie* to talk about *herself*. The irony nearly drove him to say something he'd regret. "How's work today?" Somehow—how, he couldn't imagine— Dean stifled a groan. *Talk about a yawning attempt at communication there.*

"Some days, I just want to quit. I mean, I like retail, but 'sales associates...'" She dropped air quotes over the job title with heavy sarcasm. "We are expected to do everything the managers do—just without the pay." She hesitated before adding. "Okay, and corporate doesn't jump down our throats if something doesn't go right, but Liz does, so what's the difference? Oh, yeah. About eight dollars an hour. That's right..." She leaned forward. "I found it online. *Eight* dollars more per hour as a manager. That's over three hundred dollars a *week*! For stuff I'm doing already."

"Then why not apply for that assistant job?"

She picked at her napkin. "I tried, okay? I filled it out, I even put it in Liz's box, but I couldn't do it. I'm not cut out for it. I don't even know if I *want* it. I just... I don't know."

Coffee arrived for both of them, and with it, Janice's expectation that they'd know what they wanted to eat. "I recommend the Hoedown. I swear, Frank came up with the *best* barbecue sauce you've ever tasted."

"Good enough for me," Dean agreed.

"Slaw?"

He winced. "Is it any good?"

"I'm not much of a slaw fan, but I liked it—didn't *love* it, but..."

She turned to ask Carlie the same thing, but Carlie shook her head. "I want the bean soup, cornbread, and fried okra. Can't afford to risk barbecue on this sweater."

The white sweater with its deep cowl would be ruined splattered with barbecue sauce—anyone could see that. But the moment Janice stepped away, he reached for her hand and said, "Protecting that sweater is important. It looks amazing on you—and you in it."

"You, Professor, are much too good for my ego." Her hand squeezed his as she added, "But I like it. I'll admit it. I like it."

"If you don't want that assistant's position, may I make another suggestion?"

She shrugged. "Sure."

"I observed you salvage two weddings. You were excellent during a crisis. You fulfilled the bride's wishes without sacrificing taste. You ensured that they didn't pay for things they shouldn't, and..." He smiled at the rosy pink that tinged her cheeks. "Since you were unaware that it would be a compliment to yourself, you also admitted that the results were *excellent*." Seeing he'd already begun to lose her, he added, "You talked about it once—about how much you'd enjoy it. You should consider a career in party planning—particularly weddings."

As he finished, her head began to shake, as if by its own volition. "I can't. You need to know people to get into wedding planning. I mean, it's stupid, but I'd want to work at the best, you know—The Agency. They are seriously the top of all wedding planning companies in the Rockland area. And I have no experience. They wouldn't touch me."

"But lack of experience isn't why they wouldn't hire you, Carlie. Aren't they a family operation? While *some* of their employees are obviously not family, I suspect the main planners are. I would think you'd prefer a company that doesn't have those kinds of restrictions—turn *that* company into The Agency's serious competition."

"That's not going to happen," she murmured. "Not because of me, anyway. I know how to fix problems. I know how not to let people push me around—"

Dean coughed.

"What?"

Use the opportunity carefully. "You know how not to let *businesses* take advantage, which is all you need in this respect." He hesitated before adding, "But you do allow people who are supposed to care about you push you around."

"I thought that was being forgiving and turning the other cheek." Carlie sipped her coffee, her eyes peering over the cup at him.

Don't do that to me, Carlie. Oh, my. How was I so blind to you all those months? Or did I know and not allow myself to acknowledge it? Regardless… you are incredible. His inner self ordered him to tell her. "You are killing me, Carlie. I'm attempting to inform you that you can't let people who are supposed to love you take advantage, but instead, you are doing crazy things to my heart."

The enigmatic smile she gave him, combined with a raised eyebrow, double-flopped his heart. However, when she said, "I'll have to remember that," fresh hope welled in him. "But I don't have enough skill or experience to make any agency want to take a chance on me. I'm just a 'dead end' job kind of worker. And that's okay. I can be the best associate I can be right where I am."

"Carlie, that isn't true." He covered their hands with his other hand and gazed at her. "You are worthy of a better job. You are worthy of an education if that's what you want. You have the right to seek that out for yourself. But the way you talk about yourself is just wrong."

Dean's phone rang before he could continue. A glance at it

showed Larry's name. "Excuse me. Larry never calls." As he spoke to his stepfather, he watched Carlie, and his words pounded his own heart. *You were too harsh with her. She's not a student. She's a woman—one you claim to love. Act like it.*

Just as he disconnected the call, Janice arrived with their meals. He waited until she'd taken her first bite and said, "I'm sorry, Carlie. I was out of line—rebuking you like that. The last thing you need is another man dictating what you should or shouldn't do." He gave her the smile that had always softened his mother's heart and quipped, "Forgive me?"

But as he spoke, Carlie waved her hands. "No, no. You were respectful—didn't treat me like a child like so many people do." She jabbed her spoon in her bean soup and murmured, "You treated me like an equal who needed to be reminded of something. I respect and appreciate that."

She makes an excellent point. How do I share why—oh, I'll just be honest. What else can I do? He took a bite of his barbecue sandwich, wiped his mouth, and nodded. "I suppose. You should know that I react to your reactions. I see you hurt and desire to pummel someone in return." He speared a bite of slaw before adding, "I'll step out of line occasionally. I'll annoy you. Please just tell me when I've gone too far."

"I don't understand. What are you talking about? You were just being nice."

Dean tried again—this time from another angle. "I used to listen to you talk about Blaine, and the things you would say told me that you didn't realize just how much you tore yourself down—how you echoed the nonsense Blaine spewed. I don't think you knew then—or even now—just how deeply entrenched you were in his wrong opinion of you." Try as he might, Dean couldn't meet her eyes. "It cut me to listen to you. So many times I ached to say, 'Don't talk about yourself like that.' Maybe I should have."

"I wouldn't have listened. You were smart to wait until you did. Sometimes it drove me nuts, but it was a good nuts." When he finally managed to make eye contact again, she added, "You didn't have to apologize. You didn't do anything wrong."

"Well, then I'll add one more thing while you'll accept it." He winked before adding, "You are a child of God, bought with a price beyond anything you can even imagine. You are precious and wonderful—not just to God, but also to me." Emotion thickened his voice and he winced. "Every time you say something derogatory about yourself, you reinforce the truth of it in your mind—despite the lie it really is."

"But—"

Dean continued, talking over her protests and repeating himself until she listened. "I don't want you to worship yourself, Carlie. That's not what I'm talking about. But I do want you to see you through *God's* eyes. That's why I purchased that book—to help you see yourself as God sees you. As it says, you are *His* workmanship—fearfully and wonderfully made. Don't let anyone convince you otherwise." At that moment, he realized that he had overrode her—plowed through her words like he'd done all his life, but as he opened his mouth to apologize, he realized he wasn't sorry. *This was the right time to do it. Now, to remember that in the future.*

"Thanks… that was the most amazing thing about that book— the way it wasn't all about *me*. It was all about respecting God's creation—which just happens to be me."

"I appreciated that as well," Dean admitted.

Carlie gave him a slow smile. "I've bought similar books—Teresa and a few of my friends have bought them, too. But 'worship myself'— that's how they've all made me feel. It's like they can't just say, 'God doesn't make junk. He made you, so you're not junk.'" She winked at the surprise Dean knew he showed. "Yeah! I read it. I get it. It's just hard not to let the voices that speak louder convince you that they are the *real* truth."

"I'd never considered that. Impressive. And you're wise not to get caught up in the self-centered nonsense."

Her head hung, and Dean knew exactly what she'd say before she said it. "I did, though. The first ones—I did. I got all self-absorbed. Like you said—worshiped myself almost. I guess my solution was to go to the other extreme—easy to do when I heard it so much."

Those words hung over the table as they finished their meal. As he asked her over for dinner at his house. As he gathered his things and got ready to leave. The disappointment in her eyes when he stood to go gave him just the nudge he needed. Dean hunkered down on his heels beside her and met her eyes. "I hope you'll hear this and let it sink deep into your heart. In the words of Elisabeth Elliot, 'Remember, you are loved with an everlasting love and underneath are the everlasting arms.'" He allowed himself just a quick kiss on her cheek before he stood and turned to go. "I'll see you Saturday night?"

"Yeah…"

If the dazed expression on her face meant anything, he'd said exactly what she needed to hear. *Yes!*

For thirty-two years, Easter dress shopping the Saturday before Easter had been a Denham tradition. *And my only consolation is that I wasn't there for the first nine or so of those years.*

Her credit cards demanded relief, and her checking account didn't allow for more than a twenty-dollar dress. *And if I buy it with cash first and the rest on credit, I'll hear about it. If I don't, I won't go back and fix it at home. So, it's more debt for a stupid dress that I don't need, to honor a stupid tradition I never liked or wanted.* Her mother and sister paused at a window, debating if they should try that store for the perfect outfit for Carlie's niece, when a universally unacknowledged truth hit her.

And I'll probably continue the stupid tradition with my own kids. That's the stupidest part of all. A random and amusing addendum surfaced next. *I also need to improve my vocabulary. I can surely come up with more varied adjectives for my opinion on the matter.*

"—think about that one?"

She knew better than to look. Carol's voice held that tone—the one that said, *"Eureka! You're gonna hate me, but I found it."* And she was always right. Carlie turned to look and sighed. "Why—why do you always do this to me? You know it's perfect. You know I love it. You know I can't resist it. And you *know* it's not in my budget!"

With an air of resignation, she pushed through the exiting patrons and went to pull her size off the rack. Carol caught up to her just as she accepted her door hanger from the attendant. "Carlie, if you don't want—"

"I do want it. You know I do. Why do you always pretend—?"

Her sister dragged her over to the corner and hissed, "I'm not trying to be difficult, Carlie. I know what you like. We're shopping for dresses. What do you want from me?"

The ire that had given her the impetus to stick up for herself fizzled. "Sorry. I just hate how much I try to stick to my budgets and something always happens to mess them up. You can't help that I have expensive tastes." Before she said anymore, Carlie pushed her way past and into the changing room. The dress slipped over her head, and even before she could find the tab of the side zipper, Carlie knew it would be a perfect fit—in every way. It only had one problem—it required a shorter slip than she owned. *That's what I get for spilling coffee on my last one. That stain would definitely have shown through. I'll get one somewhere cheaper, though. That'll help.*

At the checkout counter, the woman accepted the dress, bagged it, and handed her a receipt. "Happy Easter."

"Wha—" Carlie turned and saw her mother and sister grinning. "You didn't—ugh. Thank you."

"More genuine thanks, I've never heard," Gina Denham quipped.

"I just—" *How do I say, "I didn't mean to guilt you into buying me something," without making it sound like I actually was? Ugh!* "I feel guilty, okay? I was complaining, and if you were planning a surprise, I messed that up.

224

I'm good at that, you know."

Carol pushed her toward the door. "Does it look as fabulous as I thought it would?"

"Made for me, okay?" The ungraciousness of her tone whacked her conscience. "Sorry... it's always awkward when you have to admit something looks good on you. I feel full of myself or something."

"There's nothing wrong with admitting the truth. It's *how* you do it," Gina insisted.

"And," Carol added, "just think how *Dean* will like it."

Yeah, I tried not *to do that, thank-you-very-much! Ugh. What if he hates it? Then again, who says he'll see it? It's an* Easter *dress.* "Well, I don't know when he'll see it, but I hope—"

"Bring him home for Easter. We want to meet him. And it's such a busy time that there wouldn't be awkward moments or anything." Carol steered her toward J.C. Penney's. "Don't you need a new slip? Last time you wore a skirt that needed a light, shorter slip, you spilled coffee all over yourself."

Only you would remember. It's like a talent that no one should ever have.

Gina interrupted before Carlie could reply. "Oh, do it! Bring him. We all want to meet this guy." She lowered her voice. "I think we should, Carlie. Your track record for picking men is less than stellar, you know..."

Her eyes rose to the ceiling of the mall, and she implored the Lord for help. *Just get me out of here without saying something I'll have to apologize for the rest of my life for saying. Okay?*

The latest album from Dean's favorite group filled his apartment but did little to drown out the thoughts and memories he so ached to escape. *Not now, Lord. please...*

When prayer and praise did little to help, he turned up the volume a little, stepped out the front door, and closed it. The hall remained perfectly silent. He opened the door, bumped the volume up a couple of notches, and tested it again. *Perfect.*

The mind-numbing experience lasted for about a minute and a half. Then the memory—or was it a dream—of Carlie's lips on his invaded his mind again. *No! I can't allow myself to think about it, Lord. She's not ready. I'm not ready—and much too ready,* he forced himself to admit.

The table—set. Steaks—almost room temperature and ready for the Foreman. Asparagus—ready to bake. Mushrooms... Dean groaned and pulled them from the fridge. *A date at home always means I don't have to leave; therefore, I don't have to rush. And, because I don't have to leave, I'm flustered as I wait.*

225

Just as he finished slicing the mushrooms, the doorbell rang. Dean grabbed the remote and turned down the music as he hurried to the door. A quick glance in the mirror reminded him to remove his apron. *Excellent attempt at making a fabulously blah impression, Dean.*

His throat went dry as he opened the door. *Wow... just—* Dean shook himself. "Sorry. I was thinking to myself, 'Wow, she looks amazing.' Again, my new habit—not one any of my friends would ever believe—of *not* saying what's on my mind fails us both." He smiled before adding, "So, I'm determined for you to hear it. You look great."

"Thanks..." She gave him a once-over. "So do you."

As he led her to the kitchen, he hooked the apron loop over his neck. "And now, I ruin it."

"My mom says nothing is more attractive than a guy with an apron—as long as there are no ruffles."

Dean gripped the counter in an attempt to resist, but failed. He reached into his cupboard and pulled out a clipped bag of chips. "Well... I've got Ruffles..."

Carlie snatched the bag and pulled a chip from it. "Thanks. I'm starved."

"Don't spoil your appetite. I've slaved over a hot—" He shook his head. "Sorry, can't do it. I tried, but a man has his pride."

She stood close, watching as he seasoned the meat and put it on the grill and slid the asparagus in the oven. "Do you like to cook?"

With the oven closed, he turned and poured her a glass of lemon water. "I do, actually. I learned as a child after growing weary of takeout. Mim isn't much of a cook."

Carlie smiled as he spoke. That smile sent nervous flutters through his heart. "So, what was little Dean like—or should I say Cecil?"

"Oh, I shouldn't have told you that. I regret deciding against the name change."

"Where'd you get it—aside from the obvious?"

Dare I tell her? He eyed her as he slid the mushrooms in a pan of melted butter. "My mother assumed it was what the C stands for in C.S. Lewis."

"It isn't?"

"No. His name was Clive Staples, which is nearly as obnoxious as Cecil Dean." He couldn't resist teasing, "There was once a boy called Cecil Dean Sager, and he almost deserved it."

The reference meant nothing to her. "Why Dean, then?" Carlie bent over the pan and inhaled. "Man, that smells good already."

He shook the pan before answering her question. "My father insisted." He hesitated once more before adding. "My dad refused to give his son a name that sounded like a British way of saying 'sissy.' So, he demanded Jake instead."

"Jake to Dean—seems like a leap."

"It does, doesn't it? My mother went through every baby name book she could find—all of which had Dean in them, by the way—but one provided a list of intellectual sounding names. She liked Dean because of the education connection. Dad approved it because it sounded more masculine…" He reached for a plate and slid the mushrooms on it. "Would you be so kind as to retrieve two forks from the drawer on your left?"

"Sure."

They munched on mushrooms while waiting for the steaks. Dean shifted the asparagus. The steaks grilled themselves to perfection. They ate. But after dinner, when they moved to the living room, Dean felt everything shift as he plopped down on the other end of the couch. She tried to talk—and clamped her mouth shut. He tried to compensate, but every word sounded even more inane than the last. The crazy pall of their first date settled over him until he nearly threw caution to the wind and kissed her as a diversion.

Impossible idea! Just change the subject—Easter. Ask what her church is doing. At the look of misery in her eyes, Dean remembered that she couldn't read his thoughts. "So, what does your church do for Easter?"

"I don't know—and I won't be going there, so I may never know." She relaxed. "Funny you should mention Easter. I've been trying to figure out how to bring it up."

"Why?"

At first, he didn't think she'd answer. Something in the way she chewed her lip and refused to meet his eyes told him that she wasn't comfortable. But then the words spilled out, flowing, tumbling, flooding the room with random thoughts that slowly began to make sense. "—this tradition. Why do people have those anyway? I mean, they're just guilt things, right?"

"Or meaningful events that people choose to repeat in order to build upon other memories to create a collective picture of a life."

"You would like it." Despite the derisive tone, Carlie smiled. "Anyway, we were at the mall shopping for Easter dresses—stupid tradition—and my sister asked when they'd get to meet you, and then my mom said you should come for Easter, and I was going to say no…" She closed her eyes. "That sounds wrong. It's not that I don't *want* you there. Honestly, it would be a relief. It's just that it's so awkward for you, and—"

"Carlie?"

"Yeah…"

He inched closer until he could take her hand and cover it with his. "Is this an attempt to invite me to your parents' house for Easter?"

"Um..." She sighed. "Yeah."

"I'd love to."

Her head snapped up so fast Dean nearly suggested a neck brace. "Really? I mean, some people get all freaked out about the 'meet the family' thing. So I didn't know..."

"If you don't want me to come, I'll understand. But otherwise, I'd like to meet them." He grinned. "I like people, remember?"

"They'll ask even more questions than I do."

He laughed. "That won't be hard. You persist in attempting *not* to ask, while I try to discern what things you *want* to know."

A line out the door did not bode well for the day's lunch crowd. A few complained as Carlie wove her way into the front, but she ignored them. One woman grabbed her arm. "Get in line like the rest of us."

"Let. go. of. me." The moment the woman dropped her hand, she forced herself to smile. "Sorry you have to wait, but my friend is also waiting—for me, in there at a table."

A string of profanity followed her inside, and even there, Carlie had to fight her way through people to get around the corner. Dean's grin, however, made the experience worth just about every second. "Hi! Crazy out there."

"There was a fire at Vincent's last night, and Frank is being hammered by the overflow."

Guilt hit her. "We could eat fast and take a walk... it's nice out there..."

Dean passed her the menu. "I recommend the special. Those always come fastest."

A glance at the advertisement for a BLT and chicken soup was enough for her. "Done."

Janice breezed past. "Done what?"

Before Carlie could speak, Dean nodded. "She agreed."

"Be right back with it. Thanks!"

Carlie leaned back, crossed her hands over her chest, and leveled her best "did I just get played?" look at him. "I can't believe I fell for that."

"Well, the walk was your idea. I was going to suggest dinner since we didn't get to have much of a lunch."

As much as the suggestion appealed to her, the idea of a walk had grown on Carlie. Still, she decided to take whatever he had to offer. "Okay. That works, too."

"Carlie…" It took her a moment to meet his gaze, but when she did, he said, "What do *you* want to do?"

"I—"

He reached for her hand and stopped her. "I see it in your eyes. You're going to tell me what you think I want to hear. I'm asking what *you* want. Do you want to take that walk? Have dinner later? Both? Neither? You aren't trapped between just two options, you know."

"Then I want to walk. And…" A new idea occurred to her just as Janice appeared with their food. "We'll see about the rest afterward."

The low rumble of voices played background music for their silent meal. Percussion in the form of occasional laughter kept the steady spoonful of soup and crunch of teeth into bacon-loaded sandwiches from becoming monotonous. Carlie finished first and flushed as she realized that he watched her. "That's embarrassing."

"What is?"

"You watching me eat. I probably dribbled soup down my chin or have mayonnaise on my cheek."

His hand stretched out with a slowness that almost rivaled a football replay. Dean's thumb stroked the side of her lip to the corner of her mouth, and he stared at it—examined it. "Nope. Nothing."

"Oh… you got me!" *Man, did you. That was crazy romantic in a weird, "whoever-thinks-of-that," kind of way.*

"I would say, 'Any man would try anything to touch your lips,' but that would be inappropriate, so I won't."

"Such a gentleman." Carlie pointed at his bowl. "Finish! We're leaving early, remember?"

He stood, without hesitation, and grabbed his messenger bag. "I'm ready."

"But—" She frowned. "Just for that, you're buying me ice cream."

Though she couldn't be certain, Carlie would have sworn she heard him murmur, "That'll be another chance at cleaning your lips for you…" She blinked. *Nah… he wouldn't.*

Weaving through the throng still waiting for tables was even more difficult than when she'd arrived. But when they burst outside, Carlie relaxed. "It is such a gorgeous day."

"Good setting for you then," Dean murmured.

"You've got to stop being nice to me. Even my cats aren't this nice." She snickered. "They're seriously ticked off at me right now. I burned cookies last night—literally. The whole apartment smells like an arsonist attacked a bakery."

"What kind of cookies?"

"Carbon crunches?" At his snicker, she added, "I shouldn't be telling you this. I mean, you're the chef around here. You make amazing meals that should be served in restaurants, and I burn salads." She gave him a sidelong glance and, before she could talk herself out of it, added, "You know, when I was little, all I wanted to be was a homemaker and mom. I thought it would be so cool to spend all day cooking and making a house pretty. I would learn to sew and make cute clothes for my kids—boys too—and make Donna Reed look like an amateur."

"I think most little girls dream of that at some point—before they discover other exciting occupational options or are convinced that the idea is somehow beneath them."

"Yeah, well retail is better for me. I'm a failure at anything domestic. I try and I flop. Every time. It's like there's something wrong in my wiring or whatever."

She felt him stiffen beside her, but instead of pulling away as expected, he reached for her hand and said, "You are 'fearfully and wonderfully made,' not because of the skills you learn or even your natural God-given talents. You are wired just how the Lord wants you to be, because *God* is amazing, and He made you. You—we—everyone is flawed—make mistakes." He pulled her a little closer and murmured, "I have faults and weaknesses—but those aren't God's faults. They don't strip me of my worth in His eyes."

"Tell that to my brother. He's always saying that God broke the mold with me—in an attempt to spare mankind from further decay."

"I—wait a minute, what?"

Carlie stopped in the middle of the sidewalk and stared at him. *What, what? You sound ticked. What's wrong with you?* Aloud, she finally managed to say, "I don't understand. What's wrong?"

"Your brother—you said he says unkind things as well. Does your whole family do this?"

"Do what? Point out every single everlasting flaw of mine? Yeah. Duh."

He steered her around the corner to the ice cream shop and continued as if she hadn't answered—as if she wasn't even there. "I wonder if somehow you encouraged this in them." He stiffened again. "Maybe this is why you're drawn to men like Blaine—men who shred your self-confidence. You were brought up to do it—indirectly, but still..."

Dean's words seemed crazy—almost melodramatic, but the more they sank into her mind, the more she wondered. "So, what if you came down with me Saturday? Stay the whole weekend, instead of just

Sunday. I want to know what you see."

"You want me to analyze your family dynamics?" He shook his head. "I'm not a psychologist, Carlie. I can only tell you what I see—not what is really there."

"That's all a psychologist or therapist can do anyway. They can only respond to patterns, right?"

Her heart warmed and her emotions waltzed her around the streets of Rockland as Dean wrapped an arm around her again and said, "And you act as if you're unintelligent. That, my dear Carlie, was an excellent critical observation regarding the therapy process." He kissed her cheek as he pulled open the door to the ice cream shop and added, "But, of course, I'll go. It would allow me to spend another day with you."

Carlie took inventory of her luggage while she waited for Dean's arrival. "Suitcase, makeup case, gifts for kids, scarf for Mom, Max Lucado book for Dad—all there."

She checked the litter box—again—and the fridge for feeding instructions. *Teresa should be fine. Should have just brought the cats with me.*

A knock jerked her out of second-guessing herself and into action. She grabbed her purse, threw it over her shoulder, and reached for the handle of her suitcase. But as she opened the door, Carlie dropped it. "Wha—why are you here?"

"I wanted to be here when he got here." Teresa squeezed through the semi-open door, and grinned. "I want to meet this guy."

"But—"

Teresa thrust a spiral-bound book of index cards at her. "I want you to ask him every one of those questions on the way—every one. Write down any answers that you want to talk about more." She reached into her pocket and pulled out a pen. "Here. Now you can't claim you couldn't find one."

Before Carlie could absorb her friend's words and take in the information, Dean peered around the half-open door. "Carlie? Are you ready?" He stepped in and smiled at Teresa. "I suspect you're Carlie's friend—Teresa?"

"Yeah." The woman gave him a quick once-over before offering her hand. "Nice to meet you, Dean."

Carlie'd had enough of it. "Isn't it, though?"

Her friend and her boyfriend—that thought stopped Carlie in her tracks. *Is he my boyfriend? I mean, he must be, but—wow. I hadn't really thought about it.*

"Earth to Carlie…" Teresa hugged her. "Have fun. Ask questions.

I want a full report." To Dean she added, "This is seriously one of the most amazing girls on the planet. We're not putting up with anyone else hurting her."

"Excellent. Neither will I."

Carlie's eyes swung back and forth before she threw up her hands. "I'm still here! Right here. I can hear you. I'm not invisible. I'm not an idiot..."

Dean grinned at Teresa and held his hand up for a high five. "Step one to overcoming a problem—admitting the truth. Step one: accomplished."

Illogically—and she knew it—Carlie seethed as they loaded his back seat with her stuff and drove toward the Loop. Dean tried to interact, but when she froze him out, he gave her space. *Which totally ticks me off and impresses me at the same time.*

The moment she realized the incongruity of that thought, Dean stated the annoying obvious. "You're mad at me."

"Astounding observation."

"Can I ask why?" Before she could respond, he amended the question. "I should say, *may* I ask why. Somehow, I suspect you'll inform me that I'm capable of it, certainly."

"Don't mock me," she growled. *And seriously, who does that?*

What she expected, Carlie couldn't say. But she didn't expect him to reach for her hand and lace their fingers together. "I didn't mean to mock you. I'm sorry."

"Stop it! Don't—fine. Whatever. You want to do Teresa's questions? We'll do them." Carlie dug into her purse and pulled out the index card book and pen. "Okay, why did your last relationship end?" She reread the question to herself, certain Teresa wouldn't have led off with that one. But there it was. "Sorry. That's a bit... personal."

Dean didn't shift at all. His thumb stroked the back of her hand for a moment before he said, "Um... College, and it ended when I found out that I was just a joke to the girl. After that, I steered clear of relationships. It helped that I was busy with college, getting my masters and Ph.D. I thought I'd have time later. Then I just didn't meet anyone."

"Until me."

"You and Gabby."

It took a moment to realize that he'd dropped another name intentionally. "Who's Gabby?"

"One of my students—now. She wasn't when I met her. I was going to ask her out at the end of this semester."

But what? Why—I don't get it.

"Feel free to ask why. I brought it up."

"Okay then," Carlie retorted. "Why? Why were you going to ask

233

her out? Why didn't you? Why did you ask me first?"

Only the slightest squeeze of her hand hinted that she'd asked exactly what he'd hoped for. "I noticed her—liked her humor and her intellect. So, when she was no longer a student, I thought I'd ask her out. I was interested. Then, I realized why."

When he paused, she shook her head. "Don't make me ask."

"You didn't come one week, and I had to consider why that bothered me so much. Then, when I realized that it was because I was falling for you, I had to examine my interest in Gabby." He cleared his throat. "I'm relieved that I did before I asked her. It would have been unkind."

"Why?!"

Dean grinned, released her hand, and maneuvered around a weaving car in front of them. Just as he reached for her again, he said, "Because the things I found interesting in her were all things that I like about you. I found it easier to recognize that outside the restaurant. I'd allowed myself to consider our lunches as my project—consciously, anyway. Meanwhile, underneath it all, I was becoming an emotional, gooey mess every time I thought about you."

"That shouldn't be as endearing as it is." She read the next question and smiled. "Easier one. Favorite color."

"Easier answer. Whichever color you're wearing."

"This?" Carlie stared at the brown polka-dot shirt she wore and eyed it critically. "I've never heard anyone say brown was their favorite color."

Dean's head shook even as she spoke. "No... I said whatever color you're wearing. Today it's brown. Tomorrow it might be pink or blue or green." At her stammers of protest, he insisted, "No, it's true. I've never had a favorite color—never. But I notice them more since meeting you. So, it's true."

"You can't do that, Dean. You can't say things like that. It—never mind. I'm sorry. I'm being rude and stupid as usual."

His silence unnerved her. A mile passed, two. It took her the better part of the third to realize he'd been praying. *Do I say something? Wait? I don't know. God, I don't want to blow this, but I don't know how to handle someone so nice. He's too nice. I feel like I'm walking on eggshells, waiting for him to crush me.* A quiet voice in her heart said, "Tell him." But Carlie couldn't.

By the time Dean did speak, she was so relieved, she apologized again. "I shouldn't—"

"Carlie? I need to say something. This is important. I sense that you want something from me but are unwilling to ask. And that makes it easy to ignore something I may find uncomfortable." He took a deep breath. "I don't mean to try to place the blame of my faults on you. Not

234

at all. But I would really appreciate your help with that. Please stand up for yourself—say what you need. Ask what you want. Please stop apologizing for your existence."

"I guess I don't understand." *And here's where he dumps me.*

"I just find it easy to take advantage of your insecurities without meaning to. I want to be the kind of man you need—not another jerk who keeps you hopping trying to make him happy."

Her eyes stared out over the yellow-green spring countryside. Trees held a tiny haze of green around the branches that looked like streaks across the sky as they passed. At last, she sighed. "I don't know what you mean. What am I doing so wrong? I'm trying—"

When he interrupted, yet again, Carlie finally saw what he meant by his tendency to talk over someone. She started to mention it, but his words caught her attention. "—makes it easy to be unkind to you or take advantage of you. I don't want to do that. I'm just asking for your help. I see you overlooking—right now even. You're irked that I interrupted you, but you didn't say anything."

"Only because interrupting you is just as rude as you interrupting me."

"Yes!" Dean pounded the seat with their hands. "Exactly! That's what I want to hear. Be yourself, Carlie. You're not going to push me away if you irritate me."

"Shouldn't I learn to get over it, though?"

He shrugged. "I'd usually say yes, but for you... I don't think so. When you put up with my faults instead of calling me on bad behavior, you actually encourage me to treat you badly. That's..." He gave her hand another squeeze. "That's not the man I want to be. Not for you. Not for anyone."

"You might regret that," she muttered.

As Dean followed Carlie's clipped directions, he tried to resist the urge to laugh. *It's not a joke to her. She's furious that you didn't...* And therein lay the problem. He didn't know. One minute they'd been talking to the pastor of her parents' church, and the next he'd felt her go cold. *What was I saying? Told him what I do for a living, how we met, how amazing—seriously. No. She can't be angry that I told someone I think she's wonderful. That's...* Understanding lit his brain like a sign on the Las Vegas Strip.

"So, you're angry with me."

"Brilliant deduction, Cecil."

That was low. Yes. I was right. He steeled himself against the coming blast that any woman would give him for his next question. *They hate it when we can't read their minds—even if they can't read them either.* "Well... sorry, but I have to ask the question that will prove how dense I am, but how did I offend you?"

"So, you make *me* explain *your* issues. That's rich."

He tried an attempt at humor. "Can I guess?" When Dean saw her lip twitch, he relaxed. *Whew.*

"I don't know, *can* you?"

"I would like to note that right there you have proven that you will be an excellent mother. No woman can fail at motherhood who knows and appre—"

"Stuff it."

He waited.

"Well?"

"Well, what?" It was almost *too* enjoyable.

"I thought you were guessing."

And I thought you told me to stuff it. Yep. I nailed this one. He waited until they got past the intersection that sent them toward the Denham's neighborhood before he said. "I made you uncomfortable when I complimented you to Pastor Willers."

"I—that's—" She lapsed into stony silence.

And she's probably preparing for round two. Dean decided to preempt the conflict. "You need to know something about me."

"What's that?" Her voice sounded just a trace less antagonistic.

"You can't push me into a fight. I'm not going to be that man for you."

"I'm not—"

At that moment, he had a flash revelation—one of those moments that explains the meaning of the universe—or reveals a tiny truth of it—in a mere fraction of an instant. "No, Carlie. You are. It's a coping mechanism, I think, but I'm not going to play. You can get mad at me, chew me out, push me away, pick a fight—but I'm not going anywhere. I'm not going to help you self-destruct. I won't be that man for you." He waited for her to relax. Seconds ticked into the better part of a minute before he saw any sign—just as he'd convinced himself that he'd really blown it. "Left here?"

"Yeah, sorry."

"There's one more thing, Carlie."

Dean waited for some sign that she'd listen. But Carlie relaxed completely and reached for his hand. She held it in a way that seemed different—more personal—than any prior touches. "Dean, can I say something before you—" She sighed. "Don't give up on me, okay?"

"I'm not giving up on you. I'm going to be the man you need to the best of my ability, and you do not need that man—the jerk who goes off on you because he can't see that you're hurting. You don't need that man. He's done enough damage over the years."

Dean pulled up in front of the Denham home and parked the car. Children spilled out of the front door and raced to meet them as they walked hand-in-hand up the walk. Carlie glanced up at him, back at the children, and then gazed into his eyes. "I don't deserve this."

"But you're *worth* it, and that's all that matters."

"We're going to hunt eggs! Daddy says to stop trying to make him run away and hurry up."

There it was again—the wince. There had been enough of them to make him take notice—to watch. *It shouldn't hurt that much. The boy is just repeating a joke, right? But look at her. She's truly wounded, and I don't think she's as overly sensitive as I once thought. So why?*

"—coming. Let me slip on some flats first, okay?"

That's when he realized he'd missed something. So, at the door, with the retreating squeals of children growing fainter by the second, Dean stepped back, leaned against the siding, and gave her a thorough examination. "Since I neglected to say it before, I'm saying it now. You look amazing—that dress. Wow." He winked at her blush and added, "I'm going with, 'I was struck speechless earlier and have only now managed to find a way to tell you.'"

One eyebrow rose in that infuriating way that those with the necessary talent manage to do—turning ordinary moments into impressive ones. "That's your story, huh?"

"And I'm sticking to it."

The door opened and James blurted out, "Can you just get in here? The kids are driving us nuts. They want 'Aunt Carlie' and 'Dr. Dean' to find eggs, too."

"Coming… just need to change my shoes."

"Just wait'll you get married. You won't have to torture yourself to try to get a guy. He'll be sunk already." James beckoned Dean into the house. "The things women do to try to be attractive. Don't they know they are without three-inch spikes and a hundred bucks in makeup?"

Have you ever told her *that?* Though he thought it, Dean kept his mouth shut and watched the unfolding festivities.

While Carlie helped toddlers and preschoolers search for dyed eggs under scraggly shrubs that showed more than they hid in the early spring foliage, Gina brought him a bottle of root beer and urged him to sit down, relax. "She'll stay out there with those kids until they wear her out—probably ruin her dress, too. But she loves it."

Gina sank into a chair next to him. "All Carlie ever wanted to be was a mom—a wife. She's spent her whole adult life trying to overcome that. I can't get her to realize that there's nothing wrong with that. I mean, except for the past eight years, I was 'just' a wife and a home-maker—a mom. I loved it. But I can't say that to her. No girl wants to be like her mother."

"I think Carlie does." Dean waited for Gina to respond, but when she didn't, he added, "It seems to me that she's under the impression that being a professional of some kind is the only way she'll gain her family's approval. It's why she hates her job and loves it at the same time. She's good at it, but she thinks it should be beneath her, so she resists it."

"No... not Carlie. She loves that job."

Dean started to protest—but it occurred to him that perhaps Carlie preferred to hide that side of herself. "I agree that she loves it, Mrs. Denham. I just see a side of her that also thinks she shouldn't. Perhaps it's just my perception, though."

James carried a crying toddler to his mother's side and, as Carlie followed with her niece, said, "Well, I'm glad Carlie finally met a guy with half a brain." He nudged Dean. "I like you. I'm just sorry that her track record doesn't bode well for your relationship."

"James! C'mon. Don't be like that." Carlie rolled her eyes at Dean and said, "Ignore him. He's still mad that I never went out with his high school friend like he thought I would."

It sounded like normal sibling banter—something that, though Dean had never experienced for himself, had always seemed to be full of innocent digs. Carlie engaged in equally sharp repartee, but while her siblings let her words roll off their shoulders, each of theirs wounded her.

D ean's phone rang just as he settled down with a book he'd been aching to read for weeks. But the irritation that flared with the first note of the ring tone fizzled as it continued. He smiled at the sight of Carlie's name on the screen, put it on speaker, and answered. "Hey, how was today?"

"Good... but I realized something while I sat here recovering from the shock of two—count 'em *two*—mice lying in Pouncer's bowl. I think Moros is trying to bolster the kitten's confidence or something. It's not working. Pouncer is too smart—sees right through it. Just like I saw through my dad letting me win at checkers when I was little."

"Well, most parents do that at some point. I imagine that you shocked him the day you won—the day he forgot to 'let' you."

"How'd you know? I'll never forget that day! He was so... so... *dumbfounded* that he almost gave it away."

Dean would rather have asked about the "revelation" that had caused her to call, but he knew she'd get there eventually. *Patience. She needs you to have patience.* He found it difficult to share that last game with his father, but Dean tried. "A similar thing happened with my father. It was the last time I saw him."

"What?"

Carlie, have you any idea how hard this is? You don't, do you? How could you? Lord, right here—this right here—anyone who knows me at all would know I love you just with this. He gathered up his emotions, stuffed them in a box in his heart, and tried sitting on it. "I'll never forget it. We sat by the window of the apartment on Weston. The window was open, sheers fluttered in the breeze, cars honked outside. Dad got this look in his eye, and I knew it meant he was going to play to win. I crushed him. His face got this really stern, immovable look to it. He gave me a kiss, squeezed my shoulder, and walked out." Dean swallowed the lump in his throat and added, "I never saw him again."

"What? I don't understand." Thickened with emotion, Carlie's voice hinted that she might cry. "He never saw you again? Why?"

"Turns out that was Dad's agreement with my mother. He would leave and sever all ties with me, and my mother wouldn't sue for alimony, child support, or any other financial compensation." Before he knew what he'd done, Dean spoke the words he'd never said aloud. "For most of my childhood, I believed that he left because he was mad that he lost."

Her silence soothed his heart. *I know what you are thinking. I love that it matters to you that I know better now. Thanks.* But as much as he wanted to, Dean wouldn't say it aloud. *She needs to be comfortable talking about it first. She'll bring it up when it's time. It'll work out.*

When she didn't say anything, Dean offered her an out. "So… you said you realized something. What was it?"

"Oh! Sorry," Carlie exclaimed. "Forgot. I—yeah. So, anyway, I realized that you were going to tell me what you thought of my family— how… you know."

The fact that you don't even want to say it speaks the proverbial volumes. After a quick prayer, Dean asked a question of inane proportions. "So, you wish to hear my opinion?"

"Um, duh! That was kind of the question…"

And right there, you did exactly what hurts you. I really wish I knew when it started. It would explain so much.

"Dean?"

"Sorry—distracted. Well, I think their teasing is normal—it's what almost every family I've ever seen does." Her silence killed him. *Don't panic yet. Listen.* "However, what isn't normal…" Dean waited for her to acknowledge him before he continued. "—is that they don't tone it down when you don't respond well to it—when it's obvious that it's hurting you. That's what doesn't seem normal to me. Or," he added after a moment, "if it is normal, it shouldn't be."

"So, all families tease, but when I don't get into it, it's all my fault and they just keep going?"

"That isn't what I said or meant. I just noticed that you tease back *sometimes*. But other times you don't. Other times it's obvious that you're not enjoying it, but they keep going. I—" He sighed. "Do you really want to hear this?"

"Yeah. I do. I don't understand what you're saying, so maybe if you just keep going it'll click somehow."

Dean grinned. *She wants to see the good in it all. I knew she would.* "Well, okay. So, James jokes about your nose. You tease him about his ears. Everyone is having fun, right?"

"Okay…"

"Then Carol or your dad comments on your shoes, and for whatever reason, you don't think it's funny. You can't get into it. Maybe the shoes hurt or cost more than you should have paid—something that sits wrong with you. And I think this is where the dysfunction sets in. They continue trying to include you in the joking, so they keep pushing. They don't *want* to hurt you, but they obviously—to an outsider anyway—do. They need to learn how to stop."

"Really…" Carlie's voice grew quiet. "But how?"

"I think I can show them—teach them how to hear what you're trying to communicate. They learned it from your father, you know. He does the same thing to all of you—and to your mother. He's not comfortable voicing affection, so he just mouths off."

"Dad!?" She laughed. "I don't think so."

He hesitated, not wanting to make the offer but knowing he should. Right trumped preference and Dean said, "Let's go back in a couple of weeks. I'll show you."

When she didn't respond, Dean expected her to eventually say no. But after several seconds—long, grueling, agonizing seconds—Carlie agreed. "Okay. But if I have to hear one more time that you're going to figure out how much better off you'd be without me, I might just deck them both at once."

"You'll have to beat me to it," Dean warned.

Once more, nerves attacked him as Dean waited for Carlie's arrival. Thanks to the Easter break—he had no papers to grade, no work to do. Of course, that only made the wait longer and more miserable. A book lay open on the table before him. He hadn't looked at it since he arrived.

Even coming half an hour later didn't help. Oh, Carlie. You know how to make me anxious.

"Hey, mister. Mind if I join you so I don't have to wait in line?"

A grin nearly exploded in his heart and eventually reached his lips. "Glad to have you." He leaned forward as she seated herself and added, "Did I ever tell you that I was pleased you asked? You made a boring lunch grading session interesting. I was sorry to have to leave."

"No, you didn't. Because you refused to *talk* to me!" She grinned. "But since you didn't, I kind of opened up to you. So that's good. I

241

mean, you really got me through a bunch of stuff. That really means a lot to me. I'm glad you didn't—now. I wasn't so glad back then. It drove me crazy at first—only because you talked to other people sometimes."

Dean started to speak, but she continued. *Poetic justice, perchance?*

"Best thing is that you are helping me with the sibs. I mean, that means so much. Besides, if you can prove to me that my dad shows affection by cutting me down—"

"Note:" he began, as he took her hands in his. "*He* doesn't think he's cutting you down. He's teasing."

"Right. Whatever. Anyway, if you can help me see that, maybe I won't dread going home so much."

There's your opening. Take it. Before he could second-guess himself, Dean leaned back and fiddled with his napkin. "Sooo... I met your parents. Would you care to come with me to meet my mother and stepfather?"

She gave him a strange look—one that made him more nervous than he would have expected. "Um... Dean? I have. At the hospital, remember?"

Technically he'd remembered, but not practically. He knew they were there—had spoken to her even—but it seemed like a foggy dream rather than reality. "Yeah... but that's not *really* meeting them, is it? I mean, didn't Larry talk Mim into leaving?"

"Yeah..." She smiled. "He talked to me, you know."

"He did? When?" Something about it sounded familiar, but Dean couldn't decide why.

"After I left." She grinned at the surprise Dean couldn't hide. "He told me that if I thought about it, I'd figure out that you did *communicate* with me. You just didn't talk. And, that if I kept coming, you eventually would." Her eyes softened a little, sending little beats skipping over the surface of his heart. "He was right about that, too."

A server who introduced herself as Kimber stepped up to the booth with a perky bounce. That changed when she leaned close and growled, "Janice just got a call about someone in the hospital. She said I better not ruin this, or she'll make my life miserable, so if you two decide you hate each other, can you just pretend you don't until *after* next Wednesday? I've got enough misery without Janice doing her part to compound it." The perkiness resumed as she flashed a semi-plastered on grin and said, "So what can I get you?"

Carlie gave him a curious glance. "Do you know what the special is?"

"No, I—"

Kimber, eager to please, jumped in. "Today we—"

"No. Stop." The girl nearly choked on her own words as Carlie gestured for silence. Carlie gave Dean a challenging look and said, "Feel daring?"

"Uhhh…"

Taking that as a yes, she turned to Kimber and said, "We'll take the special. Just don't tell us what it is." The moment the girl left, Carlie added, "And of *course* I want to 'meet' your parents. I want your mom to sit me down and show me all your embarrassing childhood photos— like when you sneaked into the kitchen and made a mess of the cake for dinner or—"

"You won't find anything like that. Those are the *last* pictures my mother would take or save." He could see, from the smirk around the corners of her mouth, that Carlie didn't believe him. "Look, I know it sounds like I'm just trying to get out of a little personal humiliation, but really. You kind of need to understand my mother before I take you. I think Mim has blocked most of that day at the hospital out of her mind—blacked it out. She does that with crises. But…"

"What?" Carlie reached for his hand and gave it a squeeze. "What is it? She's a nice lady. I met her. She was so worried about you. It was cute."

"Carlie, you need to understand something about her. I love her— I do. But my mother is a little shallow—not unintelligent, but in her perceptions of people."

The relief on Carlie's face told him this would be a tougher conversation than he'd imagined. His other girlfriend had been confident, too—*and Mim crushed her. Yeah, she kind of deserved it, but still. Carlie doesn't.* "I should begin with the positives. My mother will be predisposed to like you because you're beautiful."

"Oh, please. I'm not repulsive, I know—"

"Oh, no," Dean interjected. "No. You don't have to think you're attractive, but you do have to allow others their own opinions. Mine is—and my mother's will be—that you *are* beautiful. Deal with it."

"Well, I love that you think so. I do. Thank you."

A gracious acceptance—something you've worked hard on, I suspect. Dean allowed himself to sit back and watch her for a moment—right until she turned a lovely shade of pink. "I'm serious. I need you to know and feel just how beautiful I think you are. It's important to me that I communicate how I feel about *all* of you."

Dean could have sworn her lip trembled as she said, "That's— that's really sweet."

"Good," he said as he tried to find a gentle way to share the rest of his concerns. "Please focus on that, because there's more."

"Uh oh."

Just tell her. "You just need to understand that my mother's opinion will be based upon appearances. If we arrived now, she would find you wonderful. However, if we show up after an intense game of racquetball or volleyball..." He gave her an apologetic look. "It would change—her opinion of you. It'll improve again later, but um..." Dean winced as he added, "But it would never be as high again."

"You're exagg—" Carlie's eyes widened as she watched him. "No... really? Why? And why are you telling me this?"

"Because I know you'll sense it. At some point, you'll know, and it'll hurt." As much as he didn't want to say it, Dean knew he needed to be honest. "Carlie, you're not excessively sensitive about everything, but in a situation like this, you'll desire to be liked and respected. Anyone would. You'll enjoy her approval and later, feel the change. It'll hurt, and I don't want you hurt."

As he spoke, Carlie shook her head. "Aren't you exaggerating just a little? I mean, it can't be *that* big of a deal."

"It's happened before—with other friends. Guys, girls, me— never matters." His stomach clenched when he came to the one thing that would make Carlie see the seriousness of it. *Just do it. Just get it over with.* He cleared his throat. "It's why my father left us. He couldn't handle the lack of respect."

Her eyes bugged. "No..."

"Yes," he whispered. "Carlie, aside from this, she's a wonderful person. I love her. But in this area..." Dean shrugged. "It's terrible to say, 'If my mother sees a stain on your shirt the first time you meet her it'll taint her opinion of you.' But it's true. I wanted to prepare you for it. If she shows some kind of..." He struggled for the least offensive word. "... distaste? I just want you prepared. You already think the worst of yourself at times. I don't want you seeing any perceived flaws through her warped eyes."

Confusion flooded her eyes. "If you didn't want me to meet—"

"No, no. I do, Carlie. I believe you will love her—eventually. If you can just overlook any unkind reaction if she happens to see you dribble ice cream on your shirt, all will be well." His heart sank as he realized he'd need to warn her about Larry. "And as for Larry..."

"Great, he's not going to accept me either?"

"No... he will. He will love you. I think you saw that at the hospital, didn't you?" The small smile that tugged at the corners of her mouth gave him the encouragement he needed. "He... Carlie, I'm closer to him than anyone in my life. He's the truest father I've ever had. I love him. And yes, he will love you, but he won't show it until he thinks you're comfortable with him. He's completely honest—doesn't play games. So, when he feels it and knows you're ready—and not before— he'll show it."

A sense of unease pricked Dean's subconscious, and he realized that Kimber stood there. A glance up broke the strange spell that had come over them. "Um… is that ours?"

"Yeah, oh!" Kimber flushed. "Sorry. I—well, you were so serious. I couldn't interrupt. And then I was listening, and then I really couldn't interrupt. I'm sorry."

Carlie accepted the New England plate with its crab cakes and clam chowder. "This looks delicious! Great special."

A blessing that neither of us is allergic to shellfish. Dean waited until Kimber left and said, "Are you sure that's what you want?"

"Defini—oh. You don't like it. I'll—"

Dean shook his head. "It actually sounds delicious. Just making certain." Something she'd said prompted him to ask, "Mind if we pray?"

Of all the responses she'd have, tears were the last he expected. "That's…" A sniffle. An embarrassed flutter of her fingers to brush away another tear or three. "I—" Her emotions choked her.

"I didn't mean—"

"No!" Carlie gave herself a little shake and forced a weak smile. "It was good, okay? I've wanted you to pray with me again. Guys just don't do that. Even Jared didn't do that, except at the church thing, of course."

The moment the prayer ended, and she dipped her spoon in the chowder, Carlie said, "So, how did your parents—Larry and your mom, I mean—end up together? They sound really opposite."

"They are." He took a bite of soup before Dean added, "You should understand something. I learned how to treat people and show them how I feel from Larry. He taught me how *not* to be like my mother. I was already headed that way when he married her."

"Why *did* he marry someone like that?" Her eyes widened. "That came out so wrong. I'm sorry."

"No, I understand," Dean assured her. "But outside of her silly shallowness—which is probably rooted in some latent insecurity that only her therapist understands—outside of that, she's a wonderful woman. Larry chose to see past the flaw and focus on the rest. He's just fortunate enough that he can overlook that one. Dad couldn't." Dean sighed. "I couldn't."

"Wow. To be able to endure that kind of constant disrespect…"

Dean shook his head as she spoke. "But see, that's just it. He doesn't feel disrespected because she sees his physical flaws now. Her constant trips to the cosmetic surgeon for just 'a little lift here' or whatever—they don't bother him like they would me."

"Yeah, I couldn't do that—marry someone like her. I mean, I know you said she's wonderful, and I saw that at the hospital. But…"

"I couldn't either, but you have no idea how grateful I am that Larry could. If it wasn't for him, I wouldn't have anything to do with her. By now I probably would have hated her—and probably ended up just like her."

As he'd been speaking, Dean had noticed something in Carlie—a growing question that he couldn't anticipate. She smiled at all the right places, nodded. But when he finished, she asked, "Is that why you dress the way you do? Is it *her* style?"

Great. Now she thinks I'm just led about the nose by my mommy. He tried to explain. "Somewhat. It helps her respect me." Disbelief in her eyes made him open up further. "You see, I went through this rebellious phase once—trying to shock her out of her issues. I was confident she'd get over it if *I* was the one to do it. It almost destroyed our relationship—took years to recover from it. Larry finally stepped in one day and said, 'You might want to reconsider how you handle it. She's your mother, and you can show her respect for whom and where she is while still being yourself. You don't have to react to her faults. That just makes you at fault too.'"

"Wow. So, you went for stained clothes—"

His laughter brought a few odd looks their way. Dean winced. "No, no. I had let my hair grow shaggy and wore graphic tees and jeans."

"Wow—can't imagine you in jeans at all."

"I'll have to wear them next time we go out."

She gave him that look—the one that hinted she didn't believe him. "Why do I get the feeling you'll have to stop by the mall on the way home and *buy* some jeans?"

"Perhaps… or not. The point is, that I did adopt a style that was all me but would also make my mother comfortable."

The look she gave him warmed his ears, his neck, his cheeks. "Well," she said at last, "it does suit you."

"Thank you."

"So, when did this thing happen with your mom—the rebellion thing? How old were you?"

"Right after I started college. I was fourteen."

"You started college at *fourteen?* Wait." Her forehead wrinkled as she thought. "Actually, that sounds familiar."

Dean cut into his crab cake as he shrugged and said, "I think I mentioned once before. I was something of a prodigy…"

Nerves turned Carlie's stomach into a jumbled mess of knots that would make any tatter cringe in horror. Fishermen would weep and howl like babies deprived of sustenance. She stood at the door fidgeting with the hem of her top, desperately wishing she'd chosen something else. *I look like an Ellie wannabe from "Up!" It's*—

Dean's arm slipped around her waist and his lips almost brushed her ears as he murmured, "You look wonderful. It'll be fine. Relax and enjoy it."

"Easy for you to say," she hissed. "You're not on the chopping block."

"That's just it," he insisted. "I am. Every time I see her. She'll always love me, but she'll lose—"

The door opened, and the man who stood there looked much more robust and a bit devastatingly handsome compared to the haggard, worried stepfather she'd met at the hospital. "Carlie, welcome. Lynn is just changing. She got a water spot on her silk blouse, and you know how that goes…"

That sounds like code for something! But what? Wha—

"—to finally get to meet you properly. We were all a bit shaken at the hospital that day." The man nodded at Dean. "Son."

It took a moment for the words to register. *He's talking to me. What do I do again?* A glance at Dean and a squeeze of his hand jerked her back into the present. "Oh, it's great to really 'meet' you, too. But you were wonderful that night. I never forgot it."

A woman breezed in from the hall with the kind of air that is usually reserved for divas with daggers for fingernails on daytime soaps. "Dean! You're finally here—late as usual."

"He's right on time, Lynn," Larry insisted. "As usual."

"Oh, true. I had to change—that new sink splashes dreadfully." Lynn turned to Carlie, who felt her throat go dry as the woman gave her the ultimate in once-overs. "Carlie…so beautiful!" Dean's mother gave her a quick hug. "I am so happy to finally meet you. I mean, I know I saw you at the hospital, but I can't remember *anything* about that awful night. The reporters and the nurses." She shuddered. "But I know it meant a lot to Dean. He has spoken of it often."

Oh, you have? She raised an eyebrow at him. "He never mentioned that to me."

"Well, he wouldn't, would he?" Lynn led Carlie to the couch and patted the cushion next to her. "It's what told me that he'd lost his heart to you long before he figured it out."

Carlie gave an awkward smile and glanced around her. A slight twitch of Larry's lip seemed to intimate that he and not Lynn had figured out Dean's feelings for her. *Makes sense. He seems like an intuitive guy.*

"—that you had a nice trip down to Morganfield. I so wish I had considered more children. Family occasions like that would be so much fun. Planning little egg hunts and shopping for frilly dresses." She leaned close. "I didn't like the stretch marks and the puffiness. I had preeclampsia, you know. Dangerous times, but…" The loving look she gave Dean proved that whatever her faults, she did adore her son. "I'd say he's worth it."

"I would agree."

The woman's eyes turned back to Carlie and the poor girl's throat went dry at the subtle scrutiny Lynn put her under. "That's a lovely top, you're wearing. I really think the nouveau-retro chic is a great look for most women. Don't you?"

And there goes the terrifying idea that we'd have nothing to talk about. Carlie pounced on that. "I do! It's all so very feminine, but most aren't fussy, so flattering for all types. That touch of tailored with the softness of fabric choices and style. It's my favorite." She leaned close and murmured, "I'll admit that I did stand out in the hall and think, 'Why did I dress up like that girl from "Up!" She'll think I'm an idiot.'"

"I think you're lovely. And I haven't seen that, but I'll have to now. If that girl dresses with such good taste, I want to know more."

Dean sat beside them and put his arm across the back of the couch. His hand stroked his mother's shoulder for a moment before he said, "Mim, "Up!" is an animated film—a cartoon. Adorable cartoon, but…"

"If Carlie likes it, I'm sure I will, too." The woman's head cocked. "You really are such a beautiful girl. Where *did* you get such an amazing complexion?"

"Genetics?" Carlie gave Lynn an apologetic shrug. "I don't know. I was fortunate *not* to have acne as a teenager. My sister didn't either, but poor James…"

"Dean had a horrible case of acne. Nothing touched it. We tried all the conventional—and a few unconventional—treatments, but time alone healed it." She winced at a memory before adding, "Then came the horrors of trying to fight the scarring. It took a combination of dermabrasion and laser treatments to rid him of the effects of the disease."

Disease? It's acne, not bubonic plague! Carlie tried to be sympathetic. "I know James keeps a hint of a beard to cover most of his scars. We couldn't afford much in the way of treatments either before or after he finally outgrew most of the acne."

Beside her, Dean stiffened. *Oh, great. Now she's predisposed to dislike my brother. This is ridiculous.*

But Lynn surprised her—Dean too, it seemed. "I can only imagine how difficult that must be for your mother—and for him. What a clever way to cover it. I've never been very fond of facial hair myself, but some men do look quite ruggedly handsome with a few days' growth."

Larry asked a question. Lynn countered with another. They made lunch and talked of Dean's academic career. They ate and talked of Carlie's position at Skyline. They drank wine on the couch afterward—or rather Larry, Lynn, and Dean did, while Carlie sipped at hers and pretended not to hate it. All the while, Lynn bragged about her son and grilled Carlie on everything from her childhood to her future dreams. Nothing Larry or Dean said or did could stop her, and by near dinner time, Carlie sagged against Dean, exhausted.

"Mim, thanks for lunch. It was great. I loved it. But we really need to go. I promised her a quiet evening tonight—just a movie and some cheap, disgusting food."

"Oh, bring her back soon." Lynn pulled out her phone. "May I have your number? We could get lunch one day. I'd love to take you to my favorite restaurant. Would that be okay?"

Well, you can't say she doesn't like me. Carlie took the phone and punched in her number. "Call anytime. And I'd love to have lunch."

The woman nearly squealed. "Oh, this'll be so much fun. I can't wait to tell Liz about me having lunch with my son's beautiful girlfriend. Oh, you'll have to meet her. She's a fabulous person—works with all kinds of charities. Oh!" Her eyes flitted to Dean. "Didn't you say Carlie was a whiz at event planning? Maybe we could recruit her for our next dinner!"

"Perhaps," Dean agreed. "But you can call or text her about that *tomorrow*. We're *going* now. I'd like to have her to myself for a bit, as well."

Larry and Lynn stepped out into the hall and waved until the elevator doors finally closed Dean and Carlie off from view. Carlie exhaled with excessive slowness. "How was that both the most wonderful lunch and the most exhausting?"

"She likes you. So did Larry." The pride in his voice choked her.

"I still can't imagine why." Carlie gave him a wicked glance as they stepped out into the lobby. "Must run in the family."

It worked. Dean's arm slipped around her waist as he propelled her out to the front where his car waited. "That it does."

All afternoon, something had niggled at her. Once seated and buckled, Carlie pulled a mirror from her purse and stared at it. Dean put the car in gear but waited. "What's wrong? Is there something in your eye?"

"She really thinks I'm beautiful—not just passable, but beautiful. I never thought I was ugly, but wow. I've never seen it. My family always talked about my funny nose and my tiny ears. My sister hates my naturally curly hair. She's into the straight look."

"Has it ever occurred to you that your sister is jealous—that perhaps they tease you because they love you—and maybe are a little jealous?"

"Nah..."

"I am serious," he insisted. "I think I saw it when I was there. I thought it was just usual family joking. The way families tease out of love and affection—but looking back, they did tease you like people do when they're trying to hide jealousy."

Carlie began to argue—almost dismissed him completely, but he'd been right enough that she couldn't—not yet. "I don't know, but maybe."

Carlie ignored the guilt producing ten o'clock that flashed on her phone as she pulled it from her pocket and punched Carol's number. Seconds ticked past—three—before a groggy Carol answered. "Are you okay? What happened?"

"I'm fine. Sorry it's so late—"

"You scared the number two out of me!"

My goodness, you're such a mom. That's hysterical. Gotta tell Dean. "No, sorry. I just really want your honest opinion. No joking, teasing—no excuses. Just straight up honesty, okay?"

"Fine. Whatever. Just ask so I can get back to sleep. I have to be up for church at eight!"

"Do you think I'm pretty?"

Carol's snort could mean anything from "definitely" to "are you kidding me, no way!" Carlie couldn't decide which fit. "C'mon, Carol. Just tell me."

"Duh! Yeah! You're gorgeous."

"Seriously? Why didn't you ever tell me?"

A low murmur told Carlie that her brother-in-law had awakened. Just as she started to apologize, Carol spoke again. "Sorry. Look, all you had to do was look in the mirror."

"What! Like that would help. I see what you guys always say."

"What do we say?" Carol groaned and muttered something about leaving the room before adding, "What are you talking about?"

"My whole childhood—the *entire* time—all you did was tell me how ugly I am. How my nose is weird, and my ears are too small."

"Uh, Carlie? That's like when you've got a seven-foot-tall guy and call him tiny or some scrawny dude and call him Big Al. It's who we are. Denhams joke to hide how we feel."

"Has it always been that way? Did you always say the opposite of what you meant?" Carlie struggled to stamp down the rising emotion in her voice. "So, you don't think I'm stupid and worthless?"

"Carlie—no!" Carol's voice caught. "How did you never get that?

You didn't know? How did you never know that we're proud to death of our little sister?"

"Because you never say anything but how pathetic I am?" When Carol protested again, Carlie stopped her. "No, listen, Carol. You've spent my whole adult life telling me what a loser I am for *just* being a stupid retail clerk, for not going to college, for picking loser boyfriends."

"Well, the last one is true. I have to admit that. Dean's great, though. I hope you keep him. But the other stuff—we're just a bit jealous that you had the guts to do what you wanted rather than letting yourself get bullied into college and a career."

"You guys told me I didn't have what it takes!"

Carol's protest came through clearly—and with volume no one could mistake. "Now you wait right there. *You* said you didn't want to go to college. *You* insisted that it was too much money when you didn't want to be anything that would turn you into a slave of your job. We supported you—joked about how you'd never cut it in college. But it was to *support* your decision!"

"Yeah, well, all it did was convince me that you thought I was stupid."

"You were almost a 4.0 student in high school. How could you possibly think that you were too stupid to hack it in college? C'mon!" When Carlie didn't reply, Carol's voice grew quiet. "I'm sorry, Carlie. I didn't know. I thought you understood. You always seemed to." She sighed. "Look, I guess I can see it. One minute we joke about you being an idiot and the next we tell you what you already know—that your boyfriend is a creep, and you have bad taste in men. I suppose I would have gotten messages mixed too—maybe. I don't know." Carol's voice dropped a bit more—became a bit softer. "Carlie, maybe I should have said it more—probably should have. But I'm crazy proud of you. I love you—so does James. Mom and Dad think you're awesome, and if we all tease you a bit too much, well. It's how we show it. I'm sorry."

Long after Carlie disconnected the call, she sat staring at the phone. At last, she sent Dean a short text. TALKED TO CAROL. YOU WERE RIGHT. WOW.

251

Fog clouded everything. Carlie stumbled along a path, tripping over cracks and bumps in the sidewalk, and called out for someone—someone she couldn't name. "Where are you? I can't see you?"

Step by step, the fog began to clear, and her eyes began to focus once more. "My bedroom? Why is there fog—?" The Turtles blasted through the room, wiping out the rest of the fog, as "Happy Together" signaled a phone call. Her hands fumbled for it while her brain tried to tick off the potential calamities on the other end of the call. "'ello?"

"I got a new job *and* a new apartment—furnished with *nice* furniture. It's tiny, but it's temporary—*rent free!* All I have to do is help with housekeeping on weekends."

"Hannah?"

"Oh! What time—oh, man. I'm so sorry, Carlie. I—"

She rushed to interrupt before the young woman disconnected. "No! I'm glad you called! What's this about a house?"

"Okay, so my sister is a freshman at the university, and she was talking to her sociology professor about whether she could write about my situation—how my parents have disowned me, how my neighbors hate me, and how the rules for welfare mean it costs society *more* to help me through the system than straight help would. It's crazy. Anyway, the professor said to come back today."

"Aaand..." Carlie's toes and fingers tingled with excitement.

"They called me from his office. We met downtown at a diner and talked for *hours.* Michaela had to take my kids home—they got a bit out of hand."

Carlie's eyes rolled before she could stop them. Grateful Hannah couldn't see, she said, "I would expect so! *One* hour at a diner is a lot for four little kids."

She heard it—that shift from embarrassment to relief that happens when parents realize they aren't total failures if their children happen to act like it sometimes. "Yeah. That's true. Thanks."

"I'm still waiting to hear about this..." Carlie hummed the theme from Jeopardy until Hannah laughed and spoke again.

"Well, so this woman was there with Michaela. Her name is Megan—amazing woman. She runs this B&B and her basement tenant just moved out. So, she's giving me that basement, rent free—oh, Carlie. I saw pictures! It's gorgeous. It's not *that* much smaller than our current place either. *And!* There's also a bathroom on the first floor we're allowed to use."

You know you're a mom when the number of bathrooms in an apartment defines its worth. Aloud, she just cheered. "I am so happy for you. So, what's this about a job?"

"Well, Michaela's professor needed an assistant—his old one is moving—so he hired *me!* I get benefits that *include* two free classes every semester! It'll take until all the kids are out of elementary school, but who cares! I can get a *degree!*"

"And with free rent, you can save up for your own place." Carlie's brain spun with the thought. "How did they pull this off so fast?"

"I don't know, but man, I'm grateful. This is going to be awesome!" An awkward pause preceded Hannah's next words. "I just want to thank you and Dean for being there for me. You were the last people who should have wanted to help. And you did it without making me feel worse."

"What happened isn't your fault," Carlie began. "And it wasn't the guy we knew either—and yet it was..." she murmured.

"What!"

Realizing how it sounded made Carlie backpedal. "No, listen. Steve wanted to take care of his family. That's all it was. It wasn't like him to hurt people, but he didn't really try to, did he? The investigators said that he shot *above* people in the restaurant. He wasn't trying to hurt us. Dean scared him, I bet."

"That's nice of you to say, Carlie. But Steve shot the guy in the kitchen."

"He probably panicked when someone saw him. Doesn't make it right," Carlie hastened to add, "but I think we all know he wasn't usually a violent man. He wanted to take care of you and thought this way he could. He felt like a failure." Her throat swelled. "He wasn't, but he felt like it."

"Yeah... anyway. Thanks."

"Hannah?" Carlie waited for a response before adding, "We don't blame him—none of us do. Frank hates that this happened. The employees miss him."

The phone disconnected half a second after Carlie heard a whispered, "Thank you."

Her clock glowed at her. 12:08. The hesitation lasted only a few seconds before she tapped the screen and waited. *Bet he sounds cute sleepy.* His voice came through the airwaves almost immediately—quiet but concerned. "Carlie? Are you okay?"

"I'm great, actually. Sorry to call so late—wake you up..."

"You didn't. I was just reading."

"Oh brother." Her heart sank a bit. "Another area where we're opposites. You're a night owl, aren't you?" His chuckle did warm, delightful things in her heart. *I like him. I really like him. It's not just rebound or whatever other horrible things Rhonda is telling everyone. Yes!*

"I am, I'm afraid. But I'm more concerned about you. Is everything all right?"

For a moment, Carlie almost suggested a quick Skype session so she could see his face, but when she patted her head, revealing hair height and width that would rival any eighties country star, that notion died a swift and decisive death. "Hannah got a job—and a new house. Benefits—everything. She just called all excited! Isn't that great?"

He didn't respond. Carlie waited for some reaction—any—but Dean said nothing. Several seconds passed and with each, her irritation blossomed into anger. "Look, you don't have to do a jig, but I thought—" Understanding hit before she could continue. "Oh, man. You're going to make it impossible for me not to fall in love with you, aren't you?" she whispered.

Still, another second or two passed before he spoke. "Sorry, what?"

"You were praying, weren't you?"

Dean cleared his throat. "Yeah... didn't mean to zone out on you. I—"

"I know. It's who you are. I think I've seen that happen at lunches before. I thought you were just irritated at me, but now... not sure."

Again, a quiet hush came over the conversation until Dean murmured, "Did I happen to hear what I think I did?"

Carlie felt her face flame as she realized that she'd spoken aloud. "Don't know what you think you heard, but I've never known you to make up stuff in your head. Goodnight." Before he could say anything else, she disconnected the call. "Whew. Awkward. Nice..." she mused.

"Yeah, but still awkward."

A little box, wrapped in pink paper with a tulle bow, sat at Carlie's place when she breezed in that second week in April. She dumped her bag and coat on the seat and slid in, eyes taking in Dean's attempt—failed as well—*not* to watch her reaction. "I see you watching. Give it up."

He stacked his papers and slid them into the messenger bag with a fluidity and familiarity that opened yet another door of her heart to him. "A man can try…"

"So, what's this for? My birthday isn't for another two mo—and you didn't know that. Drat."

He pulled out pen and paper and scribbled something. "Thanks. No, that is a combination gift and proof that my mother likes you."

"Oh?"

"I received a call on Monday. She informed me that she had overnighted that to my office and wanted to ensure that I received it and paid for it immediately."

"Wha—if she wanted to get me something, why did she make you pay for it?" Carlie blinked. "That's just weird."

His eyes—the way he looked at her. Carlie waited, holding her breath as she did, until he spoke. "I'm unable to explain until you open it."

She almost hated to do it. Carlie toyed with the box and fluffed the bow until Dean chuckled. "If you're trying to drive me crazy with the wait, it won't work. I could watch your hands all day."

"You've got to stop being so perfect."

She tugged at the bow but stopped when he said, "But that's my goal. To be perfect *for* you." At her pointed look, Dean added, "Carlie… you handed me that one."

"I did." Carlie pulled the tulle off and wrapped it around her neck like a scarf. "I can't believe you bought pink—oh, your mom did, didn't she?"

Dean shook his head. "No, I was taught to make any package reflect the gift and the recipient. I couldn't find a nice sunny yellow polkadot, so I got pink lace. It worked."

At his words, she peered closely at the wrapping paper and sighed. "I didn't even notice the lace."

Janice's voice at her shoulder made her jump just as she went to slide her finger under the paper. "Are you going to open it or what?"

Carlie jerked her finger from the package and stared as she waited for blood to appear. It never came. A glance at the package showed why.

"You folded it under! What *guy* knows to fold it under?" She thrust the box in Janice's face. "Look at that!"

"He told you his mother taught him well. I tell you, if you don't keep him, I'm going to steal him from you." Janice glared at her with mock indignation.

Dean's murmur of, "Couldn't do it, Janice. No offense…" sent delicious shivers up and down her spine.

"Don't blame you," the server muttered. "Still… someone has to scare some sense into her!" Janice took their drink orders and hurried off, leaving Carlie to open the box.

She pulled a tiny yellow and green polka dotted dress from the box. "Oh! For Cecil? It's gorgeous! And so "Up!" How'd you find—or she—how—?"

"I told her about the 'bear' of a date we had. I got Mimmy points for that date, I might add. Anyway, after you were at the condo, she said, 'You need to get a cute retro outfit for her dog.' I informed her that there were no such cute 'retro' outfits at the store. So, she took it upon herself to go on Etsy and find one. She had that dress overnighted from *France,* of all places. 'She should have it *this* week. Yes, it cost you more, but it's worth it.'" His falsetto, while a pathetic imitation of Lynn's voice, did prompt a smile from her.

"So… why again, are you paying for *her* gift?"

He took it from her and stuck two fingers through the neck hole and one through each arm. His voice climbed into the most ridiculous falsetto she'd ever heard. His hand danced back and forth as he sing-songed, "Because, my dear, Carlie. She knew I wanted to give you a gift that wouldn't be excessive so soon, and it's not a gift from me if I don't pay for it, now, is it?"

"Well, thanks… I love it. Cecil will, too. I'll have to raid my niece's doll stashes for a matching purse. They'll think that's great." She reached for his hand and laced their fingers together. "What a great day. Silly how something that seems as inconsequential as a dog dress can make everything seem beyond perfect."

The mall teemed with shoppers more reminiscent of Christmas than spring as Dean waded "upstream" against the throng that seemed only to need to push toward the doors. For a blip of a moment, he wondered if he'd missed a fire alarm. At the fountain, the tide turned with him, and Dean found himself nearly pushed along. *Good thing I am not trying to get into any of these stores. This is worse than a train in Tokyo!*

Carlie had asked to meet him at the food court at four o'clock. Now, five minutes after, Dean practically ran to avoid being any later.

But, when he burst through the press of shoppers, Dean found himself standing quite close to where Carlie spoke—nearly yelled, to be more precise—at Blaine.

"—not interested. I've said that half a dozen times. *Three* guys have offered to make you go away. Can't you get it? We're done."

"You know they're just trying to get—"

"Don't even say it, Blaine. I don't care what you think. I'm not. interested. in. you. And that's all that matters."

The first words Blaine growled, Dean missed in his desire to throttle the man, but the next nearly sent him through the roof. "He's only using you, Carlie. The guy is a *professor*. People like him do not get serious with girls like you. They want someone educated—intelligent."

Once more, just as Dean started to intervene, Carlie's words stopped him. "I think you really believe that. And I used to believe you when you said stuff like that, but I'm learning that I'm not as pathetic as you want me to think I am. I'm not stupid. I'm not pathetic, and I'm exactly what Dean wants."

"Why—"

"That's none of your business." She waved him off. "Just go away. You can't convince me I'm worthless anymore. Dean's convinced me that I'm not."

Cheering inwardly, Dean rushed forward and swung her in an arc. "How's my favorite Carlie?" As he sat her down, he allowed his eyes to rest on Blaine. "Oh, did I interrupt? I can take a walk if—"

"We're done," Carlie assured him. Without even a glance back or a trace of uncertainty in tone or expression, she added, "Blaine was just going."

"Then let's get moving. I need to purchase a couple of things before we go to the restaurant."

They hadn't taken three steps before Blaine's voice blasted over the din of shopper conversation and mall muzak. "She's a prude, you know. You won't get her into bed without a ring."

"Excuse me." She tried to stop him, but Dean gazed down at her as he touched her cheek. "Some things you let go. Others, not so much. Be right back."

He stood before a smug Blaine, hands loosely shoved in his pockets, and didn't speak—not at first. The guy began to squirm under his gaze, but only when Blaine opened his mouth did Dean respond. "Only a bully and a coward would pull a stunt like that. I'm not in love with Carlie for what I can get *from* her. I care about what I can give *to* her."

"I'll bet—"

"Don't," Dean growled, as a new, raw, *primal* side of him emerged—one that almost scared him. "Speak of her that way. Ever."

As he turned to go, Blaine snickered. "Yeah, well, if *purity* is what you want, she's not it. I talked her into consenting—*twice."*

Dean turned back and folded his arms across his chest.

"Yeah, that's right. Your precious Carlie isn't a *virgin,* if that's what you're looking for."

He fought back the urge to fly at Blaine like a kid in a schoolyard. In his mind, he saw it—Blaine crashed to the ground, him straddling the wriggling mess of humanity and pummeling the idiot's face into a bloody pulp. But, despite the anticipation of such satisfaction, Dean kept his hands to himself. Instead, he stepped forward a little, eyes trained on Blaine's, and said, "Coerced consent isn't consent, you animal. It's rape. Stay away from her or I'll do everything possible to convince her to get a restraining order against you."

No one could have been more astonished than Dean when only the steady drone of the mall followed him to Carlie's side. A glance back showed Blaine slinking away, defeated. But Carlie wouldn't look at him. Everything about her had changed. The confidence she'd shown talking to Blaine—gone.

Ideas flooded his mind as he tried to decide just how to handle it, but none seemed appropriate. Unsure what else to do, he laced his fingers through hers and tugged her toward the bookstore. "I need to purchase a book Mim wants me to read."

"A book—what?" They passed the corridor to the restrooms, and she jerked him inside. "Dean, I would have—"

He stopped her before she could say it. "Don't let him do it to you again, Carlie. I heard you tell him off. I heard you stand up for yourself. He knows how to get to you, and he did it again. Don't let him win."

"But it's true," she rasped. "I did let him talk me into—"

"Then I'll tell you what I told him." He stepped back into the press of the shoppers and pulled her with him. As they walked, he talked—probably more than he should have. Once started, he didn't seem to be able to stop. But it worked. Step by step, he watched her relax. *You have no idea just how much I wanted to beat him for doing that to you.*

"I have a bit of one. I saw your eyes." She giggled and leaned into him. "I didn't think you could *get* that mad!"

Dean blinked and shook himself. Understanding dashed him with the cold water of truth. "I didn't mean to say that aloud."

"I'm glad you did. I kind of needed to hear it. And you're right. He's just messing with my head. He's good at it. But I'm done with that. So done."

Before he could respond, they passed the accessories store where Dean had overheard her and her friends that fall. "Oh, I lost an earring

I got here. Mind if we go in and see if they have another pair? They're my favorites."

"I saw you that day," Dean admitted.

Carlie stopped mid-stride and stared at him. "Saw what?"

"You were here with Teresa and a girl who *has* to be Rhonda. You tried on a hat that you said would look good on me, and you held up earrings to see if you'd like them." He flushed at the stunned expression on her face. "I wasn't *trying* to spy on you. I was trying to keep you from seeing me, but I ducked into the wrong store. Of course, I couldn't just leave because you might see me. Then you said that you liked my style, and I didn't *want* to get out anymore."

"I can't belie—you were *in here?* That day. Seriously?"

He saw it... the frantic rush to remember everything she'd said. After half a second of agonizing deliberation, he murmured, "I also learned that I have... how did you put it? Um, '*killer* aftershave.' Is that true?"

For a moment, Dean was certain she'd slap him. Her eyes searched his face. Her hand rose and her fingers twined in his hair. *She wouldn't kiss me right here, would she? After I just confessed to sorta-not-really-but-kind-of stalking her?*

When her face leaned close, he took a deep breath. Her breath, warm on his cheek and ear, sent his heart waltzing, but her words turned it into more of a tribal dance. "Yeah. Definitely."

He choked, swallowed, and blinked before croaking out, "Let's find those earrings."

"And you tell me why your mom wants you to read a book for her."

"Oh, boy." Dean reached for earrings on a rack. "Aren't these the ones?"

"How did you remember? They are!"

He led her to the counter, set them down, and pulled out his wallet. "I told you. That day made a big impression on me. You wore them the following Wednesday—and many Wednesdays since."

Carlie stood there, agape; not even noticing that he'd paid for and accepted the earrings from the girl behind the counter. As he led her out of the store, she stammered and fumbled with words, until at last she said, "You liked me—really liked me. I mean, you didn't *like* me, maybe. But back then I really thought you were just putting up with me." She searched his face before adding, "You weren't."

"Not at all. Wednesdays were—and sometimes still are—the highlight of my week."

"Sometimes?" She elbowed him. "I think I should be offended."

Dean steered her into Price & Bradbury Booksellers. "But some weeks I get to see you on other days. Those trump Wednesdays because we're not quite so limited…"

"Smooth. Very smooth. So, what book are you buying, and *why* are you reading it again?"

Oh, Lord, help. Yet another test of her fortitude. Still, she rebounded nicely after the Blaine setback. I should tell her. He led her to the Christian romance section, and as he did, said, "Before I explain Mim, I want you to know how impressed I am with you today. I've seen Blaine shake you up for days! And look at you."

"You're going to think it's pathetic…" She glanced up at him and back at the shelves before them. "Or maybe not. But, anyway, I was talking to Teresa the other day, and she said something that really struck me." When he didn't reply, she growled, "Are you even listening?"

"I am. I'm just waiting to hear these fabulous words of wisdom." Dean reached for the book and turned to go. "So, what did she say?"

"Lynn really wants to make you read…*Forsythe Hall in the Highlands?* Seriously?"

Dean tried not to wince as he shrugged. "We have a unique relationship. I'll explain *after* you tell me what Teresa said."

"Fine." She grabbed the book and started reading the back. "Sounds kind of interesting, actually—sounds like a mystery. Oh," Carlie passed it back to him. "Teresa. Right. She said that she thought it was stupid to reject your opinion of me for Blaine's. We know Blaine is a liar, and you've never lied to me that I know of. Why wouldn't I trust your opinion? Especially after talking about stuff with Carol—again, thanks to you. So, I'm choosing to do that."

His eyes closed and he paused right there—mid-stride. "That," Dean murmured after a moment's pause, "is probably the best compliment I've ever received. Thank you."

"So… can I read that after your mom?"

Dean stood in line and waved it. "You may read it first if you care to. She'll expect it when I have time. It might be nice to get your opinion before I read it. Perhaps I can convince you to assume my pre-reading chores if you end up with similar opinions."

"But why does she have *you* read it?"

"She despises getting into a book and discovering things aren't happening how she thinks they should. So, if there's a twist in the middle that appears to lead it in a disappointing direction, she wants reassurance that it will end well."

Carlie stared at him, dumbfounded. When she finally found her voice, she asked, "Isn't that the point of reading the book?"

"Not for Mim. She truly hates finishing a book she dislikes. It makes her resent reading."

Her laughter rang out. "You're kidding? That's hysterical. I—I think I'm really going to get a kick out of your mom. I've got to invite her to lunch after I read that. Oh, my word. What books did she like?"

But Dean shook his head. "Oh, no. You ask *her* that. It'll be a nice conversation starter." He slipped an arm around her waist and murmured, "Love that you want to spend time with her. I was afraid I'd make you wary of her."

"You did," Carlie admitted. "You did. But I realized that she's just more honest than most people. A lot of us do that—judge people on how they look or if they're well-dressed, et cetera. She just doesn't pretend otherwise like the rest of us."

Oh, no. Don't do it. Don't think you can just— The salesclerk called for next in line and Dean stepped forward. As he pulled out his credit card, he turned to Carlie. "I agree on one level. But it will happen. And it will hurt. I just want you prepared for that."

"Now who thinks I'm too fragile?" She took the bag from the guy behind the counter and pulled his hand. "C'mon. Tell me more. What other things have you not told me?"

He waited until they got outside the store before he asked, "What things?"

"Like… I don't know, who was the first person you told about me?"

Dean thought for a moment. "I think it was my Wednesday night Bible study group."

"And who told you that you liked me—the first one?"

"Larry. Often. And then after our date, he assured me you'd return the next week." A memory sparked a snicker, and Carlie demanded to know what prompted it. "This one's embarrassing, but he swears you'll love it, so if you never speak to me again, I'll wind up in jail once I'm finished with him."

"Oh, c'mon and tell me." Carlie laughed and wrapped her arm through his. "This is fun."

"Well… after the disaster otherwise known as our first date, I was trying to explain what a mess I'd made of it and generally made a blubbering fool of myself—"

Carlie stopped abruptly and stared at him. "You cried?"

"*Emotionally* blubbering fool. I don't think I actually cried, but I wanted to. However, Larry said he knew what was wrong and why it had been such a mess. So, I said, 'I'm listening with an open mind and a bleeding heart.'" Dean tried to urge her forward, but Carlie refused to budge.

"That—that's actually beautiful, in a tragic sort of way."

I'd prefer that to be the last our little tragedies, okay, Lord? "I'm pleased you don't hate it."

"I don't. It... I don't want to say I like it, because you were hurting, but I like how you *put* it."

"That is a compliment. Now, shall I mortify myself further and buy me some new briefs, or may we move on to dinner? I'm famished."

"And trying to dodge the subject," Carlie added with a laugh. "But yeah. Dinner over underwear any day."

The longer she waited, the more nervous Carlie grew. In her attempt to avoid being late, she'd managed to arrive a full twenty minutes early, and now as she sat in the waiting area of the restaurant, Carlie struggled against the irrational feeling that she *needed* to pick the polish off every single one of her fingernails. *She'll notice. She'll talk Dean out of being with you. Don't blow this because you're ridiculously nervous about it.*

"Carlie! Well, I love a punctual woman." Lynn reached for her, gave a quick hug and, much to Carlie's amusement, added "air kisses" to the mix. "That is a fabulous top! You have the best taste in clothes. We *have* to go shopping sometime. I just know you'll see gems in things that look like duds to me."

Without waiting for Carlie's response, she turned to the hostess. "Rivers, party of two."

The young woman behind the desk didn't hesitate. "Right this way. You requested the east window?"

Without answering the question, Lynn turned to Carlie. "And this is why I adore this place. I never have to wait, they *always* get things right, and look how lovely it is!"

And how this lunch will cost as much as my entire month's budget for food. I knew they had money, but this is a bit much. To distract herself from thoughts of inadequacy, Carlie smiled at the hostess and thanked her. "It really is a beautiful restaurant."

Lynn ordered the "house water," whatever that meant, and Carlie decided to follow suit. Before Carlie could ask what was in it, the smiling

263

woman turned her attention to the menu and asked, "Did you have to wait long?"

Okay, I either need to be me or start off one messed-up relationship with this woman. And that'll only make things worse for Dean. So here goes, and Lord... She raised her eyes heavenward. *Help!* "I got here crazy early—so I wouldn't be late. Then I became so crazy nervous that I almost picked the nail polish from my fingers." She closed her eyes and sighed. "And for what? You're nice. You're not going to bite my head off or tell me I'm stupid for wanting my boyfriend's mom to like me." As soon as the words left her lips, panic washed over her. "Oh, no... I did *not* just say that."

The confusion in Lynn's eyes both comforted and terrified her. The woman laid down the menu and folded her hands in her lap as she leaned forward and asked, "What didn't you just say? I didn't hear anything that you should be ashamed of."

"I—" *Just do it and get it over with. This is what you get for thinking you could handle this.* "I just called Dean my boyfriend like we're some serious item or something. He's never said—"

Lynn's expression cooled and her words came out like icicles. "I understood that he had told you that he loves you."

"Um, yes..."

"Then why, may I ask, would you assume that he *doesn't* hope to be your 'boyfriend.' I would have thought that any presumption in that regard would come from him, not you." Lynn sat up straighter than any human should be able to and pursed her lips before she added, "If you are not interested in my son—"

"I am!" Carlie blushed. "Sorry, I didn't mean to interrupt. Well, I did, but I didn't mean it to be rude, and, of course, it is. I just..." She sat, chewing her lip and wishing she were anywhere but there.

Lynn's face softened a fraction. "I think I understand. You are in a bit of a spot, aren't you?"

"I am?"

"Of course!" The woman reached across the table and held out her hand. Carlie, stifling the urge to vomit from the nerves that had clearly stripped her of her senses, offered a shaking hand in return. "Oh, Carlie. I don't want you to be nervous around me. I like you. You're so good for my Dean. I always hoped he'd find someone...well, very much like you. I used to think he'd marry a blonde like me, but you're too beautiful as you are."

Marry? I don't think either of us is ready to get married—or at least, I'm not...

"I'm not trying to pressure you, Carlie, but let's face it. Relationships usually go that way, don't they? Either you break up or you get married. Since my son loves you, I'm obviously hoping for the latter."

"Sorry... I have to admit, hearing 'marriage' kind of freaked me out for a second." She doused the burning panic in her heart and forced herself to think rationally. "But I sort of understand. I mean, you're right. It is what happens." Before she could chicken out, Carlie leaned forward and murmured, "Do you think Dean..." She couldn't do it. "Sorry. Never mind."

"If you are wondering if my son hopes to get married at all, the answer is yes. He hasn't dated much—rarely, actually. He's going to want to enjoy this, but he also wants a family. I don't know if you've seen him with children, but he becomes a different person almost! He didn't get that from me!" Lynn dropped her voice and leaning forward with a conspiratorial whisper, said, "I am not a very maternal type. I wanted to be, but..."

"I always wanted to be a mom... June Cleaver and Donna Reed wannabe, you know? Fix breakfast before the kids go to school, clean the house while they're gone, sew a cute dress or fun PJ bottoms, put cookies in the oven just before they get home, help with homework while I make dinner..."

A strange look came over Lynn's face as Carlie dreamed aloud. Once more, panic welled up in Carlie's heart as she wondered what she could have said this time. But Lynn's words drove it out again. "I don't suppose you like things like..." her voice dropped to a horrified whisper. "*Camping?*"

Just be honest. You can't let it get to you! "Actually, I do. Sorry."

"Sorry? Why? I can't believe it! A girl like you—could you *be* any more perfect for my crazy son? He loves camping. Did you know—I shouldn't tell you this—he actually said once that his dream honeymoon would be in a camper in the mountains all alone?"

"No way." Carlie's throat went dry. "So, help me, if I didn't know I don't have a blog so it's impossible, I'd swear you were stalking me online or something. That's *my* dream honeymoon. I mean, if a guy can still love me after a week of camping, our marriage is rock solid."

The woman didn't speak. She just sat there for several seconds before reaching for her glass of water—water Carlie hadn't even seen delivered to the table. *Wow. They are amazing here. I wonder if they'll ever take our order or if they read our minds and then show up with what we want?*

"Carlie, you said you wanted to be a homemaker—what people call a 'stay-at-home-mom.' Do you still want that, or did that go away with new opportunities after high school?"

"I never went to college, Mrs. Rivers—"

"Oh, call me Lynn. Please. I do hate Mrs. Sounds so old and ugly." She dropped her voice to a whisper and added, "It's why Dean calls me

'Mim.' I wanted Lynn, he wanted Mum. I compromised on that one."

Carlie grinned. "I can see that. That's cute. I've wanted to ask so many times, but it felt rude—like I was criticizing." She took a quick cleansing breath and tried to redirect the conversation again. "Okay, *Lynn*, I didn't go to college. I don't have a great career. I'm just a sales associate at a nice store. That's it. I'd want to *try* the homemaking thing, I think. I don't think I'd be very good at it. I can't cook much at all. What I can is good," she added quickly as Lynn's highly-expressive face shifted again. "But most of what I try ends up charred and inedible."

"But that's because you haven't had any training—I assume. Did your mother teach you how to cook and manage a house?"

Carlie shook her head as Lynn spoke. "No. She didn't. I should have asked—or at least listened when she tried. But I always thought she didn't like the idea of me not having a good education and career, so I kind of steered clear of her in high school."

"Well, I'm not an expert on such things," Lynn admitted with almost a rueful air. "But I would imagine that you don't have much time to learn now, and not everyone is a natural like Dean. I don't cook much myself. I never liked my hands in raw meat or slimy tomatoes. It's all very disgusting to me. So, I made wise decisions and married men who loved to cook and could afford to take me out when they didn't care to. Dean's father was a fabulous cook. I suspect that's where Dean acquired the knack. I don't ever remember him burning anything—even at eight! And that's just not normal, is it?"

She hesitated to say it, but Carlie couldn't quite help herself. "He was a prodigy, though. Apparently, it extended beyond academics."

Carlie knew immediately that she'd said the right thing. Lynn began to speak and paused. "If we don't order, we will never get you back to work on time. I doubt your manager will accept a late notice from your boyfriend's—" Lynn paused. "If that's all right for me to say, anyway."

"It is. I was just being ridiculous—as usual. I'm good at that."

"Okay... from your *boyfriend's* mother." Lynn picked up her menu and smiled again. "And you're not ridiculous, dear. You're *cautious*. There's a decided difference."

One look at the menu sent Carlie into new levels of feelings of inadequacy. Prices were located below each entree item—centered and only two—and occasionally *three*—digit numbers. Her throat went dry, and Carlie gulped down a drink or two of her water before she closed the menu. "I can't decide, and I have no idea what is good and what isn't. So, will you please just choose something for me?" When Lynn's eyes rose above her menu and focused on Carlie, she found herself admitting in a mortified whisper, "I'm not used to lunches where the prices are in such tiny print that they jump out and slap you upside the head. I can't read for seeing them." A blush—a kind way of describing her flaming cheeks—punctuated the sentence. Carlie sank back in her chair, mortified, and waited for the signal that meant Dean's mother had officially written her off as hopeless."

"Carlie Denham, I like you. You're quite refreshing, you know? No wonder my Dean thinks you're about as perfect as women come."

"He knows I'm not and likes me anyway. I'd say that is more of a testimony to *his* perfection, but thank you—for saying you like me. I was sure I'd walk out of here today with an 'if you know what's good for you, you'll leave my son alone' warning."

The woman's eyes scanned the room and returned to Carlie. "Quite the contrary, Carlie. I suspect I'll be sending my son a text message that will read something to the effect of, 'I like her. Don't let her get away.'"

For the first time in six months, Dean watched the time in dread rather than anticipation of Carlie's arrival. Pages of definitions lay stacked before him—worthless. He hadn't touched them since he'd pulled them from his messenger bag—and wouldn't. *Lord... help me with this. I don't think she truly comprehends that Mim can and will flip on a dime.*

"Hey! Wha—are those *all* still needing to be done?" Carlie reached for his water and murmured, "Can I? I'm soooo thirsty."

"Sure."

Carlie stopped mid-sip and stared. "You're upset. What'd I do?"

"You didn't *do* anything, Carlie, and I'm not upset. I'm a bit... *concerned,*" he added after she tossed him an expression of disbelief. "But not upset."

"And what are you 'concerned' about?"

She doesn't believe me. Great. Another thing to overcome. "You were so excited after your lunch thing with my mother—so was she, by the way—I just don't want you to lose your guard with her."

"You can't protect me from all pain, Dean." Carlie's smile softened the curtness of her words. "Besides, we talked about it."

"Is that what Mim wouldn't tell me? She called and said, 'That girl is wise beyond her years. Don't you dare let her go.'"

Dean's fears that his mother's words might be a bit overwhelming deflated into a whizzing balloon of nothingness when Carlie laughed at him. "She said she would." When Janice appeared to take their order and drop off drinks, Carlie rested her elbows on the table and settled her head in her hands. After a long sip of Italian soda, and a "thanks" for him pre-ordering it for her, Carlie continued her story. "She called after lunch—while I was on my way into work. She made me late, actually. I had to step back outside, and Liz was seriously ticked. But it was worth it."

"I'm sorr—"

"Shut up. Let me tell this story." Carlie winked before she continued. "So, she told me again how much fun she had and that she knew we'd be great friends. I couldn't get what you said out of my head, so I stopped her—totally interrupted her. Anyway, I told her that I really like her and want to be friends with her, but she needed to be prepared for catching me in a bad spot. I wake up with bedhead and bad breath. I sometimes get food on my clothes or go without makeup when I have a pimple." She stared at Dean. "I seriously hope that doesn't gross you out, but—"

"Impossible."

"Good. I thought you'd say that but still... Anyway, I told her I didn't want to be paranoid about how she'd react if she saw me like that."

After that last sentence, Dean's heart ceased beating. His lungs refused to inflate. He gaped at her until his vocal cords restarted his vital organs. "Oh, no..."

Her wink almost sent him into cardiac arrest. "She said you'd say that." Carlie reached for his hands and played with his fingers. "We talked about it, Dean. She's prepared for me to call her on it, and I'm prepared to accept that it might take her a little while to look past it. She knows she does it, Dean. She's not proud of it. But no one has ever really called her on it."

"That's not true, Carlie. We've all—"

"No, Dean. I've done a lot of thinking about it. You've *reacted* to it and told her how wrong she is, or *shown* her how wrong she is, but no one has said, 'I accept you as you are, but I expect you to do the same for me.' I think Larry has tried—probably done it, actually, but you're both too close to her. I think I managed to say it in a way she could hear it and not get defensive."

"Whoa... wow. If I didn't love you before..."

"Now that's the kind of talk I like to hear." Janice set their California soup and salad platters on the table and grinned. "I seriously better get an invite to the wedding."

Dean's heart sank at the panicked look on Carlie's face. "We'll be sure to let you be in the first... thousand or so to know."

"Hmph. Eat up. That dressing is to die for." Janice winked at Carlie and stalked off in a mock huff.

"Carlie..."

"Since she brought it up too, I'm going to ask. Have you even

268

thought about marriage—to me, I mean? Your mom said—"

"Oh, no... Mim!" The words flew out of his mouth before he could stop them. "Carlie, I—"

"No. Just answer. Is that in the plans for you?"

He took a moment to steady himself, prayed like a crazy man, and waded into miserable territory. "If you mean to ask whether I ever intend to marry, the answer is yes. If you wish to know if I'm going to propose tomorrow, the answer is no."

"That's not what I asked. Is that where you see this going—assuming you don't figure out that you could do so much better?"

Her words cut—right until he saw her wink at him. "You..." Dean grinned. "I'm pleased you can joke about it. Now. That's quite impressive."

"Dean, it's a joke, sure, but it's true. Couldn't we *all* do *'better'* than what we choose to do? I mean, c'mon. It's impossible to pick the absolutely perfect thing every time."

"I think we're off topic," he argued. "And I can't do better than you, if you're all I want. Just putting that out there. As for marriage someday, yes. If I'm honest with myself, and with you—absolutely. That's what I want. But I never would have brought it up this early. You still don't truly know me. Perhaps if we'd both been interacting all this time—six months isn't absurdly fast. But for you—this is just a month or so. It would be unrealistically precipitous. I wouldn't do that to you."

She nodded as he spoke, but Dean saw in her something he'd only seen from his perspective—someone only listening to formulate their next argument. Carlie proved it by pouncing almost before he finished. "You need to know that that freaks me out."

He blinked. "'Freaks you out' because you think marriage is horrible and you want nothing to do with it, because you think marriage to *me* would be horrible, or you have some other issue with marriage that my brain can't conjure right now?"

"At this minute—all of the above." Carlie chewed her lip between bites of salad—all while she tried to explain. It resulted in a choppy, somewhat garbled mess of words. "I don't mean that *you* are the problem. You're a great guy. But I've never been with a guy I could ever consider marrying. That idea is freaky to me. I'm used to guys who are *not* marriage material. You're more of every girl's dream."

"You just jerked me from panic mode, into breathability, and back again," he admitted. At her confused expression, he attempted to clarify. "What I mean is that you told me that you once dreamed of being a wife and mother. Now you say that you've never considered marriage. I'm...confused." He attempted to spear a grape tomato and watched it fly across the room and land on an empty table. "Oops. Anyway, just to reiterate, I am *not* considering marriage this week, month, or even necessarily this *year*. But your opposition to the idea makes me nervous."

"Why?"

"Um… because if you *never* want to get married, or if you can't see yourself ever married to *me,* then what would be the purpose of changing our lunch dates to something more personal?"

She picked at the salad and shoved it aside. With a spoon in one hand and the bowl before her, she waded into it with gusto before spitting it out again. "Aaak! Hot!"

Dean passed her the water glass again. "You okay?"

"No." She looked up at him. "I didn't know going out with you was such a serious commitment."

With a mouth dry and a heart withering, Dean croaked, "I didn't mean for it to be, but I also wasn't aware that there was no hope of it ever becoming one."

"That's not what I said—or meant. I just—" Carlie frowned at him as she sat lost in thought. "What was the question you asked again? I had a response, and now it's gone."

"I said that if there's no hope of us having a more permanent relationship, then why try to make it more personal?"

"Yes!" Her eyes lit up. "Whew! I knew it'd come back to me. I have a brilliant response." When he didn't respond, some of her enthusiasm wilted. "I was *going* to say, 'We're seeing if you can change my mind.'"

Clarification—he needed it. "So, are you saying that dating me is an attempt to discover if we even like the idea of a journey, much less the destination, but we may find we never want to get in the car?"

"Oookay…" Carlie shrugged. "Sorry. No clue what that means."

She'd dashed his hopes and shattered them into irretrievable pieces. "It means that I'm trying to understand if you think your mind *can* be changed, or if we're just hanging out for the fun of it." As Dean waited for her to finish chewing her salad, he sipped his water, prayed, and gave himself a super-sonic pep talk regarding the possibility that he would have to rein in his emotions even further. *If she's adamantly opposed to the idea—ever—then what is the point? I'm asking to have my heart crushed. Then again, is she worth that risk? Of course, she is. What do I do, Lord?"*

"It's not that I'm not ever going to want to get married, Dean. Like I said, I've just never been out with a guy who is marriage material. I'm having a hard time shifting from knowing that it shouldn't happen with the guys I go out with, to seeing if maybe it could. I mean, my head knows that you're probably perfect in every way. But the idea that you could just spring some kind of proposal on me…" Her eyes widened. "So, help me, if you do some huge public thing to me, I'll kill you."

"Wouldn't consider it," he promised. Amusement—repressed laughter, in fact—bounced the previous panic out of his heart as he solemnly assured her that he too considered proposals to be private affairs.

"Whew. Blaine loved hearing about the wild things guys did. Made me glad that he didn't consider *me* marriage material." Just as Dean considered whether he should mention that she was exactly the kind of woman a controlling man like Blaine would eventually marry, Carlie's eyes widened, and she grinned. "Okay, I know how to make this work to make both of us comfortable."

"And I have to say that it's a little disconcerting to realize that dating me is *un*comfortable."

"Thank your mother for that. If Lynn hadn't brought it up, I know you wouldn't have, and we'd be talking about seeing the tulips on Sunday or something."

Dean grinned. "I'll make a note of that. Sunday with Carlie. Sounds like a perfect day to me."

"*Meanwhile*," she growled. Suddenly, her confidence faded. Dean watched it vanish with a sinking heart. But something—a deeper, stronger side of herself—rose up within her, wiping away the insecurity he'd seen trying to emerge.

"That—whatever just happened in you right there. That was beautiful."

She started to protest—her lips opened with the words already formed, but Carlie stopped herself—again. "Thank you." She continued, without even a pause between sentences. "So, this is how it's going to go. We're just going to sorta pretend like this conversation never happened—like your mom didn't freak me out with her dreams of my being the next mommy blogger and Pinterest diva. I'm not going to panic that if we get closer, it'll turn serious before I'm ready, because I'm going to *tell* you when I'm ready."

It didn't make sense. *You'll never do it, Carlie! You know it.* Dean shook his head. "But you wouldn't. I can't see you saying one day in the future—in three months, six months, three years even, 'Okay. I know you're the one for me. We can talk marriage now.' You won't do that."

"No..." She smiled that slow, secret smile that had already become his favorite.

"If you knew the things that smile does to my heart..."

"Good! So, listen close." Carlie shoved her soup and salad aside and leaned forward. "I don't care if I fall in love with you tomorrow or next year. Doesn't matter. I'm not saying it until I'm ready—until I won't panic if you use the 'M' word again." She winked at him before adding, "And I'm telling your mom to forget it, too. Just warning you."

The idea—if she could manage to do it—would make for an

271

interesting relationship. Dean, however, didn't have confidence that she'd ever say the words he wanted to hear, knowing that they held that kind of weight. "Carlie, do you think you can do that? Do you *truly* think you will be able to tell me you love me—assuming you ever do, I'm not so arrogant as to assume you will—if you know it means you're also saying, 'I won't panic if you bring up marriage now'?"

Her face fell, and Dean nodded. He started to tell her he understood and perhaps suggest a specific date in the future to reopen the topic, when she said, "I hoped you wouldn't think of that. Yeah, it's going to be hard. But I think if you can wait—possibly indefinitely—for me to get there, the least I can do is put myself out there a bit, too. It's the right thing to do."

Dean had no choice but to trust her—and the Lord. "Okay then. It's a deal, but I warn you." He waited for it and was not disappointed. Her left eyebrow rose, and as it did, he added, "I'm going to do everything in my power to make it happen."

"I have no doubt it will."

Lunch out on Monday with Lynn, lunch with Dean on Wednesday, and dinner with him on Friday meant that, when Teresa called in the middle of their date Friday night, Carlie suggested that she make lunch for them at her apartment. She'd been nervous about being able to make anything nice, but as Dean helped her chop up the chicken, onion, celery, and dill weed on Saturday morning, Carlie's panic shifted to excitement. "This is easier than I thought."

"I had considered the possibility that it might be the source of your cooking woes."

"What?"

Dean nudged her aside while he reached for the Dijon mustard. "A lack of confidence resulting in over-doing things. I suffered from the same 'affliction' when I first started cooking."

"When you were *eight!*" Carlie rolled her eyes at him and reached for the package of strawberries. "Besides, your mother says you were a natural at that too. You've got overachiever issues."

"She has selective memory. She chooses not to recall the time I thought the cheesecake would never get done and turned the oven up to *five hundred* as a solution to the problem." As she reached for a knife and began to slice off the top of the strawberry, Dean stopped her. "Wait... do you own a potato peeler?"

"What? *Peel* my strawberries?"

"No..." He rummaged through her utensil drawer and pulled out the peeler. "Do you see this tip? It's perfectly suited for hulling strawberries. Hook under the 'top', apply a little force..." The top popped off in his hand. "And presto—one hulled strawberry without the loss of half of the berry."

"Wow." Her eyes bounced from Dean to the topless strawberry. "Did you figure that out on your own or what?"

Dean's grin sent uncertain but quite happy butterflies dancing on her heart. "Ahh... no. I enjoy reading kitchen tips and hacks. I learned that one a couple of years ago. I've always enjoyed strawberries, but I disliked the waste of half a berry. Now I eat guilt-free." He handed her a forkful of chicken salad. "How does that taste to you?"

After a taste, she frowned. "I think it needs more salt—and pepper."

"Yes! See! I was certain that you had good instincts. Hint: it needs a tiny bit of garlic, too."

Carlie watched as he added salt, pepper, and a few shakes of garlic powder. "So, did you leave it out deliberately?"

"I did." His eyes shifted to the clock. "Okay, Teresa should arrive in fifteen or twenty minutes. It's time for me to leave." Dean washed and dried his hands, did a side-step dance to avoid stepping on Moros' tail, and paused beside her as she arranged strawberries in a bowl. "Will I see you tonight, then?"

Her eyes met his, and a riot of emotions swirled in her. *I am so going to fall in love with this guy. I'm already, "in like," as Dad always calls it.* Carlie leaned against his chest and murmured, "Mmm hmm. I'd give you a hug, but my hands are all strawberry-juicy, and well, I know you're going to see your mom."

The pressure of his lips on the top of her head—*could it get any better? Blaine would be all over me if I did this. Where would I be if I hadn't asked him if I could sit with him that day?*

"What?"

She tilted her head up and looked at him. "What, what?"

"I felt you stiffen. If you'd rather I didn't—"

"Oh! No. I was just thinking about how different you are from Blaine, and how glad I was that I got the courage to ask you to share your booth that day. Teresa had tried to get me to do it for months, but that day... God is good to me, I guess."

"He blessed me, too," he murmured. "You ladies enjoy yourselves." Dean hunkered down on his heels, scratched behind Moros' head, and hurried out the door.

Just as the door closed behind him, Carlie noticed yet another difference between her current boyfriend and the last. "Blaine wouldn't have been willing to help me and then just *go*. He would have expected to get to stay—and push Teresa out early." Her eyes rolled as she carried the strawberries to her little table. "Who am I kidding? He wouldn't have been willing to *help* me do anything."

By the time Teresa arrived, Carlie had the table set and Dean's "famous" pomegranate punch poured. She hurried to open the door, but when her friend stepped inside, Teresa said, "Why isn't the chain on? You know that was a condition of me not bugging you about moving!"

"Like a chain on the door will stop anyone bent on getting in." Carlie hugged her and added, "Besides. It was. Then Dean left, and—"

"Dean was here?" Teresa glanced around her. "Why?"

"Helping me make something that didn't taste gross. Didn't think you wanted mac 'n' cheese and little weenies."

Teresa sniffed the bowl as Carlie pulled the chicken salad out of the fridge. "Remind me to record you a nighttime sleep CD that tells you to marry this guy while you can."

Though she hadn't planned to discuss it, Teresa's comment sent Carlie on a spiral of words in a torrent of emotions. "We were *just* talking about that the other day!"

"What? *Marriage?* It was a *joke*, Carlie!"

"Well, I have known him for six months. You didn't know Eric *that* much longer before you got engaged." The dumbfounded expression on Teresa's face sent Carlie into a fit of laughter. "Sorry—you—your—oh, man. That was good. No, we were just talking about how freaked out I was at the idea of marriage at all. I mean, I never even thought about it, you know?"

Teresa switched from horrified to confused at a dizzying speed. "Wait, you *don't* want to marry him—ever? I was just thinking you were talking about setting a *date*, and *that* was a bit premature. He's everything we've ever talked about in the perfect husband. I mean, he has things even *Eric* didn't."

The truth of Teresa's words sent Carlie fleeing for her emotional life—or at least for the asparagus soup in the crock-pot that Dean had brought. "It's one thing to dream, T. It's another thing to have to live it." She set the bowls on their place mats, grabbed the plate of Triscuits and surveyed the table with a critical eye. "I think that's it. Let's eat. Do you want to pray?"

Teresa stood at the little breakfast bar and stared at Carlie. "That's it. Unless you find something about this guy you *don't* love, please. Please marry him next year or so. He's seriously good for you."

"Because I asked to pray?" Carlie murmured as Teresa sat. "What's with that?"

"Just that you used to be uncomfortable if I did. So, I stopped."

Carlie took a moment, thanked the Lord for the food and a chance

274

to spend the afternoon with Teresa, and finished with a plea for wisdom regarding Dean. The moment she said, "Amen," she returned to their previous discussion. "I told Dean that marriage freaks me out, and he was like, 'If you never want to get married, why are we dating?' I almost croaked."

"I kind of agree with him. I mean, you don't assume you're going to marry every guy you date, but..."

"But if you know you won't, why date?" She gripped her spoon with excess force and tried not to fling the contents across the table and onto Teresa's top. "So, basically, all my dating has been sinful or something?" Her emotions took control and Carlie began ranting. "Maybe you just want *not* to be a misfit. *Everyone* has a boyfriend or girlfriend. You go out as couples—do things as couples. If you don't, you're the oddball and it's awkward. *That's* why some of us date people we don't want to spend the rest of our lives with."

"And because you know you wouldn't marry someone who treated you badly, but you don't think you deserve better. So, you compromise." Teresa waited for Carlie to relax and look up before she added, "You just date them, knowing you won't ever let it go that far. Then you poison yourself against the idea of marriage in the process."

Each rebuttal she tried to form died on her lips. Not until she'd finished her soup and spooned some chicken salad onto her plate did Carlie finally manage a whispered, "Do you think...?"

"I'm sure of it." Teresa started to say something else but stopped herself. "So, tell me about this soup. Did you make this, did Dean, or did you both—"

"He brought the soup, but he showed me how to do it so I could try it next time. It looks crazy easy." A smile formed on her lips. "He also helped me with the chicken salad. Showed me what to do as he did everything, and then had me taste it—asked what I thought. It was a test to see if I could tell him what was missing. The guy is a natural teacher. He told me when he first learned to cook and figured out that it was closely related to chemistry, he almost wanted to be a research chemist."

"That's impressive. Wow." Teresa spooned chicken salad on a Triscuit cracker and took a bite. "Okay, you've got to get him to teach you more. Then you teach me. This is good. And my chicken salad isn't bad!"

"Like mine, you mean." Carlie snickered at the look of horror in Teresa's eyes. "It's okay. C'mon, last time the chicken was so rubbery we couldn't chew it!"

Something in the way Teresa spoke seemed evasive—almost secretive. Carlie watched and listened as her friend bounced from subject to subject before, she lost her patience. "Okay, you have something to tell me. What is it? Is Blaine going out with Rhonda? Oh, please say it's so."

"Don't I wish? That would be worthy of popcorn and front row seats." Teresa picked at the strawberry fork as if unsure if she really wanted any.

"You love strawberries, T. Just put some on your plate so I can grab some."

"I'm pregnant."

Carlie's fork clattered to her plate. *What do I say? They didn't want a baby for at least two years. Do I congratulate? Commiserate? What?* "Wow!"

"That's a nice non-committal answer," Teresa muttered as she speared a few strawberries. She brushed away tears with an impatient flick of her wrist. "I'm happy—really. But I just wasn't ready yet, you know? Mom said that if I wasn't ready for a baby, I wasn't ready to get married."

"She would. Why do moms do that?" Carlie growled. "They think they're helpful, I suppose, but not. Totally not helpful."

Teresa nodded as she listened. "Got that right. Anyway, Eric is totally jazzed, of course. Keeps walking around trying to figure out where we'll put a crib and a swing and a playpen and a changing table and a rocking chair—*must* have a rocking chair, you know. It's crazy!"

Despite Teresa's ranting, Carlie heard excitement in her tones. "But you're ready after all, aren't you?"

A small smile grew into a grin. "I am. I mean, it's scary as anything, but c'mon. A little person growing up calling me 'Mommy.' Baby shopping? How cool is that? Rhonda is going to pitch a *fit,* of course, but I don't think even she can kill my excitement—such as it is." Before Carlie could find a way to temper the stream of ugliness that wanted to spew from her heart, Teresa added, "Well, one thing could."

"Could what—oh, kill excitement. Right. What's that?"

"I know it's tacky," Teresa began, "and I know it's like every etiquette faux pas but, if you do not promise to take charge of a baby shower *today,* I'll kill you both the moment my hormones kick into gear."

A dozen ideas blasted into Carlie's imagination. "Whoa... that's right. Wow. A shower. *Mine!* Dibs! Whatever I have to say to get it. I'm going to have so much fun! Oh, wow. Do you want it early so you can have lots of time to shop afterward, or maybe after your sonogram? Ooooh! We could do a combination gender reveal-slash-shower! Or—"

"Carlie?"

She swallowed her excitement and murmured, "Yeah?"

"I don't care what you do or when. Just make sure Rhonda doesn't do it. That would be the worst."

Carlie hardly heard. "A baby... wow. Totally cool, T. Totally cool."

" Dr. Sager?"

"Yes?" Dean slid his finger across the page and held it as he looked up. The sight of Gabby in the doorway sent a wash of dismay over him. *You knew this day would come. How could she not have noticed that you're less... open with her?* When he didn't speak, she called his name again. Dean cleared his throat. "I apologize. Distracted. May I help you with something?"

"Well, I brought a draft for you to look at..." She passed it to him. "Can I just say how much I really appreciate how you set up your papers? It's a lot to write every week, but it makes the final paper so much easier—just combining elements and fleshing it out a little. I love it. I think it's shown me how I can do similar things with my notes in other classes. I've been rewriting them, citing things—everything. My final paper for my Principles of Translation class is half the work I thought it would be. I'd never have even..." She flushed. "I'm gushing. Sorry."

And I am likely frowning. Not acceptable. Dean managed a genuine smile as he shook his head. "No, truly. I'm pleased you find it useful. It's one constant thing I remembered from all my classes—at any level. Many of my classmates found it difficult to translate their written assignments, essays, and papers into their final paper. That word count stymied them. So, I decided to structure my classes to help them work toward that overview."

"And that's why everyone loves you."

Dean choked—not on her words, but the expression he imagined in her eyes. *No, she's not in love with you, but she's definitely hinting—that expression says she's interested in seeing if she could be.* Dean tried to shrug it off as nothing. "It's kind of you to encourage me." He concentrated on the paper before him, making a few notes in the margins as he went. "I like where you're taking this. It's a solid—wait." Dean circled half a paragraph. "You'd better check your notes on this. I think you'll find you want to change it." He flipped through his class notes and nodded. "Try week seven or eight. I believe we had several overlapping classes during that time, so I'm not confident as to which."

"Okay… thanks."

She notices that I'm not engaging as I once did. Lord, don't let me offend a sister. That's not helpful. This isn't her fault. After he finished skimming the draft, he passed it back with a smile. "Aside from that one small section, you have a strong draft there. I also made a few notes where you can add a little more evidence."

"Awesome. Thanks." Gabby took a step back. "Semester's almost over…"

"It is, and I'm looking forward to it."

She listened with a growing smile. "Yeah, I bet."

"I'm not teaching summer classes this year, but I am taking on another class for Dr. Willis next semester, so I need to prepare for that."

"Oh?" Gabby stepped forward again, curiosity showing in her features. "What class is that?"

He steadied himself with prayer and hope. *Lord, please let her be in that class.* "Intro to Hermeneutics. He's winding down to retirement, so…" When Gabby's face fell, Dean knew he hadn't misread her. "It'll make for an intense summer schedule. I anticipate a few camping trips, and my girlfriend would like me to spend a few weekends with her family. So, a lot of relaxing work—oxymoron, no? So do you have plans for summer?"

The way she fumbled with her paper and inched backward—they tore at his conscience. *You gave her every reason to think you were interested. Now look at her.* But another side of him protested. *Yes, and I was interested. Or I thought I was. I wasn't deliberately unkind, and I was careful to keep it professional.* The memory of a single flirtatious moment pricked him. *Professional… ish.*

"Well," she said once she'd reached the doorjamb. "I hope you have a lot of fun. Looks like I'll get to have you next semester then—in Hermeneutics. Bye."

Dean stared at the papers before him, his mind refusing to recall what he'd been doing before his day had been tossed in the dumpster. When all attempts failed, he pulled out his phone and sent Carlie a quick text. JUST MISSING YOU. ROUGH AFTERNOON. COULD USE AN

As Carlie slid into the booth, she smiled at Dean, but he didn't look up from the paper he read. A semi-panicked sense of déjà vu filled her as she watched him reach for the menu and pass it to her. *He said he wasn't interested in her—Gabby. He said he felt guilty that he'd sorta flirted.* Her eyes bored into the wave of hair that covered his forehead and eyes as he bent over the paper, scribbling something in the margins as he read. *I believed you when you said you wouldn't even go out with her if we broke up. But now you're over there—*

Dean looked up at that moment, his nerd glasses half-slid down his nose. "Hey…"

"Hi."

"What's with you two? You can*not* have a fight. I'm counting on you guys to provide me with all the romantic drivel my heart needs to keep pattering. Now get past it and make google eyes at each other or something."

This time, Carlie's heart squeezed into her throat as Dean said, "We'll need a minute, Janice. Thanks."

The second their faithful server was out of earshot, Carlie pounced—or tried to. "Okay, if—"

"I must expla—" He frowned. "Oh, forgive me."

"Go ahead. I'm not sure I *can* speak without yelling, so just say it."

The confusion in Dean's eyes only antagonized her further. "I'm sorry. Did I say something amiss?" He held up the paper in his hands. "I've almost finished reviewing this last paper. I must write a quick explanation as to why something is marked wrong. Do you mind?"

"Oh. No." Carlie sank back against the cushions. "Whew! You had me scared."

Again, he didn't respond. She leaned forward once more, elbows on the table and chin resting in her hands—leaned and watched. His eyes rose and met hers as Dean stacked the papers and fumbled with his messenger bag. "Pardon me, but did you say I had 'scared' you? What did I say?"

"I was just being paranoid," Carlie admitted. "After the thing with Gabby and…" She flushed. "Anyway—"

Dean interrupted, concern almost dripping from him as he reached for her hand. "Carlie, I'm afraid I don't understand. What 'thing' about Gabby are you referring to?" His fingers squeezed her hand, and for a moment, she almost expected him to kiss it. "Should I not have told you about the awkward moment in my office?"

The gentle—almost tender—concern he showed struck an oddly

funny chord in her. Carlie's laughter echoed around them and surprised even herself. "No, no!" As diners turned their way, she lowered her voice and murmured, "I just walked in here, and it was like those first weeks again. I sat down, and you didn't say anything—just handed me the menu. Then you sent Janice away without really acknowledging her—weird flashback is all."

"I suppose that would be a bit... unsettling. Again, I apologize. After my poor performance in the fall, I wanted to ensure I finished the last paper with my full attention. I had only two paragraphs left."

She dug through her purse and pulled out an envelope. "Well, now that I know all is fine with us, read that."

Dean reached for the cream envelope and a slight smile formed as he traced the return address with his finger. He began to remove the contents and stopped. "You thought we *weren't* 'fine'?"

"I just didn't know what to make of your silence again. It's nothing. I knew we'd talk it out, but you did have me a little nervous after the thing with Gabby. It made me wonder if you'd reconsidered after talking about it. That's all."

The smile grew. "I see."

Carlie snatched the envelope back and leveled her best, "Oh, yeah?" glare on him. "Just what do you see? You're almost smirking at me."

"I see that you disliked the idea of me being interested in someone else. I consider that to be... encouraging." He held out his hand for the envelope. "Now may I read Larry's note?"

She passed it across the table and signaled for Janice as she watched him remove the sheets of paper within it. "I got that yesterday. The date says he wrote it after we left on Sunday. That struck me for some reason." As the server arrived, she ordered coffee and asked for fruit. "I'm famished. Dean?"

"The coffee will be sufficient for me, too. Thank you, Janice."

"Do either of you know what you want to order?"

Carlie shook her head. "Sorry, no. Ever since Frank switched to the spring menu, I get confused. I'll try to hurry, though."

By the time Janice left and Carlie turned back to Dean, she saw what looked suspiciously like tears in his eyes. "Dean?"

"I apologize," he choked. "I love this man."

"He obviously loves you, too." She reached for the letter. "This here— 'The joy your friendship gives Dean blesses more than just him. It blesses Lynn and me as well.' That... I'm just grateful that God brought him into your life. No wonder you're such an amazing man."

Cups and saucers rattled as Janice set down their coffee and the plate of fruit. "Sorry. I've been shaky all day."

"Have you eaten?" Carlie speared a piece of melon with her fork. "Maybe you need to get your blood sugar up."

"Maybe, but I'd get fired if I ate that. Thanks. I'll try to snag some cheese in the kitchen. You might be right."

Once again, Carlie watched emotions flit across Dean's face. "Are you sure you're okay?"

"Were you aware that I did not truly communicate with people after my father left?"

"Thinking he walked out over a checkers game—duh! I wouldn't have talked either. But..." She frowned as a memory surfaced. "I thought your mother said she used to pay you to be quiet."

Dean brushed a strand of hair away from her face. "I chose the word 'communicate' with care. I spoke—often, and rarely with any purpose—but I did not converse."

"Oh… and Larry got you to…*converse?*" She captured his hand and held it against her cheek. "How?"

"Aaah… Carlie. You always know how to unsettle my heart, and in the most delightful ways."

Her own heart did a few somersaults before she managed to ask again, "But how did he get you to talk?"

"He listened." Dean pulled his hand back and clasped them together like an earnest little boy with a deep and painful confession. "I should have realized then the intrinsic value of the art of listening. I didn't. I learned that from you."

Carlie stared unseeing at the menu before her. With an impatient flick of her wrist, she shoved it at him. "I'm going to cry if I keep staring at that. You and Larry have such a special relationship. I love it." She nodded at the menu. "Just pick something out, will you? Pick something out for me to eat, and call Larry later and tell him what you just told me?"

"I most certainly will." He didn't say it—not in words or even a touch—but Carlie heard and felt his meaning clearly. *"I love you."*

The car sped away from Hannah's new basement apartment, and Carlie rubbed her shoulders, groaning as the tight, aching muscles screamed for her to leave them alone. Dean reached for her other hand and squeezed it. "Weary?"

Only Dean would use "weary" rather than "tired." It's sweet. She laced her fingers in his and inched a little closer. "Yeah. I'm exhausted, actually. But it's a good tired. Hannah's all set—those bunk beds. So cute!"

"Larry exhausted every large-family resource at his disposal before finding those. He suspected Hannah would be reticent to consider a *true* triple-bunk at her children's ages. I think what he purchased was an excellent compromise."

"And *cute!*" Carlie nudged him. "I am a woman, and cute factor comes over practical as long as it isn't *dangerous.*"

Dean's thumb stroked the back of her hand as he wove through Rockland traffic and onto Carlie's street. "I would assure you that I think *you* are 'cute'; however, considering the original meaning of the word was *bowlegged,* I am a little uncertain of whether you would take that as the compliment intended."

"It doesn't—er, didn't! No way."

"It did. Nice, is another interesting word," Dean continued. "It originally meant foolish or stupid."

Carlie shook her head as she listened. "I—"

"Forgive me, Carlie. You didn't ask for an impromptu etymology lesson. As the saying goes, 'old habits die hard.'"

"You know I like to listen, right?" She waited for him to stop at a red light before he could look at her. "I do. If you start ignoring me or talking over me, I'll tell you, okay?"

Dean merely nodded before he whispered, "Thank you."

Desperate to change the subject before it became truly uncomfortable, Carlie pounced on the first idea that came to mind. "Did I tell you Jared called to see how we were doing?"

For a moment, Dean didn't respond, and when he did, he sounded a bit absent minded. "I'm sorry, what did you say? Something about Jared?"

Carlie blinked as her mind swirled. *What's with him? He's usually more attentive. Whatever. He's tired. I forgot.* "Yeah. He said he'd been thinking about us and praying for us, and just wanted to see how we were doing."

"That is… unusual."

"What do you mean?"

The car pulled into a space at the corner of her building, and Dean turned off the engine. "Nothing of consequence. I merely noted that it is unusual for a man to call someone he had hoped to date and inquire about the progress of her new relationship—tell her that he is praying for them. I think it speaks well of him."

"It does, doesn't it? I was so sorry when I found out that I just didn't have anything *there* with him." She pressed against his arm again. "Now, I'm not so sorry, but I still hate knowing that he'd *like* to find someone but hasn't."

"I think that is a common affliction with most singles, don't you? Most of us have an innate desire to share our hearts with someone special."

A new idea clicked just as he stepped out of the car. She flung open her door, dragged her purse out from the floorboard, and met him at the hood. "Gabby!"

"Gabby?" The confused tone, combined with blank expression, gave Dean a decided unintelligent air, and the incongruity of it prompted a snicker. His eyes narrowed. "That's amusing?"

"Sorry, no. You just—it's hard to explain. Anyway. Yes! Gabby. She'd be perfect for Jared. She's studying Bible at the seminary. Jared loves nothing more than the Bible... we should totally set them up!"

He took her hand and strolled toward the entrance to her building. Only at the door did he speak. "I don't think that would be appropriate."

What caused the slow burn of ire in her heart, Carlie found difficult to pinpoint. It might have been Dean's tone—that calm, self-assured string of words could easily have been intended as a gentle rebuke. For what, she had no clue. It may have been the dashing of what seemed like a fine idea to her—probably was, if truth be told. But one other possibility slowly grew into immense proportions. "Seriously? You don't want her—or so you claim—but no one else can have a shot with her? Seriously?"

She wavered at the utterly dumbfounded expression on his face. Dean waited until she'd opened her door and stepped inside before he responded with, "Isn't that rather a ridiculous—"

"Oh, so now I'm ridiculous. What is with you?"

"Perhaps you're tired? I could get a bowl of hot water for your feet?"

Carlie blinked—twice. She shook her head and rolled her eyes as exasperation took hold of her body and began a chain reaction of events. "Hot water? Are you kidding me? Why not some Valium and a nice martini while I twirl my pearls and kick off my heels? Then I'll realize what a stupid idea it was to introduce two people who might—just *might*—find each other interesting. After all, *we* both found them interesting and then found each other interesting. Why, I'll never know."

"Carlie..."

"No. No. You're not going to sound all calm and sweet and make me do or think whatever you want me to. Just go home. Go home and think about whether you really aren't interested in Gabby anymore."

While he had started to turn as she spoke, Dean whirled back. "You think I lied to you."

"Well..." Her anger fizzled a little. "Not *lied* per se. Just don't quite know your own mind. I'm not doing this, Dean. I'm not going to be strung along as a second girlfriend again. I've been there, done that, and I refused to go into further debt for that stupid t-shirt."

"What?"

Carlie gave him a gentle shove out the door. "Go home, Dean. Call me if you really think you are interested *only* in me." She tried to smile but failed. "Because I'm not interested in another multi-whatever relationship. I'm done with that. Goodbye, Dean."

While she didn't quite *slam* the door, the force with which she pushed it firmly shut rattled the chain. Pouncer gazed at her from the top of the couch with a look in his eye that could mean anything from empathy to a demand for dinner. "I knew it was too good to be true. I just knew it."

"I think we broke up." The words sounded even worse aloud than they had in her heart.

Teresa choked on something. The rasping, gasping, strangled sounds nearly made Carlie jump in the car and race across town to... *What? Stare at her lifeless body by the time I get there? C'mon. That's stupid, even for you.*

"—are you talking about. When?"

"Saturday. We helped Hannah move into that bed and breakfast—great place, by the way. I love it. And on the way home, I remembered Jared calling so I told—"

Teresa interrupted quickly. "Wait. You told Dean that Jared called you? You *told* him that the guy who really liked you called to say, 'Hey... I've been praying for you guys. Just wanted to see how it was going... maybe ask you out again if things weren't working out.'"

"He never said that," Carlie protested. "He didn't even hint at it!"

The snort from the other side of Rockland might not have needed a phone to reach Carlie's ear. "You're kidding me, right?"

"About what? Seriously? He never—"

"Carlie! The guy liked you. He is a good guy. He wouldn't ask you out if you were with someone else, and he's probably praying like crazy that it doesn't work out for you. That's still 'praying for you guys'. Don't you get it?" Teresa lowered her voice. "He liked you, Carls."

But despite Teresa's words, Carlie refused to believe it. "He's not like that. He's one of the most sincere, genuine people I've ever met. I just thought it would be cool for Dean to know that he was praying for us. And then I got the idea that maybe we should introduce Jared and Gabby."

"Wait—Gabby the student Dean thought he liked until he figured out it was really you? That Gabby?"

"Well, yeah. They both like books, and the Bible, and are really neat people—or at least Dean seems to think she is. So, why not?"

Teresa's groan nearly smothered Carlie's confidence. "Oh, Carlie. He said no, didn't he?"

"Yes! See what I mean? It's crazy. The guy really isn't over her. You should be proud of me. I mean, I stood up to him and told him I wasn't going to be just *one* of his girlfriends. I'm done with that."

The groan intensified. "Carlie! I'd bet a week of additional puking that he wasn't talking about that! C'mon, he just told this girl that he has a girlfriend—when she had every right to assume he might ask her out in a couple of weeks. Trying to set her up with someone else would be such a slap in the face."

"Oh." The picture grew crystal clear. "Ohhhh… All I could see was me stuck with another guy who couldn't choose just one girl. So, when he said no—" Carlie choked. "Oh, man…"

"Call him, Carls. Explain. He'll understand."

Emotion thickened her voice and choked her as she considered Teresa's suggestion. "I don't know… T., he just left. He just walked out."

"When you told him to go, right?"

"Yeah, but he didn't—"

Teresa's demand for her to shush would have annoyed her at one time, but Carlie just sank against the couch cushions and listened. "Okay. Look. He told you he wouldn't fight with you. He said he would be the kind of guy you needed. Well, you needed him to wait for you to see things clearly. He's not going anywhere—not this one. So, call him."

"What if he's mad?"

"He probably *is* mad. You basically accused him of lying to you."

The words dashed cold water on her fury as it tried to reignite. "He asked that, too. Wow." A memory sparked it again. "He called me ridiculous—"

"You were!"

"And said I should soak my feet," Carlie continued without waiting for Teresa's soothing words of explanation. "I mean, seriously? 'I think you're tired. Let me get you hot water for your feet. Would you like a Valium with that?'"

Teresa's groan sounded laborish. "Carlie! You said that to him, didn't you? Oh, man. He was concerned. I seriously doubt he said *you* were ridiculous. He probably tried to show you why something wouldn't work and chose a bad word to explain it."

"Since when," Carlie growled, "do you stick up for the *boyfriend?* You're always telling me that they're treating me like dirt, so the one time I see it and call him on it, you—"

"Sorry. This time, I agree with him. Maybe *someday* it would be good to introduce them, but not until she's had a couple of weeks or months to get over the disappointment. For him, it would be like you telling him to load up a severed artery with a pound of salt."

Pouncer jumped and landed on her chest. "Ooof. You're right. *Ridiculously* exaggerating there, but yeah. Maybe."

"Call him, Carlie. He's probably miserable."

She reached for her mail as a diversion. "As soon as I get through the mail and—oh."

"What?"

Her heart raced until she thought she'd pass out from the exertion. Perspiration beaded on her forehead, and her body felt clammy from head to toe. "There's a letter from him."

"A letter? Oh, Carls... Open it while I'm here. Or I could come over. Maybe I could call him."

Carlie put the phone on speaker and fumbled with the back flap until the little envelope opened. Inside, a note card with a simple, engraved monogram stared back at her. "CSD."

"What?"

"His monogram." She closed her eyes and flipped it up. "I'm afraid to read. It looks so cold and formal."

"Well, he *is* a little formal. It's all he has, probably."

She took a quick breath and tried to open her eyes but failed. "I would have thought he would be an 'in person' kind of breaker-upper."

"Well, then, maybe he's just telling you he wants a break until... something."

But as Teresa spoke, she started reading. "Oh, man..."

"That's it. I'm coming over."

"No! Don't. Listen. 'My dear, Carlie. I am grieved by our misunderstanding. It has been difficult not to call, but I assumed you might wish some space. Please know that I am not angry and am anxious to hear from you. I should also explain that I meant to speak of myself when I said that the notion of me being unwilling for Gabby to meet someone else was "ridiculous." I only realized how it might have sounded after I arrived home. I will wait to hear from you, unless I do not see you on Wednesday. By then, I fear, I will not be able to restrain myself from a call at the very least. Yours, Dean."

Teresa's sigh echoed the one in Carlie's heart. "He does have a very... stuffy... way of speaking and writing, doesn't he? It's almost

British—old school."

"He means it. I hurt him."

"Then get off of here and call him! I'm going now. Love you, girl. *Bye!*" And with that, the call went dead.

She hesitated—pride and shame mingling in a mess of emotions that promised to make her incomprehensible. But the knowledge that it would only be harder the longer she waited prompted her to pick up the phone. Dean answered on the first ring. "Carlie? I've been concerned."

"I'm fine—now. I just talked it out with Teresa. I'm sorry."

She heard the exhale of relief and imagined him leaning back, eyes closed, hand pressed against his forehead. Her mental image was confirmed when he said, "There is nothing to forgive. I am just relieved that you called. I was unsure how—"

"It's okay. You said you wouldn't fight with me. I took silence all wrong." When he didn't reply, she murmured, "Dean?"

"I'm here." Again silence. "I'm just—just *grateful* that you called. I didn't know what I would do if you didn't come on Wednesday. There is such a fine line between giving someone space and not showing how much you care."

It's so you… "Dean?"

"Yes?"

"Don't give me *too* much space in the future. A few hours to cool down is great. Much more and…" She closed her eyes. "In my experience, it means you're gone."

Neither spoke for the better part of a minute. Dean broke the silence first. "Carlie?"

"Yeah?"

"I have no intention of leaving you unless you tell me, unequivocally, not to return."

Despite the pile of uncorrected papers in his messenger bag, Dean sat in The Fiddleleaf's corner booth and waited. Nerves kept his knees bouncing and his hands shaking, but only one thing would relax him. A cup of coffee—now lukewarm, he suspected—sat untouched in front of him. Janice had tried to draw him out, but as much as he'd tried to respond, he'd failed.

It would have been best had I tried to see her last night. Allowing even more time to pass only adds to the awkwardness.

Voices on the other side of the booth—Janice's and Carlie's—ripped him from his thoughts. "—looks like he's lost his best friend. So, help me, if you break his heart—"

"I won't. We had a misunderstanding. It's fine now." Carlie's voice dropped. "I almost drove over to his house at midnight last night—just to beg a hug."

That would have been a welcome relief.

Her skirt—the pink polka-dotted one that he thought suited her complexion so well—swished next to his leg. Dean looked up and smiled at her. He tried to stand, but she leaned on the edge of the bench with one knee and gave him half a hug. "Hey…"

Dean allowed himself a moment to hold her before he forced himself to lean back again. "You're looking especially lovely today."

"And that's why you melt my heart on a regular basis. You're good for a girl's ego, Dean—maybe too good. I may end up the most vain girl on the planet."

He shook his head as she spoke. "Hardly."

To his astonishment, as she slid into her side of the booth, Carlie dipped her finger in his cup. "Just as I suspected. Cold. You need fresh coffee."

Is it too ridiculous? Before he could second-guess himself, Dean leaned forward and grinned. "I think this is where I say—and mean most sincerely—that you are the only addictive stimulant I need or want." The delighted half-giggle, the way her eyes lit up and sparkled as she shook her head, even the faint tinge of pink on her cheeks all told him he'd said exactly the right thing.

"That was seriously one of the cheesiest compliments ever. I love it."

"I am not adept at the subtle art of flirting, so I decided to attempt overt…"

Janice appeared before Dean could find the word that eluded him. "He looks better already." She retrieved the untouched coffee and asked, "Coffee for both or something else?"

"Strawberry lemonade," Carlie said. "I saw it on the board when I came in. Sounds *great.*"

"That suits me as well. Thank you, Janice."

The woman gave each of them a warm smile before saying, "You two are seriously the highlight of my week." She winked at Dean, "And no, it's not your tips either—generous as they are."

He'd never understood the appeal of sitting across from someone and simply gazing at her. Books, movies, poetry. They all hinted at a certain emotional connection—a beauty of interconnected spirits—that came with just *being* and allowing the eyes to see deeper into another than the optic nerve was designed to see. *And now I understand. It's…* intense. *It's deeply moving.*

Carlie dropped her gaze first. The distance across the table grew exponentially in his heart. "You are so far…"

"I was just thinking the same thing! Silly, isn't it? I mean…" Her fingers reached across the table and toyed with his. "You're right *here*. Right here!" She seemed to hesitate. Dean wanted to ask if she'd like to take a ride in the park or play a round of tennis—anything to see her again that evening—but he resisted.

You have taught me that there are rewards in waiting and listening, Carlie. Thank you.

"I'm happy, Dean. I was telling Mom about it on the way to work this morning. Note for the curious," she added with a wry smile. "It is nearly impossible to hear a conversation on the subway if a little kid is screaming her head off. Thought you oughtta know. Anyway, I said, 'Mom, after talking with him again, I realized what's so different with Dean. He makes me *happy!*'" Her cheeks grew rosy again. "It sounds silly, but I never realized that I wasn't *happy* in other relationships. I liked things about them—I did," she added defensively when Dean failed to hide his disbelief. "But after the initial 'he likes me' thing after a first few meetings, I was always just happy not to be *alone*. Ugh." Her nose wrinkled, and Dean found himself fighting back a smile.

You cannot be delighted in her adorableness while she's obviously disturbed by something.

"—one of *those* girls. I keep seeing little snippets that prove it, though. I really was, wasn't I?"

"Forgive me, one of *what* girls?" Dean gave her an apologetic smile. "I don't quite understand."

"Just… I don't know, *desperate* to be wanted. Ugh. I should have more self-respect than that." Carlie's face lit up again. "And you know what, that's part of what about you makes me so happy. You…ugh. What's the word when you make it happen in someone… c'mon. I know you know it."

After a pause, Dean offered, "Foster?"

"Yes! You *foster* that attitude in me. It's probably why I'm always so eager to see you—always have been. You inspire me to be a *better* me because you…" Carlie's eyes widened. "Wow. You really think I'm that better me, don't you?"

Dean didn't respond. He didn't need to. Janice came, took their orders, and even returned with fruit and cheese, but still they sat, fingers exploring fingers, and enjoyed *being*.

When their food arrived, Carlie spoke first. "Going to pray?"

"If you wish…"

The moment he said, "amen" Carlie pounced. "Guilty—ooooh, I feel guilty. But I thought of a question, and it totally just drowned out your prayer. Sorry."

"Of all people, Carlie, I am the last to criticize someone for the lamentable habit of—"

"Oh, stop it. Look. I need to know something. Did you not want to introduce Jared to Gabby because of timing or at all?" She ducked her head for a moment before adding, "I wanted to ask last night, but I couldn't bring myself to do it."

"It seemed a bit... precipitous after I just, for all intents and purposes, rejected her."

"So, you wouldn't be opposed to it later... say, in a month or two?"

Dean shook his head. "Actually, next month might present a perfect opportunity. I happen to know that the bookstore in which she works has a book she wanted to show me. It is her opinion that I would like it. You and Jared could go on a shopping trip together to purchase something for my birthday and—"

"Wait! I just realized. I don't know when your birthday is! It's next month? What day?"

"June sixteenth."

Her fingers flew across her phone. "That's it. We're having a party that day, and you're going to meet all my friends. We'll have a picnic in the park or—oh. Sorry." Carlie flushed. "You were helping me with my scheme, and I just interrupted—again."

"It seems I have been a negative influence on you." Dean winked before continuing. "I think an arranged 'accidental' meeting might be a natural way for them to have the opportunity to talk. I could call during your visit to the store, and you would have to step outside so I couldn't overhear." He gave her a sheepish grin. "I would, of course, be happy to purchase the book myself. My mother would be appalled at the idea of me even hinting that you should purchase a gift—"

"Hogwash. I'm buying the book—and having the party." She grinned. "You just made my day."

You are a natural party planner, Carlie. Somehow, we have to convince you to try it.

He began to suggest it when Carlie spoke. "I was curious..." Before Dean could respond, Janice arrived with a lemonade refill for Carlie. She thanked their server, and the moment the woman stepped away asked, "Why haven't you kissed me? I mean, is it some religious thing or..."

"I—" His words evaporated at the memory of a three-second moment in the hospital. "But I have."

"I'm still shocked at that. It always seems a little like a dream."

Dean's heart skipped a beat at her words. "I thought so, as well."

"Why'd you do it? I never really understood."

"I can't say. I shifted and your lips were there." Dean stared at his plate of salad as he struggled to control unexpected emotions. "I didn't want them to go," he whispered. Words poured from him unbidden. "I was terrified when I saw Steve. The booth might have protected me, but you—" He swallowed a lump the size of a golf ball and tried again. "You would be—" Jaw clenched, fingers gripping the fork until it should have bent into a twisted mess of metal—Dean fought back the bile of fear that rose up in him at the memory. "Trying to stop him—I—" His eyes met hers. "I expected to die. And then in the hospital, it kept replaying in my mind. The shots—the screams—*your* scream. The fire in my chest." His lip trembled despite every effort to keep his features in check. "The blood..."

She slipped from the booth and moved to his side. Eyes swimming with unshed tears that come with unwanted memories, Dean felt rather than saw her slide in next to him and wrap her arms around him. "You seemed so brave," she murmured. "I didn't see fear at all—just a man determined to stop it. And at the hospital, you didn't seem upset."

"That," he rasped, "we can credit the narcotics for. I didn't have my first nightmare until the tubes came out of my chest."

He felt her suck in air and then exhale. "I didn't know you had nightmares. I'm so sorry."

"Perhaps I shouldn't confess it, but that kiss has proved to be an excellent sedative sometimes."

She giggled, kissed his cheek, gave him a quick hug and moved back to her side of the bench. "So *that's* why you haven't kissed me. I'm too boring."

"Quite the contrary. It has proven to be a way to have the nicest dreams instead of the worst. I thank you for that." His fork speared a slice of egg. "And I haven't kissed you since simply because I never wanted you to feel pressured."

"Why—?" Carlie gulped down lemonade before trying again. "Why would I feel pressured?"

"You know that I care for you. I thought it best to wait until you knew how you felt about me. Otherwise, you might..." He didn't know how to finish—how to explain that he would rather wait than to ever presume too much too soon. "You know I have little experience with relationships. I err on the side of caution, I suppose."

Carlie nodded and continued to eat her salad as if they had been discussing spinach rather than the affection he ached to show but refused to consider. Just as he decided to ask about another trip to Morganfield, she spoke. Her eyes never left her plate—hands never moved. But even over the ever-present noise of the restaurant, Dean heard her murmur, "Just so you know. You would never make me feel pressured. You're too good of a man for that." Her eyes rose and she repeated, "I wouldn't feel pressured."

Tucked in the corner of her couch, Dean reclined with his stocking feet propped up on Carlie's coffee table while he ignored the movie they'd so carefully chosen. Carlie sat half curled against him with a cat draped over her lap and his leg. Pouncer, on the other hand, frolicked on the floor, batting at the string Dean yanked absentmindedly. *This, I could enjoy forever.*

"Did she just really say that she thinks true love is a way for men to subjugate women?"

Dean swallowed his pride and confessed he hadn't been paying attention. "Between a beautiful woman on one side of me and a fascinating over-grown kitten on the other, how am I to be expected to concentrate on Hollywood drivel?"

"Well, I guess I can see it. That guy's a jerk. Reminds me of my high school boyfriend—Kurt."

Every time you demonstrate your utter lack of taste in men, you make me doubt that I am anything less than a monster.

"—forget the time he sprained my wrist because I refused to go to a party with him." A sigh showed that she saw it through fresh eyes. "Why didn't I see it? He was so controlling—much worse than Blaine ever was."

"I'm sorry you had to endure that, Carlie. No girl or woman should ever have to feel threatened by someone who is supposed to care about her."

She snuggled in a little closer and wrapped an arm around his waist. "I was so mad at James. He broke us up, you know."

"Excellent. I knew I liked James."

"Very funny. I was livid. Of course, now I see that he was just taking care of me. He wanted me to go out with his friend, Gerald. Gerald had one advantage, and only one."

Dean could only imagine. "He was a senior?"

"Exactly! But he was also super smart and was in the school band. His name was *Gerald.* Not Jerry or even Al, but *Gerald.* My barely fifteen-year-old heart just knew I'd be a high school reject if I even talked to Gerald. So, I said no and blamed it on James making Kurt break up with me." Another sigh escaped. "I should call and thank James. I never did that."

Pouncer bounced away after an invisible toy on the floor—a light from the TV, Dean suspected. He wrapped his free arm around her and relaxed again. "I would imagine he would like to know that you understand now."

"Yeah… I will."

The movie plot seemed to wind tighter and tighter until Dean expected the characters to explode from the repressed tension. *Or perhaps it's just you,* his inner self argued. Before he could consider what that might mean, Carlie disentangled herself from him and moved to the kitchen. "Thirsty?"

Dean followed. "I am, actually." His stomach rumbled as he spoke. "Would you happen to have the ingredients for a sandwich? I'm suddenly famished."

"Sure." As he reached for her fridge door, Carlie waved him back. "I have it. What do you want? Roast beef? Turkey? Lettuce? Tomato?"

"Surprise me, but please don't go to any great trouble."

Something in her movements—a certain grace in the way she spread mayonnaise on the bread, perhaps—struck him as particularly beautiful. The memory of Wednesday's lunch and her hint that she wouldn't be averse to the idea of his kissing her overrode his previous reticence. As she offered him a plate, Dean set it on the counter and pulled her close. "Thank you."

"If I'd known I would get this kind of thanks, I'd have made you more sandwiches," she joked.

An air of expectation grew and filled the little apartment. He saw it in her eyes—in the way she stepped a little closer and held her breath. "Carlie…" Dean closed his eyes. "I can't tell you how foolish it feels to admit that I enjoy saying your name. Just saying it."

"Is it any more foolish than my liking to hear you say it?" She leaned her forehead against his chest. "I don't hate it anymore. I can thank you for that."

By the time he'd gathered enough courage to cradle her face in his hands, Dean could hardly breathe anymore. And by the time their lips met, he didn't care. What began as a commonplace action became an infinite moment—no discernible beginning or end. When he sat on the couch and took a bite of his sandwich, Dean couldn't have said. And if the expression on Carlie's face meant anything, she was equally dazed by the kiss.

Her first words nearly made him choke on his last bite. "When are you going to say it?"

"What should I have said?"

Her impatience showed long before she answered him. "When I asked you why you asked me out that day, you said it was because you were falling in love with me."

"I did. Did that offend you? I have second-guessed that confession more times than I care to admit."

"No…" Carlie took the plate from his hands and set it on the table before settling in next to him again—closer. "You haven't said anything since. I wondered if you really meant it, or if it changed. I—"

Dean's laughter earned him a gentle punch in the gut. "I'm sorry. I couldn't help but wonder if this is where I am supposed to say, 'I told you once that I love you. I assure you that I will let you know if that changes.'"

"Very funny, professor. I'm serious. You are so different from anyone I've ever known that I don't know how to read you."

Several options lay open to him. He could explain, he could reassure, he could do both. Or he could simply share his heart and hope for the best. Of course, he chose the latter. "Do you remember why I said I hadn't kissed you?"

"Well, you have now—twice!" When he didn't continue, she growled, "Fine. Yes. You didn't want me to feel pressured."

Dean allowed himself to slide his fingers through her hair as he tried to formulate a coherent sentence. "Well, that would also be why I haven't burdened you with constant reassurances of, as my mother always likes to word it, 'my undying love.'" He relaxed a little at her giggle. "I don't want to rush you or make you *feel* pressured, even if your heart and mind assure you that I wouldn't," he added as she began to protest. "I have a distinct advantage, Carlie. I enjoyed several months of learning about you—getting to know you. I listened and observed. You, on the other hand, have had very little time—not quite two months yet—to know me. I thought just showing it as circumstances allow rather than telling…" He shrugged. "It seemed best to wait."

"I know you better than I thought," she mused. "I was thinking about that last night. While you listened to me, I watched you. Now that I know you were listening when you really wanted to talk—you know, tell me this or that—wow. That's still amazing to me." He opened his mouth to reply, but she continued. "I saw that sometimes, you know. I didn't understand *why* you wouldn't just say something. Now I understand. Now I appreciate it in a way I don't think I could have back then."

Before he could stop himself, Dean murmured, "You have a gift for encouragement. Thank you."

He felt her disappointment, and the urge to reassure her nearly overpowered him. Instead, he waited until the credits rolled before he said, "I should go. Church is only a few hours away."

"I suppose…"

At the door, Dean allowed himself to pull her close again. "So, Miss Denham, would I presume too much to attempt a second kiss, or are you strictly a 'one kiss per night' kind of girl?" Her giggle brought a smile to his lips as well. He brushed the back of his knuckles across her temple with a tenderness he suspected she needed more of in her life.

"I do love you." The words unleashed a floodgate of emotion in him, and Dean heard himself add, "I have a feeling that I will love you more every day for the rest of my life."

Carlie dropped her forehead to his chest and then pressed her cheek against him. "I think what I'm afraid of the most is that I love how you make me *feel,*" she whispered. "Will I ever know if it's a genuine love for *you?* I'm so afraid I won't see it and I'll hurt you."

"A perfectly natural concern," he assured her. "I understand completely." He tilted her chin to meet her eyes as he added, "I am content to wait—however long."

Rain drizzled outside as the October sky wept for the loss of summer. In the corner booth, Dean and Carlie sat laughing and talking about the latest mishap with her cats. "So, Moros about *killed* that little upstart! She actually *boxed* Pouncer's ears! I couldn't believe it. I didn't know cats really did that. Pouncer has been pouting ever since."

The sparkle in her eyes, the way she flipped her hair out of the way of her plate, and the graceful move of her hand as she reached for her fork stirred something new in his heart—regret. "Carlie?"

"Hmmm?"

"So often, when we're out or we're talking, I ache to tell you how beautiful you are." At her blush, he smiled and continued. "I'm not speaking only of your skin or your hair—your eyes that do crazy things to my heart—but you. Carlie Denham is a beautiful woman inside and out, and I rarely tell you."

"Why?" The question, whispered so softly he almost couldn't hear it, cut him.

"Because it makes me feel like my mother. So, I stop myself." His hand covered hers. "That isn't fair to you. Please forgive me."

A change came over her—an inexplicably ominous change. He saw it in her eyes, the way she refused to look at him, and the hint of a tremble of her lower lip. *She's done with me. I knew something had changed in the last couple of months. I'd hoped...*

When her hand covered his, Dean's discouragement swelled into devastation. *You always do that when you have bad news—like when Teresa lost*

298

the baby. Dean watched as she struggled, and his heart went out to her. *Do something. Help her!* "Carlie?"

"Yeah?"

"You know that you can tell me anything. I'll understand. Whatever it is. I'll understand." When she shifted one of her hands to cover his again, Dean nearly cried. *Yes. It's over. Lord, help me.*

Carlie tried to look at him but couldn't. After several false starts, she said, "I've needed to tell you something for a long time, but I couldn't bring myself to do it—since July or August, actually." Her eyes swept the room. "It's been a year, you know. A year of coming here every week."

Great. She is ending our relationship on our "anniversary."

"—promised myself I wouldn't wait another day."

"Carlie, you—"

"I love you."

Three words shut him up and opened up new worlds for them. Three words. "I love you."

Gratitude, joy… love. This time, those rendered Dean Sager speechless—genuinely speechless.

THE END

If you enjoyed *Corner Booth*, I'd really appreciate it if you'd take a moment to leave a review on Amazon or Goodreads.

Chautona Havig's Books

I took a moment to pull out some of the books that I think readers who enjoyed *Corner Booth* might also enjoy. Here are a few! I'd start with *Speak Now*. You might recognize Dean and Carlie in that book, but a book that is closer in theme and style to this one would be *Not a Word*.
Past Forward: A Serial Novel (Six Volumes)

Argosy Junction
Discovering Hope
Not a Word
Speak Now
Thirty Days Hath…
Premeditated Serendipity
Random Acts of Shyness
Operation Posthaste

Made in the USA
Columbia, SC
10 April 2022

58367063R00165